Quarantine Sunsets

BENJAMIN GOLDING

What a journey, thank you to those
who walked it with me.

Prologue

Most stories end with sunsets.

After all, the dipping of a golden sun below a cloudless horizon has been synonymous with the close of as many fables, myths and stories as there have been days on Earth. When the brave warrior has fought his war, slain his dragon and rescued his damsel, it is the sunset that awaits him and his lover; that dusk-tinged place where all happy couples disappear to once victory is theirs. Certainly then, there is something magical about the conclusion of the day, a radiant quality that affirms the notion that *all is well, that ends well*.

But sometimes sunsets do not always mark the end of a story, sometimes they offer just as much promise of a new beginning as the waking dawn. This is one such tale. One that finds its origins in the dying of the light, yet despite the murk, the narrative continues to look out at the troubled world with a pertinent stare; its eyes brimming with determination, a lust for change and a dire need for truth.

Chapter I

Marcus stood in the summer evening, still looking at his phone with a contented, if slightly surprised, smile playing at the corners of his mouth. It felt alien to him. Smiling was difficult given the circumstances, but he did so anyway, revelling in the small act of rebellion and becoming empowered by it. He locked the phone and slid it back into his pocket, zipping it up as he returned his gaze to the setting sun before him.

She'd said yes.

That one, tiny, three lettered word had transformed the sky from something of pretty peculiarity, into an image of comprehension defying beauty. Through a silhouette frame of jet-black trees, it looked as though someone had painted an upturned range of purple and crimson mountains. The soft, midnight blue bases emerged from the vastness of the sky, throwing violet and magenta valleys downwards until their vermillion peaks thrust out, almost scraping the ground below. It was stunning, and there in the centre of it all, slowly melting behind the clouds, was the glimmering sun saying goodbye to the glorious day it had so recently lit, and ushering in the night.

Marcus wasn't sure how long he'd stood there enraptured by the colourful sky, thinking about the implications of his conversation with Aria, but when a speeding car thrashed past on the road behind him, making him jump so far out of his skin that his soul almost landed in the field beyond the trees; he knew he'd spent too long swimming through his thoughts.

Feeling such dread for a passing car would once have been considered preposterous, but being outside during the pandemic was potentially dangerous, not necessarily because of the virus itself, but rather because of who was watching. Indeed, the mortality rate in the United Kingdom was relatively low; nevertheless, though, the Prime Minister had ordered a nationwide quarantine to be enforced by both the police and the military. With it had come a selection of rules, which ranged from inconvenient, to borderline oppressive, and the longer they persisted the more devastating the effects were becoming for the country.

Marcus had been dragged home by the authorities on several occasions over the past few months, and he'd noticed that it wasn't just the police he had to be wary of; it was the public too. It seemed the media had petrified certain minorities so much, with their false news and inflated headlines, that they now favoured the lockdown over their freedom, and would condemn anyone who attempted to live a normal life.

It was a horrifying way to live, and worse still, it was happening all over the planet. Entire countries were locked away in their own bubbles, their citizens beset on all sides by the virus, their governments and the restrictions they imposed, the lies of the media and, in some cases, even civil war. In many ways it really did feel as though the world was set to implode any day. But Marcus still had a glimmer of hope beating away inside his mourning heart, and the thirst for the truth drove him on.

He patted himself down in search of his car key and, after finding it hiding away in the left pouch of his black hoody, flipped it out and trotted across the road to the layby where his noble steed waited. Clicking the unlock button and watching the electric mirrors unfurl like small wings as he approached, he couldn't help a boyish grin from appearing on his lips. It was the only car he'd ever owned with electric mirrors and he was irrationally attached to the fact. After jumping into the car, plugging in his phone and selecting some suitably emotional, brooding R'n'B, he hit the start button and listened to the engine purr into life. With one last look at that magnificent, amethyst sky, a sunset he knew he'd always remember, he pulled out into the narrow lane and thundered towards his date with destiny.

The roads were quiet during the lockdown; so quiet in fact that Marcus deemed it irresponsible *not* to speed wherever he went. After spending years in traffic jams and waiting at red lights with that condescending ruby orb glowering down at him, willing him to slow down and remain still, how could he possibly refuse the tantalising curves of an empty road? Precisely: he couldn't. But it wasn't just the lack of other drivers that compelled him to double the speed limit, he was full of purpose and in such a rush to slam his own will into the machinations of fate, that it would've taken a natural disaster to stop him. Which is why when he arrived at the public gardens where he was supposed to meet Aria, Marcus was fifteen minutes early, despite setting off later than intended.

It was one of the very few times in his life that he'd been on time for anything and he beamed inwardly. He was happy to be early; he needed to rehearse his points and ensure he had his plan in order. Getting her to agree to meet him in spite of the imminent curfew wasn't easy, but what he had to get her to accede to next, was almost impossible, unless he played his cards with the deftness of a Vegas dealer.

Marcus turned the music off and sat in silence, considering his options, and exploring hypothetical scenarios in his mind until the world outside disappeared. His musings went on, and he was still debating with himself about how to play his first conversational card, when a sleek, black hatchback wheeled into the carpark, and pulled up beside him. The lights went out, the door opened and there she was. Aria.

The pair had known each other for almost twenty years, having met in primary school, they then attended secondary school together, and had been part of the same group of friends as they moved into adulthood too; meaning they'd always been close.

At times very close and at others, more distant, yet they'd remained in one another's lives throughout university and her years travelling the world. Then, when she returned home and they found themselves in similar boats, in parallel seas, their friendship had flourished further. Aria and Marcus weren't the type of people to talk every day and know every detail of one another's lives but they both knew, as sure as the sky is blue and the grass is green, that if one needed the other, they'd be there in a heartbeat.

When the lockdown came into place, she was perhaps the person he'd missed the most, although he wouldn't dare tell her; in fact, he hardly dared to admit it to himself. Now there they were, more than six months since the last time they'd seen each other in the flesh, and as Marcus opened his own car door to greet her, he couldn't help but smile again.

She smiled back, and in that moment something else that Marcus would never divulge to anyone else crept into his thoughts. Aria was beautiful. She always had been and he had always thought it, even when he was too young to really understand what it meant, but after such a long time without seeing her, the fact was all the more poignant.

Her name meant 'air' and was apparently derived from both the Hebrew and Italian ancient worlds. She'd taken great pride in the multiculturalism of her lofty name when they were at school, often alluding to the idea that she was an angel and, just as frequently, referring to Marcus as a turd. She falsely claimed the closest thing to the name Marcus in Italian was 'merda', meaning 'shit', and like the substance, that joke had always stuck.

The potty-mouthed, half Italian girl with the antiquated name had olive skin and a cascade of glossy, dark brown hair, but it was her eyes and lips that stole the entire show. Those eyes were two pools of ice-covered water, shining in spring light, and the easy smile she so often wore was worth waging wars over. All of that shot through Marcus's brain in a matter of seconds, and he quickly pushed the notion of her loveliness back into the box that he hid it in, before burying it in the back of his mind.

'Long time no see!' he said jovially, as he walked around the car to meet her.

'You're telling me, stranger,' she said giggling. 'I'd give you a hug, but I don't want your germs.'

'You're assuming I *want* a hug, Ari, I haven't missed you that much,' he lied.

'Whatever, loser. So, what have you dragged me all the way out here for then – you sounded pretty urgent on the phone?'

'Yeah, it's quite important, actually it's very important. I can't believe you said yes!'

'Oh please, I said yes to meeting you, not marrying you! Stop being so dramatic!' Aria said, belting out a genuine laugh.

'I know, our mothers will be so disappointed.' He sighed and they both laughed then and just for a second, it was like it used to be before the world closed its doors. 'Anyway, come on, this is serious, and the curfew hits in about an hour, you know what it's like these days. They'll be rounding people up like stray dogs, and the last thing I want is to get stopped by the police, *again*. I don't have the most inconspicuous car, now do I?' Marcus said, gesturing to the metallic yellow vehicle behind him.

'I like your custard tart, it's growing on me,' she replied, casting her eyes over the gleaming paint work. 'Right, one hour, we can walk and talk because I need to get my steps in. Deal?'

'Deal,' he agreed, and with that, they headed down the moss coated car park, towards the path beside the river.

It was a clear night in August and with the sun now completely set, the sky had become a deep cobalt wave, peppered with infinitesimally small, yet brilliant glimmers of light. It looked like a jewellery maker's workshop table, all blue velvet and diamonds. The two friends caught up on one another's lives as they walked beneath the stars, pausing every so often to marvel at the splendour of the starry sky, and its twinkling reflection in the dancing river.

They laughed, joked and ridiculed each other as friends must, but it wasn't long before the merriment subsided, as Marcus began to explain why he'd asked her to meet him. He spoke with fervour and clarity of the plan he'd been hatching for the past few weeks, remembering all his rehearsed lines, and doing his best to appeal to Aria's sensibilities. He had to make her understand, he had to make her *believe* in it as much as he did, but the dark-haired girl remained silent throughout his monologue, taking in every morsel of information, as she prepared her answers. Eventually they completed their loop of the gardens and as Marcus finished his great, endearing speech, the two of them settled on a bench by the riverbank.

They stared at each other. Her icy blue pools met his hazel green rings in utter, perfect silence, but as the stillness of their encounter threatened to spiral into awkwardness, Aria spoke. 'You're mad,' she proclaimed, with absolute certainty.

'Not the first time you've told me that,' Marcus said, a hint of a smile turning up one side of his mouth. 'But are you in?'

'The country, no, actually, almost the entire world is locked down, in a state of quarantine due to a deadly vir–'

'We don't even know if it's rea–'

'Don't interrupt me, *Merda*! You know exactly what I mean. People are dying out there. Regardless of the cause, whether it really is a virus like they claim, or whether it's something manmade, I don't know, I'm not qualified to know, but it doesn't change the fact that hundreds of thousands of people have lost their lives. And you, you want to sneak out of our country, and into God knows how many others, risking exposure to this lethal *thing*, until you find out what's going on? Like I said, you're mad,' Aria snapped, looking defiantly at Marcus, who was holding his hands up in a placating gesture.

'I'm sorry, I know you've lost people to this and what I'm suggesting must seem reckless. But don't you want to know the truth too – what if it isn't even real?' he pleaded.

'Of course I do.' She sagged, softening slightly at his tone. 'But this is all just too much. Kids are out of school, people are out of work, we're only allowed out of our houses once a day, we're not supposed to see each other. We've got curfews, we get tracked through our phones, the bloody army is on the *streets* herding people. This is dangerous, Marcus. The risks, the things we'd leave behind, I'm not sure I can commit to this ...' She paused, sensing she was starting to ramble and Marcus, seeing her anger diminishing and turning to something sadder, seized the opportunity to speak from his heart to hers.

'Me, you, all those countless people out there in the world; we were made for more than this, Aria. This lockdown was supposed to last three weeks, then it was six weeks and now it's been over six months with the measures only getting tighter. These precautions, that were once just advice, are now getting passed into law! I mean think about that for a second, how long is it going to be before the entire United Kingdom is under house arrest? We get lied to every single day by the media and the governments across the world who tell us to *stay home and protect the vulnerable* and it's complete shit! People are dying and we don't know the cause, we're losing our freedom one slow, painful day at a time and we don't know why because they're hiding the truth from us.' He was on his feet now, pacing, unable to remain still.

'I know, Marcus, I do, bu–' Aria tried to interject, but Marcus steamrolled her response and carried on with his passionate ranting.

'I've already lost my job, I've used most of my savings just to stay alive and all the dreams I had before this happened have been rendered pointless, useless, and fucking worthless. This isn't a movie, Ari, this is real life, and whoever is at the top of the food chain is running the human race into the ground and I *need* to know *why*.'

She opened her mouth to speak again, but he carried on before she had the chance.

'You always told me to live more, do more and be *more*, but don't you see? All those opportunities are disappearing before our eyes and unless someone steps in to stop it, they'll keep disappearing until there's nothing left. It gets worse every day, and how long is it going to be before all those peaceful protests turn into riots? We're on the brink of something terrible, Ari. Think about the people we know, our families, our friends, they're all falling apart, and I just can't sit here and watch. I can't sit here and wait to die. So, I'm going out there and I'm going to make a difference.' He was hoarse and tired when he slumped back onto the bench beside her, his eyes still pleading with hers. The words had hit their mark and Marcus knew it; something in her had changed, but there was still scepticism painted across her delicate European features.

'I know, you're right, and you know I feel the same. I hate every single day of this lockdown and all the lies it's brought with it, just as much as you do. The entire world seems to have gone mad and me, you and billions of other people want this to end, but are we really the ones who are going to fix this?' She let out an exasperated growl and put her hand on her head. 'I just can't wrap my head around it … you're asking me to sacrifice *a lot* to do this with you and for what? Who knows what you'll find, if anything at all?'

'I understand that it's a huge ask and there's a lot you'd be leaving behind. There's your parents, your brothers, your cousins, and I know how you feel about leaving your sisters for a day, let alone a week, a month or however long we'd be gone. But it won't be forever and the world they're growing up in, is it even worth growing up *for*? We could be part of the process that changes everything, we could give them, and everyone else we love, a future.' Marcus finished with an appealing smile and she huffed a small laugh at his last comment.

'You're such a hopeless romantic, I can see your heart falling out of your sleeve from here,' she said, flashing him a smile of her own.

'I can't argue with you there.' He snorted in amusement. 'But I believe in this, Ari and besides, it's not like we'd be out there by ourselves. We'll have help.'

'So you've said,' she countered, narrowing her eyes into cynical slits. 'I don't know what vain dreams this *friend* of yours has planted in your head, Marcus, and I don't know how you plan on changing the world by flying to Sweden either, but you seem to have a lot of faith in him. So, who is he, you still haven't said?'

'I can't tell you,' he said hesitantly.

'Why not?'

'I'm under strict orders not to reveal his name.'

'Are you kidding me? You can tell me the entire wacky plan, but you can't tell me *whose* plan it is? Bullshit, Marcus.'

'He's an artist. That's all you're getting.'

'Wow. Seems like the perfect person to join for a weekend of illegal, international espionage. You're out of your mind,' she mocked angrily, her temper rising again.

'Look, I don't have all the answers, I know there's massive flaws in this plan and you probably think I've lost my mind, but this is the closest thing I've got to the hope of a future right now.' Marcus said, his anger growing to match Aria's.

She could see the pain and frustration in his eyes and let out a long, irritated breath before replying.

'I get it, and you're right, it's far from perfect but it's *something*. As insane as this entire conversation has been, and as much as I hate to admit it, I do think there's some sense in what you're saying. But we're not revolutionaries, Marcus, you're an artist, as is whoever came up with this idea, and I sell insurance policies. We're just ordinary people.'

'Exactly!' he said putting his hand on hers. 'People assume that there's this unspoken rule that says you have to be someone special to make a difference in the world. It's not true. We're all ordinary people at the heart of it, some of us just spend too much time thinking and not enough time doing. Please, Ari, come with me.'

'Why me?'

'What?'

'Why are you asking me to come with you? There's a hundred other people you could ask.'

Marcus took his hand back and was quiet for a moment. There was a minute voice whispering a ludicrous and unutterable truth in the back of his mind, that if he did go out there and he was going to die, if this really was the end of all things, as the media so frequently liked to remind them, then he wanted to spend his last moments with her.

Only her.

Fearing that he might let that notion slip from his mouth, he shook the thought from his consciousness, and stuffed it down into the most remote part of himself before it had the chance to resurface.

'There's no one else I trust more than you, and there's no one else who thinks like me, so it has to be you. *Or*, I have to go alone.'

'Fuck! Don't go delivering ultimatums to my door; this, you, are not my responsibility,' Aria said harshly, raising her voice in the darkness.

'No, no that's not what I meant,' he said, stumbling over his words. 'I'll still go alone, I've made up my mind, I need a purpose, and this is it. I won't begrudge you for not coming and I won't think any less of you,' he said with a faint smile.

She knew he meant what he said, and that her decision wouldn't taint his perception of her, but there was something about his words that burrowed into her mind and refused to let go.

'I need to think about it, Marcus,' she said shaking her head in tiredness, obviously irritated that he'd managed to get under her skin. 'How much time do we have?'

'The plane leaves for Sweden in seven days. It'll fly from a little airstrip in the Scottish Orkney Islands. All the instructions about how to prepare are in here, if you want to come with me. I've arranged to be picked up from this car park actually, so all you'd need to do is meet me here next Friday at 6 AM,' he said, handing her a note that had been folded so many times it looked like a postage stamp.

'Christ, you make it sound like it's so *easy*,' she said, daring him to reply, but Marcus knew better than to ignite those particular fireworks. 'I can't believe I'm even considering this.' She groaned.

'Just mull it over, yeah?' He smirked.

'Alright.'

'Alright.'

Marcus threw his arms around her and held her tightly.

'Fuck your germs,' he said, and she laughed, squeezing him back.

They returned to their cars and exited the carpark just three minutes before the curfew. Marcus tore out of the carpark, his excessive acceleration causing the exhaust on his car to pop and bang like a war drum, echoing the powerful beats of his heart as he blazed through the night. Doubt assailed him as he drove the short distance home, and a singular question proceeded to dart back and forth inside his head, even as he left the car behind and made his way inside. What had he started?

Chapter II

The week had passed by with that bizarre, meandering pace that can only be experienced when one is both extremely busy, and also living in dire anticipation of something. Some days it seemed like the hours passed by with such velocity, that there'd never be enough of them for Marcus to complete his preparations. Other days, time crawled by with the morose pace of a funeral procession, the black seconds marching by, carrying his dwindling self-belief in an even blacker casket atop their wizened shoulders. It was a difficult few days, yet in spite of the emotional peaks and troughs the clocks had dragged him through, he'd overcome the first obstacle and was now sat on a tree stump, in the same gardens he'd met Aria in seven days ago.

The sun was quickly making its ascent into the sky, despite the early hour, and there were few clouds to interrupt its climb. Shimmering droplets of dew coated every blade of grass and leaf-strewn bough, even the daffodils beneath the trees were almost incandescent in the morning light. The scent of fresh cut grass pervaded the air, along with that distinct earthen smell of a summer morning in Britain; one that declared with certainty that the day would be a hot one.

It was a gorgeous scene, and the nostalgia of it hit Marcus with a ferocity he wasn't expecting. He thought of all the years he'd spent walking those paths with both friends and family alike, feeding bread to the ducks in summer, avoiding the floods in spring and drinking cans of pilfered beer and cheap wine with his school mates under the bridge, long before they were old enough to even enjoy the taste. Now Marcus was twenty-five years old and he didn't know where all the time had gone. His reverie soured further when he remembered that all those joyful, carefree days, once considered normal, were now lost to them all. Normal had changed forever.

He fidgeted with the locks on his traveller's rucksack to distract himself and ran his fingers over the taut, khaki coloured canvas. It reminded him of a painting and Marcus wondered then, for perhaps the first time, just how much he'd miss the oils and the brushes of his profession during the trip. A lot, he concluded, but his foray into the unknown wouldn't be without its creativity, partly because it was simply in his nature to be artistic, but more importantly because he'd packed his camera.

That would be one of his most important tools in the days to come, and in his mind, Marcus had envisioned himself on more than one occasion, photographing clandestine government officials in hushed meetings, snapping shots of mysterious laboratories hidden in rural villages, and unearthing all the world's secrets through the eagle eye of his lens. His Hollywood dream of changing the world was, quite frankly, absurd; and he knew it. However, before Marcus could begin dwelling on how damaging the self-indulgent grandiosity of his hero complex was, the sound of footsteps approaching from the river path stole his attention.

When Aria rounded the corner of the treeline, and walked through the carpark towards his stump, Marcus had to bite down on the inside of his cheek to stifle a laugh. Some of the hilarity was caused by relief that she'd actually turned up, the other part was due to the fact that the pack she had strapped to her back, was almost as big as she was.

She kept moving, and even the severity of her almost entirely black outfit did little to stave off his amusement. Indeed, the dark jeans, rugged black boots and solemn charcoal top she wore only accentuated the silliness of the situation. Eventually he gave in, crumpling at the waist and bracing his hands against his knees as the laughter shook him.

'Oh wow, I haven't laughed that much in at least six months,' Marcus said, as he stood, wiping his eyes as she came within a few feet of him. 'If you need a grown up to help you with your luggage, give me a shout.'

'Glad to see your sense of humour is still intact,' she said rolling her eyes. 'But for the record, if I needed a grown up, you'd be the last person I'd ask.'

'And I'm glad to see your wit is still intact, *malady*,' he said, doffing an invisible hat and taking a wildly exaggerated bow.

'Please, Marcus, I had enough of your Shakespeare shit last week, you can keep your *maladies* and your *soliloquies* thank you very much,' she said light-heartedly, as Marcus straightened up and mimed placing his invisible hat back onto his head. Unfortunately though, the airiness of their conversation evaporated at the mention of last week's meeting, which slammed them back into the seriousness of their predicament with jarring speed.

The pair looked at each other with strained smiles. Marcus broke the accumulating tension with a sigh before it had time to become anything more significant; and began to speak.

'How did you get on then, did my instructions make sense?'

'Alright I suppose, I've left home a few times over the years but never quite like this. I still can't believe I'm here, if I'm honest, but I'm doing my best not to focus on that. The packing was pretty easy and the instructions…' She trailed off briefly and arched an eyebrow. 'Were very clear and very easy to follow, which means that *you* definitely didn't write them. So, who did, your mysterious friend?'

'God, was it that obvious? Yes, it was my *friend* actually, and he's also our driver, I'm hoping he'll be here soon,' replied Marcus, checking the brown leather-strapped watch at his wrist. 'Obviously he's in charge of this little *excursion*, let's call it, and he outlined everything he wanted me to do. I just passed everything over to you; the only thing I had a hand in was the route you took to get here.' 'Right, so that's why it took me almost two hours to walk just over a mile. Do you have any idea how early I had to get up to drag myself here?' she said with that lovely, easy smile returning briefly to her face, before her features reset into an equally brilliant frown.

'Yeah, sorry about the early start, but I couldn't risk you being seen,' Marcus countered with a shrug. 'Although with a bag that big you would've been hard to miss. You look like you've got a small village on your back.'

'Honestly, Marcus, is there any limit to your comedic genius?' Aria joked. He opened his mouth to interject what would've doubtlessly been another sarcastic comment; but she crushed his response and kept speaking. 'Who is he then, this smuggler of yours – surely you can tell me now that I've actually agreed to come on this suicide trip with you?'

'Well you'll be meeting him in a few minutes, so it can't hurt,' Marcus offered gingerly.

'He must be well connected if he's got the means to get us out of Britain during the lockdown?' she asked dubiously.

'Well it's probably not what you'd expect. He's another artist, like I said last week, I met him in London a few years ago and we kind of, hit it off, I guess,' Marcus began, his words irregular and clipped, as though he didn't know how to compress the complexity of his tale into only a single sentence.

'Go on,' Aria encouraged.

'Well, he's a lot older than us and he took me under his wing, I suppose. Imagine him as my mentor if you like, you know the sort, the kind that's always talking about philosophy and science, and trying to make you view the world in different way.'

'Sounds pretentious.'

'Again, he's probably not what you'd expect. Anyway, I owe him a lot and when he mentioned this idea to me, about getting out there and finding the answers, I couldn't say no. To be honest, he's actually quite famous. Have you heard of Knox McRae?'

'Knox McRae?' She pondered for a moment. 'Isn't he the guy who blacked out London as part of an exhibition last year?'

'Yep. Might have hacked the National Grid, might not have.'

'And the same guy who draped that gigantic Chinese flag over the Houses of Parliament when the virus first broke out?'

'That's the one.'

'Jesus, Marcus, you didn't tell me we were going on a fucking five-hundred-mile road trip with a deranged political artist? We'll be lucky to make it there alive! What if he gets halfway and decides to make a tapestry out of our skin and call it "*Untitled Three*". Besides, the guy's been in the news every other month for the past decade at least, he's hardly a discreet choice of accomplice, for Christ's sake. Could you not have mentioned this last week? And why have you never told me that you and Knox-bloody-McRae are best buddies?' she squawked, hurling her questions at him with a venomous force that left Marcus's insides reeling. He couldn't lose her now.

'Ari, look it's really not like that, I never mentioned it because I just didn't think you'd be that interested. Please just wait until you meet him, I promise it'll all make so much more sense when you do! And when he explains everything to you the way he did to me, all the pieces will fall into place,' he said hurriedly, knowing his argument was as feeble as a seed in the wind.

She stared at him with fury in her eyes as Marcus scrambled through his disarrayed thoughts, looking for the right words to say, when he was saved by an ambulance screeching into the carpark.

It was a very old model, the kind that would've been in service all over the United Kingdom in the 1980s and early 1990s, but in the modern day, it looked almost like a caricature. It was a significantly smaller, squarer jawed beast than its present-day counterparts and, unlike the newer, luminous yellow and blue vehicles, was almost completely white other than a bright orange band that ran the length of both sides and the rear door. This particular example was pristine and although it gleamed as though it was new, there was no escaping the fact that it was an automotive relic.

However, no matter how obscure the pearly ambulance looked in the small, wooded carpark so many years past its sell-by date, it paled in comparison to the strangeness of the wiry, steel haired man who sprung from its cabin and into the sunlight.

Knox McRae was a tall, terrible visage of a man in his early sixties. He'd been born in Glasgow in 1958 and had once said during an interview, when he was a younger and significantly happier man, that he *had been raised on whisky and adventure*. Whether or not that self-stereotyping was actually true, no one but the man himself knew; however, he certainly had lived a philanthropic and, if his stories were to be believed, wild life. Looking at the ravines of wrinkles that crossed his face, the hard lines that formed the shape of his head and the strong, yet frightfully thin, angles of the body upon which it sat, one would be hard pushed not to believe the stories.

The histories of Knox's life were adorned on his flesh like twisted letters scrawled onto a piece of coarse parchment; the opposing extremes of his past unmissable. Poverty and luxury, sorrow and elation, celebration and war; he had at some point experienced them all. Yet, if those features alone didn't supply enough proof of the type of life McRae had led, then his eyes would undoubtedly put the nail in the coffin, perchance, even, a stake through the heart.

They were green – maybe in another time they would have been emerald vistas but now, they were two sun bleached jade totems, so pale they had turned an unnerving grey. Staring into the Scot's eyes would reveal no window to the soul, only broken glass, waiting to pierce the flesh of anyone foolish enough to intrude. That meant that only the people who were *invited* in ever got a chance to glimpse the man beneath that armoured exterior.

Marcus had somehow found himself on the inside of those barricaded walls, during a trip to London shortly after completing his degree, several years prior to that meeting in the carpark. He'd been exhibiting one of his paintings, alongside works by a plethora of other artists, at a small gallery on the outskirts of Camden. It wasn't a particularly prestigious event, nor was it that well-advertised, so when one of the most renowned British artists of the 21st century clomped through the door and started perusing the space, everyone present entered a state of disbelief.

Marcus remembered the experience well, and recalled how, after several minutes of McRae stalking silently between the paintings, he had eventually stopped in front of his piece and scrutinised it with his lethal glare.

Those agonisingly slow, slithering moments whilst the great artist examined his work without so much as an audible breath, made the hairs on his neck prickle. Then, with an abruptness that cut through the noiseless anxiety in the room faster than a bullet from a gun, McRae spun to face the young painter. 'I like this,' he said, in a voice that was so unlike anything Marcus had ever heard before, that he almost laughed in bewilderment.

It was a deep, husky burr, that combined the staccato separation of each syllable found in the Glaswegian dialect, with the cockney drawl of every vowel. Jarring and smooth, it was all at once the satisfying sound of a knife through hot butter and the wincing rasp of barbed wire on metal; a juxtaposition that Marcus had always thought summarised the man's personality as much as his voice.

'Yes. I do like it, but tell me, young man, do you always lie so openly?'

'Erm I … Well … There's …' But Marcus's words died in his throat, and he did little more than redden in response.

'Look,' Knox said, gesturing to the painting. 'It appears as though you've attempted to paint a vaguely optimistic abstract here, with your airy yellow hues and your – rather enjoyable, I must admit – shades of teal. But the marks you've used to lay the colours down look like they were made by a rabid animal, lad. So, either the colours are lying, or the marks are; which one is it?'

'I'm not sure what you mean, Mr McRae, I'm confused,' he uttered meekly. 'That I can tell. You see, you can parade around with your nice colours and that big smile of yours as much as you like, but there's something dark inside you, sunshine, and it's clawing to get out. If it wasn't, your canvas wouldn't look that!' he said, raising his voice and thrusting a crooked finger toward the painting.

The words struck like punches and Marcus felt as though Knox's eyes were boring holes into his chest, exposing his ribs, and the violently thrashing heart behind them. In that moment McRae held the whole room captive and it stretched on and on until, mercifully, he retracted the daggers from his glare, and looked at Marcus with what seemed like approval. Was that a test; had he passed? 'I strongly advise that you embrace that side of yourself, that side you won't show anyone,' the older man intoned, as he put his hand into the pocket of his navy trench-coat, to remove a small scrap of card. 'I would also advise that you stay in the city tonight and meet me at this address tomorrow, around noon.' He extended the piece of card to Marcus, who took it sheepishly, and hoped the gesture didn't look as pathetic as it felt.

Knox McRae left the gallery and its stunned occupants without another word, causing Marcus to become a minor celebrity for the rest of the evening. For one night only he became a legend, the young painter who'd stared down the fire breathing nostrils of *The Great Knox McRae* and lived to tell the tale. However, it was swiftly forgotten the following day when he arrived at the studio of the aforementioned artist, and began to travel down the road that would, ultimately, lead him to that fateful day that he now found himself living.

Marcus and Knox hadn't seen one another in person since the lockdown began as it was too difficult to move undetected in the capital. So, despite the terror he still struck into the younger man, Marcus shone a smile at his white-haired, bushy-eyebrowed mentor as he strode over the gravel towards the spot where he and Aria stood. Knox allowed himself a small smile in return, but couldn't resist a quick jibe too. Such was his way.

'Still wearing that obtuse smile, are we, Mister Barnes? Either your face is getting smaller, or your mouth is getting bigger, lad, because you look at least twice as ridiculous as you did the last time I saw you. Although...' His guttural voice trailed off as he moved to fix his full, startling attention on Aria for the first time. 'Mayhap I was wrong about you, that unsightly face of yours seems to have attracted you a mate. You didn't mention that your *companion* was a girl? What might your name be, lass?' he enquired, prompting an amused scoff from Aria, and a blush from Marcus.

'Firstly, Knox, it's a pleasure to meet you. I'd like to say I've heard a lot about you, but Marcus failed to mention anything about your, *acquaintance,* for almost, oh I don't know, four years? And secondly, there's more chance of us walking to Sweden than there is of me and Marcus being anything more than *friends,*' she said, with a kind of ruthless finesse that made it seem both charming and threatening, in the same instant. The way she said *friends* knotted Marcus's stomach, and deepened his pink blush, until his face resembled a beetroot.

'Straight to the first name, a smattering of cynicism and even a flourish, as you shot our wee Marcus's dreams right out the sky without so much as a twitch. Delightful!' he huffed, in not entirely mock admiration. 'Oh, I think we're going to get along famously, young lady. But you still didn't tell me your name?'

'How rude of me,' she said with escalating sarcasm. 'It's Aria.'

'Hmmm, Aria, the name of the air.' He swooned, looking her dead in the eyes. 'Dimmi, cosa vuoi di più dalla vita?' said the Scotsman in fluent Italian.

Hearing the abrasive rasp of his voice change into such a velvet gloss was almost as jarring as a slap in the face, and for how effective it was at disarming Aria, it may as well have been a physical blow. She stood there, jaw agape for a moment, before recovering some of her composure.

'I don't speak Italian, I only know a few words,' she said, still attempting to sound defiant.

'Well, you should learn some more. I just asked you one of the most important questions of your life.'

'I…' Aria began, but her words were swept aside by a deft flick of McRae's hand.

'Enough. We need to get moving and you'll have naught but time on our journey north, you can ponder my question to you then.'

With that, he turned on his heel and trod the short distance back to the ambulance with surprising speed, for a man his age, and hopped back up into the driver's seat. When he glanced up, Marcus and Aria were still standing in the same spot he'd left them. The expression his crevassed face moulded into was so commanding and fierce, that it set the pair of them scurrying towards the vehicle liked frightened mice, without him having to breathe a single word. They both hurtled towards the passenger door of the cab, but another wordless scowl from Knox, and a sharp tilt of his head, indicated that they should ride in the back.

Marcus opened the rear door, thinking quietly to himself that both the handle and the hinges moved with remarkable ease for a vehicle that was so old. Had McRae serviced them before the trip? Was it actually a much newer ambulance in disguise? He had to stop himself at that point, before his mind spiralled down a pointless and excruciating tangent about the lifetime of a door hinge; and the old artist's prowess as a mechanic.

Aria pushed past him, knowing that the slightly glazed look in his eyes meant he'd got himself stuck in a loop of severe overthinking, and she wasn't prepared to wait for it to end. Instead, she grabbed his arm as she stepped up into the raised interior of the ambulance, hauling Marcus in behind her but leaving the door ajar.

It was bright inside. The walls were a combination of shiny white plastic and reflective metal panelling, with a single strip light running across the ceiling that cast a sterile light in all directions, making a mirror of the polished linoleum floor, and illuminating every tiny crevice of the space.

The porter beds were gone, as was all the medical equipment, replaced instead by two static, padded benches and a cage like contraption for storing luggage and other equipment. Above the cage, there was also a sliding hatch set into the wall that allowed communication between the front and back sections of the ambulance; and beside that, stood a man.

He was below average height and had a lissom build that made him look somehow agile, almost fluid, even when he was stood still. This was further punctuated by the lean, sinuous arms that were crossed over his small chest. His features immediately marked him as being of Far Eastern origin; high cheek bones, dark eyes surrounded by little plumes of delicate lashes, and a head coated in silky obsidian hair. He was striking to say the least, and Marcus recognised him immediately.

'Cyril!' He grinned. 'I almost forgot you were coming. How are you?'

'Marcus, I am well and it is good to see you, my friend,' Cyril said in his honied, well enunciated English. 'It has been many months since we last spoke; helping Mr McRae with his preparations has consumed all my time. I am excited for the journey ahead!' he told them, his doll-like mouth curling up into a warm smile, as he unfolded his arms in an emphatic gesture to signal his enthusiasm.

The gesture, along with his tapered blue jeans and plain white t shirt were distinctly Western, and somehow clashed with Cyril's straight-backed, Eastern heritage. It was almost like watching a nobleman don the outfit of a court jester, and it incited a loud chuckle from both Marcus and Aria.

'Well I'm glad you're here, that's for sure,' Marcus said through a smile. 'This is Aria, she's the crazy friend I mentioned to you – remember when we used to work in Knox's workshop together? I managed to persuade her to come!'

'Indeed, I do. What a pleasure it is to make your acquaintance, Miss Aria. You are just as beautiful as Marcus described you to be.'

'He said I was *what?*' Aria guffawed, as Marcus's eyes widened in shock.

'Beautiful. Many times, in fact he even said—'

'Ok, well, that's enough,' Marcus swiftly interjected, severing the other man's sentence before it spawned any more truth-spewing hydra heads. 'I have no recollection of saying *anything* even remotely like that, I think you must be confused, or maybe just thinking of someone else?' The question was rhetorical, and thankfully its intention wasn't lost on Cyril, although Aria, bemused by the exchange and not particularly interested in it, changed the subject anyway.

'So is Cyril your real name then?'

'No, no, my real name is Chan Cōng-ming,' he said with pride.

'Sorry, I didn't catch that?' she replied, stunned.

'My apologies, it is difficult for the English to pronounce, which is why nobody uses my true name here. Mr McRae suggested Cyril as an alternative; I believe it was the name of his family dog when he was young, and still lived in Scotland. I quite liked the idea of being named after a dog – they are honourable creatures. Anyway, forgive my digression, my name, you say it like this: Ch-aen Tsoong-Meeng.'

'Ch,' she repeated uncertainly.

'Yes.'

'Aen.'

'Yes.'

'Tsoong.'

'Good.'

'Meeng.'

'Fantastic!' He laughed; it sounded just as serene and controlled as his speech. 'At this rate, Aria, we will have you speaking fluent Mandarin before we even reach Glasgow.'

At the mention of his native city, Knox swung open the hatch and poked his head through to address the group.

'As lovely as it is hear you three are getting along, we have to get moving, so if it's not too much of an inconvenience for you children, shall we crack on?' he barked, his harsh voice all the more unsettling after hearing Cyril's graceful tones. He didn't give any of them the opportunity to speak; instead, he proceeded with his orders.

'Cyril, you can finish your lesson once we're on the move. Now, lock the back doors and brace all the luggage in the rack, make sure it's locked in tight, lad. This could be a bumpy ride and I don't want any of you dying under your own backpacks before we've even hit the border.'

His words made the young Oriental man spring to life, and with incredible rapidity, he swung both doors shut and twisted the locking bars across them with a decisive click. Then, with even more assiduous speed, he took both Marcus and Aria's large packs in his strong arms and positioned them in the baggage cage. He managed all this in roughly the same time it took Knox to take a breath between sentences, and both of his companions were transfixed by his movements. McRae, however, continued his next instruction without any acknowledgment.

'I need you to brief these two en route. Passports, currencies, who we're meeting and where we're going. As none of us have any phones, or other modes of GPS, I'll be doing the driving as I'm the only one who knows the way. I don't intend to stop more than once if we can help it,' Knox said decisively. His orders weren't cruel, but they were sobering, and his authority removed the playful atmosphere the three young accomplices had shared less than two minutes beforehand, replacing it with an acute focus. The older man glanced at the clock set into the scratchy grey plastic of the cab's dashboard, drawing Marcus's eyes to it as well, allowing him to see that the sickly green digits showed the time as 6:17 AM.

'It should take us roughly twelve hours to get to the northern tip of Scotland. If we don't run into any trouble, that'll mean we'll arrive at around 6 PM. From there we've got a boat ride through the Orkney Islands which will take us around the bottom of South Ronaldsay, we'll then skirt the east edge of the mainland, where we'll eventually dock at Copinsay. How long it takes depends on the temperament of the sea. But that's where our plane is and that's where the real fun begins.'

A dour smile cracked Knox's face at the final comment, and he took the time to stare its many meanings into the eyes of each of his companions, who were all equally rapt by his description of the road ahead. Without another word he closed the hatch and turned the engine over.

As the ancient beast rattled into life, so too did the thoughts inside Marcus's head. They collided and combusted like the fuel inside the engine, and he knew the others, in their own way, were experiencing the same thing. They took up seats on the benches as the wheels turned the first corner and remained quiet; each of them adrift in the deep, turbulent oceans of their minds.

The die had been cast. The game had begun.

Chapter III

As the wheels rolled on, the minutes ticked by and Knox's erratic driving threatened, on more than one occasion, to induce some rather serious bouts of motion sickness, Marcus and Aria gave up on the idea of sleeping the journey away.

The combination of their restless night of preparations, the excitement and terror of meeting McRae, and the constantly looming gravity of what they were doing, had exhausted them. However, after several failed attempts to doze, which had resulted in little more than a few seconds of peace before the ambulance veered off in some unanticipated direction, reducing them to a tangle of limbs on the floor, they had resigned themselves to endure the perpetual torment of being awake.

And torment it was.

The windowless, antiseptic box they were in was much too bright to provide any comfort, and too sparsely furnished to offer any real distractions. So, they both retreated into their own thoughts, searching for comfort, but what they found instead was a gaping chasm; filled with a pernicious mass of writhing moral ambiguities, and coiling serpents of self-doubt.

They teetered there, on the edge of the drop, trying to wrestle with the magnitude of the choices they'd already made and the ones still left to come, but it was a dangerous game in such a tired state; when one does not have the energy to fight the negativity. It wouldn't take much to be sucked all the way to the bottom of that dark hole and they knew it; so with trepidation, they stepped away from the pit and found new ways to cope with their boredom.

It was the need for diversion, along with the help of their irritable yearning for sleep, that led the pair to the realisation that they had both started to harbour a secret, but not malignant, dislike for Cyril.

As they sat there with heavy lids that they couldn't close for fear of becoming heaps on the floor, the handsome young man perched on the bench opposite them with his sublime posture, eyes blissfully closed, and barely moved a muscle; despite the ambulance's lurching movements. With every peaceful rise and fall of his chest, the envy in Marcus and Aria burned hotter and hotter. They began to murmur their conspiracies about him, trying to figure out what could possibly be the source of his uncanny powers of stillness.

'Maybe he's not even human?' Aria suggested.

'What do you mean, like he's a ghost or something?'

'No!' she said too loudly making them both cringe, but fortunately, Cyril didn't stir. She lowered her voice and continued. 'I was thinking more along the lines of a robot. Like, what if McRae built him to be his personal helper or something?'

'Hmmm, I don't know. I'm not sure robotics is Knox's cup of tea, besides how would a robot age?' Marcus dismissed. 'What if he's some kind of expert martial artist?'

'Oh, good call! Like a ninja?' she offered, before scrutinising him for a moment. 'Yes, definitely a ninja.'

'I think you will find, Aria, that ninjas originate in Japan,' Cyril said as his left eyelid slid up, revealing the dark iris beneath.

Marcus and Aria felt as if they were fixed in a gorgon's stare, shocked and embarrassed; they sat unmoving, transfixed by that beady eye. 'I, however, am Chinese. Perhaps the question you should be asking yourselves, is not how I am able to stay so still, but rather how Mr McRae can drive so badly, in a straight line?' he said, opening his other eye and propositioning them both an honest, uplifting smile that dispelled the awkwardness and set them all laughing.

'You were awake the whole time, weren't you?' Marcus tittered, putting his hand over his eyes in faux despair.

'Of course, even I cannot sleep through Mr McRae's incessant changes in direction. It does not matter how many times I travel with him, I never get used to it,' Cyril said in his Queen's English, as his giggling subsided. It was a good laugh; high, truthful and infectious.

'I can't imagine how many times you must've been put through this ordeal. How long have you been with Knox now, twenty years? You're lucky you've survived this long,' Marcus joked, as he stifled another bout of laughter.

'Wait, you've known Knox for twenty years?' Aria chimed in with genuine surprise.

'Twenty-two years this November I believe, yes. My father and Mr McRae have been friends for a very long time, and he decided that I would benefit from having the artist as my teacher, and counsellor. I was seven years old when I came to London and from then on, it certainly has been an *interesting* time.' There was warm reflection in his voice, and its richness helped to elevate their moods further.

'I can't believe that!' exclaimed Aria, and Marcus knew from the tone of her voice, and the glint that shone in her crystal blue eyes, that she was utterly fascinated by how Cyril had come to England.

As a girl who was, and had been for as long as he'd known her, obsessed with travel and adventure, she couldn't resist the exotic allure of his tale. She demonstrated her barely contained enthusiasm by bombarding him with a volley of questions in such quick succession, that he scarcely had time to think, let alone reply.

'So how did you get to England? Do you ever go home and visit your family? What's it like out there? Is it really as polluted as they say it is? And whereabouts in China are you actually from?' she enquired invasively, leaving herself breathless with anticipation, and Cyril holding up his hands to defend himself from her assault. He let out a short laugh, waited a second longer to see if she would release another barrage, then, when none came, he continued.

'I am amazed, and flattered of course, that you are so interested but it is a long story,' he stated, in an attempt to worm his way away from Aria's pressing enquiries. Ever the humble assistant, Cyril was not used to telling his own story, and he found the intensity of her attention quite awkward.

Marcus, noticing, and partially enjoying, how Cyril was starting to squirm under her inspection, did what any good friend would do: pushed him back into the firing line.

'We've got nothing but time; why don't you tell us?' Marcus said with a smile that was simultaneously sarcastic, and genuine.

'Very well,' Cyril replied, with a single shake of his head and smirk for Marcus. 'I will tell you my story, but first, I must go over Mr McRae's orders and instructions with you.' He stood up.

Then, battling against the tremulous driving of the Scot with incredible balance, Cyril made his way over to the luggage container, and removed a small black satchel from it. Pivoting neatly, he then retraced the four short steps he'd taken over the polished floor, and resumed the seat opposite his two companions, the bag in his hand jangling with a metallic twang, as he did so.

The noise the bag made wasn't a result of its contents, but rather of the incongruous collection of padlocks, that were being used to keep those contents safe. The double zip across the top of the bag had two tiny brass locks looped through it, which was arguably excessive enough. However, beyond that there were seven other locks, of varying size and colour, punched through the leather on either side of the zip, like the mismatched earrings of a weathered pirate.

That unconventional, if not completely ludicrous, system for keeping something closed was typical of Knox and his unique mind, which was equal parts genius *and* lunatic. Marcus held no doubts that this particular creation, had emerged as a result of the latter.

Whilst Marcus and Aria examined the satchel with expressions of perplexed curiosity dancing across their features, Cyril rolled the hem of his t shirt up to reveal a thin wire, with nine tiny keys strung across it. The wire itself had been sewn into the shirt, with both its ends tied into looping knots, to prevent the keys from falling off.

He uncoiled one side and slid each of them off into his palm, keeping careful track of the order in which they came off, and then set to work on removing the locks with his nimble fingers. As the last padlock clicked open and was pulled free from the puncture wound it left behind, Aria spoke, unable to restrain her queries any longer.

'I met Knox-bloody-McRae today, and that—' she said, motioning towards the bag in Cyril's hands— 'is still the weirdest thing I've seen all day.'

'Mr McRae was very specific about the protection of the items within this pouch. His methods may be, unconventional shall we say, but they seem to work and most importantly, they keep him happy,' replied Cyril, sharing a smile with his friends.

'So, what's in there, exactly?' Marcus probed.

'Ah, wait, before we get into all that, there's a question I've been dying to ask all morning,' Aria interrupted. 'Why are we in an ambulance that looks like it's been around since the dinosaurs?'

'Oh,' the two young men said in unison, as Aria looked between them with suspicion in her eyes, curious about the knowledge they shared, and the facts that she was not yet privy to.

'Marcus, I will let you explain this one,' Cyril said, as Aria raised an eyebrow to urge him on.

'Gladly! So, and I'm sure this won't really come as any surprise, but this information wasn't really spread openly via the mainstream news. I think it was mentioned once, in May? Anyway, apparently the virus is putting such a strain on our healthcare system, that the government has had no choice but to recommission all the old medical service units, to help deal with the increased number of cases. That means that an ambulance of this age, or any other really, is one of the only vehicles that can move freely, without getting checked.'

'Right,' said Aria after taking a second to absorb the information. 'I had no idea they'd gone that far. Christ, it seems like I don't know *anything* these days. So how have we ended up in one then?'

'Well,' Marcus continued. 'Back in the late 90s, Knox set up a huge installation in Rome. He essentially took a busy London street and recreated it in the middle of the Italian capital. It was incredible, the detail and the accuracy of it really was something else; I wish I'd been more than three years old at the time but hey, you win some, you lose some.'

'Your point, Mr tangent?'

'Oh yeah, sorry! My point is that this ambulance was part of that piece and McRae has had it in the garage under his studio ever since. Luckily for us, we now have the perfect way to sneak all the way to the Orkneys without anyone giving us a second thought.'

'Surely it can't be that easy?' Aria said in disbelief. 'This is 2020. There must be a hundred ways of tracking this thing? What about the number plate, there must be loads of cameras between London and Scotland – won't they all record our movements?'

'That is why Mr McRae wants to stop near the border, to change the plates over, that way it will look like a different ambulance in each country,' Cyril responded in a calming voice, sensing Aria's unease.

'Plus, because of the age of this thing, there's no tracking system at all. So even if someone had the time to spend looking for us, which they don't if the pandemic is causing as many issues as they claim, they'd have no real way of doing it anyway,' Marcus added cheerfully.

'Fuck!' she said abruptly, wiping off the soothing balm of the young men's words, and hurling it at the wall. 'I already feel like I'm in over my head with all of this, and we've barely started – how do we even know if any of this is going to work?'

Neither Marcus, nor Cyril, knew where her outburst had come from, or how to respond to it, so they chose instead to remain quiet, in the hope that the paroxysm wouldn't be followed up by another. An uncomfortable moment passed before she sighed heavily and spoke again.

'I trust you, I'll take your word for it ... sorry,' she mumbled before hurrying on. 'What's in the bag anyway, Cyril?'

The young man visibly relaxed then, and his oriental face returned to its state of tranquillity, as he began to pull a series of envelopes from the bag. He quickly checked the brown paper fronts of each package before handing them both one. They were heavier than they appeared, Marcus thought, as he and Aria took and then gingerly unsealed them, before warily extracting the contents. They glanced once at the materials, twice at each other and then as one, turned their astonished eyes towards Cyril.

'There are three false passports for each of you, they all have the same image of you inside but a different name; these should not be needed but will be useful as a precaution,' he said, expecting an interrogative hailstorm from Aria, which thankfully never came.

Still fearing its arrival though, he proceeded, trying to pre-empt some of her questions before they arose.

'Marcus provided the photographs and Mr McRae was owed some favours from a very good forger; if you were curious as to how I had them made. There are also one thousand British pounds' worth of several currencies. You will find them in the smaller white envelopes, and if my memory serves me correctly there should be roughly twelve thousand Swedish Krona, ninety-one thousand Russian Rubles, one thousand two hundred American Dollars and lastly, just under nine thousand Chinese Yuan.'

That information, coupled with the tactility of the soft envelopes in his hands, seemed to somehow cement their futures in place and although the details were still imprecise, it was the inevitability of it that scared Marcus. With the cogs of his mind spinning rapidly, he felt a wicked anxiety begin to creep over him but he, like Aria, remained silent whilst Cyril finished his explanation.

'I am sure you are wondering why there is so much money, but in actuality, we are very unlikely to need any of it. It is simply another form of insurance. The people we will be meeting in Sweden are Mr McRae's associates from all over the world and it may help to – how does he say it? – *grease the palms* of these acquaintances, should it be required.'

Just like that, the murky waters of reality rose, precipitous, powerful, and full of ice-cold dread; they threatened to drown Marcus where he sat. All too quickly, the bigger picture became too large to comprehend; instead of seeing more, he saw less, until the notion that the entire escapade was simply too much to handle rendered him completely blind.

The dark things in the pit of his thoughts had been unleashed, and as their shadowy bodies slid over him, the freezing water crept ever higher, distorting his vision, dimming his perception, and pushing Marcus to doubt everything.

Aria had been right, he was an ordinary person and he should have stuck to doing ordinary things; he had no business greasing palms and unravelling mysteries. He was an oil painter from a small town in the British countryside, not an international emissary – what on Earth had he been thinking? Then something else began to scrabble around on the outskirts of his cognition: guilt. But before he had the chance to address it, the ambulance swung off the road and shuddered to a violent halt, throwing him, Aria and even the statuesque Cyril, around its interior like pieces of discarded litter in the wind.

'For fuck's sake,' Aria moaned from where she'd landed next to the luggage rack. 'Who taught him to drive?'

'I think he taught himself,' Marcus joked, almost thankful for the disruption of the tumble, and the way it had thrown the troubled thoughts from his mind. He clambered to his feet and, rubbing a tender spot on the back of his head where it had collided with something hard, offered Aria a hand. She took it, and sprang up.

'Let us be thankful he is not teaching anyone else!' said Cyril, as he too rose from the floor. That caused them all to laugh for what felt like the first time in an eternity, and it was a sweet indulgence, but one that was cut short when Knox wrenched open the rear doors, annoyance etched into every crease of his face.

'We have a problem,' he announced, moving to one side and marshalling the others out of the ambulance. Marcus wanted to ask if it was his driving, but the expression McRae wore was so thunderous, that he didn't dare.

They filed out of the vehicle to find themselves standing on a grassy verge beside the motorway. The infinite blue ceiling of the sky was clear above them, save for a few downy clouds shuffling across its limitless expanse, and the sun shone gloriously. The searing midday heat caused waves of distortion to emanate from the empty ribbon of the road, and even Knox's bleak statement couldn't dampen its beauty.

Having not seen even a morsel of the outside world since they had departed over four hours ago, they all relished the opportunity to escape the jail of that surgical box, and bask in the light. It was also the first time any of them had been so far from their homes since the quarantine was imposed; and the sense of freedom wasn't lost on them.

Examining their surroundings as McRae led them past their transport, and to the peak of the verge, it didn't take much to discern that they were at the Scottish border. In the direction they had come from, the land was mostly flat and sprawling; in the other, the fields began to rise into rolling foothills which would eventually lead to mountains, and if there was still any doubt in their minds about their location; the enormous blue sign that read "Welcome to Scotland" provided the final piece of incontrovertible evidence. Knox stopped his march just beyond the sign, in a knot of trees and foliage, and from that vantage point the problem he'd mentioned became obvious to them all.

'There's a roadblock,' remarked Marcus, making it sound almost like a question.

'Aye, it would appear so,' Knox snarled, which sparked a phenomenon rarely seen. On the top of that rise, four people, from four different backgrounds, cursed in four different languages.

'What does *la shee* mean?' Aria asked Cyril, with an intrigued smile.

'Lā shǐ,' he repeated, looking slightly embarrassed. 'It means excrement.'

'It means shite, lass; don't let Cyril's impression of an Oxford professor fool you – he's got a foul mouth like the rest of us,' he said clapping his apprentice on the shoulder, in a display of surprising warmth, for a man carved from stone. 'Now, enough chatter, we need to figure out what's going on down there and how the hell we're going to get past it. It looks more like a military checkpoint than a roadblock and what's more concerning, is that it looks like it's been there a while.'

He paused to think for a moment. Squinting against the sunrays, the light made rough cliffs of his features, making his shifting brow resemble two tectonic plates grinding together, with the currents of his mind whirring beneath. Then his rugged face turned from the sun and back to his companions.

'There'll be options for us if we know where to look, of that I'm sure, but first we need to do precisely that: look. Cyril, head back down the bank and get the binoculars from the ambulance, would you, lad, then we can see what we're dealing with.' The young man obediently turned to retreat down the verge but before he could leave, Marcus grabbed his arm.

'I need to document this, Cyril – could you grab my camera for me on your way?'

'Sure,' he said easily, before making his way to the ambulance with alarming speed. Barely even out of breath, he returned, handing Knox the chunky, black binoculars, and stepping back to join Marcus and Aria where they stood beneath the shade of the trees. Cyril offered Marcus his camera, and the three of them watched nervously, as McRae ventured across the open crest of the hill and into another leafy thicket. There he braced himself against a solid trunk and began to survey the blockade.

In the meantime, the three younger members of the party began to speculate over the roadblock and its implications, as they waited for Knox's analysis, which came far sooner than they'd expected. The spindly artist was back with them in what seemed like only seconds, distracted as they were in the thrall of their hushed conversation.

'We'll continue as planned. Those concrete slabs might have been there for some time, but the security is half baked at best. My guess is that they're mainly there to scare people off,' McRae said, the certainty in his voice compelling. 'Saying that, we might have got here at just the right time – if we'd tried to do this even a month from now, I reckon we'd be scuppered.'

'What makes you say that?' questioned Cyril.

'It looks to me like Scotland is trying to wall itself in.'

'What?' Marcus asked in bafflement.

'Take these and see for yourself,' Knox replied, thrusting the binoculars at him. Marcus took them and began scanning the scene below, taking photographs as he went.

'There's walled checkpoints all across the border,' he said, concern furrowing his brow, as he passed the binoculars back to the white-haired artist.

'Correct, and my guess is they're going to attempt to connect them whilst they think no one's looking.'

'How has this not been on the news? And why would they do that?' asked Aria, with a confused expression.

'Nothing important is ever on the news,' he sneered. 'And I'm not sure if you're familiar with Scottish politics, lass, but the relationship between England and Scotland has been less than amicable for quite some time. The outbreak of this virus has pushed that relationship to breaking point, it seems, and I would assume that the Scots are wanting to weather this storm alone; and sever their ties to the rest of the UK in the process.'

'That seems ridiculous,' Marcus argued. 'Barricading yourself in, just to gain your independence and send a message to your neighbours? It's a bit extreme.'

'You'd be surprised what people will do for independence and freedom, Marcus,' he said with a grim, knowing smile. 'The other difference here, is that *they* might know what's coming. We, on the other hand, do not, and unless we get ourselves to that plane we might never find out. So, my recommendation is that we get back to the ambulance, change the plates, top up the fuel, and get on with the mission. Do I have any objections?' He glowered, daring any of them to challenge him.

'What about the guards patrolling the checkpoint – I saw at least half a dozen down there and there's bound to be more?' Marcus added sheepishly.

'Well spotted, your eye is as true as ever I see, but they don't look like much of a threat. Besides, we have the advantage, a Scottish driver with his blues and twos roaring shouldn't have too much trouble getting back into his own country now, should he? And in the unlikely event that we do get stopped, I'm sure my wit and charm will *woo* whoever is on duty.' He grinned, acerbity glinting off every one of his sunlit teeth.

Hearing Knox tell a joke was such a rare occurrence, that none of them actually knew whether it was a joke at all. When no one uttered so much as a snicker, he shook his head and began leading them back down the hill, mumbling about how his humour was lost on them. When they reached the ambulance, Knox's next round of orders came in the quick, burst-fire rhythm of assault rifle rounds.

'Cyril, grab the fuel cans from the luggage cage and top us up; the tank is behind the passenger door. Marcus, you can put that unhealthy automotive obsession to good use and change the number plates, and Aria, you can supervise.'

'I hope you're not patronising me, Knox?' she retorted with contemptuous bravery.

'I wouldn't dream of it, *poppet*,' he said, as he opened the cab door and climbed back into the driver's seat.

Once inside, he removed a set of latex gloves and a surgical mask from the glove box and started to put them on; if this was going to work, he needed to look authentic. The two young men sprang into action then, finding that rooting through the storage cage for their required items was made pleasantly simple, thanks to Cyril's meticulous packing strategy, and in just a few minutes the ambulance wore a fresh set of registration plates and had filled its belly with diesel. McRae rammed the key into the ignition and awakened the slumbering machine, whilst his three young accomplices returned to their seats in the back, and locked the door firmly behind them.

Then, they were away, hurtling off the rutted bank and back onto the smooth tarmac of the motorway. Marcus, Cyril and Aria remained rigid and silent, their nervous eyes darting around the claustrophobic room, as their ears were filled with the rumble of the road, and the hammering of their hearts. Their collective nervousness was beginning to grow into a physical, palpable thing and when Knox clanged the hatch open to speak with them, the sudden noise caused them to snap their heads around with enough savagery to give themselves whiplash.

'Christ, you look like three little deer trapped in the headlights!' He huffed, looking at them in the rear-view mirror, and fiddling with the face mask. 'Just relax, let me do the talking and do not open that door *for anyone* but me. Understand?' They nodded. 'Good.'

Then he was gone; the cold metal of the access panel stared back from where his face had just been, and the piercing wail of the siren ripped through the air, with the same unpleasantness of a fingernail gouging skin.

Blind though they were, sat in the confines of that windowless room, they all knew that the checkpoint was less than half a mile away, so when the ambulance kept accelerating, they allowed a flicker of hope to flare inside themselves. "They were going to make it, they weren't even going to be stopped", that tiny seed of optimism breathed into their ears, like the sweet nothings of a private lover. Then the brakes hit, and with every crawling metre from then on, the enchanting intonations receded, until they came to a complete standstill. When the ignition was turned off; the spark died entirely.

Almost immediately, there were several people speaking outside the ambulance. Their Scottish accents were thick, making their words almost imperceptible, muffled as they were, through the metal layers of the ambulance. There was no mistaking the aggression and unyielding nature of their tones, however, and Marcus, Cyril and Aria became springs, the pressure of the situation winding them tighter and tighter. Then Knox's booming snarl cut the other voices off in a startling offensive.

'I haven't got time to listen to your bullshit, lads – what do you think this is? A fucking ice cream truck?' he bellowed, the sword of his condescension slicing through the words of the other men. 'There are people dying in the back of this *ambulance*, and I need to get them to the hospital.' One of the men on the ground somewhere to the right, Marcus thought, responded with a question that he couldn't make out.

'Which hospital is none of your business, pumpkin; it could be on the fucking moon as far as you're concerned. Let me through, let me do my job and we can all get on with our day, aye?' This caused a brief uproar, and the click-clack of safety catches being removed from weapons, swiftly followed. Marcus and Aria, who had been smiling at McRae's boldness, found themselves suddenly grimacing. They gritted their teeth and waited.

'Right, so now you're going to shoot a man trying to save the lives of other people? Tell me, how many brain cells do you lot share between you, three? Lift that barrier and I'll be on my way.'

The soldiers were incensed by this, and Marcus winced at the comment, wishing he'd stop pushing the armed men outside as their mob grew louder, and more restless. The others were tense too, and Aria flinched when a set of footsteps echoed on the road, and stopped, right behind where she was sitting.

'Get back here, you scabby bampot!' McRae bellowed. 'Didn't you hear me? There are people *dying* from the virus onboard. You go in there, you catch it too, spread it to the rest of your boneheaded squad, and then what? You're all fucked, lad. Do you want that blood on your hands?'

Then another voice entered the maelstrom, deeper and more controlled, it was the sound of someone with authority. Cyril, straining to hear, whispered that whoever it was, was telling his men to stand down.

'About fucking time! It's nice to know that at least one of you has their head screwed on.' There were a few calamitous replies to that, but they died out quickly.

The sound of footsteps on the tarmac, close to the driver's side door made Marcus tighten his grip on the bench, but nothing other than a quiet conversation ensued, so quiet in fact, that Knox wasn't even audible despite being only a few feet away.

In the back of the ambulance, which had become stifling in the heat, the uneasiness grew as the conversation between McRae, and the presumed officer in charge, stretched on for what seemed like hours. The three unlikely travellers listened intently for any hints as to what was going to happen next, but it wasn't another voice that broke the silence, it was the unexpected sound of the engine coming back to life.

As they moved off, the cool wind of relief swathed them all in a joyful caress. Then, their speed climbed, the siren wailed back into life and just like that they were through. They had leapt the first hurdle.

Chapter IV

Being driven through the verdant Scottish countryside by someone as demented as Knox McRae was akin, Marcus thought, to being shot into Heaven from a cannon.

In an attempt to distract himself from the alarming way in which McRae flung the ambulance around the precarious rural lanes, Marcus started handing out cheese and ham sandwiches from his bag. It had been hours since they'd eaten and he, Aria and Cyril devoured their crusty delicacies in greedy silence. The taste of bread – something he didn't eat particularly often – brought him back to his childhood, and it wasn't long before he found himself trawling the seas of his past as Knox propelled them northwards.

Marcus had visited Scotland many times when he was growing up due to the fact that his parents were both avid climbers and hikers. As a boy, the undulating terrain had always captured his imagination, plunging him deep into fantasies of courageous knights, fire breathing beasts and corrupt kings. He recalled many days spent trudging along muddy passes, with his mother ahead of him and his father behind, and the promise of a dragon's nest at the mountain's peak his sole motivation. However, each time he reached his destination, he was greeted with nothing but dull rocks and other walkers.

Thus, the country had become, in the eyes of a nine-year-old Marcus, the land of lies and false hopes. That glum shadow had hung over his memories for years, his childish perceptions tarnishing them, in the same way water rusts iron. It wasn't until that very moment, stealing glimpses of the glorious crags and raging blue rivers through the hatch in the wall, that he had learned to truly appreciate the country's splendour. His head may have been heavy, but his heart was light with the fluttering wings of change, and with every lolling shake of the ambulance, the oxidised thoughts from his past fell away. Scotland had transformed into the land of dreams.

Their journey north had been, much to everyone's relief, significantly less eventful after passing over the border. Other than the blockades along Scotland's territorial boundary, they had seen almost no sign of the military at all.

The air of tension generated by Knox's verbal assault of the soldiers, and the unlikely cooperation of their captain, had taken many miles to dissipate. Fat leeches of fear had clung to all of them, the terror of being followed, stopped and dragged back to England provided the blood for their dreadful mouths, until McRae had shaken them all loose with another bout of unexpected humour.

After half an hour of listening to the torturous wail of the siren, and praying they weren't being pursued, Knox slowed the pace of ambulance. The three younger companions watched hopefully, as he extended one of his long, hooked fingers and pressed the button to silence the crying banshee on the roof. The reflection of his pallid green eyes in the mirror revealed that he was as thankful for the peace as the rest of them.

'Well, I thought that went very well indeed!' Knox said, the escarpments of his cheeks rising into a smile.

'You certainly do have a way with words, Mr McRae.' Cyril laughed, visibly relaxing.

'That's one way of putting it,' Aria added, with a snigger of her own. 'You do have quite the pair of balls, Knox!'

That even earned a chuckle from the man himself.

'How many of them were there anyway?' Marcus asked, still pent up.

'Five when they stopped us, six if you include the captain.'

'What on Earth? So, you pulled up to what was essentially a fortified military roadblock, on an illegal mission to escape the country, and decided the best thing to do was to start shouting at six armed men … Are you sure you know what you're doing?' said Marcus in exasperation, his voice rising.

'Marcus, in matters like that, it's very important to know who and what you're dealing with,' the old artist said, becoming momentarily serious. 'Those men were young, inexperienced and clearly scared. In a simple clash of wills, sometimes, it genuinely is all about who can shout the loudest. Intimidation is a tool and a useful one at that, providing of course that you have the testicular fortitude to use it, as Aria has so articulately pointed out.' His tone eased again at the mention of her comment.

'I just think it could have been handled, *differently*, that's all,' Marcus retorted.

'That is because you, and I, are not the same. You'll avoid confrontation at all costs, even when it is necessary or, Heaven forbid, actually the most sensible option. You are, in that regard at least, the proverbial doormat, lad, and you know it.'

McRae delivered those blows to Marcus's ego without any panache or malice; to him they were simply facts, and statements like that were just another piece of the dispassionate puzzle that formed the great man.

As a blush crept up Marcus's cheeks, Aria began to laugh at him too, and even though he knew it was coming, its effects couldn't be diminished. She had told him, more times than he cared to recount, that his ability to defend his sensibilities was pitiful at best. But expecting to be stabbed, and being prepared for it, are two separate things, and every crease of her beautiful face and sound of glee that escaped her lips drove the knife deeper.

'Oh, come on, Merda, there's nothing wrong with being *soft*!' she jibed, observing the pensive look on his face.

'Exactly, you know what else is soft?' Marcus retorted, hoping to salvage the situation.

'What?' asked Cyril.

'Puppies, and everyone loves puppies.'

'I'll tell you what then, next time we run into trouble, I'll shout and you roll on your back and ask for a wee belly scratch, aye?' said Knox, thwarting Marcus's attempt at a self-deprecating comeback, and filling the ambulance with his rattling laughter. All three of them joined in then; even Marcus laughed in spite of himself, and although he wouldn't admit it, after the debacle at the Scottish border it felt good.

When their mirth petered out the entire cohort, with the exclusion of Knox who was still driving with infallible resolve, found themselves careening towards drowsiness. Still coming down from the exhilarating heights of their prior confrontation, and trapped inside the now sweltering ambulance with full bellies, they had little choice but to surrender to their fatigue.

Aria was the first to submit. Knowing that McRae's driving would likely be the death of her if she fell off the bench, she staggered to the storage hold, removed the large canvas packs that she and Marcus had brought with them to use as cushions, and wedged herself into the corner. She was asleep within seconds.

Marcus shook his head, amazed and slightly jealous of her ability to doze off so quickly, and then glanced at Cyril. The young man looked as composed as ever, the only tell-tale sign that he too had succumbed to the irresistible plea of sleep, was a slight tilt of his head as it rested against the wall. He was glad to see Cyril relax; he felt as though he deserved it. After all, he and Knox had left London at around 3:30 AM, some twelve hours ago; and they were still more than a hundred miles from the Orkney Islands.

He wished he could drift off himself, but the residual burning in his cheeks from McRae's scathing comments, and Aria's laughter, wouldn't allow it. He shifted his hazel eyes to where she was slumped in the corner like a rag doll, limbs akimbo in her makeshift nest, and let out an almost imperceptible sigh as a thousand thoughts of her rushed to the surface of his mind.

Each one was an irate reporter; and he was an alleged criminal leaving a courtroom. They clambered over one another in a desperate attempt to scream their question the loudest; meanwhile, he bobbed and weaved through their masses, trying urgently to reach the black car that would inevitably drive him to safety. But when the car sped off without him, Marcus had no choice other than to turn and face the rabid horde, who had now merged together to form one collective voice, all chanting that same, bitter word: *soft*.

He hated it, despised it, loathed it, abhorred it, detested it, and could not embrace the fact that it was true. Marcus had always wanted to be tough; he idealised the notion of being respected because he was strong and able, should the need arise, to take care of the people he cared for. As a child, he had fallen in love the with the ancient warriors battling across the pages of the books he'd read, and the warring clans he'd watched in cartoons on the television. The issue was that he'd never truly separated himself from those fantasies.

Throughout school he had strived to be athletic, proficient in sports and continuously tried, and miserably failed, to usurp the bigger boys from their thrones of popularity. It seemed to Marcus that the ideology of his childhood had failed him; he wasn't any of the things he wanted to be, and what he possessed instead were traits that placed him at the opposite end of the spectrum to his heroes. He was a talented artist, a kind-hearted joker full of compassion and, more often than not, selfless to a fault. Yet, worst of all for Marcus was the fact that he, as Knox had so eloquently phrased it, hated confrontation. How was it that he could want to be one thing, yet all his intrinsic qualities pointed him in the direction of another?

That was the riddle that had cleaved Marcus in two from a young age; and haunted him for all the days thereafter. After spending more than a decade attempting to balance his every deed between impressing others and remaining true to his own thoughts, he'd found himself to be pitifully unhappy.

It was that same unhappiness that was beginning to skulk out of the recesses of his mind at that very moment, leading Marcus towards a memory he knew all too well. He cast his mind back, through the exhausted haze of the day's events, and dredged up a conversation from one of his and McRae's very first encounters, in his London studio.

'Which side are you going choose?'

'There's a choice?'

'Don't insult your own intelligence, lad, you know there is, but you're too scared to choose one, in case you lose something you can't get back on the other,' said Knox, sounding infinitely knowledgeable.

His bludgeoning delivery had rendered Marcus silent, and he felt exposed under the penetrating eyes of his mentor, finding himself unable to summon words.

'You're a coward … and the sooner you admit that to yourself, the sooner you'll be able to work on becoming who you're supposed to be,' McRae remarked with stoic impassivity.

What he'd said had not meant to wound, only to inform, but the threatening jaws of reality were scraping agonisingly close to the bone, and Marcus's pride was screaming.

'How could you possibly presume to know so much about me?' he replied tersely. 'We've only met on what, three occasions? You don't know me, and you shouldn't assume you understand me. Assumptions are a dangerous thing, Mr McRae,' Marcus spat, as an uncharacteristic wave of anger began building inside him. He wanted to patronise the older man, to shake him from his judicious perch, but his response came out petulant.

'Assumptions *are* dangerous, I couldn't agree more, and I'd like to say I admire you for countering my statement, but that's not you talking, lad, it's your ego.'

'What do you know?' he cried, the hurt shining in his eyes.

'I know that there's a little voice in your head, a little voice that's been there for as long as you can remember, that tells you that you're different, that no one understands you, appreciates you, or could ever possibly love you as completely as you love them. It makes you the victim,' Knox crooned with absolute certainty. 'But – and this may come as a shock – that voice is lying. You've just capitulated to its will; those thoughts don't belong to you, they belong to *it*.'

Marcus swayed as though he'd taken a punch to the face. His temper subsided, leaving him weak, and forcing him to flop onto one of the wooden stools in the workshop. He braced himself for the next verbal onslaught, but McRae's truths overwhelmed him, nonetheless.

'Most egotists inflate themselves to unimaginable proportions, until the shadow of their self-professed greatness is so large, that it consumes them. But some egos don't explode, they implode. Yours is one such case; it's taken you in the opposite direction to the norm. It has locked you in a cage and convinced you that it's for your own safety. It wants you to believe that it's protecting you – the world is a terrible place, after all, but human beings aren't supposed to live their lives in boxes, Marcus,' Knox stated, the intensity of his glare unwavering. 'That war you've been fighting, those battles that no one can see, where the two sides of you roil against one another whilst you try to please everyone, do everything and not compromise a single thing along the way, they can't be won. What you need to realise is that you can't be all things to all be people. It's impossible to be who you think they want you to be, *and* be who you want to be, *and* expect to make it out alive. That's not how life works.'

'How?' Marcus croaked, feeling as though McRae's words were eviscerating him. 'How do you know all this?'

'I've lived almost three of your lifetimes, lad, experience counts for a lot, but beyond all that it's still not hard to see. You tell your story every time you put your brush to the canvas, that confused knot you've tied yourself into, that's the darkness I saw in you that night in Camden. You need to face it, cultivate it, civilise it and then show it to the world! So, I would encourage you to stop trying to be who you think you should be, for other people; and for God's sake lock your ego back where it belongs. Start choosing sides and start looking for the truth, or the lack of it will fill you with hate.'

Marcus closed the door on the harsh recollection and allowed Knox's words to ruminate in his mind. That particular monologue had wedged itself into Marcus's subconscious like a hatchet, and he often found himself referring to it because, as difficult as it was to admit, every word of that speech had been true. He'd been working hard on McRae's advice ever since that day and, more often than not, the fruits of his endeavours had been sweet. There is always at least one anomaly, however, and in this particular circumstance, it was Aria.

He blinked away his stare, and returned his gaze to the girl that was, in his mind, perhaps the most perplexing thing in the universe. Where she was concerned, it didn't seem to matter if he tried to amaze her with falsehoods, or impress her with his honesty and openness, she remained unreadable; like a book written in red ink on even redder paper. She continued to be the dazzling ray of confusion in his otherwise placid night but, for reasons still not entirely known to him, he wanted to be, to her, the most incredible thing in the world.

Marcus had been lost in his vivid recollections for far longer than he'd thought. When he finally broke free from his internal parenthesis, and searched his surroundings for a new diversion, he noticed that not only had the light outside begun to change, but through the hatch, the shimmering sea was now visible too.

Taking care not to wake the slumbering Cyril, he stood up, stretched his tight limbs as quietly as possible and made his way towards the hatch. He tested the strength of the storage cage by pressing both his palms against its metal clad top, then, satisfied with its integrity, propped himself up on it for a better view through the windscreen. It groaned slightly at his weight making Marcus freeze, but Aria, who had now retracted her arms and legs and was folded into a tight ball, snored on indifferently. He let out a relieved breath and turned his attention to the view ahead.

Knox gave him a nod but didn't say anything.

'What a view,' Marcus said quietly, looking out towards the ocean, and the sunbeams that danced across its rippling surface.

'Aye, it is. Few things in life captivate the creativity in us like the sun and the sea.'

'And what do you think?'

'I think it will lead just as many people to their deaths, as it will to their salvation.'

'It doesn't seem to matter what we're talking about, you never seem to say what I expect you to.'

'That is the art of good conversation, lad. If you always knew what I was going to say, you'd have no reason to talk to me, would you?' The stone smile appeared on Knox's face then and they both chuckled.

'Where are we anyway? We can't be far now.' Marcus was starting to grow restless.

'We're just coming to a place called Latheron, which is right on the eastern coast, hence why we can see the sea.' Knox paused, flinging the steering wheel to turn a corner and head further inland. 'In fact, we've been driving up the coastal road for over an hour – if you weren't so deep in thought you might have noticed.'

'Was it that obvious?' The younger man sighed in resignation.

'Hah! Marcus, you think so loudly you could wake the dead,' McRae said, laughing again. 'Very funny. How long until we reach our destination then?' Marcus said, not wanting to discuss his private musings.

'Less than half an hour now, we'll be slightly late but it won't matter – Hugo has his instructions. He'll wait.'

'Hugo?'

'Aye, he's is one of my closest friends. By my reckoning only a few years older than you actually, but it's his father whom I have a history with.'

'How long have you known him? Hugo's father I mean.'

'I forget. A while though, he's even got some of my early works, well, providing the old bastard hasn't binned them yet.' He snorted.

The mention of McRae's international friends suddenly remined Marcus of the unusual selection of currencies that he'd been given earlier that day. He wasn't sure why, but the thought of them settled uncomfortably in the pit of his stomach, where it proceeded to use his innards as playthings.

'You do seem to have a rather exotic group of friends, Knox?' The statement was a question in disguise; but McRae chose to ignore it.

'Ever the social butterfly, you know me,' he said evasively. 'Anyway, we're close now, I suggest you wake our friends.'

Before Marcus could reply, however, there was a muted rustle from the bench behind him, and he turned to see Cyril let out a cat-like yawn and open his eyes. He smiled, rose to his feet and stretched without a sound. His timing was impeccable, and Marcus once again questioned the theory of him actually being a robot.

'I think Cyril must have heard you,' Marcus said, gesturing over his shoulder.

'Perfect, that just leaves sleeping beauty then,' Knox jested.

'You've got more chance of flying to the sun on a paper plane! She doesn't take well to being woken up,' Marcus warned, with a thread of genuine fear laced around his joke.

'Do you *have* to talk so loudly?' came a groggy complaint from the floor.

'Much easier than anticipated,' refuted Knox, as Cyril almost succeeded in holding back his laughter.

'What can I say, it's time to get up?' Marcus said, winning him a surprisingly painful punch to the thigh from Aria, as she whined and hauled herself free from her warren. He massaged the spot where her fist had smashed into his leg and shuffled to his left, allowing her room to rest her elbows next to his on the luggage rack. Cyril joined them then, and three pairs of eyes, frost blue, burnt hazel and glossy black, followed the route of the ambulance as it crested a hill, and began to descend towards a secluded cove on the shoreline.

The Orkney Islands themselves were visible now too, some appearing extremely close, but others were nothing more than spectres on the gilded horizon. The evening sun was beginning to fall through the sky, not quite ready to set though, it hung lazily and threw out an orange light which engulfed everything in a molten, ochre blaze. None of them, besides Knox, had ever been this far north before and it felt to them, as though they were about to drive off the end of the Earth.

They were close to the cove now, but the road ended abruptly, with a high bank that shielded the beach on the other side. Marcus supposed that they would have to abandon the ambulance and proceed on foot which, given that they hadn't seen a soul for miles, was probably safe to do. However, as he opened his mouth to ask why Knox wasn't slowing down, the terrible realisation that McRae was going to drive straight over it dawned on him, snapping it shut before he'd uttered a syllable.

'Better hold on,' Knox said, with remarkable nonchalance, and far too late to be of any use. In a flash of mere seconds, that in actuality felt like a lifetime, they hurtled off the tarmac, scaled the rubble-strewn bank and flew through the air, before crashing onto the sandy, shingle beach with an almighty thump. The suspension groaned as the vehicle hopped along, trying to gain traction after the impact, and a harsh rattle near the rear axle indicated to them all that not everything had survived the impact. McRae limped the injured ambulance along, aiming for a small archway carved into the cliff that led through to a smaller inlet on the other side.

'Are you shitting me, Knox?' Aria admonished. 'Please tell me someone else is flying the damn plane?'

'Forget the plane, what about the bloody boat?' Marcus said, still regaining his bearings.

'I have *no idea* what you're complaining about, but you can untwist your underwear; I won't be piloting anything more extravagant than this ambulance.'

'What a relief!' Aria said, as they drove beneath the great stone arch and emerged on the other side where they were greeted by a large, khaki green landing craft, which appeared to be a relic from the storming of Dunkirk.

'That's our boat?' Aria guffawed.

'What were you expecting, sweet cheeks, a superyacht?' McRae rebuked.

As they drew closer, the immense, riveted haunches of the green beast became increasingly imposing, and Marcus found himself slightly in awe of its size. Its dense hide was dotted with the scars of war; bullet holes, flayed armour and most notably, there were two deep gauges along its right flank, the corrosion around their edges making them appear to be infected wounds that hadn't healed.

The loading ramp hung open like a great maw ready to devour them, and the cabin was painted in the same deep green as the hull, with most of the craft looking weathered at best, and almost derelict at its worst. In that tiny, isolated bay, with the peaceful decline of the burning sun behind it, the boat looked almost iniquitous, the decaying straightness of its edges seeming abrasive in contrast to the loveliness of its surroundings.

Marcus quickly dug through his bag in search of his camera, and snapped a few images of the stalwart vessel, certain he'd never see another quite like it.

'It looks worse than I'd imagined, Mr McRae,' Cyril admitted.

'Aye, she's seen better days, of that I'm sure. But the old girl is still seaworthy, or she wouldn't have made it here,' Knox replied, as he aligned the ambulance with the mouth of the great brute, and began to drive aboard.

'You never mentioned that we'd be taking the ambulance with us?' Marcus questioned, craning his neck to peer through the hatch.

'That's because technically, *we're not*,' was McRae's ambiguous reply.

As tired as he and his companions were, they didn't even bother to pry any further, knowing that the answers to Knox's enigmatic puzzles were rarely worth the hassle. Once they were completely on board the boat, McRae pulled the handbrake and turned the engine off.

After so many hours with the diesel-powered lump chugging away in the background, Marcus found its absence to be quite disconcerting, and started to scuff his feet against one another just to fill the quiet void. Fortunately, Knox had no intentions of sitting still.

'Right then, children, everybody out. We need to meet our captain,' he said and popped open his door to walk out on the deck, just as a large, bearded man exited the boat's cabin and strode towards them.

With their vehicle still, Cyril removed the locking bar from the rear doors, and led his friends around the ambulance to where Knox was stood with their new ally. The young Chinese man moved with the grace of a panther, but Marcus and Aria found their legs to be stiff and uncooperative, making them lope forwards with jerky, unnatural steps. They ambled up to stand with McRae and Cyril who, apparently already acquainted with the stranger, greeted him with an enthusiastic handshake. Then Knox spoke again, and his next words tore their attention away from their achy limbs and prised their mouths open in disbelief.

'Aria, Marcus, allow me to introduce you to my friend, Prince Hugo of Sweden, Duke of Jämtland.'

Chapter V

Prince Hugo of Sweden, or just Hugo as he preferred to be called, was an imposing yet extraordinarily gentle figure.

After a series of warm introductions on the deck, their would-be captain enlisted Cyril to help him secure the ambulance in place, and then raised the great jawbone of the ramp to seal them in. The burly Swede then guided them into the cramped cockpit, the deteriorating architecture of which echoed the perishing metal of the landing craft's exterior, making it feel gloomy. The dark wasn't helped by the odour in the room; where a mixture of the sea's salty tang, a metallic scent, and a dusty, plastic musk made the air seem unusually thick.

Hugo turned to the helm, settled his broad back into one of the cracked, misshapen chairs and set about casting them off. Marcus watched the chair compress under his bulk and observed a small, yellow piece of stuffing as it bulged and rippled from a tear in the bolster. Knox took up the equally decrepit seat to his right, and the two began to converse in whispers, whilst Cyril moved into a leaning position against the left wall, and peered out of the clouded glass at the swelling sea below.

Marcus stood beside Aria at the back of the room, adjusting his stance as the boat rocked in the shallow waters, and watched with genuine admiration as the Prince skilfully operated the boat's controls. The array of flashing buttons, movable switches and spinning dials which covered the dashboard seemed immensely complex, and the components were so densely packed together that they looked, in the early evening light, like a bird's eye view of a miniature city.

'This guy's got to be in the military, right?' Marcus said, nudging Aria and nodding toward Hugo. 'I've never seen anything like it.'

'Yeah definitely, how else would he know how to steer a boat like this? It's not exactly the sort of thing you see every day, is it?' she replied, without taking her eyes off the Swede.

'I can't believe he's part of the bloody Royal Family either. Just when I thought this day couldn't escalate any further, it just did.'

'It really is bizarre and he's certainly … *something*,' came her wistful reply. Marcus, curious about the tone of her voice, turned his head to see her ogling Hugo with a devilish smile playing on her lips.

'Wow. I really can't take you anywhere, can I?' he teased.

'What?' she said indignantly. 'He looks like the love child of a Michelangelo painting and a Viking Lord; it's not my fault he's so handsome.'

'Whatever you say.' Marcus snorted, trying to sound amused, whilst secretly quelling the spite bubbling in his chest. Her words had formed fingers and they plucked, ever so lightly, at the chords of jealously that surrounded his heart. He moved his eyes from her soft face, to examine more closely the man who had so quickly become the object of her infatuation.

Prince Hugo was tall, roughly the same height as Knox, but where the artist was gnarled and thin, he was square and strapping; even sitting down he almost seemed to loom over McRae as they spoke. He was dressed in green combat trousers, which nearly matched the colour of the boat, tan brown boots and a ribbed, white top that accentuated his physique.

His chestnut hair was slicked back on the top of his scalp like a sculpted wave; the sides, however, were cut much shorter and ran down until they met the voluminous mass of his trimmed auburn beard. The jawline beneath that beard was almost as muscular as his arms, and was complemented by a strongly bridged nose, thin lips and eyes the colour of crushed chocolate biscuits, deep brown and flecked with gold.

For a fetching man, with such evident physical prowess, it would've been extremely easy for him to swagger around wearing his self-importance like brilliant, shining armour. But Hugo, from the little they had seen of him thus far, carried himself without even a hint of braggadocio. In fact, the contrary seemed to be true; he almost seemed shy, and that only deepened Marcus's irrational dislike for the man.

In spite of that, however, he managed to wrestle his ill feelings towards Hugo into submission, addressing their nonsensicality, and vowed to get to know him before he made any further judgements. He shifted his focus to the hazy windows, and watched, as the vessel turned away from the beach and out towards the sea.

After only a few minutes traversing the waters between the isles, it became apparent to everyone aboard that although the journey wouldn't be a long one, it certainly would be a rough one. The route they were taking to the tiny scrap of land called Copinsay, required them to manoeuvre close to the cliffs of the larger islands, in order to use them as cover. Unfortunately, their proximity to the stony overhangs meant the sea was constantly tumultuous. The waves crashed into the rock walls with roaring violence, bouncing back and striking the hull, which sent merciless, reverberating tremors through the craft, like a thousand fists beating against its steel underside.

It wasn't a pleasant sensation for any of them, and as Aria and Marcus gripped the wall to stay upright, it occurred to him that Cyril had remained totally motionless, and silent, since they had arrived in the cockpit. Despite that being his natural disposition, there was something troubling about how he stood, and Marcus eyed his friend with a flash of concern. He noticed his shallow breathing, the sallow appearance his face had acquired, and the greenish tinge that had started to dampen his regal features.

'Cyril, do you get sea–'

'Sick?' he finished, predicting Marcus's question. 'Yes!' he said, rushing from the room in a sudden explosion of energy.

Aria leapt back out of his way as he made for the door, one hand clasped over his stomach, the other over his mouth. She looked at Marcus and they both winced knowingly. Hugo and Knox were so deeply engrossed in their conversation that they barely noticed Cyril's dash to the starboard railing, but when Marcus followed to check on the fate of his friend, the Prince lifted his head. He pointed out a few specific levers and buttons to McRae, entrusted him with the navigation of the boat, and left to join the two young men outside.

Cyril collapsed to his knees and retched hopelessly into the sea. His fists were clenched about the guard rail so tightly, that the blood had drained from his knuckles, making the skin on his hands match that of his ashen face. Marcus patted him on the shoulder, in an attempt to soothe his distressed friend, and quickly whipped his head out of the way every time the wind threatened to shower him in vomit. The sound of heavy footsteps approaching snatched Marcus's attention away from the liquid projectiles, and he was surprised to see that it was Hugo who'd come to their aid. He offered Marcus a neutral half-smile and then addressed the miserable form that was Cyril.

'Come now, master Chan, must you be ill *every* time I take you out on a boat?' asked Hugo in a voice that was soft and melodic.

The English came out flawlessly and Marcus gaped slightly, surprised at how such a smooth voice could be so charismatic. He was also becoming increasingly intrigued by Cyril and Hugo's relationship and in an effort to learn more, refrained from speaking, hoping that if the two conversed that they would reveal more about their past.

'Once.' Cyril gurgled, dragging himself into a standing position. 'Once I was not sick. When you took me to Tallinn, remember?' he finished, gritting his teeth.

'Ah, maybe I am a liar after all. I do remember that trip, the Baltic Sea was like cashmere that day, I haven't seen it that still since!' Hugo conceded, reaching out with of one of his giant paws, to steady his fragile companion. 'Today we've got no such luck, but don't fret, Cōng-ming, we'll be back on solid land within the hour.'

'I may expire before then,' Cyril moaned, although some of his colour was returning.

'You're getting weak in your old age, little brother,' Hugo taunted affably.

'I am still south of thirty, unlike you, *big brother*.'

'Still just as quick though, it seems,' Hugo said, letting out a rhythmic chuckle, and reaching his other hand around to grab Cyril in a playful headlock which he avoided with feline precision, despite his nausea, verifying the Prince's point. They both laughed then and Marcus, who couldn't help but be delighted by the authenticity of the exchange, joined them.

'Come now, we need to get you a bucket and we should probably get you lower down too,' Hugo announced, signalling towards the loading deck, where the ambulance resided. 'It will be less turbulent down there.'

Cyril nodded his approval and began heading in the direction of the steps with slow, cautious movements. Marcus smiled and turned to re-enter the cockpit when Hugo spoke again.

'Marcus, why don't you wait out here? I'll only be a minute; we should have a chat when I get back.' It wasn't a question, but equally, there was no menace in his words.

'Sure, why not?' Marcus said easily, now thoroughly fascinated by the enigmatic Prince. He couldn't resist grinning, as he watched Hugo and Cyril wander off and disappear down the slick, metal stairs. They were complete contrasts in appearance, one a nigh on seven-foot boulder of a man, the other hardly over five feet and possessing the figure of a rattlesnake, and yet they complemented each other perfectly.

There is something to be said of the transcendental quality of true friendship. Its blatant disregard for race, colour and creed, in favour of the harmonious union of two similar minds and hearts, can be magical to behold. That's what the world was missing, Marcus thought, more friendships like that.

Listening to the two men talk had left Marcus feeling ebullient; but it had also filled him with questions. There seemed to be an eclectic web of people formed around McRae that Marcus had previously been oblivious to, and it was beginning to gnaw at him, that Knox appeared to be the spider in the centre of it all.

Perhaps he was overthinking the issue, as was the case with the vast majority of things that entered his head, but why was he such good friends with the Prince? Why had he raised a young man from China? Why did Cyril and Hugo act as though they'd known one another for years – had they? His head was spinning with the ambiguity of it all, and just as he prepared to throw in the cognitive towel, the thumping footfall of the Swede approached again, disentangling him from his thoughts and bringing him back to reality.

'How's Cyril doing?' Marcus enquired.

'Cyril? Oh, you mean Cōng-ming, sorry, I forget that most people don't call him that.' He smiled. 'He'll be fine. I don't know why, and it doesn't matter how many times I introduce him to the ocean, but he has yet to gain his sea legs.' The bigger man sighed and in that, Marcus saw his first opportunity to glean some information from Hugo; and seized it.

'Maybe the sea isn't for everyone,' he said non-committedly. 'But it sounds like you've known each other for a long time?'

'We have. We grew up together, in a way,' replied the Prince.

'Really, how?'

'Knox and my father, they've been friends since before I was born and they frequently visit each other, well, they used to, before the world came crashing down. Naturally, when I was old enough to go with my father to London, I did, and when Cōng-ming was apprenticed to Knox, he started to come to Stockholm.'

'That's crazy! A Chinese boy, living in England, and a Swedish Prince become best friends through their mutual acquaintance with a mad artist?' He huffed, starting to laugh.

'You couldn't write it!' Hugo replied, equally amused. 'But not all brothers are those of our own blood.'

'Don't you have any true siblings then?' Marcus asked, keen to know more.

'Oh no, I have many. The Swedish Royal Family is, complicated, shall we say.'

'I can't say it's something I've ever looked into.'

'Well, if you do,' Hugo said, with a grin stretching his handsome features, 'I'd advise you to bring several calculators, at least one historian and enough coffee to last you a week.'

'That bad?' Marcus tittered.

'That bad,' seconded the Prince.

There was a quiet moment then, as their laughter slowed and the conversation dwindled. Marcus used the time to adjust his hands on the rail and plan his next question; but it was Hugo who spoke first.

'So, how did you meet Knox then?'

'What?' asked Marcus rudely, caught slightly off guard.

'Well I knew you were coming, and your friend, but I always find it interesting to hear how people find themselves in Knox's life. The man himself never reveals too much, you see.'

'You could say that, he can be quite devious at times, I've noticed,' Marcus said, seeking to move the trajectory of the discussion away from himself.

'I think it's a trait he's carried over from his military days,' Hugo replied, with a hint of his tuneful chuckle colouring his words. 'You could get the blood from a thousand stones before Knox McRae gave you a straight answer to a question.'

'Too true,' Marcus agreed, deciding that he quite liked the brawny Swede after all. 'I don't know much about his time in the army. I mean, you can read all about it on the internet, but I've never asked him directly.'

'If you get the chance, ask my father about it, he's got so many stories about Knox. They even fought together once I believe.'

'You're joking?' Marcus asked incredulously.

'Perhaps *fought together* is a bit far-fetched, it was something to do with an assassination attempt in Geneva. I don't remember the details exactly,' he replied offhandedly.

'Wait a minute, Knox McRae defended *The King of Sweden* during an assassination attempt? When?' Marcus yelped, flinging the questions at Hugo, becoming suddenly abashed by just how little he understood about the man he thought he knew so well.

The Prince considered his answer for a second, his face intense, as he searched for the correct date in the vaults of his memories. But much to Marcus's dismay, the question remained unanswered, as Aria came bounding up on the other side of Hugo and shattered the moment.

Ignorant to the damage she'd done to Marcus's campaign for information, Aria smiled coquettishly at Hugo, and refused to acknowledge the irritation plastered across her old friend's face. His thoughts formed a storm inside him, so tempestuous, it made the waves below seem like a tranquil pond, and the last thing Marcus wanted was for his confusion of feelings for Aria to cloud his mind further. So, with considerable effort, he composed himself and took his leave, using the excuse that he was going to check on Cyril as the reason for his departure.

He made his way down the stairs towards the loading deck, steering his train of thought away from her flirtations, and back towards what he'd learned from the Prince of Sweden.

Marcus took up a seat on the bottom step, out of sight, and grappled with the questions as they came to him, despondently finding himself ill equipped to answer any of them. What concerned Marcus the most, was that as McRae's list of known international associates became bigger, so too did the proportions of the situation he'd embroiled himself, and Aria, in.

When he'd been offered the chance to find the truth, to strike back against the powers that be, he'd snapped Knox's hand off without a second thought. He'd trusted, and idolised, McRae, he thought he knew the old artist well but as is typically the case, one only sees what they want to see. Time would tell if he'd made the right choice but, as he felt the first miniscule fibre of doubt begin to unspool from its bobbin, he knew it would keep unravelling until he had his answers.

Tired of thinking, guessing and not knowing, Marcus left the step and walked around the side of the ambulance until he found Cyril, who was sitting on the floor, bucket in hand, with his back against the vehicle.

'Looks like you've seen better days,' he said, addressing the sorry state of his friend on the floor with an apologetic expression.

'You could say that,' Cyril replied, trying to smile, but still looking defeated.

'Do you mind if I join you?'

'Feel free, I would be glad for the company, just please do not expect any riveting conversation from me.'

'I think I've had enough conversations for one day, so don't worry, I won't be chewing your ears off,' Marcus joked, making his way past Cyril to take a seat on the floor a few feet to his right. Without another word, he leant his tired head back against the ambulance, closed his eyes and let the rocking of the boat persuade him into a light sleep.

There was no way to tell how long he'd been there, afloat in the twilight world between wakefulness and dreams, but the respite it provided from his corporeal body, without its aches, pains and needs, felt like numb ecstasy. Marcus roamed the great plains of that hazy place, hoping to fall down a rabbit hole that would eventually lead him to a sincere, restful slumber.

Lavishing in the peacefulness of his quiet state, he couldn't help but think that the sliver of paradise he'd been granted was as a kind of reward, perhaps for staying awake throughout the entirety of Knox's perilous drive north. But just as Marcus was about to drift off completely, a noise broke the stillness, a siren song pulling him back towards the land of living, calling his name.

He followed it, wanting to hear more, wanting to know the face behind that sweet serenade. However, as his lucidity transformed into consciousness, the music turned shrill and, prising his eyes open with a herculean effort, he found no ethereal siren; only Aria standing over him with a triumphant smirk on her face.

'Wakey, wakey Marcus, payback's a bitch, right?' she said in jubilation, pleased to have had her revenge so soon.

'Oh, piss off, Ari!' he snapped.

'*What can I say, it's time to get up?*' she sneered, repeating the words he'd said to her, just a few hours earlier in the back of the ambulance.

He kicked out at her legs but she jumped back, causing Marcus to slide down the back of the ambulance until he was nothing more than a pile on the floor. Aria's infectious laughter rang out then, leaving Marcus and Cyril no choice but to giggle along with her.

'I'm assuming that, as you've so kindly woken me up, we're almost there?' Marcus asked, his voice rife with sarcasm, as he uncrumpled himself and got to his feet.

'Clever boy!' she replied, miming stroking a dog and throwing an invisible ball.

That caused Cyril to laugh hysterically, and Marcus shot him a glance that could've been a bullet; but it did little to stem his amusement.

'God, sometimes you just make it too easy, Merda. Yes, we're almost there, you see that chunk of land poking out behind that stack of rock, that's Copinsay,' Aria said, pointing to a very flat island, not far from their position.

'I can't believe we're finally here. I think this has been the longest day of my life,' muttered Marcus in response.

'I could not agree more,' added Cyril, as he put the bucket down and rose on wobbly legs, causing Aria to turn to him with a pitying look.

'What I want to know, Cyril, is how McRae's driving barely fazed you, but less than two hours on a boat has put you at death's door?' she questioned humorously.

'It is a mystery.' He shrugged. 'I will just be glad when the ground under my feet is not bucking like a wild mule.'

With that, the three of them made their way back into the dim cockpit, willed the last few moments of the journey away, and watched the light wane through the filthy windows. They arrived in only a few minutes, and as Hugo directed the craft into a pebbled hollow in the cliffs, Marcus started to appreciate just how small Copinsay was.

The island comprised two, nearly separate, wedge-shaped landmasses which were connected by a strip of zigzagging earth, no wider than a single-track road. Although the cliffs were lower than the boat where they were, on the opposing side, the brooding grey stone shot up out of the water in sheer, vertical faces which rivalled those of the mainland in height.

The skeleton of a lighthouse sat atop the bluffs, and though it appeared to have been in ruins for some time, its sentinel glare still made him feel uneasy. Trying not to think of the ghosts dwelling in that dead tower, he concentrated on the vibrations through his feet, as the bow, and then the hull scraped the rocks hidden beneath the surface of the water.

The section of the island they would be disembarking onto was the larger of the two; and it looked completely barren. Its only denizens were grasses, rocks, and, bisecting the uneven ground from one craggy tip to the other, was a gravel runway. Noticing this, Marcus and Aria pressed closer to the windows in search of the plane that might carry them to freedom, and the truth.

Aria had been disappointed by the unexpectedly dishevelled state of the boat that awaited them in Scotland, and she was wearing a similarly disenchanted expression as her eyes found the aircraft.

It was relatively small, somewhere around fifty feet long, Marcus estimated as he squinted at it. Its riveted body was an off-white, although whether that was by design or simply as a result of its age, couldn't be determined in the dusky light. There was also a blue line running horizontally down the flanks of the plane, just below the row of windows, and another which ran across the front edge of each wing.

Most notable though, was the coat of arms, which was in actuality the Swedish Royal Crest Marcus would later learn, adorning the vertical fin of the tail. The golden lions of the emblem shimmered in what little remained of the sun's glow, and although there was a subtly aged look about the plane's service-worn body, nothing could tarnish the fact that it was a rather impressive private jet.

'What's up with your face?' Marcus asked Aria, with a troublemaker's smile.

'I don't know,' she said, with a quizzical furrow of her brow. 'I guess it just isn't what I was expecting, somehow. When you said we were catching a flight, I think I'd imagined a full sized plane.'

'Ari, we're about to be flown out of a quarantined country, by a Prince, in what is probably a royal jet, for a secret rendezvous with the Swedish King ...' He trailed off, his eyes widening at her as he spoke. 'Let that shit sink in. This is real. Maybe you need to adjust your expectations?' He laughed and nudged her impishly.

'When you put it like that ... I hate it when you're right.' She giggled and pushed him back. Then her laughter faded, and her smile was replaced with a thoughtful frown. She turned to McRae who, along with Hugo, was rising from his squeaking chair and preparing to leave.

'This should be good,' Marcus muttered under his breath, knowing that she was about to ask a question that could, quite literally, be anything.

'Knox.' He looked up, at the mention of his name. 'What the hell are we going to do with the ambulance?'

'We're going to sink it,' he replied, his tone suggesting that sinking ambulances in the North Sea was an everyday activity.

Cyril remained passive at the remark, Hugo, likely aware of the plan, was unfazed but Marcus and Aria both looked at the Scot as though he was a madman. McRae rolled his eyes.

'Let me explain before you try to send me to the loony bin, aye? We couldn't leave it in Scotland, despite the fact that there is no one living anywhere near that beach; I knew it wouldn't be safe. I'd planned for this, that's why I asked Hugo to bring a landing craft.'

'That's all well and good, but if it's not safe to leave an ambulance on a beach, how is it safe to leave the boat on one? Or are you planning on flying it to Sweden with us?' she challenged.

Hugo, apparently not used to seeing people confront the older man in that way, let out a small, chuckling snort.

'No. We're sinking that too.'

'Seriously?' Marcus interjected, taken aback by his candid reply.

'It's simple Marcus, honestly,' Hugo said smiling, his voice making Aria attentive. 'Once we've unloaded everything we need, I'll place a small, timed explosive in the storage room below the cockpit, rig the throttle and controls so the craft manoeuvres back into open water, and then bang!' He made an explosive gesture with his hands. 'The charge will blow a hole in the hull, and the water will claim them both.'

'You really do make it sound so stress-free.' Marcus exhaled, unable to argue with the straightforwardness of his explanation.

'So that's why you brought a boat that's already on its last legs – you were going to sink it all along,' Aria said, more to herself that anyone else, as the realisation struck her. 'Won't people notice an explosion though?' she wondered aloud.

'No,' Knox said immediately. 'As I said, the population around here is almost non-existent and even if word did somehow get to the right ears, no one has the resources to go fishing right now. We're safe,' he concluded. 'Anyway, now you've had your masterclass in ship sinking, shall we get a move on?' McRae asked rhetorically as he made his way out of the cockpit.

'Wait, wait, wait, how are we going to get home?' she cried after him, but he didn't indulge her with a response.

Cyril was the first to follow Knox, the allure of dry, solid land beneath his feet propelled him onwards with speed. Marcus went after him, leaving Hugo holding the door open for Aria, who seemed quite delighted by the small act of gallantry.

Together they retrieved the numerous bags, cases and packs from the storage cage and carried them up the rock-scattered beach. Before they could reach the runway, however, they had to ascend a small, but practically vertical outcrop. Hugo, using his height and strength to his advantage, vaulted up the rock face, whilst Cyril sprang up behind him, with wasp like agility.

Marcus handed them their cargo, piece by piece, and then found himself being hauled up as well, just as the bags were before him. Knox came next, his lean frame meant his was light, and Marcus and Cyril lifted him with ease; meanwhile, Hugo flung Aria up with a sweep of his powerful arms. Her black-brown hair billowed out behind her, and she landed with her hands in his, a mirrored grin splitting both their faces.

Marcus pretended not to notice, even as the musical thrum of jealousy's harp began to fill his head with its ghostly notes.

Having made it off the beach, each of them loaded themselves up and began to make their way towards the plane, with the exception of the prince, who was now jogging back down the beach to attend to the funeral rites of the boat. They walked towards the front of the aircraft which, at that close a propinquity, Marcus had decided was undeniably a form of private jet. Knox lifted a small cover to the right of the door to reveal a numbered keypad with aluminium buttons, into which he punched a six digit code, that caused the door to pop open with a creaking whoosh as the seals were released.

Instead of entering though, they turned collectively, and watched as the landing craft sputtered back into life one last time. Hugo, barely more than a silhouette now, with the sun half melted into the horizon, jumped over the raised ramp and landed with an audible thud, narrowly missing the water. Breathing heavily from his dash up the hillside, the prince made it back to the rest of the cohort, and swung around quickly to the see if his mission had been successful.

The boat slogged its way away from the shore, almost looking resistant to the pull of its engines, like a beast being herded to the slaughterhouse. It had barely made it a hundred feet into the water when it rocked with a sudden, violent seizure, spraying shattered glass and fragmented metal in all directions. As the delayed thump of the blast hit their ears, Marcus pondered on what type of explosive their Swedish friend had used, to cause such damage, without any of the bright lights and licking flames that were always so prevalent in the film industry. He made a mental note to ask Hugo when the next opportunity arose, and then lost the thought as he reached once again for his pack, hoping to seize his camera, before the craft went down.

Marcus took a few successful photographs as the setting sun vanished entirely beyond the horizon, leaving nothing but a couple of fiery trails streaming across the indigo sky, like the tail feathers of a giant phoenix. Then the boat, and the ambulance, were gone, and as they plummeted to the sea floor to rust and rot, the veracity of what he'd just seen revealed itself to him. There really was no going back now; they had no choice but to keep moving forwards.

Chapter VI

Marcus woke with a start.

He rubbed at his sleep encrusted eyes, trying to remember where he was and how he had got there, when he suddenly, randomly, became very aware of how comfortable his seat was. A mystified look passed over his face as he began to pat the sumptuous, leather upholstered chair he was reclining in, but his sleep addled brain did little to help him reclaim his lost bearings. Sitting forwards in order to rouse himself properly, Marcus began to reacquaint himself with his surroundings, watching the mists of fatigue dissipate as he did so.

The interior of the Royal plane was opulently designed. The floor, and a few feet of the walls before they hit a narrow shelf, were clad in a warm stained pine, which made the space feel almost like a chalet. The portion of the walls above the shelf, and the ceiling, were the colour of soft vanilla ice cream, made all the more delicious by the mellow glow being cast from the brushed aluminium lights above.

Marcus himself was sat in one of the four high backed, luxuriously padded chairs which were positioned on either side of the passenger compartment. Each pair of seats faced one another, and was separated by a large foldout table, made from creamy, gold speckled marble. It was undoubtedly the most palatial mode of transport that he had, and probably would, ever travel in and Marcus found that he was almost disappointed in himself for falling asleep; and not savouring the experience.

He let his eyes rove around one more time, following the line of the thickly piled rug that ran up the aisle until his gaze met the backs of his companions, where they crowded in the doorway of the cockpit. He stood and made his way towards them, stretching as he went and noticing for the first time, how black the night was beyond the windows. Letting out an obnoxiously loud yawn as he approached, Marcus swung a brotherly arm around Cyril's small shoulders to lean on him.

'Are we getting close yet? I'm starving!' he declared, making Cyril snicker.

'Welcome back to the land of the living, we thought we'd lost you there, lad. You dropped off so quickly it looked like you'd died,' Knox rasped in his thick, guttural voice.

'Nice to know you'd miss me, Knox,' Marcus joked, feeling rejuvenated by his nap.

'Miss you? Not a Chance, I was glad for the peace.'

'I second that, you're much easier to like when you're asleep,' Aria quipped.

'I mean, I think you are *ok*,' Cyril added.

'Wow guys, you really are *the best* of friends,' Marcus said, feigning being shot through the heart as he laughed.

'Pay them no mind, Marcus!' Hugo bellowed from his seat in the cockpit. 'We can find you some new friends in Stockholm, and hopefully get you fed.'

'Sounds good to me,' Marcus answered, pushing the unwelcome image of Aria's hands in those of the Swede out of his mind as it resurfaced.

'And to answer your earlier question, yes, we are very close now. You see those lights ahead of us?' Hugo continued, gesturing out of the curved windows ahead of them. 'That's my city, the beauty on the water.'

'The beauty on the water?' Marcus enquired.

'Yes! It is an opinion of mine, that people who have never visited the city before don't associate it with the water. But the Swedish archipelago, I hope I've said that right, which Stockholm is built on, actually has more islands than the Caribbean!' Hugo said, his animated hand movements punctuating the words, as he spoke pridefully of his homeland.

'Seriously? That's unbelievable,' replied Marcus genuinely surprised.

'That sounds like perfect pub quiz trivia to me,' Aria said with a smirk.

'Honestly, go to the windows and take a look; even in the dark you'll be able to see it,' Hugo said, making shooing motions at them over his shoulder.

Knox remained where he was, having little interest in seeing a view he'd already observed a hundred times before, but Cyril, who was also very familiar with the Swedish capital, still seemed excited by the prospect of laying eyes on it again. He accompanied Marcus and Aria as they hurried enthusiastically towards the passenger windows, where they clambered onto the seats, and pressed their faces as close to the plastic as possible. None of them wanted to miss a thing as they descended into Scandinavia.

'It does not matter how many times I see those lights, they never stop being beautiful,' Cyril said, sounding almost reverent, his earnest intonation enchanting his two friends.

Nearly all major cities, in Marcus's experience at least, looked rather astounding from the air, particularly at night. Their great masses of lights, the dark ribbons of water that signified rivers, the wide, weaving roads streaked with tiny dots of traffic; it was always incredible to see the great feats of human civilisation as a bird might. But Stockholm was unlike anything he'd seen before.

The landscape itself, although blurred by the early morning darkness, was still distinct. The structure of the coastline suggested it had once been a single, solid mass but it had somehow become shattered, as though a colossal hammer had struck it and sent shards of Sweden flying into the sea. The capital city was further inland and spanned a number of islands, but it didn't sprawl greedily like an American city, or follow the regimental code of a Roman one; instead it trailed out almost organically; like a monolithic kraken come home to roost.

Its heart lay in the densely packed city centre and from there, numerous bridges spanned the gaps over the water like tentacles, as if the creature of Stockholm was in fact fighting the currents beneath and holding the land together. The little spots of light that comprised its body spread far and wide and formed an asymmetrical pattern until, at last, they fizzled out at the tips of its stretching appendages. The view was absolutely gorgeous; and Marcus was besotted with the place before he'd even stepped foot in it.

He backed away from the window, energised by thoughts of what might be in store for them in the city below, and turned to see his sentiments reflected in Aria's glassy eyed stare as she proceeded to gaze into the night. Feeling Marcus's eye on her, she shifted on the chair, and pulled away smiling.

'I can't believe we got out! And we're going to a place I've never been before,' she said with bubbly enthusiasm, in spite of the late hour.

'I know, not an easy thing to do these days, little miss nomad.'

'Yes, Marcus mentioned that you liked to travel, Aria; where have you been?' Cyril asked, his superbly spoken English fitting of the plane's lavish décor.

'Where hasn't she been?' Marcus huffed.

'I don't know where to start, India is definitely my favourite country! But I've also been to Thailand, Cambodia, parts of the Philippines...' Marcus rolled his eyes and let out a chuckle, knowing that Cyril was completely naïve to the conversational can of worms he'd just unleashed, and led his friends back towards the cockpit.

Aria was in full swing, reeling off countries she'd been to and monuments she'd seen with a lightning quickness, whilst Cyril, ever the kind soul, listened intently and smiled along with her. Knox, however, impatient and weary, had no tolerance for her incessant chatter.

'Aria, what are you doing, lass, reading Cyril the entire encyclopaedia of the world from memory? How about you give it a rest, aye?' he said in an unusually placid tone.

'Who put a penny in you?' she retorted, displeased to have her passionate recount interrupted by the old artist. It wasn't her finest choice and McRae turned then for the first time, pulling himself up to his full height, and loomed over her.

'I've been awake now for almost thirty hours. I've driven just shy of seven hundred miles, whilst *you* rested your delicate eyes in the back. I've driven a boat, and remained awake in the cockpit as you, *once again,* did nothing but lay down and catch up on your beauty sleep,' he seethed through gritted teeth, the unblinking fire in his eyes melting the defiant ice in hers. 'So, forgive me if I'm a little tetchy, it's been a long day, *pumpkin*.' He grimaced; the inflection in his voice made Aria flinch.

She gave a single nod, in faux indifference, and folded her arms like a schoolgirl being told off by a teacher. The silence pressed on for a few moments after that; none of them, not even Hugo, wanted to disturb Knox's peace for fear that they too, would end up face to face with the serrated edge of his fury. In the end it was Cyril, with his idiomatic serenity, that ended the quiet spell with a question.

'Which airport are we landing at, Hugo, will it be Bromma?'

'Not this time, my friend. Tonight, we're landing at Arlanda, in the north.'

'Why so far out of the city?' Cyril queried.

'It's a matter of public relations, I suppose. Even though Sweden isn't under quarantine, it would still cause an unpleasant stir amongst the people to see a royal aircraft in the skies during such a time,' the prince answered, in his almost song like speech.

'So how far out of the centre will we be?' came Aria's voice, in a significantly quieter tone than usual.

'Only around fifty kilometres.'

'What's that in real money?' Marcus added.

'Roughly thirty miles. It won't take us long, maybe an hour.'

'And where are we going?' Aria and Marcus asked, nearly simultaneously, but McRae cut in before the prince had a chance to offer them an answer.

'Hugo, for the sake of my sanity and their safety, please just tell them the plan. If I have to hear another question, I might just pop the airlock and throw them out one by one,' he growled, scrubbing his tired eyes, and sweeping back his wild white hair. Their eyes widened at that, the older man's tone as flat as ever, leaving them all powerless to discern whether or not he was joking.

'Of course,' Hugo replied, intervening in the potential murder of his passengers. 'As I've already said, we will be landing in Arlanda. There are a few private hangars belonging to my father there, where we can land safely and store the plane. Fortunately, there are also some of the royal family's cars held there too, we'll take one and travel into the city by road, which will be much more discreet.'

Marcus was practically bursting to ask more about the Swedish King's car collection but refrained; a mental picture of McRae hurling him from the plane making him cautious.

'I'll be dropping you off at the Hotel Diamant and then, well, you sleep!' He laughed. 'Once you've had some rest, I will come back to collect you and show you some of this wonderful city, before we meet my father tomorrow to talk business. Sound good?'

'It sounds like someone else's life,' Marcus said, dumbstruck by how causally Hugo had described a sequence of events which he'd never expected to ever hear uttered, let alone be a part of.

'Indeed. In Sweden, you are our guests, and you are free people. Enjoy the respite, whilst it lasts,' he concluded, his beaming smile visible in the reflection on the windscreen.

'Now that story time is over, you should return to your seats, children, we'll be landing soon,' Knox said, the look in his hard, jade eyes alerting them to the fact that it was an order, not a suggestion.

The three young travellers complied with his wishes, returning to their seats, and reintroducing their bodies to the delightful plushness of them. McRae didn't follow them into the passenger section and take his seat; instead he chose to remain in the cockpit and see out the remainder of the journey in the co-pilot's chair.

Marcus poked his head out from time to time in an effort to catch any stray snippets of conversation from the prince and the artist, but their whispers were indecipherable at that distance. The only word his ears seemed to latch onto was "victor", which he noticed was being repeated quite frequently; however, without any context it meant nothing. He abandoned his eavesdropping then and returned his attention to the city beyond the windows, his lust for knowledge throbbing harder in his veins, as they drew closer and closer to the ground.

Some thirty minutes slid by before the rubber of the landing gear made contact with the smooth asphalt of the runway. Hugo brought them down with expert precision, and Marcus found himself once again fascinated by the prince's abilities.

They'd landed some distance away from the main terminals, on a thinner runway, that led towards two hangars made from dark corrugated metal. As they moved nearer, Marcus could see that the enormous doors wore the same crest that ornamented the tail of the plane, and his anticipation to see what other wonders the Royal hangars held swelled inside him.

Hugo turned the plane to face the doors of the leftmost hangar, its headlights illuminating the way ahead, revealing two previously unseen guards on either side of the building. The bright glare of the lights washed the colours from everything, but both men seemed to be wearing some kind of formal, military dress.

Their heads were covered in navy blue, almost grey, berets adorned with a circular golden emblem which Marcus couldn't fully make out. Their jackets and trousers were the same ambiguous blue, with gold buttons and accents to match the beret, which glinted in the light like fireflies. Each of them held a rifle in their white gloved hands, and saluted the prince, as he signalled for them to open the hangar.

Marcus's view was somewhat restricted from his side window, but as the plane pulled forwards into the mostly hollow room, he watched the soldiers march to Hugo's command, and thought they seemed, rather oddly, too friendly to be guards. They moved expertly, like well-oiled machines and yet, somehow, they just didn't appear threatening; moreover they appeared to be the antithesis of every blockbuster combatant he'd ever seen. Indeed, if such men existed in the armed forces, these two would be the sort of killers that asked questions first; and shot later.

Tearing his distracted mind away from the soldiers, Marcus looked about the hangar, as the plane was parked against the right wall. Cyril, Marcus and Aria stood then and immediately went about collecting their bags from the disorganised pile they'd left them in by the door. Hugo powered down the aircraft and then he, and Knox, emerged from the cockpit to unseal the door and lower the steps to the ground.

The air inside the vast, metal shell was cool but not unpleasantly so, and smelled of engines, oil and the sweet, appetising fragrance of carnauba wax. To Marcus the scent of something so delectable, and so familiar, only served to reinforce the near perfect portrayal of the country that he was conjuring in his head. Falling in love too quickly was one of his worst vices though, and he cautioned himself against it. Nevertheless, he adored the little he had seen so far and thirsted for more. To that end, Marcus began to explore the Royal hangar; and it did not disappoint.

He walked away from the jet they had arrived in and started to examine the others in the row next to it, which were also parked neatly and resembled giant, slumbering birds. Each of the four aircrafts were almost identical, wearing the same white and blue livery with the golden crested tail fins, except for the one at the end of the line. That one sported a navy livery with gold accents; much like the uniforms of the guards and Marcus unconsciously made his way towards it; like a magpie drawn irresistibly towards a shiny object. His feet carried him forwards without thought, until the sound of Hugo's voice broke the spell and returned him to the moment.

'Marcus, this way! If you want a ride in the King's personal jet, I suggest you ask him first.' The bear of a man laughed, the commodious room amplifying the musicality of it, making Hugo sound like an ersatz opera singer.

Marcus smiled through his embarrassment and obediently scurried back towards his companions, which was when he became aware of the glorious array of classical cars on the opposite side of the hangar to the planes, where his friends now stood waiting. In another life, under less fraught circumstances, he would've spent hours there, fawning over every elegant detail and beautifully sculpted panel, but this wasn't another life. If it was, would he have found himself in that room at all?

He watched the prince, Knox and Aria enter a much newer but equally impressive limousine style car and made his way around its glossy black body, to where Cyril was loading their bags into the boot. Together they squeezed in their bulky luggage, and then joined the rest of their unlikely group inside the vehicle.

The interior was as equally well-appointed as that of the plane they had arrived in. An amalgamation of high-quality varnished woods, soft leathers, and delicate hand stitching graced every surface from the door inserts, to the champagne chiller between their seats. As Marcus nestled into the car though, he suddenly started to feel overwhelmed and exhausted by the relentless pace they had kept up, and the obscure path they had travelled to get to Sweden. Curious to see if it was only him who was feeling the strain of the day, he glanced around the car as Hugo set it into motion.

The seating arrangement meant he could see everyone, as the two benches faced one another. Cyril was sat to his left, gazing out of the heavily tinted windows at the empty roads, with a subdued expression on his face. McRae rested heavily in the seat across from Cyril with his spindly limbs crunched up like a spider's, his countenance that of a barely dormant volcano, threatening to erupt at any moment; and directly opposite Marcus, sat Aria.

She slumped low into the comfortable grasp of the leather, the bags that had formed under her partially closed eyes betrayed her tiredness but didn't diminish how pretty she was in the slightest, and he let his own eyes linger on her for a second; before turning to look out at the scenery.

Although much less erratic than Knox, Hugo still drove quickly, which blurred the view outside into a vague alternation of luminescent white streaks, caused by the city lights, and intermittent strokes of dark green countryside. Even if he'd had the energy to take in at all in, which he certainly didn't, the

Prince's hasty driving made Stockholm look more like a Cubist painting, than a place where people lived. So, Marcus stared blankly at the passing streets and trees, with a dull awareness that the buildings were getting taller and more densely packed, until the limousine stopped without much warning and jolted him back to life.

Hugo turned the car off, its engine almost inaudible in comparison to that of the ambulance they'd endured so many hours in, and was out on the cobbles in mere seconds. He flung the doors open for them to exit and made his way around to the rear of the car to unload their baggage. Marcus tapped Aria on the knee to stir her into action, and as he followed her out of the car, he couldn't help but wonder why Hugo was in such a rush. Then it occurred to him, that somewhere throughout the course of the day's events, he had completely lost all sense of time.

He checked his watch as he bolted around the vehicle to collect his bags, and was shocked to see that it was close to 2:30 AM. It was a disorientating realisation, he couldn't tell if they'd made good time or not, perhaps they were late, maybe they were early; but the peculiar hour had to be the reason for Hugo's sudden urgency.

It took considerable effort to drag themselves up to the top of the grand stairs, and through the enormous glass doors of the Hotel Diamant. It would've been significantly more arduous though, if a black uniformed concierge hadn't dutifully run to them to carry their packs, and possibly harder still, if another darkly attired doorman hadn't so formally opened the way for them.

Once inside, the concierge who had brought in their belongings proceeded to load them onto a gleaming silver trolley, with a dark wooden base.

'Is it safe to let them take our *things*?' Marcus said quietly to McRae, surprised to see him give up his bags so easily, knowing the importance of their contents.

'Aye. This hotel is owned by the Royal Family, it only caters for their personal friends and associates. We're safer now, in here, than we have been all day,' he muttered wearily. Marcus raised his eyebrows and nodded but didn't pry further; sensing that now wasn't the time to interrogate him.

As the concierge made his excellently postured way towards an elevator, which looked large enough to swallow an entire London bus and still have room for leftovers, the clicking sound of high heeled footsteps started on the marble behind them. Marcus spun towards the noise. The rhythmic precision of the tread snagged his attention, stirring his senses after the drowsy journey from the airport, and allowed him to appreciate the splendour of the hotel's lobby; and the stunning woman who now awaited them at its centre.

'Lilly!' Hugo beamed, striding towards her, and encircling her in a brief but sincere hug; which she didn't return. 'I feel like I haven't seen you weeks.'

'That's what you get for being daddy's errand boy,' she mocked, in a cool voice.

'*Daddy's errand boy*? Does that mean…' Aria whispered to herself, far more loudly than she'd meant to. Hugo, hearing her comment as easily as the rest of them, made to introduce the enigmatic Lilly but she brushed passed him, intent on doing it herself.

'I am Princess Lilly of Sweden, Duchess of Gotland,' she said imperiously, glowering down at them from the lofty heights her heeled shoes afforded her.

Marcus gawped at her, arrested by her unique, glacial beauty. Lilly's pale blonde hair framed her perfect alabaster face and cascaded down the back of her dark outfit like a frozen waterfall, all the way to the small of her back, where it pooled in luscious curls. She was tall, imposing and exuded a regal atmosphere that was most prevalent in the depths of her Baltic, blue eyes. Never before had Marcus seen anyone so exquisitely beautiful, or so utterly devoid of loveliness – she was a ray of sunshine trapped forever under the impenetrable ice of an Arctic sea; and he battled to drag his gaze away from her.

Aria had taken an instantaneous dislike to the icy woman; she never had dealt well with conceit, and her rapidly rising temper was now almost palpable. Marcus, having been on the receiving end of it several times, knew that the dark-haired girl's rage could be quite spectacular, and he hoped that given their situation, she'd keep herself under control.

'As I was going to say, my sister!' Hugo clarified, with a contrite smile.

'And you are?' the princess asked, ignoring her brother.

'Aria.'

'Marcus.'

'A pleasure,' Lilly said with scornful disinterest.

She shifted then, dismissing them as though they were nothing more than inconsequential pieces of detritus, merely the biproduct of Knox's presence; which was where her attention was now focused.

'Well if it isn't the star of the show and his apprentice. How are we, Mr McRae, Cōng-ming?'

Cyril chose to remain quiet, simply smiling dumbly at her with a fanciful twinkle in his tired eyes. It was a look that Marcus knew all too well, and it astounded him, to think that a soul as tender as Cyril's, could possibly be attracted to someone as tyrannical as Princess Lilly. Knox, on the other hand, entertained no such feelings.

'All the better for seeing Stockholm's very own ice queen in the flesh, you're looking as bitter as ever,' came McRae's cheery reply, his words not matching his tone. 'How is hell anyway, have you managed to freeze it yet?'

'Oh Knox, you do flatter me,' she replied, the smile on her lips unable to disguise the evil in her eyes.

'I do my best.' He shrugged, continuing to push her, but Lilly's concentration had already moved away from the Scotsman. She appeared to be counting them, her eyes flicking from face to face.

'There's one missing,' she stated, with a sense of detachment towards the fact she was speaking about human beings, and not inanimate objects. 'I was expecting another?' The question was hard edged and directed at Hugo, whose eyes widened in sudden remembrance.

'Yes, that's where I'm heading now, I'm expecting him in around twenty minutes,' he replied hurriedly.

So that was the reason for the frantic dash from the car, Marcus thought internally, as he speculated over who the prince could possibly be collecting at three in the morning, during a global lockdown.

'Right. Enough with the pleasantries then.'

'Which part of that was pleasant, might I ask?' Knox jibed, but Lilly ignored him again and proceeded with her instructions.

'Hugo, I'll meet you back here when you're done. McRae, you and your *vermin*, will be staying on the second floor. You'll be in your usual suite on the east wing, the rest of you are in the three adjoining rooms.' She spurned, producing four, black chrome key cards from the inside pocket of her tightly fitted jacket and handed them to McRae. 'Knox, you know the way, I trust you are able to get there by yourself?' she asked superciliously.

He didn't reply. Instead, the old artist took the cards from her outstretched hand and loped off towards the elevators, without waiting for the others to follow. Hugo sprinted for the doors calling back over his shoulder, as he flew over the highly polished floor.

'Marcus, Aria, meet me in the breakfast room at nine thirty, I will show you the city!'

Then he was gone, speeding back into the summer night, on a mission to collect his undisclosed quarry. Princess Lilly also left them then, and Marcus couldn't help but watch the seductive sway of her hips, as she made her way across the lobby like a viper. The clipped sound of Aria tutting broke the spell, but he was too tired to care or comment, instead falling into line behind her and Cyril as they moved towards the elevator where Knox waited.

McRae hit the hexagonal button for the second floor as they entered and distributed the key cards amongst his young companions. Marcus observed as the huge doors glided shut, noticing at the same time how unusual the design of the room was. The walls and ceiling were covered in an irregular blanket of black glass, mirrored plates and brushed metal shards; each surface reflecting off the others, splintering them all into a thousand, tiny pieces. It was incredible and sickening all at once; it was, Marcus imagined, what it would be like to be trapped inside the diamond of an engagement ring. `

To his relief the ride upwards was over almost as quickly as it had begun, and he all but ran out onto the landing. McRae scowled at him before leading them all down the grey carpeted hallway, towards the furthest corner of the east wing; where they were greeted by large windows which overlooked the glorious city below. Each of them checked the number on their cards before entering it into the slot on the corresponding door, the wonderful prospect of a sweet night's sleep tugging at them as they did so. However, before they could toss their responsibilities aside and enter the joyful embrace of their dreams, Knox addressed them one last time.

'Get some rest, you'll need it. Make sure the two of you go meet Hugo in the morning; Cyril and I have some business to attend to, so we'll meet you later on. I'll be gasping for a whisky by then.' He almost laughed. 'And make sure you stay away from the princess … she's poisonous. Are we clear?' McRae growled.

His heavy brow crunched together then, darkening his words, and sending a chill up Marcus's spine; as though the princess herself had breathed her wicked frost in his ear. They all nodded in turn, and once satisfied that they understood him, the Scot turned and slammed his door. Aria and Cyril quickly followed suit, albeit with less aggression than Knox, leaving Marcus alone with his thoughts in the silent corridor.

Chapter VII

The quality of the beds in the Hotel Diamant had to be, without a modicum of doubt, the finest in the world. That was the conclusion Marcus had arrived at, having slept with such tranquillity, that he had awoken feeling several years younger.

He sprawled his lean body over the white sheets as he stretched and yawned, looking to each side of the marshmallow-like expanse, and wondering if there would still be room to spare if he laid horizontally. Fearing that he might waste too many precious minutes indulging his obscure imagination, or that he may already be running late, Marcus sprang up to check the alarm clock. In a former life, his phone would've acted as his alarm, and it was then that he realised that he was still coming to terms with its absence. The last time he'd used it was roughly a week ago to call Knox in order to confirm their plans; now it was lying in a drawer back in England, sim card-less and inactive.

In the 21st century, where a phone could contain a person's entire life behind its smooth, dark screen, Marcus found it at once both liberating and debilitating to be deprived of it. With that being said, his experience of the physical world had definitely been heightened, without the distraction of the digital one in his pocket; and what a world he'd found himself in.

The clock, he noticed as he moved to check it, was itself a minor work of art. It was a three-sided pyramid made from a glossy, black plastic that concealed the screen so well, that the crimson digits appeared to be floating across its slick surface. To his relief, those tall red numbers revealed that it was still only eight o'clock; thirty minutes before the time he'd set it to. He didn't stop to question how, after only just over five hours of sleep, he felt so spritely; instead, he got up and began to investigate the rest of the room.

When he'd opened the door in a state of exhaustion the night before, Marcus had done little more than throw his bag down, undress and collapse on the bed, leaving no time to appreciate his incredible lodgings. He immediately headed towards the lavishly embroidered curtains and threw them open, excited to see the sun-soaked city beyond.

The view from the window was staggering; and made all the more beautiful by how unusual it was to be staring at a foreign land during such unprecedented times. Enjoying it completely was difficult though with the concern of being late for his meeting with Hugo playing on his mind, but as it turned out, ripping his gaze away from the vibrant array of bridges and spires was no mean feat. Nevertheless, he did so, somewhat begrudgingly, and reminded himself in a conciliatory voice that the quicker he got ready, the sooner he could be out there to experience it properly.

That notion was swiftly side-tracked, however, when he realised that there were two floors to his hotel room. He made his way to the upper level, enjoying the cool glass beneath his feet as he ascended the staircase, and, leaning on the silver banister at the top, surveyed the room as a Roman Emperor might survey his kingdom.

Much like the rest of the hotel, his suite was a magnificent blend of industrial metalwork, geometric cuts of glass and dark wood, all detailed beautifully with silver accents. The furniture was designed in an industrial chic style, each rivet and weld displayed a wonderful level of craftsmanship, but it was the light fitting that, ironically, eclipsed all else.

It was suspended from the high ceiling by a multitude of almost invisible wires, making it appear like a firework caught in time and space, its tangle of latticed metal and trailing filaments rushing out in all directions. Marcus's eyes wandered over it, exploring its intricacies, and he decided that if Gustave Eiffel and Thomas Edison had ever collaborated; that light fixture may well have been the result. Convinced that he would never see anything else quite like it, he padded back down the stairs, and rummaged around for his camera.

Once content with the photographs he'd taken, he placed the camera on charge, gathered his toiletries, and made for the marble walled bathroom to prepare himself for his first day in Stockholm.

After he'd showered, dried and clothed himself, Marcus styled his pecan brown hair and filled a small backpack with his camera, sunglasses and the Swedish currency Cyril had given him. He checked himself one last time in the mirror, and then left the hotel room with a broad smile on his face, before walking across the corridor to rap his knuckles three times on Aria's door.

'Room service!' he yelled in a high-pitched accent which, he hoped, sounded Eastern European.

'In a minute!' she snapped from within.

'Hello? This is room service. May I come in?' he persisted, knocking again more loudly.

'I said hold *on!*' Aria shouted back, the frustration rising in her voice. Marcus continued pounding on the door, the amusement he was holding back starting to bubble out of him as her footsteps drew nearer.

'Oh my god, will you just–' Aria swung the door open with such speed, that Marcus almost punched her in the face as he made to knock again. She flinched out of the way, only marginally missing the blow, as Marcus burst into laughter.

'Are you fucking serious!' she bellowed at him, the vehemence in her stare doing nothing to quell his tittering.

'What? I just came to see if you were ready for breakfast,' he said innocently.

'You are *beyond* annoying,' she fumed, swatting at him through the doorway.

But his glee was contagious, and it wasn't long before she too was laughing. Aria dipped back into her room to put her shoes on, whilst Marcus waited by the door, then the two of them headed towards the lobby.

Feeling refreshed after their comfortable sleep, and aware that they had done nothing besides sit down throughout their entire trip from England to Sweden, both of them opted to take the stairs. They arrived on the ground floor to find it considerably busier than they'd expected it to be, and they were quite taken aback to see such a large quantity of people so close to one another. As they navigated their way towards the breakfast room, each of them started to question how things could possibly be so different there.

The quarantine that had been established in the United Kingdom, and indeed throughout the majority of the Western world, had conditioned them to believe that human contact was wrong; and unhygienic. It was truly baffling to consider that less than a thousand miles away, Scotland was attempting to wall itself in from fear of its public contracting the virus, and yet in Sweden, life breezed by as if nothing was happening. It was a shocking contrast to behold, and it reminded Marcus that although he had every right to enjoy his freedom in that foreign land, first and foremost, they were there for answers.

Someone clapped Marcus on the shoulder then; it was a heavy gesture and it caught him unawares causing him to stumble, but before he toppled completely, that same weighty hand pulled him upright again. He whirled around viscously, unimpressed by the rough handling, and wrenched himself out of the grasp of his unseen assailant. Following the arm that had held him to its origin, Marcus saw Hugo's handsome face looking back at him; the expression on it caught halfway between apology and ridicule.

'Bloody hell, is that how the Swedes greet each other in the morning, with a punch in the back?' Marcus said, deciding that making a joke out of the incident was probably the best way to mask his humiliation.

'I'm so sorry! Honestly,' Hugo muttered, still unsure whether to laugh at, or console, his new friend.

'It's fine, really, it is. Just know that there'll be a nice thump waiting for you tomorrow.' He smiled, giving Hugo the green light to let out his booming laugh.

'Oh please, you wouldn't hurt a fly,' Aria chimed in, also giggling.

'Well, luckily for me, the Prince *isn't* a fly,' Marcus replied sardonically. Hugo made a mock gesture of surrender at this and calmed his laughter before replying.

'Tonight, my friend, as an apology, the drinks are on me. How does that sound?'

'Like a good start.' Marcus grinned.

'Perfect. But before all that, I have a fantastic day planned for you, and it starts with breakfast,' he intoned, taking on the role of a gracious host.

With their odd reintroduction dealt with, Hugo encircled Aria and Marcus in his powerful arms and led them into the dining room.

The three of them were seated by another of the hotel's congenial, black uniformed staff members, in the furthest corner of the grand room. Their position offered them both privacy for themselves and a fully disclosed view of the rest of the diners, which pleased Aria greatly as she could practise one of her favourite pastimes: people watching.

As their coffee was being poured, Marcus set about examining the ornate cutlery, attempting to decipher what one could possibly need three forks for, that early in the day. Meanwhile Aria shot several rather obvious glances around the room, no doubt intending to be discreet but failing; she didn't waste any time in raising the subject of Sweden's evident lack of quarantine.

'I haven't seen this many people in one place since, I don't know, last year maybe?'

'Aria, there can't be more than thirty people in this room, it's not many,' Hugo replied, sipping his black, unsweetened coffee.

'That's what I mean. It's not a lot at all and yet in the UK, if you're seen outside with anyone who isn't from your household you get escorted home by the police. Or worse, the military,' she replied, her passion rising, but the prince said nothing.

'Think about Spain,' Marcus added, glad to be getting straight to the point. 'Their authorities are forcing people into their homes at gunpoint, the same in France. Germany is on the verge of a civil war between its government and its citizens…' He trailed off, shaking his head, allowing Aria to pick up where he'd left off.

'Greece's economy has completely collapsed, as have those in most of the Eastern European countries, because their workers can't travel. Italy has lost almost a tenth of its population since the virus took hold. A fucking *tenth*,' she said, the pain evident in her voice, as she recalled the family members she'd lost during the pandemic. 'And that's just the tip of iceberg. America, the Middle East, Australia, parts of Africa, if any of the news we've been given can be trusted at all, then they're all falling apart.'

'Ari's right. This is a global catastrophe. *But* in spite of all that, China and apparently Sweden, seem astonishingly unfazed. So, what the hell is going on?' Marcus demanded, brandishing his resolve like a sword, becoming unjustly angry at the prince for living a normal life whilst the rest of them suffered, died, or were lied to.

He could feel Aria to his left, seething with the same indignation and together they stared intensely at Hugo, willing the truth to spill from him like the squeezed juice of a fresh orange.

The prince flicked his eyes between his young companions without saying a word. Then he looked to the high ceiling above with its hundreds of twinkling lights and let out a long, breathy sigh before speaking.

'I cannot tell you everything,' he stated simply, making Marcus and Aria's mouths drop in perturbation. Seeing the disappointment and confusion mingling on their faces, the prince hurried on. 'If I could, I would, but I myself do not know all the details and beyond that, I am under orders from my father not to share certain pieces of information.'

'Why a–' Aria attempted to butt in, before Hugo cut her off with a stern hand.

'Wait,' he said with a curt authority which neither Aria nor Marcus were expecting, cooling their anger rapidly and reminding them that were talking to a member of the Royal Family, not a common person. 'Tomorrow yourselves, Knox and Cōng-ming will be meeting with the king at the Palace, if you have the patience to wait, you'll find your answers then. But, as I'm sure that will be a struggle for you, I'll share three pieces of knowledge with you now, under one condition,' the prince offered, as a roughish smile pulled at the corners of his mouth, twitching his beard.

'Which is?' Marcus asked curiously.

'If I tell you, there must no more questions on the matter until tomorrow. Today, I want to introduce you to Stockholm, and offer you a day of sanctuary before the impending storm,' Hugo said, his impish smile becoming an honest, meaningful one.

'How are we supposed to enjoy ourselves whilst the world ends around us?' Aria questioned, in an utterly despondent tone.

'It is precisely *because* the world is ending that we must enjoy ourselves!' Hugo replied, becoming his usual, animated self once again. 'Tomorrow could be our last day, but instead of moping around and cursing our misfortune, surely we should make the most of every second we have remaining? Perspective is important, it shapes our lives far more than the events we endure; you will both do well to remember that over the coming days.'

Marcus and Aria were stunned into silence by the prince's words. In the short time they'd known him, they'd come to see Hugo as an easy going, relaxed man, and although they'd never doubted his intelligence, neither of them were expecting such a philosophical outpour from him. Sensing that he had their attention, and assuming that their quietness was in fact their acceptance of his conditions, Hugo proceeded.

'So, I have three facts to share with you.'

'Three? I thought you didn't know that much?' Aria interrupted before he could say more.

'Well, luckily for you, I'm feeling generous this morning. Now that's enough questions or the deal's off,' the prince said, winking at her.

'Fine,' she replied, offering Hugo a smile that made Marcus uncomfortable.

'Very good. Ok, so firstly Sweden is not the only place that hasn't been affected by the virus,' said the prince, pausing momentarily to see if they would give in to their desires and shower him with questions; but when they remained silent, he carried on. 'Secondly, the data and statistics being given to the public are largely false; what's actually happening is that the key governments of the world are fabricating information to suit their own narratives. And my third and final piece of information for you, is that the roots of this pandemic lie in China.'

Marcus contemplated Hugo's words and although they didn't provide him with masses of new facts, the prince had confirmed many of his suspicions, and saturated his head with speculations. He opened his mouth to speak but the prince stared him down.

'Don't do it, Marcus,' he warned, not entirely in jest.

The thoughts raged in his mind then, assaulting his tight jaw as they attempted to break out through his mouth and form words. He wanted to shout, to ask all the burning questions that had set his mind alight, but before he could say anything brash, Marcus found himself saved by the waiter who, in the nick of time, set their breakfasts down in front of them.

None of them had eaten a proper meal in hours, and the sight of the delicious array of traditional, Swedish open-topped sandwiches caused their stomachs to rumble; and the clawing questions to subside. Thankful for the distraction after the seriousness of their conversation, they each refocused their attention on the food, examining their plates with hungry eyes.

Each slice of thin bread was topped with lashings of creamy butter, cured ham and wafers of hard cheese which they jubilantly savoured; only pausing to wash them down with coffee and juice. Once they had filled themselves to the brim with sandwiches, or Smörgås as Hugo informed them they were called in Swedish, the three of them left the table, crossed back through the lobby and made for the city streets.

The air outside was already warm in comparison to that of the Hotel Diamant's perfectly moderated atmosphere, and as they trotted down the stairs, the smell of hot pavements and the Scandinavian summer permeated their nostrils.

That scent was lost on Marcus though. With no more edible distractions, he once again began frantically trying to piece together all the information in his head as Hugo led them out from under the hotel's impressive porte-cochère, and around the corner to the right.

He watched the prince's heavy boots as they connected with the ground, using the rhythm of the larger man's stride to regulate his mind, which was quickly becoming an inscrutable whirlpool. Not for the first time, he found himself so over encumbered with thoughts, that the sheer weight of them made him blind to his surroundings. If it hadn't been for Aria and Hugo stopping to marvel at the titanic mass of stone, that was in fact the Royal Palace, Marcus would've likely walked right past it and sustained his negligent march until he found himself paddling in the Norrström river.

He turned to face the Palace, tracing Hugo's pointing finger as he highlighted certain parts of the architecture and told them an abbreviated version of the building's history. It was an undeniably striking building due to its sheer size and density, but it lacked the flourishes of the Royal abodes found on the European mainland.

Indeed, to Marcus, the whole thing seemed to have been built with function over form as its supreme principal which, for him at least, made it appear quite bland. Nevertheless, he still found some enjoyment in the spectacle, and following the lines of the brickwork and the decorative windows, helped him to return to the moment. He took a few photographs and reminded himself that he was, after all, being given a tour of Sweden's capital by a member of the Swedish Royal Family, and he had no right to squander such an auspicious opportunity.

Hugo, satisfied that he had bestowed enough facts upon them, started to move again, directing them past the front of the Palace and towards the Old Town district. Marcus shifted his gaze from the massive building to follow their guide, but as he did so, his eyes locked with Aria's, and the two of them shared a look that was filled with both reassurance and confusion. They needed to discuss what they'd learned so far in private, and he hoped at some point that day, maybe in the evening, they would get a chance to do just that.

With that telepathic message successfully communicated, the two of them raced after the prince, who had covered an alarming amount of ground in just a few short seconds; and caught him just as he rounded the next corner.

Once around the bend, they moved away from the water side and into a forest of tall, brightly coloured buildings. Their group travelled through the narrow, cobbled streets of the Old Town, winding their way between the high structures in relative quiet. Hugo occasionally stopped to point out a few random buildings and quirky shops, the handmade chocolate store piqued all three of their interests, its sweet aroma making them salivate long after they'd gone past it.

Eventually they arrived in the Stortorget, which was a stylish and picturesque open square, situated behind the Palace. The prince announced with great pride, that it was built on the site of the original settlement that would one day spawn the expansive city they now walked in. He showed Marcus and Aria to the slightly off-centred fountain and sat them on a nearby bench to soak in the rich diversity of the plaza's design.

Despite the asymmetric location of the water feature, which Marcus learned had once been a well, aggravating his aesthetic preferences, the vibrancy of the buildings that lined the square were dazzling. There was a veritable rainbow of colours splashed across their facades, ranging from scorching reds, to lustrous oranges, a green that changed from olive to almost teal depending on the light, and an abundance of yellow shades that extended from lemon rind, all the way to buttercups, and back again.

Coupled with the peppermint blue sky which was awash with rolls of thin white cloud, the scene was a visual carnival; and Marcus relished every second of it. He drank in that rare moment of stillness, soaking himself in the peace and quiet it brought to his thought ravaged mind, not wanting it to end. With that notion, the urge to hold onto the moment grew almost urgent, practically forcing Marcus to remove the camera from the bag on his back, and set about capturing the square through its lens before they moved on.

Feeling noticeably calmer than he had when they had first set out, Marcus trailed slightly behind Hugo and Aria, as the prince guided them out of the Old Town Square and towards the Southern bridge. He watched the fast-flowing water of the river Söderström crash into the buttresses of the towering walkway as they crossed it, excited to be leaving the island of Gamla Stan behind, and to be entering a new area of the capital.

From there, their route took them west through the province of Södermalm, where they followed the gradual incline of the road as it rose high above the river. The views from that particular path were spectacular in the bright sunshine, and they could even make out the shining glass dome of the Hotel Diamant, as it peeked its distinctly contemporary head out from amongst the rows of its classical stone siblings.

Hugo would sporadically veer away from the river and take them into the bustling side roads to show them a random building, a statue that he found particularly interesting, or perhaps one of the elaborately wrought churches. He clearly knew the city like the back of his hand, but the convoluted route he was taking them on seemed dizzying in its complexity to the two outsiders.

Aria walked side by side with the prince, asking questions about both him and the city as they strolled. Marcus noted her childish grin and their closeness with as much detachment as he could muster; but his private orchestra of jealousy still squeezed out a note or two, before his objectivity silenced the players once more.

He had to remind himself that he and Aria were only friends, the best of friends, but still nothing more and he had no right to garner such covetous feelings. Fortunately for Marcus, as their small group angled north again and traversed the long bridge that connected Södermalm with the equally sizable district of Kungsholem, his favourite form of diversion came to his rescue once again.

The first whiff of succulent, grilled meat hit his nose whilst they were still on the bridge and as they walked off it into a small, wooded park, the mouth-watering scent only grew stronger. The source of the smell was revealed to be a small burger truck parked on the outskirts of the public garden. Hugo, clearly hungry himself and a great lover of burgers it seemed, wasted no time in altering their course to visit the vendor.

Inside the van was an elderly man and a younger one, who was presumably his son, both of whom looked up from their cooking in amazement at the sight of the human mountain that was Hugo. It was the first time Marcus and Aria had really discerned any noteworthy reactions from the Swedish people towards seeing a member of the Royal Family amongst them; and it was quite amusing to watch.

The prince ordered beef burgers and a bottle of water for each of them, smiling graciously at the starstruck men as they left, treasuring each bite as they went. Naturally, Marcus had requested two burgers, fearing that one just wouldn't be enough to stave off his insatiable appetite. That earned him a respectful pat on the back from Hugo, and an apathetic eye roll from Aria, as he wolfed them both down before she had even finished her first.

Fuelled by his early afternoon meal, their Royal tour guide increased his pace for the final leg of the journey, meaning that Marcus and Aria practically had to jog to keep up with him at times. Hugo's relentless marching soon led them to the metropolitan area of Norrmalm, which they had to pass through in order to finish their loop, and arrive back at the hotel in Gamla Stan.

That part of Stockholm was filled with high rise office buildings, traffic-laden roads, banks, and large corporate headquarters coated in glass. It was busier, louder and far more active than any other section of the city they had previously seen, and the sight of so many people doing mundane, everyday things like walking, working, driving, even *breathing* without the ever-present menace of the virus was mind blowing; and it imbued Marcus with a renewed sense of hope.

'I love it here,' Marcus said, speaking his thoughts aloud.

'Yeah me too, it's awesome,' Aria agreed.

'I knew you would!' Hugo beamed, at last slowing his pace.

'I have to ask though. You're a *prince*, why have you spent half of your day showing two lowly British tourists around?' asked Marcus, quizzically.

'Lowly? Speak for yourself,' Aria huffed, eliciting a short laugh from Hugo, who shook his head before answering.

'If we are fighting for the same cause, then we are equal as far as I'm concerned; my station doesn't matter. You are friends of Knox and therefore you are friends of mine, it really is that simple.' The burly Swede smiled. 'Besides, I love this city too, and I don't often get to walk the streets and eat burgers just for fun!'

Marcus and Aria smiled back at him, finding his honesty endearing, and the three of them chatted happily as they made their way back around the Royal Palace. They ended their tour where they had started, in the lobby of the Hotel Diamant and when they stopped, Marcus realised just how much his legs ached. He flicked his wrist up to check his watch, raising his eyebrows in disbelief.

'Christ! We've been out for hours.'

'Time flies when you're having fun,' Hugo responded, evidently pleased that his companions had fallen for Stockholm. 'You should go relax for a while, perhaps catch up on some sleep. We'll meet again this evening around eight o'clock in the dining room,' he said, gesturing to a wonderfully discreet doorway they'd not yet been through, its black glass face barely distinguishable from the walls.

They said their goodbyes and made their way towards the elevator, leaving Hugo behind, but before the doors closed, he called something to them.

'Don't be late, Marcus! If you are, those drinks I promised you might end up with someone else.' Then the lift slid shut with silky precision, closing out the prince's laughter, as Marcus and Aria ascended back to the second floor.

Several hours later, after a brilliant day in Stockholm, a wonderfully undisturbed nap and an exquisite dinner in the Diamant, Marcus felt truly happy for the first time in recent memory. He was in the bar, sat in a black winged-back chair which, after several single malt whiskies, had become nothing short of a throne in his eyes.

To his left, Knox had folded himself into a similar seat and across from them, lounging on an enormous Chesterfield sofa covered in the same, remarkably soft leather, were Aria,

Cyril and Hugo. Between them was a dark wooden table, which by that point in the evening's festivities was littered with a selection of fine crystal tumblers, empty wine bottles and a small mound of tissues; which Aria had unsuccessfully used to mop up a spillage.

The atmosphere between them had been light and good humoured, and under Hugo's orders that they wouldn't discuss the worlds affairs until tomorrow, even McRae had managed to conjure up a smile or two. Cyril and Knox had answered circuitously, when Aria asked what they'd been doing that day, however, and their reluctance to discuss anything further troubled Marcus. Yet in spite of their disinclination to reveal their whereabouts wreaking havoc in a small corner of his mind, Marcus had still managed to embrace the hedonism of the night. As the saying goes though, all good things must come to an end.

Marcus drained the last of the whisky from his tumbler, accidentally inhaling an ice cube in the process and crunched it clumsily as the Prince stood to speak.

'My friends!' he boomed, opening his arms in a courtly gesture. 'It's getting late and there is much work to be done tomorrow, *but*, before we call it a day, I propose a round of punsch,' he said, looking jubilantly at the circle of faces staring back at him, making for the bar before they had a chance to reply.

'What's punsch?' Aria questioned, trying vainly to stop the wine from slurring her speech.

'Lightly distilled horse piss, lass,' McRae growled.

'You know what, Knox, I think I've missed you,' she replied with laughter in her voice.

'I wouldn't get too attached. If you're planning on having a tipple of punsch, this might just be your last day alive,' the Scot rumbled back, but his stony lips were smiling.

'So, what actually is it?' Marcus asked, leaning forward in his seat to join the fray.

'It is a traditional Swedish liqueur, and Mr McRae is right, it is rather *pungent*,' Cyril clarified, his words sounding remarkably sober, considering how much he had drunk.

'What they mean,' Hugo said, slamming a tray of chilled glasses down onto the table, 'is that it tastes delicious and you should try some.' They all eyed the dark liquid swirling inside the glasses with hesitation, but equally, they knew that it would be an offence to say no. Aria, never one to back down from any challenge, least of all those containing alcohol, grabbed the tumbler closest to her. Each of them followed suit, taking a glass and raising it at Hugo's instruction.

'Skål!' the prince shouted.

'Skål!' they echoed and threw the drink down their throats.

There was a mixed reception upon tasting the liqueur. Knox looked nothing short of incensed; and mumbled quietly to himself about how it paled in comparison to the whisky of his homeland. Cyril winced, shuddering once before regaining his composure; meanwhile Marcus grimaced as though he'd eaten a wasp and Aria gagged, looking like she might be sick at any moment. The prince laughed heartily at that and, now satisfied that they'd indulged him, said goodnight as he retired for the evening.

Knox and his apprentice also rose from their seats, gathering their jackets in the process as they turned to leave. Cyril looked uncharacteristically shaky on his feet, and Marcus couldn't help but chuckle at his friend as he bounced between the tables, scarcely avoided a collision with a waiter and, at last, fell through the door to the lobby. McRae sighed and tutted.

'Right, I'm going to make sure Cyril doesn't break his neck. Don't stay up too late, tomorrow's important,' McRae said, fixing them with his menacing stare, before making his way out of the room. Marcus and Aria watched him go, then turned back to their table.

'And then there were two,' Marcus said, grinning at her.

'I didn't think you'd last this long if I'm honest, you're normally heaving your guts up in a club toilet by now.' She laughed, recalling all the times Marcus had embarrassed himself in the past.

'It happened once!'

'Sure, if by once, you mean *every* time we went out. After tonight, I'm never drinking with you again.'

'No way! You promised me cocktails when this is all over, remember?'

'Do you think this will ever be over?' she asked solemnly, the sudden change in direction sobering them both.

'I don't know what to think, other than this mess is *a lot* bigger than I, we, first thought.' He breathed, feeling the weight of it all for the first time since breakfast.

'It's crazy. Every answer we find gives us twelve more questions; I can't help but think there's so much more to Knox that he's telling us, right?'

'I know. Before this trip I really thought I knew him. But I suppose I'd only gotten to know him as an artist because that's all I needed to know, at the time. And as I'm sure you've seen, he's hardly forthcoming with his secrets.'

'You really didn't know what we were getting into?' she asked, with just a hint of suspicion flickering across her features.

'No,' Marcus answered, meeting her eyes. 'He said to me, in the very beginning, that he didn't think this virus, or whatever it is, was going anywhere soon but he had a friend in Sweden who might be able to help, all we had to do was get there. That was more or less it … and I said yes because part of me idolises him, I guess. I trust him, and I just wanted to do some fucking good in the world,' he said, taking a swig of wine from a half empty bottle.

'And that friend turned out to be the Prince of Sweden?' she pressed.

'Yeah. So, Knox McRae, an *artist* from Glasgow, fought some kind of secret war when he was in his twenties, befriended the king of Sweden and later his son, then essentially adopted a Chinese son of his own and raised him in London as his apprentice … that's a ridiculous list of things, and none of them make any sense but I know they're connected,' he said, running his hands through his hair in frustration.

'Don't you think it's odd that Knox has a connection to both Sweden *and* China, the two places that are now apparently free of the virus – surely that can't be a coincidence?'

'No, it can't be, there has to be more to this. Did you know McRae once saved the Swedish King from an assassination attempt?'

'No, I bloody didn't!' she sputtered. 'That man is literally bonkers.'

'I couldn't agree more.' He laughed. 'And another thing, I'd love to know who Cyril's dad is,' Marcus said, more to himself than Aria.

'And I'd love to know why the fuck I've got a pocket full of Dollars and Russian whatever-they're-called,' she countered with a snort.

'What a nightmare, Ari, let's hope we find the truth tomorrow, and then we can get back to England.'

'To truth,' Aria said, raising her wine.

'To truth,' Marcus repeated, grabbing the remainder of the bottle, and clinking it against her wineglass. She drained her glass and poured herself another, as Marcus guzzled down a sizeable portion of his own bottle before returning it to the table.

The pair drank on for another hour or so, becoming progressively louder and more intoxicated as the minutes ticked by. They prattled on about how they missed being at school, and all the lazy, carefree days they had taken for granted. They reminisced about friends, their families, lovers and all the humiliating moments they'd shared throughout their long friendship. They laughed, sang, and revealed things to one another that their pride wouldn't have allowed them to, without the wine and whisky coursing through their veins, and only when their eyelids began to droop, did they haul themselves up on unsteady legs to leave.

The fact that Marcus and Aria made it back to the second floor landing without either of them collapsing, vomiting, or falling asleep, was nothing short of a miracle. They wobbled their way along the corridor, clutching one another for dear life and giggling at absolutely nothing, until they found themselves outside their rooms.

'Goodnight, *pumpkin*, may your dreams be sweet and full of turds.,' Marcus said, doing his best impression of McRae, as he scooped Aria into a bearhug.

She let out a loud, shrieking chuckle at that, and Marcus rushed to cover her mouth with his hand to quiet her. Apparently not going down without a fight though, she licked his palm, then when he recoiled in disgust, she planted another wet stroke of her tongue across his cheek. It was a trick she'd been doing for years, and as Marcus wiped her spittle from his face, he questioned for the umpteenth time how he never saw it coming.

He attempted to pull away then, but she drew him back in with astonishing force. They were silent for a moment, drunk, tired and propping one another up like fallen scarecrows in a field of wheat. Then Aria broke the quiet and with only a few garbled words, set off an explosion in Marcus's mind so profound, that it made his bones burn.

'You know Marcus, I've never loved anyone, as much as I love you.' And with that, she vanished into her room and to bed, as if what she'd said was the most casual, inconsequential thing in the world. Yet to Marcus, that sentence seemed to be the fulcrum upon which his entire future turned.

Chapter VIII

Hangovers weren't really something that had ever troubled Marcus. Aside from a few notable occasions, the most momentous of which typically involved spontaneous, rash decisions to go for mid-week cocktails and the abandoning of all rational thoughts and inhibitions in the process, he usually handled his alcohol quite well. It was a gift of sorts, one that had proved invaluable as he'd grown up, and he quietly praised it as he readied himself for what could prove to be the most pivotal day of his life.

He left his room, slid the gleaming key card into his bag and approached the door to Aria's room with a cacophonous racket of thoughts inside his head. As he knocked lightly on her door and stepped back to wait for her to surface, his mind frolicked over their parting words from the previous night.

He was dancing in the ballroom of possibility, where truth, hope, confusion, doubt and even the black gowned cynicism all vied to be his partner, but he gambolled around them all, unable to choose just one. Then when the heavy sound of the door unlocking hit his ears, the internal music stopped, the ballroom evaporated, and Marcus found himself back in Hotel Diamant. However, the ghoul that emerged from within that dark corridor, was barely identifiable as Aria.

It crept out of the room, dressed in a mostly black outfit, with the exclusion of a cream-coloured blouse, and slid a pair of dark sunglasses over its partly bloodshot eyes. With those in place, the creature looked up at Marcus as it tied its long, dark hair up into something that bore resemblance to a bird's nest. Marcus had seen that very beast numerous times before, and knew it to be both deadly and emotionally indigent, but that had never stopped him from poking fun at it in the past; nor would it now.

'Aria, is that you?' he asked, doing his utmost to sound genuinely concerned.

'Does it look like I'm in the mood for you today, Merda?' She groaned.

'What? It's just that you look so lovely today, that I almost didn't recognise you.'

'If I thought you were worth the effort, I'd punch you.' Aria grunted, but she couldn't help a smile from tickling the corners of her mouth, as the two of them started to move towards the elevator as they talked.

'I'm sure you're going to make a great impression on the king looking like *that*,' Marcus said with a chortle.

'He's a king, he must have at least seventeen wives, right? I'm sure he's seen a girl with a hangover before,' she replied, adding her own wheezing laugh to his.

'Shit, what was in your wine, Ari, shrapnel? You sound like you've been chewing gravel all night.'

'I'm blaming Hugo's stupid punsch, that stuff was like petrol! Now, with all due respect, can you shut up please? You're not making this headache any better. Just get me downstairs, get me a huge pot of coffee, and I'll be back to my usual ray-of-sunshine-like self, ok?'

Marcus nodded and made to reply, but Aria stilled him by making a zipping motion across her mouth. They continued their short journey to the breakfast room in silence, choosing to use the elevator rather than the stairs on account of Aria's condition, and in the quietness, Marcus couldn't help his mind drifting, once again, to what she'd said to him the last night.

As he stole glances at her out of the corner of his eye, two questions presented themselves to him. The first, the more impartial of them, was did she remember what she'd said? And the second, tainted by the colours of acrimony, was did she mean those words at all?

He knew, however, that such delicate enquiries, if he had the courage to present them at all, would need to be timed and placed carefully. With that notion prevailing over the others contending for his attention, he blocked out the static of his rambling mind, and focused again on their more immediate situation.

The pair of them regrouped with their companions at the same table they had eaten at the previous day, and their reception was somewhat diverse. McRae noticed the state Aria was in and set about making a mockery of her before she'd even had the chance to pull out a chair.

'Christ, lass, what happened to not staying up too late? You look like you've lived through a week of Saturday nights,' he said, the tone of his voice suggesting he was equally annoyed, and amused.

'I'm not sure if that's a compliment or an insult, Knox, but surely if I survived a whole week of Saturday nights, I must've done something right?' she grumbled, as she took a seat beside the old artist, and donned a false smile.

'I think that depends on your ambitions, poppet – if your aim was to make yourself look as though you'd just climbed out of a grave, then yes I'd say you'd *done something right*.' He chuckled gruffly, whilst Aria set about pouring herself a cup of the rich, dark coffee she so passionately desired. 'Mind you, Cyril hasn't fared much better,' Knox added, taking a sip from his own cup, and raising his rugged eyebrows at his apprentice in condemnation.

'I assure you, Mr McRae, I am absolutely fine,' Cyril said, attempting to sound convincing, but his voice was thin and the bags under his eyes told another story. He and Aria shared a look of mutual pain and understanding through the black visors of her glasses; and then proceeded to aimlessly stir their drinks.

'Maybe punsch is not for everyone?' Hugo offered with a grin, reminding them all of the perilous liqueur that had more in common with crude oil, than it did with a beverage. 'But you, Marcus, you seem to have handled it like a champion,' he said, nodding approvingly.'What can I say? It's one of my many talents,'Marcus responded, feeling a small wave of pride pass over him.

'Many talents? Don't talk wet, lad,' McRae chastised, but before he had a chance to finish whatever derogatory joke he'd concocted, the waiter appeared with a shimmering tray of food.

Marcus wordlessly blessed the waiter for his timing and inspected the steaming bowl of creamy, honey swirled porridge that had been placed in front of him. He inhaled the delicious smell of his breakfast, added more honey and a touch of orange marmalade to the bowl and impatiently whisked the cooked oats around, waiting for them to cool. After pausing for what cannot have been more than ten seconds, Marcus burnt his mouth on the first bite, deemed it a necessary evil, and wolfed the rest down without pausing for breath.

Hugo ate with a similar determination and finished just as quickly. Meanwhile, Knox added salt to his porridge, a Scottish tradition, as the two more fragile members of their party, suffering their post-intoxication blues, nibbled at theirs like timid mice. Once they had finished their meals, and Cyril and Aria had consumed enough caffeine to keep an elephant awake, the five unusual accomplices rose, and left the Diamant behind.

After exiting the glass-coated hotel, they strode down the sunlit promenade, enjoying the cool breeze from the river as they headed in the direction of the Palace. Along the way, Hugo informed them that the museums and public attractions situated within the Royal abode had been closed temporarily as a result of the virus.

'As you all know, there are only a handful of cases of the virus here in Sweden, and as you have probably guessed by now, the figures we've released to the public aren't true. To help the situation appear more believable, we've had to close a few major public venues around the city,' the prince explained, as he marched them up the inclining slope which led to the great edifice, and towards the large stone archway that was its entrance.

'In spite of keeping everything else open as normal?' Marcus probed.

'There are a few other light restrictions in place that I didn't mention yesterday. Unless you're a native of the city though, you're very unlikely to notice. We're talking trivial things such as limiting public transport, the number of people in restaurants, cafes and the like, but overall, it's caused almost no disruption.'

'I wish we could say the same about our country,' Aria griped, looking substantially better, but apparently not feeling it.

Hugo moved them through the archway, and into the enormous courtyard that lay at the heart of the gigantic building. He pointed out several distinguished features as they passed through, which Marcus assumed were for his and Aria's benefit considering Knox and Cyril had visited countless times before, and he listened intently as the prince spoke.

The rough, grey cobbles eventually gave way to a polished marble floor, as they entered the interior of the Palace for the first time. The marble itself was a milky white in colour, shot through with lightning bolts of a pale lilac, and as Marcus traced those racing streaks with his eyes, he realised that almost the entire room was made of the same material.

At the centre of the atrium was an enormous double-sided staircase, easily wide enough to fit all five of them abreast, that ran up both walls and finally met beneath a column-lined doorway. As their footsteps reverberated off the smooth stairs, making a drumbeat of their traversal, Marcus scanned the ornate carvings on the ceiling and suddenly felt the great heft of the building bearing down on him.

The sheer bulk of all that stone and marble, coupled with the gravity of their reasons for being there, made the expansive hall feel as though it were no bigger than a rabbit's warren. His legs grew heavier with each plodding step, and there was a pressure mounting between his temples as though two pistons were slowly compressing his skull. It was frightening, and in that moment, he wanted nothing more than to be wrapped in the reassuring familiarity of his home.

The feeling persisted as they advanced through the first floor, the opulent furniture, gilded picture frames and rich lacework that adorned the rooms they passed only serving to antagonise it further. It wasn't until they had reached another set of stairs, these ones marginally slighter in stature than the flight they had previously encountered, that Marcus found a kind of relief.

Hugo stopped at the foot of the staircase and, putting out a hand to lean against the column which formed the base of the bannister, turned to face Aria, who had just asked him a question. 'What did you say, Aria?'

'I just asked how much further we've got to go. As incredible as it is to be here, I feel like we've been walking for hours,' she said, trying to disguise her frustration in the praise; and not seem ungrateful.

'Not much further.' The prince smiled. 'We'll be meeting the king in the White Sea Hall, which, conveniently, is just at the top of these stairs and is a little less *formal* than the meeting rooms,' he finished, his Swedish accent made the English language sound dulcet, and Marcus latched onto its soothing notes.

'I mean we've passed enough rooms, could they not have picked one on the ground floor?' Aria jested, sparking a laugh from the entire party.

'I'll tell you what, Aria, next time we host a meeting in the Palace, I'll make sure my father writes ahead to ask you which room to use. Does that seem fair?' he replied, matching her wit, and winking at her before he resumed his climb.

Cyril followed the prince, treading so lightly that his steps were almost soundless, making Aria's stomping seem all the more ungainly. Marcus made to proceed after them, but as his foot hit the second marble step, Knox's hand ensnared his arm. He whipped around to face the older man, shocked not only by the unanticipated invasion of his space, but also by the shackling immensity of McRae's grip.

'Must you always look so aghast at everything? Close your mouth, lad; if you open it any wider you'll swallow the Palace,' he quipped, but there was no humour in his lichen green eyes.

'What's wrong?' Marcus asked, now looking less shocked and more perplexed, and taking his arm back as the Scotsman released it.

'When we go into that hall, you're going to be given information that will, undoubtedly, leave you with questions. Reserve your judgments about what you hear, and who you meet, until your emotions have subsided. *Do not* act rashly on account of your feelings. Alright?'

'What are you talking about?'

'Take heed, lad.'

'But I don't understand.'

'You will. We'll talk afterwards, you have you have my word.'

'Why do you always have to vex me with your riddles at the *worst* times?' Marcus said through gritted teeth, but his words slid off McRae's impenetrable hide like water off a duck's back, and the older man swept past him without another word.

He watched Knox disappear through yet another stone arch, at the end of the landing, and ground his jaws together in annoyance before pursuing him. He found his companions waiting beyond the archway in front of a colossal pair of richly coloured, wooden doors, their surface buffed to an almost reflective lustre.

So, this was it, Marcus thought. On the other side of those marvellous doors, all the world's secrets lay in wait for them to discover. The unendurable months of decline, the covert weeks spent scheming with Knox, and the uncertain days of travelling had all been leading towards that singular, inexorable moment.

Yet now he was there, Marcus didn't know how to feel or what to expect. Perhaps that abstruse emptiness was, in actuality, a blessing, for he knew that if one's expectations and realities did not coalesce, chaos would be the result. So as Hugo grasped the golden handle and pushed his way inside, Marcus reminded himself of a little saying his mother used to tell him when he was a child.

'Hope for the best, expect the worst,' he muttered under his breath, before looking forwards, pointing his eyes in the direction of Aria and the open door. Watching her remove her sunglasses, Marcus met Aria's cerulean gaze for a fleeting second, smiling his hope into her and when she nodded her understanding, they traced Hugo's steps over the threshold.

The White Sea Hall was an unashamedly massive room. The door they had entered through opened out into its left side, leaving the vast majority of its expanse to their right. Marcus walked lightly over the varnished floor, inspecting the geometric patterns which decorated its maple syrup surface, before they disappeared beneath an ornate rug. The baroque walls were swathed in white and gold pillar-like designs, which eventually led up and over an ornamental border, to an incredibly detailed renaissance scene that had been painted on the ceiling. He and Knox craned their necks to appraise the work of art; however where Marcus's face conveyed a look of awe, McRae's showed something closer to disdain.

The further they moved into the hall, the more encompassing its golden facades and crystal chandeliers became, until they culminated in a sense of almost overpowering wealth. It seemed odd to Marcus that such a large room, brimming with so many of the material objects that men aspired to own, could be utterly stifling.

'What's this room used for, Hugo, I've never seen anything like it?' Marcus whispered curiously, not wanting his voice to echo.

'Many things, my friend. It has been a ballroom, a dining hall, a drawing room and today, it is a meeting room,' said the prince as he stopped a few paces ahead of their group, and with a flourish of his arm, stepped aside.

With the mountainous Swede now out of his line of sight, Marcus could see that three very distinct men were sat in the red, quilted chairs opposite them. Although he had no way of knowing anything with certainty, Marcus tingled with a kind of premonition at the sight of the unforeseen visitors, as he inferred from their presence alone that there would be more than one unexpected roll of the dice that day. Instead of giving voice to his anxieties though, he adhered to Knox's advice, letting the scene play out without his interference.

Aria, Cyril and Knox gathered to fill in the gaps between Hugo and Marcus, finding themselves arranged in a semi-circle of their own which mirrored that of their hosts. Once assembled, the man on the central chair stood, revealing himself to be considerably taller than he appeared when seated, and spoke to the group.

'Friends new and old, it is a pleasure to host you here in the Royal Palace,' he warbled in a sonorous, well spoken voice. 'Of course, there are several introductions to be made, and some rather unpropitious matters to discuss, but before all that, let us have some tea.'

'Do you have to be so formal?' Knox rasped, as a male and female attendant entered the room with silver trays of tea in their gloved hands.

'Can a king not address his court, in his own Palace, in whatever manner pleases him, Mr McRae?' he replied haughtily.

'Aye, of course, just let me know when you've climbed down from your high horse, so that I may kiss your feet, your *highness*,' Knox said, as a huge grin formed a fissure in the rocky plateau of his face.

Marcus and Aria stood agape, unable to believe Knox's audacity, but to their relief, everyone present erupted into laughter. It was a clamorous medley of sound that ricocheted around the space, saturating it in a thousand tones, before it receded into a playful snickering that left all of them smiling.

'Oh Knox, I've missed your indecorous ways! Come, have a seat,' the king said, swooping his arm towards several more ruby coloured chairs, which had been arranged by the male attendant.

Marcus studied the king as they each took up a seat, admiring the accurate way in which he pronounced his words, and the erect posture he upheld in spite of his age. It was hard to discern exactly how old he was, but Marcus estimated that he must've been born around the same time as McRae. However, where his mentor had grown knotty and sharp as he moved towards his expiry date, the king had ripened.

His receding white hair appeared stately, there was a svelteness to his physique which lent him a kind of grace, and his strong face bore an uncanny similarity to Hugo's. He caught

Marcus scrutinising him, as one of his attendants poured tea from the decorative china pot into his cup, and smiled at him with his radiant blue eyes, causing the younger man to colour.

Marcus averted his gaze then, just in time to watch Cyril pull up a chair besides the man to the king's right. They dipped their heads towards one another in a respectful nod, and Marcus observed that underneath his wispy moustache. the stranger was undoubtedly of Oriental descent. That discovery set his mind in motion as he attempted to see, and then connect, the constellation of dots that he'd found himself in the centre of. He felt as though he was on the cusp of unearthing the mystery, when the king politely dismissed his servers, and ground Marcus's gears to a halt with his voice.

'I hope the tea is to your liking, Tak-hing?' the king said, aiming his enquiry towards the man closest to Cyril, who upon further inspection seemed to be the most elderly person present.

'Very good, thank you,' he replied with a heavy Eastern accent.

'Splendid. Now then, Knox, why don't you introduce us to your two new *disciples*?'

'Disciples? Please, we all know that I'm about as far from holy as you can get.' He snorted. 'They're my students, let's say, Marcus and Aria, and they're here for the same reasons I am.'

'A pleasure to make your acquaintance, and let's get to the heart of the topic then, if these students of yours are to be trusted?' the king asked, glaring at Knox with a sudden seriousness.

'On my word, Oliver, they're to be trusted.'

'He's right, Father, they're good people,' Hugo added earnestly.

'Are you so sure?' the man to King Oliver's left snarled vociferously. 'What place do two inadequate *children* have in affairs like these?' His voice was guttural, the foreign twang in it making his words sound like blades hacking through bones, and Marcus struggled to place his accent. Though its violence curdled his stomach.

'They're with me, Viktor,' Knox replied tightly.

'What justification is that? They do not belong here.' Viktor spat.

'Enough!' the king bellowed, shutting down the argument before it could fully germinate. 'We are allies, and respectable men; calm yourself, Viktor. There are enough wars being fought out there, I will not have another waged in my dining hall, are we clear?'

'On your head be it,' came Viktor's grimacing reply.

'Very well.' The King sighed and smiled wearily. 'Let us not dally any longer then, we must discuss the grave state of the world. Knox, I know you and your companions have travelled a long way, I hope what I have to offer you will prove worthy of the journey.'

Marcus's pulse raced at the truculent exchange between Knox and Viktor, and he sensed that there would be more than one confrontation before their time with him came to an end. In the meantime, however, he needed to concentrate on whatever knowledge King Oliver and his cohort were about to impart. He resisted the urge to reach out and take Aria's hand, instead folding his own across his lap, and listened intently.

'As you're likely aware, the relationship between China and the majority of the Western world has become increasingly fraught over the past decade or so. The decline, however, has been going on for much longer, and what we are witnessing now is the culmination of almost forty years' worth of decay. As China's wealth and power have grown at an exponential rate, so too, has the rest of the world's dependency on them. The crux of the problem is the greed of their current government.' He paused to sip his tea, and so enthralled were his spectators, that none of them made a sound as they waited for him to continue. 'They know that they are one of the central spokes of the wheel that keeps our planet turning, but they do not want to be a humble spoke, they want to be the hub. That is why their leaders continue to push harder against the West, demanding more and more, in exchange for less and less. In their reckless pursuits though, they have alienated many of their former allies, and others they have beaten entirely into submission. I fear that may be the fate they wish on all of us.'

'And the virus, where does that fit in?' McRae asked, intensity written across every ravine of his face.

'It is a threat, a means of control and—'

'It is a weapon,' the elderly Oriental man next to Cyril hissed. It was a chilling sound, and despite lacking the anger or volume of Viktor's outburst, it was equally menacing.

'What do you mean, Tak-hing?' Knox pressed.

'When the American President came to our country to discuss new trading laws last year, he had our government backed into a corner. What he proposed was fair, and in my eyes at least, would've provided mutual benefit to both nations, but it also ensured that power would remain in the West. Our Prime Minster did not take well to that and, knowing that he could not reject the offer made by the Americans, he chose to delay any further negotiations. However, instead of using the time to develop new strategies for diplomacy, he chose the opposite, and began researching a way to take the world by force,' 'Tak-hing said in slow, methodical English, as though he were reading from an instruction manual.

He sat back in his chair then, appearing tired after his speech, and Marcus couldn't help but wonder who the mysterious man was; or how he came to know such hidden truths.

'Shite,' McRae intoned, as if it was a type of fact. 'So, we know it came from China, do we know why it's taken the path it has, what its purpose is? Surely as their Defence Minister, you must know?'

'Defence Minister! You're the Chinese Defence Minister?' Aria cut in, unable to hold her tongue any longer.

'Don't you tell your dogs *anything*?' Viktor scoffed.

'Quiet, Viktor. And yes, Tak-hing is the Defence Minister of China, and has been since 1975; now save your questions, lass, there'll be time later,' Knox scolded, causing Aria's will to wilt, as she shrank back into herself.

Yet, there was something about the speed of McRae's reply, a type of desperation to quiet Viktor, that rattled the cage of Marcus's trust, and there was something else too. He'd heard the Scotsman say Viktor like that before as they were landing in Sweden, but he'd confused the word for a noun, not a name, and that also tickled his uncertainty.

'I tried to dissuade them many times, but my authority is in its twilight days, I was overruled without a second thought. What they have made is an abomination. It is a uniquely manufactured virus, formed from several strains of other more common ones, and the way in which they have spread it throughout the world is even more barbaric,' Tak-hing said, sounding pained, the sorrow of not being able to do more to prevent the events that had transpired becoming palpable as he continued. 'They targeted members of the Chinese public, infecting them with the virus as they travelled across the world, by releasing it through the air circulatory systems of the aeroplanes they were in. That is how they directed the concentration of it to specific regions, hence why the United States, and all her allies, are suffering the most.'

Knox rubbed his forehead with unease at the startling information. It was the first time Marcus had ever seen him so apprehensive, and it felt like watching the first crack appear in the walls of the house he'd built his entire understanding of the world upon. But the fear that his perceptions may be on the brink of collapse was superseded, by the budding anger that resulted from McRae's secrecy.

Marcus knew that Knox knew little more than he did in the relation to the virus, but he had omitted so many crucial facts about himself, his associates, and their oracular positions, that he was starting to resent his mentor for his mendacity. Perhaps more concerning, was the likelihood of that resentment growing larger, with each new revelation that came to pass.

'So, the Chinese Government used their own civilians to disperse the virus? That's ingenious and ... well, *monstrous*,' the old artist remarked.

'Quite. But it wasn't just our people,' Tak-hing proceeded. 'The Chinese intelligence had access to information regarding every passenger on those planes. That meant they could rely on the tourists to transmit the virus throughout public locations, and the natives of those countries travelling home from China, to spread it within more localised communities and minorities. They bided their time, and chose their travellers carefully, to ensure that the widest possible cross-section of the targeted populations was hit.'

'But whatever they've made isn't proving fatal to the majority of the populace, only the elderly and infirm, so what's it for?' Knox questioned again, evidently ravenous to get to the bottom of the fallacy.

'That's not strictly true,' Viktor remarked, but was quietened by a wave from the king before he could elaborate further.

'At first, I thought they had simply rushed their experiments, missing whatever vital ingredient was required to make it lethal, but to my understanding it is that way by design. After all, what is the point of ruling the world, if there is no one left in it to oppress? It was produced to weaken China's adversaries, by destroying their economies and stretching their resources so thin, that they had no choice but to ask for help. What's worse still is that the Chinese Government sacrificed nearly four hundred thousand of their own people, and forced the remainder to live like lab rats, just to make them appear like victims of the same crisis. When, in reality, they are the authors of the entire tragic tale.' Tak-hing's voice had risen with his passions, and the silence of its absence filled the White Sea Hall, as he crumpled back into his chair.

Cyril shot out a consoling hand, murmuring soft Chinese words to the older man as he did so, and the tenderness of the gesture was not lost on Marcus. There was definitely more to their relationship which he was yet to discover, but at that moment, there was more to learn of the world's affairs.

'Am I right in presuming that the old allegiance is what's keeping Sweden safe from this cataclysm?' McRae probed, looking as though each new piece of evidence he'd received had aged him a decade.

'You are indeed, and the early closure of our borders,' King Oliver answered sombrely. 'Although our ties to China are crumbling, thanks to Tak-hing, our country and a few others – Nigeria, Angola, Japan, Korea, Argentina, and perhaps more – have remained untouched by the virus.'

'So, the hands of the players are finally revealed.' Knox breathed.

'They are, and there you have the origin of the blight, and the reason for the global quarantine, but sadly that is still not quite the full picture.'

'We believe that now China has its enemies on their knees, they are mobilising for all-out war,' Viktor said spitefully.

'What? That is insane, I can't believe this is actually happening … won't the Chinese soldiers just contract the virus themselves if they invade other countries though?' Marcus said, his voice an amalgamation of frustration and hopelessness.

'The dark truth at the heart of all this, Marcus, is that the Chinese have had a cure, and a preventative vaccine from the start. That may prove to be an even greater means of control than the virus itself,' King Oliver stated bleakly, quieting the younger man.

'What, exactly, makes you think they're now preparing for war?' Knox asked Viktor.

'Thanks to Tak-hing's intelligence and our own scouts, we have seen them massing huge amounts of troops in the remote areas of their northern territory. It's the same in many regions of Mongolia, and in some places, the *cheeky ublyudoks* have even started to cross the border into Russian territory!' he griped, melding his native tongue with his English, and finally giving Marcus the answer to his origins. 'They will make their move to take my homeland soon, if they haven't started already, but as for the rest of the world I am unsure. Despite not being completely allied with America, Russia is still a major threat to their agenda, and as such is now maybe the sickest of them all. This virus is rotting my people, and many cities, including St Petersburg, are completely lost to us now, but Moscow will never fall. It is already being prepared, as you will see if you're still planning on accompanying me home, McRae?' the Russian said with wrathful inflection, directing his ire at no one in particular.

'You're planning on going to Russia?' Aria said, looking astounded.

'You've never mentioned that once, Knox?' Marcus added, feeling somehow betrayed.

'Mr McRae, you didn't tell them?' said Cyril, sounding similarly shocked.

'Be still!' Knox boomed gruffly, but Marcus had reached his limit for lies and being told what to do that day, and he ignored the old artist.

His brain felt overloaded, and trying to digest all he'd just heard was as impossible as forcing an anvil through the eye of a needle. He needed to escape the pressure, the uncertainties, the veiled deceits, and he felt himself being drawn ineluctably towards the door. With the thought of escape on a conquest through his mind, Marcus thrust his chair back, got to his feet, and strode out of the grand hall without a pause.

Feeling elated, he increased his speed as he retraced his steps through the labyrinth of the Palace. With liberation fuelling every step, Marcus found himself close to the double staircase that led down to the main courtyard, in no time at all. However, there was a miscellany of footsteps thundering over the marble behind him now, and the implication of being chased stoked the flames of his already hot irrationality. He pelted down the stairs, skidding on the slick floor at their base, and hurtled through the doors, only to be met by a surging horde of aggravated people.

Completely dumbfounded, and with the spell of his false freedom shattered at his feet, Marcus stood there and gawped as cameras began to flash. He might have stayed there indefinitely, caught perpetually in that absurd moment, if it weren't for several pairs of hands clasping him, and wrenching him back inside the Palace.

Chapter IX

The marble was chill beneath Marcus's body, providing a welcome reprieve from the heat which was now inundating the Royal Palace, as the roaring sun reached its zenith.

He was slouched over the bottom few stairs, gasping for air, like some marine specimen yanked from the depths by a fisherman's net, as he tried to establish a foothold on the day's events. Hugo, Aria and Knox stood over him with an assortment of expressions, the former showing mild concern; and the latter looking characteristically disparaged. Marcus himself still appeared to be entirely flummoxed by the vacillating mob that had awaited him outside the doors. Their cries, although unintelligible, were still resonant from the courtyard and he couldn't fathom a reason for their presence.

'What are they saying, Hugo?' asked Marcus, consternation evident in his voice.

'A range of things, none of them good I'm sorry to say,' he informed them grimly, moving closer to the door to listen more intently. 'Expel the immigrants, lockdown is salvation … close our borders and, I'm sure you'll enjoy this one, kill the foreigners,' he said, making light of the despicable slogans. 'Who are they, and what on Earth are they doing here? There was no sign of them before?' Aria questioned, sounding fretful and partially defiant, clearly angry at the throng beyond the door who hungered for their blood.

'Judging by their banners, I'd say they're part of a group of Swedish far leftists who are extremely upset by the lack of any quarantine in our country, as you can hear. They call themselves the En Röst which, in your language, pretty much translates to "The One Voice",' the prince said, as he prised a halberd from one of the medieval suits of armour and slid it between the handles of the door to bar any intruders. 'They've been hounding the city for months with their protests and I expect *they're* here because *you* are. These people are hellbent on locking the country down, and as you can likely imagine, seeing several foreigners in the Royal Palace when it's supposedly closed, probably isn't sitting too well with them.'

'But how did they know we're here?' Marcus added, pulling himself up from the steps. 'And more importantly, how do they know we're not Swedish?'

'That's what I can't figure out. There's no way we could've been followed,' Hugo said, raking a hand through his thick beard, in deliberation.

'It has to be a set up,' McRae barked resolutely.

'How though?' Aria stuttered.

'That pack of degenerates must've been tipped off. There's no way that many En Röst members could've coordinated themselves so precisely,' the old artist ranted, punctuating his words by flinging his gnarled hands towards the courtyard. 'Not to mention the number of journalists and photographers amongst them – that's hardly a normal occurrence – and come tomorrow morning our faces are going to be slapped across every news outlet in the city, perhaps even broadcasted internationally!'

'Fuck! What does that mean for us then?' Aria asked urgently.

'It means going home isn't really an option right now,' he replied with a clenched jaw.

'You weren't planning on taking us back anyway,' Marcus argued, the pain of his mentor's treachery heating his voice.

'Reign yourself in, Marcus, your lack of self-control has already gotten us in enough trouble today,' Knox reprimanded in a punishing tone.

'You can't possibly be blaming me for this?'

'If you hadn't have stormed out like some querulous child this mess would've been easily avoidable, but as a result of your pitiful inability to keep your emotions in check, we are, to put it bluntly, fucked, lad!' The barbs of McRae's words hurtled towards Marcus, set to impale him, but the young man used the frayed edges of his nerves like a shield, protecting himself in a shell of resentment.

'And what if you'd have just told us the truth from the start, wouldn't that have prevented all this from happening in the first place?' he countered, the fire in him rising, turning his hazel eyes to lava.

'This isn't the time to discuss that. We have more pressing concerns,' Knox snapped.

'How *convenient.*'

'He's right, Marcus, our priority should be to find out who's behind this scheme,' the prince stated, siding with McRae in the process.

'What reason have I got to trust you any more than those maniacs outside?' Marcus spluttered, hammering out his words with ardent ferocity.

'We are not your enemies, I assure you, but the more time you waste treating us like we are, the less we have to focus on our true goals,' Hugo reasoned in a firm, yet compassionate, tone.

Marcus didn't fight back this time. He felt wretched, like a rabid animal backed into a corner and his thoughts contradicted one another with such pertinacity, that he feared their strife might flay the very skin from his body.

Knox took his silence as defeat, and as Aria stepped to Marcus's side in a gesture of reassurance, the old artist deemed the matter concluded.

'Lilly,' McRae rumbled.

'Pardon?'

'Think about it, Hugo, she's the only other person who knew about our meeting, and you can't be blind to her scorn?' he said, his eyes narrowing into raptor-like slashes. 'She's been trying to sever your father's ties to us, *common folk*, for years and now she might have succeeded.'

'You can't be suggesting–'

'That my daughter is responsible for this travesty? Tread carefully, Knox, I love you like a brother, but blood will always remain thicker than water, my friend,' came the majesty of King Oliver's voice from the landing above.

He was stood with Viktor, the two Chinese men presumably still upstairs in the White Sea Hall, and they both glowered down at McRae, their objection to his claim visible in their expressions. The old artist's hard face was still contracted into an igneous mask, but he withheld his thoughts, nonetheless.

'I'll hear no more talk of this today; we will adjourn for now. I'd advise you all to wait here until my guards have moved this rabble on.'

'Aye, Oliver.' Knox sighed resignedly, though the resolve etched into his face remained unwavering.

'Return to the Diamant when this is dealt with, and make your plans. I fear Stockholm may not be a safe haven for yourself, nor you companions, for much longer. We will meet again on Tuesday; until then remain inside the Hotel,' the king requested; his voice decisive.

'And what of Viktor, and the Chans?' Hugo queried.

'They will be going with you. Now I bid you all farewell, until Tuesday, be safe,' he said, as he turned to leave.

Marcus watched his arrow straight back recede through the archway, as he conjectured to understand how Hugo had referred to Cyril, and the elderly Chinese man. When he finally apprehended the missing link, the penny dropped with the force of an anchor; almost toppling him.

Tak-hing was Cyril's father.

He didn't know what kind of web Knox was weaving, but its threads spanned several continents, and over four decades of covert dealings; whatever he was concealing, Marcus had to uncover it by Tuesday at the latest.

Viktor descended the stairs and stood close to McRae, which seemed to Marcus an odd decision, considering they'd done nothing but disagree with one another at every turn. Cogitating over their strange relationship, he noticed that the pair were alike in many ways. They looked like two twisted trees ripped from the same soil, or a set of cantankerous relics from a begotten age, whose acrimony towards life was so profound that it immortalised them.

Having so much of the board now revealed to him, meant that it wasn't difficult for Marcus to guess that Knox, Viktor, King Oliver and the frail looking Tak-hing, were all linked to the same point in time. The details of what had brought them together were still shrouded in mystery, but McRae had referenced a year, 1975, and Marcus deduced that it held some relevance. However, he was tired of speculating and assuming, he wanted the facts now and he intended to get them. For the meantime though, all any of them could do was wait.

Before long Cyril and Tak-hing reappeared from the hallway above them, making their way steadily down the stairs to re-join the rest of their sundry group in the atrium. The more senior of them moved daintily, his stooped posture a contrast to that of his son, and together they endured the long minutes, eager for the calamity outside to abate.

None of them were sure if they had waited for hours or merely seconds, but each of them experienced a feeling of relief, when a tremendous banging on the door signalled the end of their confinement. Hugo removed the halberd he'd placed between the handles and returned it to the arms of the hollow knight, before opening the door to the guards.

They were wearing the same regal uniforms as the men stationed at Arlanda airport, and the prince exchanged a few words with their blonde-haired lead who had pounded on the door. From his stance it appeared he ranked above the other three men assembled behind him.

The guards, they were told, had established a perimeter around the Royal Palace and the Hotel Diamant, allowing them to move freely from one to the other. In a bid to appear as inconspicuous as possible, their numbers were spread thinly, however, and it was for that reason that they didn't travel as a single entourage. Alternatively, they were to cross the short distance to the hotel in several unassuming groups.

With their plan established, Knox stalked out immediately, followed by a grouchy Viktor, who displayed his irritation by uttering Russian profanities with every step. The placid Cyril went next, guiding his father across the cobbles by his elbow. In a world that seemed, of late at least, to be brimming with depravity and human impertinence; it was refreshing to witness such a sincere, caring act. Maybe humanity was redeemable after all, Marcus thought sceptically. He had no time to dwell on the matter though, as he found himself, and Aria, being rushed out of the door by Hugo's bough like arms.

Outside, the courtyard was bathed in mid-afternoon sun; its radiance bleached the towering building around them, and caused myriad refracted light beams to bounce off the smooth stones on the floor. Marcus squinted against the blinding light, as they moved away from the Palace and down the sloping street which would take them right to the steps of the Diamant.

There were no traces of the En Röst to be seen along their route, other than a solitary banner littering the pathway near the bridge. It amazed both Aria and Marcus, to see how efficiently the king's guards had dispersed them, and they entered the shaded safety of the hotel's splendid portico without a single hitch.

The ever-present doorman, who seemed to be immune to the sweltering heat, in his completely black outfit, opened the door for them, allowing them to enter the cool oasis of the lobby. Once inside, Hugo accompanied them to the wide mouth of the lift and used the time whilst they waited to address what had happened at the Palace.

'I know your heads are probably spinning, and I'm sorry that between us we have kept so many secrets from you,' the Swede said, with a hint of culpability tinting his voice. 'But these issues are hardly trivial, my friends, they had to be handled with care.'

'I don't know what to think anymore. I just feel like whatever's going on, it's too big for us, and we have no place here,' said Aria despairingly, as the three of them entered the lift.

'Aria's right, this situation is getting bigger by the day. I don't know why Knox even considered bringing us,' Marcus added, making fists, and then unfurling them as he spoke. 'I just want the truth, that's all I ever wanted.'

'Talk to McRae, both of you, it will help,' the prince offered, before departing onto the first-floor landing. He extended a small, conciliatory smile, and made to leave but Marcus lurched forward to hold the door open.

'Where are you going, Hugo?'

'Viktor and Tak-hing have been set up with rooms on this floor, I have to check on them.'

'What about the En Röst?'

'We'll get to the bottom of it, Marcus, don't worry. Now, is my interrogation over, or are you going to handcuff me and walk me to the gallows?' Hugo joked, providing the antidote for the tension in the air and Marcus, despite his niggling mistrust, couldn't help a chuckle escape his lips.

Aria joined in, chortling away beside him and just for split second, it felt as though nothing was wrong at all. Content that he'd made some progress towards regaining their faith in him, the prince smiled once more, and marched off down the corridor.

'Are you ok, Ari?' Marcus enquired warily, as he let the doors close.

'I haven't got the words to describe how I feel, Marcus,' she replied, without meeting his gaze, as her giggles morphed into a sigh.

'I'm sorry I left you in there, I just, lost myself.'

'I can't say I'd have reacted much differently in your shoes,' she huffed, as the doors opened onto their floor.

'That doesn't make it right though,' he said, but Aria didn't respond as they disembarked and trudged off towards their rooms. 'We'll find a way out of this, I know we will, I pro–'

'Don't do it, Marcus, don't make promises you can't keep. Let's just find Knox later and try to put all the pieces of this fucking jigsaw together,' she said decisively, swiping her key card and entering her room without giving him a chance to reply.

'I'll see you soon then,' he murmured quietly to the patch of air, where his friend had just stood.

He felt the searing prick of tears fill his eyes as he opened his own door, and used his fingers to hold back their swelling tide, as he closed himself in.

Eyes swimming, Marcus dropped onto the bed and stared up at the light fitting that he'd become so obsessed with; using its kaleidoscope of lines to distract himself from the feelings of futility, incompetence and misery that assaulted his jaded brain. Sadly though, even that infinite spectrum of diversion, couldn't assuage the distress he felt over the situation he'd plunged himself and Aria into.

The blame inside him was crippling, but as with all emotions allowed to run rampant through one's mind it became exaggerated, inflating like a balloon until it finally burst, spilling its putrefying lies all over his rationality and poisoning the voice of reason with its odorous vapours.

Marcus lay there for some time, moving through the various sentimental stages a person experiences, when their life appears to have burnt down around them. The convulsive surge of sadness came first, accompanied by that most deplorable of notions: self-pity. Then, at the very bottom of the well when one can no longer sink any lower, the sorrow ebbed and Marcus's head broke the surface of the water.

Disorientated and gulping for air, he thrashed around aimlessly until his grief died, and was replaced by a misguided anger that brought the liquid to a boil. Thus, the unreasonable questioning and blustering began.

Why had Knox kept so much from him? How could he have been so reckless; surely Aria must hate him? If he wasn't such a terrible person, would he even be in such a mess? Those insufferable enquires persisted, only coming to an end when they had exhausted themselves of energy, and sense, and all that was left of the water was steam.

It was there, standing in the bottom of the dry well and gazing up towards the light at its rim, that Marcus began the process of objective acceptance. Seeing the state of affairs as they were, not tarnished by the colours of his ego's bias, he was afforded his first, invigorating taste of illusory hope, and so, his ascent out of the well commenced.

He dragged himself from the soft embrace of the bed's covers with a dogged resolve, checking the time on the alarm clock, as he made for the bathroom. It was 5:49 PM which, if he got his act together, still gave him plenty of time to see McRae and acquire a firmer grasp of what was going on.

After splashing cold water across his cheeks and tidying his unruly hair, Marcus started to pace around his sizable suite, putting events in order as he walked. The movement helped to balance his mind and he likely would have worn holes in the thickly piled carpets, if a small tap at his door hadn't disturbed his indoor marathon.

He redirected himself towards the entrance to the room, considering who might have knocked so lightly; and was surprised to see Aria on the other side of the door.

'That was a very delicate knock; normally you'd have hammered it down,' he said with a smirk. 'Is everything alright?'

'If you'd class having a meltdown, screaming into a pillow and being stuck God knows how many miles from home with a collection of the craziest people on Earth, *alright*, then yes, Marcus, everything is bloody marvellous,' she replied, with the most satirical nuance he'd ever heard.

'Meltdowns are great, don't you think? I've just had one myself and it was, quite possibly, the best one of my life,' Marcus said, punctuating his words with overdramatic gestures, as he joined in her mordant game.

'Fancy adding some more ingredients to this shit stew?'

'Sounds delicious, what did you have in mind?'

'How about a sprinkling of Knox McRae's aged secrets?' she offered.

'It's like you're reading my mind! I'm sure that'll go beautifully with the side dish of international fuckery I've been preparing,' he gushed, breaking out into raucous laughter, with just a hint of hysteria beneath its surface.

Aria laughed madly too, and both of them exhaled their burdens into that cloud of ironic humour.

'I think we've finally lost it, Merda.'

'I'm not sure we ever had *it*.' He beamed, and the two of them shared a look then that conveyed what even a hundred words could not.

In that tiny fragment of time, no more than an existential snap of the universe's fingers, they knew that there were no ills between them.

Restored by the knowledge that Aria didn't hate him, as he had so acutely, and childishly, feared, he locked the door to his room and followed the dark-haired girl to Knox's suite. When they arrived, she pounded on his door in a manner that was much more typical of her fiery temperament, and they didn't have to wait long for the Scotsman to appear.

'I was wondering when you'd turn up. I'm almost disappointed, I imagined you'd be here sooner,' the old artist said by means of a greeting, but something seemed off about him.

He'd spoken with his usual patronising wit, and his voice still sounded like metal being cut with a chainsaw, yet he was downcast in an unfamiliar way.

'You could've always come to us,' Marcus stated.

'And where's the fun in that, lad? Come in anyway, I'm sure you've got questions, and I did give you my word that I'd answer them. Although, you hardly kept up your end of the bargain, did you?' he rumbled over his shoulder, as he turned back towards his suite.

The question was aimed at Marcus, and he knew Knox was referring to how he'd thundered out of the White Sea Hall earlier that day.

'What bargain?' Aria asked curtly, as they made their way into the living room area.

'I told Marcus to, how did I put it? Reserve his judgements about what you heard in the Palace today and that we'd discuss it later, but as you saw that *didn't* happen.'

'That's hardly a fair offer considering what we learned,' she remarked protectively.

'If you spend your life waiting for it to be fair, Aria, you'll have a sour existence, let me tell you.'

'Don't try to undermine me, Knox, that isn't what we came for. You owe us the truth and you know it,' she criticised, and Marcus couldn't help his lips from twitching into a smile, in admiration of her nerve.

'She's right, Knox, we haven't come for an argument,' Marcus concurred. 'We just want to know why you kept so much from us.'

Knox paused for a moment, chewing over his choice of words before speaking. It was an odd thing to witness as he was ordinarily so quick to react, but as his face flickered in deliberation, Marcus thought he saw just a fraction of the impervious, rocky shell fall from McRae; and expose some of the human beneath.

'Have a seat then,' he said, breathing out heavily. 'Do you want a drink?'

'A cup of tea wouldn't go amiss,' Marcus responded, slightly alarmed by the courtesy.

'Not tea, a real drink!'

'Hugo's punsch has put me off alcohol for life.' Aria scowled.

'Fine. Marcus?'

'I suppose a dram won't kill me,' he conceded with a shrug.

'Very good,' Knox drawled. 'The whisky's on the sideboard over there, get it yourself,' he finished, pointing towards the kitchen, as he nestled himself comfortably into a sizable leather armchair.

Marcus knew he'd been duped but chose to go along with McRae and fetch the spirit regardless; finding pleasure in the normality of the situation. It reminded him that, in spite of what his pride presumed, he didn't despise Knox and his trust in the man was only wounded, not broken.

He gathered the whisky, a rather charming Speyside single malt, two tumblers, a chilled bucket of ice, and returned to the main living space. Placing his goods onto the wooden coffee table, Marcus proceeded to drop three, almost perfectly cuboidal, chunks of ice into his glass and poured two fingers of the amber liquid over them. McRae snatched the bottle then, filling his glass almost to the brim, and consumed every last drop in one, remarkable gulp, before wiping his mouth and topping it up again.

'You're a monster,' Aria said, looking at Knox with a caustic expression.

'I've had better compliments and worse insults, lass, try harder next time,' he retaliated with a wry smile. 'Now, I realise you're probably wondering what my connections are to the Swedish Royal Family, and why I know, and raised the offspring of, the Chinese Defence Minister so I'll st–'

'And Viktor,' Marcus pointed out, his features stern.

'And Viktor. So, I'll start at the beginning, in the Autumn of 1976, when all of us first met,' McRae said, with his proclivity for sounding ominous on full display.

Marcus settled down next to Aria on the charcoal coloured sofa and prepared to be absorbed into the tale of his mentor's past. The strata of Knox's face bent into one of his hard, mirthless smiles, and then he began.

'Actually, before I get to the details, allow me to set some context. In 1949, after quite a long period of unrest, the People's

Republic of China was born. That is significant because that change in China's political climate, is ultimately what brought myself, and the others, together. Once they'd reformed, the people in charge of the country were eager to form a network between themselves and the West, and as it happens, the Swedes were the first to establish official democratic relations with them.'

'Is that the *old allegiance* you mentioned today?' Aria enquired, begrudgingly intrigued by the histories he spoke of.

'Aye, lass. Oliver's father, who was the then king, became close friends with China's Prime Minister, or Premier as they're called. For twenty-five years, everything progressed nicely. Trade flourished, industry boomed and the connections between the East and the West were strong. However, as I'm sure you're old enough to know, there's opposition in everything.' He paused to sip his whisky, savouring the smoky bite of it, before continuing. 'There was a summit held in Geneva, sometime in the October of 1976, I can't remember the exact date, where several of the world's leaders were meeting to discuss all the usual political tripe. Wars, borders, trade and the like. I just so happened to be one of the lucky few that got an invite to that, *prestigious* event.' He grinned derisively.

'What? Why were you there?' asked Marcus in bewilderment.

'I was in the military at the time, as you may or may not be aware, and as it was an international event, there were army personnel from all over the world there. It was luck of the draw, quite literally. My regiment were selected by the powers that be and then between ourselves, we just plucked names from a hat. A month later, at the tender age of eighteen, I was in Switzerland wearing my best uniform and watching the world's elite talk about a lot of things that I didn't understand. The meetings were set to last a week and I was, in all honesty, enjoying myself. It was easy work.'

'I didn't know you were capable of enjoying yourself Knox,' Aria jibed.

'That silver tongue of yours is going to get you in trouble one of these days, lass.' The Scotsman struck back with a single growl of laughter. 'Anyway, on the fourth day, the entire thing went belly up. The summit was concluded for the day, and as all the diplomats and bigwigs left, a group of terrorists made an attempt on the lives of the members of the Chinese Government. Most of the Chinese officials were already out on the streets, which worked in our favour, but the Premier and his two guards were blown to pieces as soon as they opened the front door. It was the first time I'd seen anyone die; and it was vile, the poor sods,' he paused, shaking his head before proceeding. 'I was close to where the Swedish King, his son Prince Oliver, and the Chinese Defence Minister – who you now know is Tak-hing – were talking beneath some trees when the gunfire rang out. So myself and another solider, which of course turned out to be none other than Viktor Stefanovich, rushed to defend them. We were pinned down in the undergrowth for what felt like hours, but in reality, it can't have been more than twenty minutes. Viktor killed three men that day, and managed to get himself shot in the process, I killed another, and between us we gained control of the situation. It remains, to this day, one of the foulest days of my life, but if the events hadn't have transpired the way they did, we wouldn't be here right now.'

'So that's the assassination attempt Hugo told me about then,' Marcus said, astounded by what he'd heard, and now able to put some of the pieces into place. 'I can't believe that's how you all met …'

'Aye, surviving an encounter like that shapes a unique bond, shall we say. I didn't know the King of Sweden long before he passed away, but myself and Oliver have remained close ever since, the same with Tak-hing.'

'There's got be a better way of making friends? What about Viktor?' Aria chimed in.

'Me and Viktor don't see eye to eye on a lot of things. He's been in the military his entire life and it's warped his views. He's cold and ruthless, but he's better as a friend than he is an enemy,' McRae replied in an honest rasp, ignoring her joke.

'Now what though? You befriended two extremely powerful people, stayed in touch, and now you're part of the *secret world defence league*?' Marcus badgered, articulating his frustration through his hands as he spoke.

'Don't be ridiculous, this isn't a fantasy, Marcus, this is real life. Tak-hing reached out to King Oliver when he learned of his government's plans to weaponize the virus, to warn him of what was coming, and to try and protect the Swedish people. Viktor is very high up in the Russian military and had intel regarding the movements of the Chinese army; knowing they could help one another, the three of them arranged to meet in Stockholm.'

'But you're neither a King, a General nor a Defence Minister?' Aria said, puzzled.

'Art has undone as many political regimes as war has, lass, I've been battling the world's perspectives for decades. Just because my weapons don't *end* lives, doesn't mean I can't *change* them. This is the biggest global crisis the world has faced since the Second World War, and I wanted to know what was going on, so here I am.'

'So, you knew what we were getting involved in, and you chose to keep it from us?' Marcus seethed, feeling his rage beginning to simmer once more as he spoke, but he fought to restrain himself.

'You said to me that you wanted answers, lad, you said you knew there was something larger and darker at work, and that you didn't want to sit at home and wait to die; so I offered you a chance to make a difference. I've provided you with the means to get your answers and have the impact you crave. But if I'd told you everything you know now back in London, do you really think you would've come?'

'I don't know … no, I just … I just didn't think it would be like this,' Marcus answered in a faltering, staccato voice.

'And what did you think it would be like, a little jolly to save the world, and then you'd simply return home as the hero? The reality we face is far more abhorrent than we foresaw; I understand that must be a shock. But nevertheless, you can't want to change the world only if it suits you to do so – where's the altruism in that?' McRae lectured. 'We can't go back to England yet, Sweden won't be safe for much longer, but Moscow should be, so that's where we're going.'

'Moscow should be safe? They're preparing for war!' Marcus rebuked in exasperation.

'He's right. We're not cut out for this shit, Knox! We need to get home,' Aria contended, shoring up Marcus's argument.

'Calm down! The Chinese forces are still hundreds, if not thousands of miles away from Moscow, and they'll never be stupid enough to launch a direct assault against the capital.

We'll be safe, I assure you,' McRae said, stymieing their responses with his autocratic voice.

'We're still heading closer to the conflict, it's hardly a sensible move,' reasoned Marcus, unconvinced by his mentor's attempts to propitiate them.

'Viktor is the only one with the means to get us back now. King Oliver can't risk sending out another Royal jet with the En Röst watching; it would be irresponsible – so unless you're planning on getting yourselves home, I suggest you come with me.'

'We're out of options then,' stated Marcus submissively, staring at the untouched whisky on the table.

'Christ, Knox, you really have fucked us here,' Aria said, her sizzling anger now nothing more than stagnant embers.

'You talk as though I've kidnapped you,' the old artist chuckled blearily. 'There's no insidious schemes here; you wanted answers, I've provided them. Say what you will of my methods, but how you feel about the truths you've been given is not my responsibility. Now leave me,' he said, unfurling his limbs, and rising to his feet in a dismissive gesture.

Knowing that there was nothing to be gained from quarrelling with McRae, Marcus and Aria dragged their subjugated selves out of his suite, and back down the corridor. Blown along like two cracked leaves in the gusts of a wind that was far greater than themselves, they could do nothing, but wait to see where they would land.

Chapter X

The following day was an unusually cold one, and as Marcus pulled back the sail-like curtains covering the window in his hotel room, he saw that the entire city had been enclosed in an overcast cocoon of grey clouds. The sun made insincere attempts to rear its flaming head, peeking out from behind its disconsolate veil for a pithy moment or two, before ducking away into the gloom once more.

The irony of the weather reflecting his mood wasn't lost on him, and there was a time in Marcus's life, when he would've given in to the misconception that the universe was indeed out to get him. Knox had taught him, however, that such things were just stories that one tells oneself, to further one's suffering.

According to McRae, it wasn't the events we endure that upset, or unbalance us, but rather our opinions of those events. Nothing is inherently good or bad, Marcus recalled him saying, as he dashed paint across an image of the UK's Prime Minister in his London studio; our perceptions make them so. It was an extraordinarily stoic thing to say, and quite incongruous, coming from the most explosive person he knew. But it was always that particular gem of reason he returned to, in times of turmoil. He turned from the window then, cursing Knox's maddening way of simultaneously providing him with solutions and problems, and left the colourless city behind.

Marcus's stomach grumbled as he made his way towards the Diamant's breakfast room; for what was potentially the last time. He admired the room's splendour as he was seated, forcing his eyes to appreciate the flamboyance of its architecture, as a dying man might savour his last meal. Today, however, he had no one to share his musings with, and he tucked into the delicious selection of Smörgas without any disturbances.

After the events of the previous day had left both of their minds in upheaval, Marcus and Aria had decided it was best to give one another some space, in order to fully assimilate what they'd learned. It was a wise choice, and as he placed the last tasty morsel of bread between his lips, Marcus felt, for the first time in days, that he had room to breathe.

It was an energising sensation, to not have such a profusion of thoughts all crushing against one another, deforming themselves into incoherence as they brawled. With the space now separating them, he could form a clearer picture of what was going on, and as Marcus drank his milky coffee, he began amalgamating everything he'd been told.

Starting with Knox's account of the Chinese Premier's assassination in 1976, he traced a line through history, all the way to the viral warfare of the present day. The issue was that no matter how well he understood the events or their implications, he still had no way of making an impact on them.

It occurred to him then, more distinctly than it ever had before, that he really had followed Knox into the abyss without considering what he was going to do when he actually got there. So sightless he'd been rendered by his yearning for freedom, so blinded had he been by the trust in his mentor, that he never considered how futile his acquisition of the truth might be. Foolishly he'd presumed that McRae had all the answers, that he would miraculously conjure a solution, and that would be that. Agitated by his own immaturity and powerlessness, Marcus finished his coffee and slammed his mug onto the table, drawing a few curious glances from the surrounding tables as he strode out of the room.

As the space between his thoughts closed back in, and his mind once again became a cesspit of rowdy malignance, Marcus paced the perimeter of the lobby. The thought of sitting still was unbearable, and as he was trapped inside the hotel, he had little choice but to walk its halls and vestibules. However, in a stroke of luck, or possibly even an instance of divine intervention, Marcus found himself presented with a rare opportunity.

From the corner of his eye, he spotted Tak-hing, easily identifiable by the traditional, black stand collar suit he wore. He was strolling towards an unfamiliar passageway out of the lobby, and under the influence of a strange compulsion, Marcus found himself running across the vast room in pursuit of the Chinese Defence Minister.

Although the older man looked to have an almost ambling gait from a distance, he moved with alarming speed, and once Marcus drew closer, he noticed that he possessed the same ethereal lightness of foot that his son did. The frailty he'd seemed hampered by yesterday was nowhere to be seen, and Marcus had to exert himself to catch up with him.

'Tak-hing, sir.' He panted, unsure how to address the Chinese minister, and praying he'd pronounced his name correctly. 'May I have a word, please?'

The stooped man didn't appear startled in the slightest by Marcus's sudden request coming from behind him; on the contrary, he seemed to have been expecting it. He circled around to face Marcus slowly, his movements devoid of exigency, and with a twitch of his featherlight moustache smiled at him.

'What can I help you with, Marcus?' Tak-hing asked patiently.

'I was hoping you could tell me more about, well, everything,' was Marcus's somewhat floaty reply.

'That would be a very long conversation indeed. Why don't you join me in the garden, and we'll see how far we can get?'

'Great, thank you. There's a garden?' Marcus stammered, disconcerted by Tak-hing's literal interpretation of his words, and the news that the hotel housed a garden.

'Come, and you will see,' he instructed, and with no further explanation, carried on walking. Marcus did as he was advised, trailing Tak-hing at a slight distance, as he was still undecided about how best to conduct himself. The corridor snaked around on itself as they progressed, almost in a complete U shape, giving the impression that they'd moved deeper into the Diamant somehow.

Following such a prominent Chinese official through the glass labyrinth of the hotel, in the hopes of arriving at its hidden, floral heart was a surreal experience; and in Marcus's contrived imagination, Tak-hing was beginning to exude a mystical quality. The impression that the elderly man was leading him to some kind of remedial oasis, was of course nothing more than a projection of his desires, but it was a captivating fiction nonetheless and he chose to it embrace for the meantime.

After taking yet another serpentine corner, they egressed from the building's interior and into the garden, which was perhaps even more inspiring than the hotel itself. Despite not sharing the same immense size as the building that held it, nor oozing the same brazen wealth, it was enchanting in a way that only natural things can be.

The space was hexagonal and couldn't have spanned more than twenty metres between its two widest points, yet rather than feeling confined, it felt cosy. Marcus looked around, marvelling at the gorgeous array of pruned trees, vivaciously coloured flowers, and ornamental hedges. The smell of pollen and sap was strong, almost making him sneeze, but it felt revitalising in contrast to the still, manufactured air of the Diamant's lobby.

He followed the path Tak-hing had taken to a bench on the outskirts of the greenery to their left, basking in the sensory gala of the garden, as he felt the supple grass compress beneath his boots. Taking up a seat next to the old man, Marcus gazed upwards as he positioned himself and saw the hotel's glass dome glistening high above them, which gave the impression that they were swimming face up in a deep pool. The bulging of Marcus's, eyes as they roved around their surroundings had not gone unnoticed, and Tak-hing let out a quiet laugh as he watched.

'Do they not have trees in England anymore?' the older man asked, making Marcus catch himself.

'Yes, loads, everywhere actually,' he answered, blushing slightly, and wondering why he seemed incapable of talking in a normal manner.

'Your face betrays you, Marcus, you would make a terrible poker player! Now, why don't you tell me what troubles you so much that you can't even string a sentence together?'

'I'm confused.'

'At this moment in time, I think most of us are, but I have a feeling there is something more specific on your mind?' Tak-hing said in an equable, soothing tone, enticing Marcus to bring his issues to bear.

'It's Knox, actually. I feel as though I'm losing trust in him.'

'Why is that so?'

'He lied to me, and he didn't tell me the full extent of his plans,' Marcus said, sounding far more whiney that he would've liked.

'Did he lie to you, or did he choose to keep information from you? Those two things are not alike.'

'Well, I suppose he didn't really lie to me then. He just kept a lot of important facts from me, facts that would've influenced my decision to come, and more importantly, my decision on whether or not to bring Aria with me.'

'You didn't *bring* Aria with you, she *chose* to come with you, don't take responsibility for that which is not yours.'

'Alright.'

'And what was it you wanted from Knox, what did he promise you?'

'He didn't promise me anything. I was frustrated, I wanted to know what was going on in the world, and he said he had a way of finding out.'

'Have you found the answers you sought?' Tak-hing enquired, extracting answers from the younger man, as a heron might pluck fish from a pond.

'Yeah, I guess I have.'

'Then what reason have you to distrust him?'

'I just …' But Marcus's words fizzled out, leaving the thought unfinished.

'From what I gather, you had a need for knowledge and it has been fulfilled; your grievance seems to be with the gravity of the situation you have found yourself in, and your apparent inability to do anything about it.'

'Exactly!' Marcus said, astounded by Tak-hing's acumen. 'If I'd have known how big this whole affair was, I would've stayed out of it. Now I just feel like I'm in over my head, and worse still, I feel guilty for dragging my best friend into this mess too.'

'So then, you are saying that when you were naïve to the magnitude of the problem, you assumed you could find a way to help solve it. However, now you are aware of its proportions, it seems too large, and yourself too ill equipped, to make a difference. If that is the case, Marcus, your issue does not lie with Knox McRae, it lies within yourself,' he replied, in an unrepentant tone that reminded Marcus of the same way Knox dealt with the telling of similar, introspective truths.

Every mentor needs a master, and perhaps Tak-hing had been McRae's, Marcus pondered, as he continued to digest every word the astute Chinese politician had to offer.

'Knox has given you precisely what you asked for; knowledge of the affairs causing the global quarantine, and in doing so, has accorded you an insight that few will ever have the privilege of seeing. If you have found yourself displeased by this, then either your judgments about the world are unrealistic, or you didn't really want to know in the first place.'

'You sound an awful lot like Knox, you know?' Marcus replied dumbly, giving voice to his thoughts.

'I doubt that's a coincidence.'

'What do you mean?'

'You are an easy young man to read, Marcus, it's likely that the two of us have simply made the same observations of your character.' He answered easily, as though the topic of one's intrinsic faculties could be discussed as insouciantly as a dinner menu. Marcus didn't reply, feeling both embarrassed and intellectually outclassed, he chose not to speak. But Tak-hing's eyes seemed to be puncturing his skin with their intensity, and when he looked up from the ground to meet them, Marcus found himself staring into to two bottomless, black pits.

'So, what do you propose I do then, what's the best course of action?' Marcus said, tearing his eyes away.

'Who am I to tell you that? I am no more qualified to tell you what to do, than you yourself are. When it comes to the matter of how we should live our lives, no one has successfully answered that question, in its entirety, since it was first conceived. Socrates couldn't tell you; Confucius was unable to summarise it; and every religion you've ever heard of is, ultimately, just an opinion. If these sagely masters cannot provide the answer, how can I?' Tak-hing responded, complicating matters further. The juxtaposition of his pleasantly hypnotic tone, and the candid way in which he delivered his ideas, was whirling Marcus's mind into pandemonium.

'Are we not off topic here?' asked Marcus curtly. 'I wanted to discuss my issues with McRae, and how best to approach the scale of this dilemma. With all due respect, I didn't come for a philosophy lesson.'

'Let me be more succinct then,' Tak-hing said, unbothered by Marcus's tone. 'You know what you think is right, and what is wrong, you are old enough to have established a system of ethical values and yet, you seem to be caught in an eternal cycle of confusion, capriciousness and self-catastrophising. I cannot pretend to know you well, my presumption is based only on what I've learned from my son, and my brief time with you, but I feel it may be correct nonetheless.'

Then there was pause as Tak-hing, apparently drained by the exchange and the imparting of knowledge, exhaled deeply. Meanwhile Marcus nursed his ego in silence, feeling as though the Chinese man's tongue was a whip, and every word a laceration upon his back.

There was no denying, however, that what the judicious old man had spoken was the truth. It was the same truth he'd been confronted with time and again, especially since he'd crossed paths with McRae. In fact, Tak-hing had done little more than reinforce what his mentor had told him all those years ago, in London. But what good had it done him, that pursuit of self-betterment and change? Insofar as he could tell, not a great deal, and as Marcus prepared to express his resentment for the scourge of knowledge, the elderly man squashed his impetus by speaking first.

'It isn't easy to analyse oneself and dislike what you've found, but remember, Marcus, everywhere you go, you'll find yourself. It won't matter how far you run, how much you know, or how many distractions you implement, *you* will always be *there*. Perhaps that is the root of your problem?'

'Do you really think so?' Marcus said, fortifying his inquest with both satire and scepticism.

'I genuinely do. Would you trust someone you hate?'

'Probably not.'

'And would you listen to the advice of someone you despise?'

'No.'

'And if a person you detested was in charge of making decisions for you, how would you react?'

'I don't know, I'd rebel against them I suppose. What are you getting at, Tak-hing?'

'Don't you see? If all you have is contempt for yourself, Marcus, you'll do nothing but fight your intuition at every turn, and so we come full circle to what I said in the beginning: the issue lies within yourself.'

'What a wonderful paradox.' Marcus groaned, thrusting his head skyward, as though his solace might be found on the glass above them.

'Wonderful indeed.' Tak-hing chuckled in his quaint, Eastern way. 'Human nature has, and will always be, a contradictory thing but you will do well to accept that and reconcile the shards of your broken self. If you can do that, it won't matter where you are or what obstacles you face, you will always be sufficiently armed for what is to come.'

'And what exactly is to come? With the world I mean?' Marcus questioned, growing tired of the philosophising and platitudinous talk.

'First you want to talk about everything, and now you want to know what is to come of the world – you are fond of the big questions, aren't you?' Tak-hing jested, showing a toothy smile, before his austerity returned. 'How it will come about I am unsure, but I believe a war is inevitable now. It is likely to be on a scale previously unseen, a seismic event, that will place a wall before the flow of the universe and change the course of history forever. I can only hope that the new path leads to prosperity, and not impoverishment.' He finished, closing his eyes for moment.

Marcus, observing that the older man was clearly drained, and likely as a result of his impetuous attitude, inferred that it was probably time for him to leave. He placed his hands on his thighs, and stood briskly, uncrumpling the creases in his mustard coloured t-shirt as he did so.

'Thanks for today, I'm sorry for acting like such a child, but I appreciate your time,' said Marcus, trying to redeem his insolence.

'You've caused me no offence, therefore, you have no reason to apologise. I only hope I've been of some use to you, but I'm sure we will talk again before this drama unfolds completely,' Tak-hing concluded, without opening his eyes.

He looked at peace, and Marcus wondered if he'd fall asleep there, in that luscious green enclave, as he himself left its sweet greenery behind.

He navigated his way back to the hotel's lobby in a kind of reverse pilgrimage, finding that the industrial modishness of the hotel was a poor substitute for the esoteric sanctuary of the hidden garden. Marcus turned his wrist up to examine his watch, as he traipsed around the enormous reception desk and towards the stairwell. It seemed the sagacious Chinese politician also had the ability to bend time, for it was well past midday and yet Marcus's last memory, prior to their conversation, was of breakfast. The fact that he now had less time trapped inside the Diamant than he'd anticipated, should've been comforting, but it also brought a portentous sense of dread along with it.

Their time in Sweden was drawing to a rapid close, and their journey to Russia was hurtling towards them with equal haste. What disturbed Marcus the most was that, in an unforeseen change of heart, going to Moscow now seemed like the best course of action. The combined words of McRae and Tak-hing had taken root in his mind, and the trees they sprouted were blossoming quickly. After all, he'd already entered limbo, why not go all the way to hell?

Part of him still fought for a safer option though, recoiling at the idea of going even further from home; and creating even more distance between himself and his old life. It reminded him of the remorse he felt for his parents, and the biting guilt of the stress his actions had undoubtably caused them. But Marcus didn't have the time to let the two poles of his personality bind him to inaction with their arguments; he had to align himself with only one of the factions and remain faithful to it regardless.

With a dangerous, and somewhat audacious, feeling of purpose blooming within him, Marcus pushed his way through the door to the stairwell and mounted the stairs. He needed to find Aria now, and he prayed that she would be in her room, and more importantly that she was of a similar mindset to his own. If she wasn't, he'd have to summon every ounce of cunning and persuasion he had to sway her obdurate will.

Descending into the depths of his thoughts as he scaled the first-floor landing, Marcus ran over a sequence of hypothetical interactions in his head, each of them, conveniently, ending with a triumph. He'd become so transfixed by the make-believe scenarios that he failed to see, or hear, the real one that was about to play out before him.

As he clasped the bannister and swung himself up the next flight of steps, he was met by a whirlwind of brunette hair and tanned skin, that struck him at chest height. If he hadn't been holding on, Marcus would undeniably be lying in a rumpled pile at the foot of the stairs, but as it happened, he'd only fallen down a single step.

However, whoever he'd collided with, was now sprawled over the landing above him at an awkward angle. Slightly winded from where the person's forehead had smashed into his sternum, Marcus approached the scrunched form, but before he could extend his apologies, it began to speak. Angrily.

'For fucks sake, watch where you're going, will you!' came the expulsion of outrage from the floor. The voice was female, and although the face of the young woman was covered by her dishevelled hair, her identity was unmistakable.

'Ari! This is perfect, I was literally about to come looking for you.' Marcus grinned, pleased by the coincidence and oblivious, or perhaps just impervious, to her fury.

'Marcus?' she questioned, flipping her hair out her face. 'Bloody hell, I should've known the only person clumsy enough to run into me in a place like this would be *you*.'

'What? You ran into me, and I've got the crater in my chest from your gigantic forehead to prove it!'

'Wow, first you push me over, then you insult me? And you wonder why I always tell you that chivalry is dead?' she muttered disapprovingly, as she clambered to her feet and rubbed her aching back. 'Anyway, come with me. I need to catch you up on what I've found.'

'What do you mean, found?' he questioned, walking side by side with her, as they progressed up the stairs towards the second floor.

'I'm not talking about it out here, this is important, and I don't know who might be listening.' Aria replied connivingly.

Marcus decided not to push her, and the pair of them moved quietly out of the stairwell and towards their rooms, choosing Aria's as their base operations.

Influenced by the peculiarly secretive behaviour of his friend, Marcus checked the corridor before following her in, and closed the door delicately behind him. He found himself feeling quite on edge, but as he turned and walked into the room, the unease he was experiencing transmuted into something closer to an entertained bafflement.

'How, please, has one tiny person such as yourself managed to create so much mess?' Marcus balked, looking around at the domestic fallout from Aria's short, but ostensibly anarchic, stay in the hotel.

Hillocks of clothes littered the floor and were draped over chairs, various toiletries and other products were strewn across almost every available surface, a selection of used plates dotted the kitchen worktops; and there was a worrying amount of hair bobbles scattered throughout the suite. It was, in short, a true feat of human obsolescence.

'If I spent all my time tidying up, I'd have no time for anything else,' she said, avoiding the question.

'Have you ever considered just making less mess?'

'No. I like it, mainly because it bothers you. Now shut up and let me tell you about what I've learned.'

'Alright, alright,' he mumbled, taking a seat on a clear patch of sofa between a can of deodorant and a pile of socks. Aria sat across from him on the heavily padded arm of the chair, and that's when he noticed just how distressed her blue eyes looked.

'I don't really know where to start, so I'll just cut to the chase: Knox was right about Princess Lilly. She's off her rocker, Marcus, and she's definitely behind all this En Röst, or however you say it, stuff.' She spoke hurriedly, with an unfamiliar twang of timidity in her voice.

'How do you know she's involved with them?'

'I followed her out of the hotel today; she met a couple of very strange looking men in an—'

'Wait, you left the hotel, how?'

'By walking out of the front door – it's a hotel, not a fucking prison. Now listen,' Aria said, her tone growing louder and more insistent. 'She met these guys, two of them; they were scary, like they looked properly unhinged. Obviously, I couldn't understand what they were saying, but between them they must've mentioned the En Röst about a hundred times. I think they're planning something, Marcus, and I don't think it's going to be anything good.'

'What the hell?' Marcus replied, unable to muster anything more constructive.

'I wish I'd had my phone, I could've recorded what they were saying and translated it! But as it stands, I haven't got a clue what was actually said.'

'What about Hugo, can't he help us?'

'Funny you should say that actually, I ran into him on my way back into the hotel. As you can imagine he wasn't pleased to find me sneaking around, but I managed to sweet talk my way out of it,' Aria responded with a cat-like smile, which gave rise to a hot flush in Marcus, whose irrational mind had twisted her words into a jealousy inducing tale of sexual promiscuity.

He quickly staunched the flames of that misdirected train of thought, lest they set him alight, and returned himself to a more factual plane.

'Ok so you batted your eyelids at Hugo, he let you off the hook, and then what? Did you tell him what you saw?'

'I tried, but he just dismissed everything I had to say, and seemed to have an explanation for everything. He's just like his father was with McRae at the Palace, really protective and completely unwilling to see any flaws in his family members,' she huffed dejectedly, and Marcus had to try his best not to smile at her show of dislike for the Prince.

'Well, it looks like we've got no chance of outing her then. And I can't see pissing off the king by trying to convince him that his daughter is conspiring against him, really doing us any favours right now,' he replied, with a similar sound of defeat in his voice.

'No, I think that's a losing battle.'

'I wonder why she's doing this, I know Knox said she's got a bee in her bonnet about the king's friendship with *commoners*, but surely that's not enough justification to organise your own political party, and a violent one at that?'

'I couldn't begin to imagine. Up until a few days ago I knew nothing about Sweden, least of all the vendettas of its Royal Family. I just think the sooner we get out of here, the better.' Aria motioned.

'I can't believe I'm saying this, Ari, but I honestly think going to Moscow with Viktor and Knox might be the best option, especially if Stockholm is about to turn into a battleground,' he said, feeling relieved to have admitted his thoughts, but equally anxious as to how she might reply.

'I think you're right. I just want to get *home*. We've seen more than enough, and if Viktor's got our tickets back to England then I'm in.'

'So, we're going to Russia then?' he asked rhetorically.

'I think we are,' she concurred, biting her lower lip nervously.

Marcus, vacillating between the impulse to cry and the one to laugh, settled for a half smile. Grasping the sentiment of his expression, Aria smiled back, but neither of them spoke as they considered the implications of travelling to Russia. Fearful that the silence might be a sign that he'd outstayed his welcome, Marcus got to his feet and prepared to leave.

'I better get going then and give you some time pack your things,' he said, gesturing vaguely at the shambolic room, as he chuckled.

'You never told me about your day?' she probed, delaying his departure.

'I can't really say that much happened to be honest.' He shrugged in reply. 'Although I did have an interesting chat with Cyril's dad,' Marcus finished, considerably de-emphasising the significance of their conversation.

'Oh really? And what did he have to say?'

'Not much that I didn't know already,' snorted Marcus. 'Basically, I need to stop victimising myself, I'm of no use to anyone if I can't make a decision, and I can't want to save the world only if, and when, it suits me.'

'That's amazing, you'd think he'd known you your whole life.' Aria laughed, revelling in the bluntness of Tak-hing's analysis.

'Tell me about it. Now, get packing, you!' he jibed, disguising his introverted keenness to be alone behind the joke.

'Fine,' she mocked, screwing her face up in a playful manner.

Marcus made for the door then, but as he approached the handle, a sudden, inexplicable vagary spun him back around.

'I really don't want to see anyone else today, and the last thing I need is another one of Knox's reprimanding sermons *but*, what do you say to a room service dinner in like, two hours?' he enquired, surprised by his own boldness.

'Why not? One last supper before we get mauled to death by angry protesters.'

'It'd be a shame to die on an empty stomach,' Marcus agreed.

'It's a date then,' Aria said, her eyes widening as she realised what she'd said.

'A date? Wow, Lucky me, I've successfully courted the *infamous* Aria Bianchi,' he joked, putting on a terribly clichéd Italian accent, and twirling his hand as though he was shaping pizza dough.

'Get out!' she cried, assailing him with a projectile of bundled socks.

Marcus did as he was told, and with her saccharine laughter still ringing in his ears, beamed all the way back to his room; like a child enjoying their favourite confectionery. It was moments like those, that despite being ephemeral, gave him the strength to weather life's afflictions, and he drew comfort from the knowledge that whatever uncertainties the following day would bring, he wouldn't be facing them alone.

Chapter XI

'Marcus,' said someone, on the vague edges of his cognition.

'Marcus, wake up.' The voice came again, this time louder and far more importunate.

He considered addressing it and shaking off the manacles of sleep that bound him, but before he could even make the choice, a pair of hands seized him. He shot up reflexively at the touch, heart thrumming, and cast his bleary eyes around for the source of danger.

'Relax! Christ, it's only me!'

'Aria?' he asked, nonplussed.

'Yes!' she answered tautly. 'Who else would it be?'

'It's pitch black, what time is it?' Marcus pressed, trying to regain his senses, as he rubbed his dry eyes.

'It's about four in the morning, now *be quiet*, there's something going on outside. Look,' Aria replied, sounding overwrought as she traversed the room on her tip toes, and headed towards the window.

Marcus followed, trying to establish if the unfamiliar pattering noise filling his ears was his own heartbeat; or something more ill-omened. They each folded back enough of the curtain to see down into the streets below, and to Marcus's astonishment, not only was it raining, but there were also hundreds of shapes shifting across the cobbles.

As their eyes adjusted to the gloom it wasn't hard to discern that they were human, but the way they scurried around in the shadows, blending in and out of the inky spaces between the buildings, made them appear as insidious wraiths. Their beguiling forms were at once both hideous and brilliant, and Marcus found himself unable to resist staring at their ethereal scuttling.

'What are they doing?' he said, straining to catch any details he could through the rain-spotted murk.

'I don't know, but I have a horrible feeling it has something to do with what I heard yesterday,' she said, her eyes wide, her tone jittery.

'Any idea how long they've been there?'

'No. I woke up on the sofa about five minutes ago, then when I heard some scuffling outside, I got you up straight away.'

'We need to let Knox and the others know. Go grab your bags, I'll get mine, and I'll meet you in the corridor,' Marcus said with a self-assuredness he didn't feel.

She nodded and spun on her heel to make for the door, but as she did so, something banged boorishly on the other side of it.

Aria leapt back in fright, smothering a yelp, whilst whoever was on the other side yanked furiously at the handle. Marcus dived forwards to protect her from whatever may have been about to rampage into the room, and they waited for the encore, or the bursting of the wood from its hinges; but neither came. He positioned Aria behind him and approached the door, counting back from three under his breath as he went, before clutching the handle and opening it a fraction.

A blade of dim light from the hallway sliced through the darkness, but there was nothing obvious to be seen, which, given how deafening the sound had been, was perhaps more concerning than if he'd been greeted by some vulgar beast. Marcus pushed the door further open, unsure what he'd find, when the unmistakable figure of Knox came into view.

'Shit, Knox, you scared us to death,' Marcus said, releasing an exasperated breath. 'What's going on?'

'Us?' the old man questioned, with narrowed eyes.

'Aria's with me, we were having dinner and fe–'

'I don't care. We need to leave, and sharpish,' said McRae fiercely, repudiating Marcus's comment. 'Cyril has gone to wake his father and Viktor, we'll meet them and Hugo in the lobby. Aria, get your things, me and Marcus will wait for you here,' the Scotsman ordered, flicking his head in the direction of her room.

She skittered past without a word, not wanting to provoke Knox with any questions, and dashed into her suite.

'Any idea what's happening out there?' Marcus asked, trying to keep his voice stable.

'Not really. My best guess is that it's something to do with Princess Lilly, the devious witch, and these fucking En Röst lunatics. They look to be surrounding the hotel, but we're not sticking around long enough to find out why.' He grimaced.

'So where are we going?'

'To the airport.'

'Back to Arlanda?'

'No, Bromma. That's where Viktor's plane is,' McRae concluded as Aria returned. He glanced at her and nodded. 'Right then, we're moving.'

Knox took charge, leading them at a trot down the corridor and towards the elevators. However, as Marcus slowed his pace, assuming they would be using one to reach the ground floor, McRae signalled ahead indicating that they'd be taking the stairs. Together they shot through the door and bounded downwards in a matter of seconds, only pausing when they reached the ground floor, where Knox held up a fist to stop Marcus and Aria from proceeding. The old artist then pressed his jagged face to the glass pane in the door, assessing the cavernous room beyond and seeing if it was safe to enter.

'We're clear, but I can't make out what's going on outside the hotel, that black glass just looks like a mirror from here. There's also no sign of the night staff, which is odd, but the rest of our motley crew are behind the reception desk, which is where we're heading too. Keep low and run. Got it?' McRae intoned in his hoarse rasp, like a captain giving orders to his regiment.

'Got it,' Aria said, as Marcus nodded to show his understanding, and then they were out in the open.

Knox darted off ahead, propelling himself at an amazing speed for a man over sixty, and the three of them covered the gap between the stairwell and the behemothic desk in a flash. Breathing heavily from their sprint, they ducked down to conceal themselves, and were received by the remainder of their cohort.

With the exceptions of Viktor, whose face looked so splenetic that he might combust, and Tak-hing who wore a mask of accepting tranquillity, they made a solemn group.

'What's the latest, Hugo? I can't see a damn thing through those reflections, and where are all the staff?' Knox enquired sourly.

'I don't know about the staff, I was thinking the same thing myself, but we've got other things to concern ourselves with. From what I've seen they're basically blocking all the Diamant's exits, and judging by the slogans they've got painted on their makeshift barriers, they're definitely En Röst,' he answered, displaying a flat, business-like tone.

'Do you know if they've seen us?' Viktor added in his hawking, Russian timbre.

'Not as far as I'm aware, which should give us the element of surprise,' responded Hugo.

'We should rush them then, and break their walls down.'

'Always so quick to find violence, Viktor. Even with your temper, we'll still be vastly outnumbered if we leave on foot,' Tak-hing said smoothly, trying to reason with his old friend.

'What about the garage? If we can get a vehicle and use it to punch a hole in their wall, then we should be able to make it to the airport before they have a chance to react,' added Cyril, reinforcing his father's statement, and shocking Marcus and Aria with his tactical aptitude.

'Likely our best option, any chance of a distraction?' Knox offered, earning a scoff from Viktor, whose aggravation was increased further by the dismissal of his more offensive plan.

'There's too many to try and outwit, we should just focus on reaching the garage, and engage them as little as possible,' the Prince concluded.

'How far is it to the garage?' asked Marcus, eager to know just how many of the fanatical Swedes he'd have to run through to reach the safety of a vehicle.

'Out of the main door, turn left, and the entrance is on the hotel's West side. It can't be more than a hundred metres.'

'What about keys? We can't start a car without keys.'

'Don't worry, Marcus, the limousine we arrived in is still down there, the keys will be under here,' said Hugo as he turned around and started to rifle through a recess beneath the desk's thick, marble surface. After a few moments of rattling around, the hulking prince shifted to face them, revealing a set of gleaming keys in his palm.

'Good. We need to move though, the longer we wait, the more time they have to prepare,' McRae advised, though it was more imperative than suggestion.

'Agreed, I'll lead the way. I'm the least likely to alarm them on sight and it might buy us a few extra seconds,' Hugo stated with finality, before rising to his feet.

Adrenaline coursed through Marcus's limbs, bestowing him with a sense of power and awareness, that was not entirely his own. With a clear mind, uncorrupted by his usual, idiosyncratic tendencies for overthought, he felt focused as he took up a place beside his companions.

They moved towards the tremendous glass exit in a single file column, the only noise the rhythmic tapping of their shoes on the marble, and the occasional shallow breath. As the doors loomed over them, Marcus felt Aria's hand slip into his own, their fingers looping together and compressing one another in a wordless conversation. In his heightened state, the touch of her skin on his was electric, and he hoped that he'd communicated enough in that final squeeze before she pulled away, to make Aria realise just how much he cared.

Hugo was at the door now, his enormous hands braced against it, ready to fling it open on McRae's count. Despite being so close to the outside world the scene beyond the hotel was still cloaked by the black glass, but the pouring rain was now audible, roaring its relentless beat.

'Ready?' the Scotsman croaked.

'Ready,' they echoed, their contrary range of accents uniting into a single voice.

'On my mark. Three.'

Marcus held his breath.

'Two.'

He poised his stance.

'One!'

Then they were running.

Hugo pelted through the door, his massive form almost cracking the glass as he charged down the steps, and slid to a crouch behind the decorative hedge that lined the valet bays. Knox joined him, followed by Marcus and Aria, with Viktor and Cyril escorting the slower moving Tak-hing at the rear. The rain whipped around them as they shuffled along behind the cover of the foliage, reducing their visibility drastically, but of course if they couldn't really see, neither could the mob.

Within the first minute of being outside they were drenched, and as Marcus brushed the flowing water from his eyes, the first shouts from beyond the hedge split the air. At first there was only one and the group kept crawling, gaining precious metres. But then a second came, and a third, until a pernicious wave of rippling yells rose all around them. The fine hairs on the back of Marcus's neck fought the streaming rain, and rose to stand on their ends, as his stomach lurched and then dropped a hundred feet within him.

'I think we've got company!' Viktor bellowed, quashing the ceaseless roar of the rain with his own mighty growl. The prince stuck his head up above the leafy parapet to gauge the situation and almost instantly dropped back down.

'They're moving towards the door; if they get there and we don't move, they'll surround us. We have to go, now!' Hugo ordered, scrambling to his feet. 'Around the building. Move!' Then he shot off, modulating his pace so the others wouldn't fall too far behind, and aimed for the corner of the hotel.

The dissonant wails of the crowd grew exponentially as the group struck out from their hiding place and dashed across the open stones. A stampede of footsteps began behind them, adding to the already riotous drumming of the falling water, to form an inconsonant chorus of repetitious bangs. The chase was on, but the path they were taking was almost completely devoid of any En Röst, and they reached the declining slope on the Diamant's West side without any hindrances.

Skidding over the slippery cobbles, their loose column made their way towards the entrance to the underground carpark. Hugo struggled to tap in the code on the access panel, his wet fingers sliding over the buttons as Knox, Marcus and Aria formed a circle around him and fought to fill their burning lungs.

There was a shrill beep then, as the shutter door barring their way began to lift, which sent a deluge of relief through Marcus. Hoping that they'd successfully averted any direct conflict with their pursuers, he watched McRae and Aria duck under the partially opened door after the prince. As he prepared to go in himself, though; when noticed that the others still hadn't rounded the corner. The extrication from the danger he'd just felt subsided, leaching from his body like liquid through a plug hole, and was replaced by a rising fear as he jogged back up the street. Unsure what he'd find, or what use he could possibly be if things did become violent, Marcus rounded the corner anyway and found the remainder of the cohort only metres away. To his horror though, they were caught in a skirmish with several members of the throng.

Tak-hing, slower than his companions, had been apprehended from behind and twisted into a cruel position with his neck trapped by the arm of his attacker. Cyril meanwhile, much to Marcus's surprise, was on the offensive, and was delivering lightning-fast blows to two En Röst members as they tried, and failed, to catch him.

Marcus watched in awe, as Cyril sent the larger of the men flying with a high kick to his chest and rendered the other unconscious with a strike of his elbow. It was incredible in a terrible way and the sight inflated Marcus's confidence, coercing him to join the fight, as more of the hostile mob leapt over the hedge. He bolted towards them, his only concern to free Tak-hing, but Viktor, apparently thinking the same thing, intervened before Marcus had moved more than a few paces.

The Russian left the unmoving body he had just been pummelling on the floor, the red blood stark on his fists under the streetlights; and launched a vicious punch into the face of the man restraining Tak-hing. The sickly, thudding crunch of bones breaking permeated the air, making Marcus flinch. Cyril caught his father as Viktor landed a follow up kick to the person he'd just downed. Then having staved off the pack of fanatics, they each put an arm around the elderly Oriental man and helped him to Marcus's position at the hotel's edge.

It was a small victory to have him back, but they were still vulnerable, with more En Röst closing in around them all the time. Further enraged by the sight of their fellow rioters on the floor, the gaggling horde looked more feral than ever. Drenched in rain and cast in harsh shadows, they hardly appeared human at all.

Marcus could see how outnumbered they were, and the feeling of being stalked like a prey animal grew in him. His nostrils flared, inhaling the reek of imminent disaster as he prepared for the worst, but fortune it seemed was not done with them yet.

As the tension broke, and the mob surged inwards, Hugo's limousine screeched up from the direction of the carpark and slammed into three thugs who were attempting to launch an assault from behind them. That unexpected move seemed to startle the raging En Röst, giving Marcus and his companions enough of an advantage to secure their escape.

Viktor handed Tak-hing to him then, and with Cyril's help they got the older man into the car through the door which Knox had just flung open. Marcus turned his eyes back to the street as he clambered in after them, just in time to watch Viktor remove an ancient looking pistol from the back of his belt and level it at the crowd; stopping them dead.

He started to back towards the car, snarling as he shifted the barrel from person to person and although he possessed the greater firepower, it would be of little use if they swamped him. Knowing they'd eventually realise that one gun couldn't harm them all, Viktor fired three, thunderous warning shots into the air before vaulting into the limousine. With the deafening crack of the shots still reverberating around the streets of Gamla Stan, and the mob now stunned into stasis, Hugo stamped on the accelerator and sped away from the scene.

With only four seats in the back, Marcus and Cyril found themselves on the floor of the limousine's passenger area, gripping onto the shifting stack of bags to avoid being tossed around as they raced through the streets. The frenzied En Röst may have had superior numbers, but their favourable edge was redundant if they couldn't catch their quarry. Infuriated by the turn of events, they launched a hail of missiles at the car as it shot by and all manner of litter, rocks, protest boards and even shoes struck the vehicle.

Besieged on all sides by crashing rain and hurled projectiles, Hugo directed them towards the northern bridge, which would give them the means to then head west and reach Bromma Airport. There were far more of the protesters, or extremists as they'd turned out to be, than any of them had originally anticipated, and it was horrifying to see just how swollen their ranks were. Somewhat fortuitously though, the presence of the En Röst dwindled as they moved away from the hotel, allowing them a fleeting moment of respite.

'Have we lost them?' Cyril asked, noticing a reduction in the amount of objects hitting the limousine.

'I think so,' McRae said with conviction, as he swivelled his head to peer out of the rear window. 'There's no way they can catch us on foot now.'

'They can if they're in front of us!' Hugo shouted from the driver's seat, making all of them crane their necks to look ahead.

Stupefied by the prince's statement and not wanting to believe it, they all stared ahead with wide eyes. As the bridge came into full view though, there was no denying the credibility of his words and the prince brought the car to a stop with a rough, tyre squealing mash of the brakes.

'There's no way they've beaten us here, it must be a separate mob.' Knox growled.

'Knox is right, that blockade would've taken ages to set up, there's got to be different groups,' added Aria, sounding tense.

'Look, over there!' Marcus shouted, pointing vigorously out of the left window. 'They're on the other bridges too!'

'Fuck this! What good will some wooden boards do? Hugo, run them down,' Viktor barked.

'No! I will not kill them,' he admonished.

'Would they show you the same mercy?' the Russian cried belligerently.

'Enough arguing. Whatever we do, we have to do it *now*. It's only a matter of time before the rabble behind us catches up and then we'll be sitting ducks,' McRae reasoned soberly.

'The South bridge,' Tak-hing wheezed, the injury to his windpipe altering his voice.

'It's as good a plan as any; with any luck the bastards won't have blocked that side of the island off,' the Scotsman said, buttressing his old friend's idea.

'The South bridge it is then,' the Prince agreed decisively, reversing the limousine. The horde of activists on the bridge showered them with a booming torrent of abuse as the car fled, but thankfully, none of them left their post.

The southern side of Gamla Stan was less than a mile away and with speed on their side, they reached their destination quickly. Their pursuers, now agitated by their failures and disorganised by the erratic route Hugo had taken through the Old Town, had fallen even further behind. For the minute they posed little threat, which was fortunate, because the jeopardy they were faced with in front of them was more than enough to deal with.

The Southern bridge, several lanes wider than its northern counterparts was, astonishingly, covered from one side to the other in an interlocking chain of people. There were no wooden barriers this time, however, and for some reason, that lack of any obvious defences made the human wall seem even more foreboding.

'What am I supposed to do?' Hugo asked through gritted teeth, the seams of his resolve at last starting to fray.

'They're only one row deep; rush them, Hugo, they'll move!' Viktor said forcefully.

'I think we're out of options, lad, do it!' McRae seconded.

'Shit, alright, alright,' replied the prince shakily, dropping the car down a gear and piling on the revs.

The car lurched forwards then, gaining momentum as the engine rumbled, and it looked as though they'd cover the short distance in only a few seconds. Marcus stuck his head up over the top of Aria's oversized pack, trying to gain a better view of the events unfolding before them by looking through the windscreen. Surely, he thought to himself, no matter how committed they were to their cause, they couldn't stand in the way of the car and just wait to be mowed down, could they?

As the limousine hurtled down the road, it appeared that Marcus was about to receive an answer to his question when a lithe, hooded figure dead ahead of them stepped forward from the line. Hugo ignored the rising of the person's hand, motioning for them to stop, and kept his foot resolutely buried in the accelerator. Still the sentinel of the En Röst did not falter, unwavering and unyielding they stood, like a sculpture formed of black granite and the night itself.

They were so close now that Marcus could discern some of the features beneath the hood, and he thought for an evanescent second, that he recognised that frigid stare. But as he squinted into the face of the stranger, and prepared himself for the impact of a soft body against the rigid bonnet, he didn't notice the unusually dark pool that stretched across the bridge ahead of the En Röst's human fortification. McRae on the other hand *had* seen it, as well as the lighter in the hand of the stranger.

'Hugo! Stop!' he cried, but the prince had noticed it too and was already spinning the steering wheel and pumping the brakes.

The car skidded sideways over the wet surface of the road, smashing its flank into the shadowy character with a bone shattering thump, before gaining traction again. In the same instant that they collided, a wall of broiling flames shot up into sky, forming an impenetrable barricade of fire from one side of the bridge to the other.

'Are they insane?' Aria screeched, partially blinded by the sudden blaze, and now thrust against the window. 'What the fuck is that?'

'Oil slick,' Viktor replied captiously. 'Hugo, get us out of here!'

'There's nowhere to go, they've got us trapped on the island,' the prince griped morosely, as he drove away from the flames and towards the road on the eastern side of Gamla Stan. The silence left in the wake of Hugo's remark stretched as they drove, when a quiet voice offered a solution.

'What about a boat?' Cyril suggested, sounding calm in spite of the chaos.

'What do you mean?' Knox questioned.

'We are on an island, why not get a boat? There are always plenty where the cruise ships dock,' he continued.

'You're not wrong, lad,' McRae mused thoughtfully.

'How are we going to get to Moscow on a boat though? Last time I checked it definitely wasn't on the coast,' Aria pointed out worriedly.

'We can dock in St Petersburg and worry about the rest when we're there. Hugo, pull us over by the railing. There, we'll take the stairs!' the old artist instructed, solving the problem posed by Aria, and gesturing to a gap in the iron bars which led down to sea level.

'How are we going to steal a boat, like, make it work I mean?' Marcus said, thinking out loud, as their cohort absconded the car and worked their way over to the hard, concrete stairs.

Tak-hing, despite currently not being at risk and appearing to have recovered his strength, was still guarded vigilantly by Knox, Viktor and Cyril, who encircled the elderly man like a miniature phalanx. Hugo, Marcus and Aria covered their backs, checking for any signs of the En Röst as McRae guided their path.

'Easy. We find one that's already occupied, they leave us the keys and we kick them off. Done,' said Viktor with brutal simplicity.

'We can't just run around forcing people off their boats, I won't have it, Viktor,' challenged Hugo vituperatively.

'Fine, ask them politely, have a nice fucking negotiation tea party, ah? Just don't expect me to come to your rescue when those *crazy Mu-daks* come for your blood,' Viktor riposted, spewing venom at the prince.

'Does your father have any boats here?' Knox asked Hugo, scanning the eclectic range of vessels moored up along the jetty.

'No, not down here, they're stored at the port in Nyn⊠shamn,' he answered.

'Then we go with Viktor's plan.'

'What? We can't.'

'What do you propose then, lad, swimming to Russia?' McRae retorted, his own patience wearing thin. 'This is the only option, and if you're that bothered, get your father to buy a new boat for whoever the unlucky sod is that we so happen to come across.'

'Fine,' the prince fumed, as his handsome face contorted into a grim mask. 'Take that one, it's got the biggest fuel tank,' he said reluctantly, pointing towards a relatively small, white vessel with sleek proportions and canopy over the cockpit.

'Oh look, the lights are on too, maybe they're expecting us?' Viktor crooned, smiling humourlessly as he brushed past the muscular Swede as if he was nothing more than blade of unruly grass. Hugo went after him, shaking his head with displeasure at what they were about to do, and was followed shortly after by the remainder of the group.

The sour-faced Russian made his way onto the boat, taking tender, creeping steps in an effort not to alert the inhabitants of his presence. Once aboard he reached into his belt and removed the pistol from its concealed holster, holding the weapon with a casual flippancy, as he progressed towards the entrance to the lower deck. The prince, seeing that as a premonition for more needless violence, prepared to board the boat himself and stop Viktor, but found himself held back by the abnormally powerful hand of McRae.

'Let him go. He won't use it, it's only to scare th–' Knox began, but was discourteously interrupted by two resounding gun shots.

'Shit!' Marcus said, flinching terribly at the explosive sound.

'I knew we couldn't trust him!' Hugo said, tearing himself from the Scotsman's grip, as he prepared to lunge onto the boat. However, before he had the chance, a semi-dressed man and woman shot up the ladder from the lower deck and ran out onto the jetty. Their faces portrayed an amalgamation of distress, anger, terror and confusion as they ran by, their bare feet pounding on the wood.

'Don't forget to bill the king!' Viktor bellowed after them, his sinister laughter echoing around the bowels of the boat.

'Damn it, Viktor!' Hugo yelled, storming the vessel.

Marcus and Aria turned away from the fleeing couple, unsure how to feel about the outrageous events they'd just borne witness too, and searched Knox's stone hewn face for some semblance of guidance. They were met, however, with little more than an ambiguous smile, the nuanced crags in his cheeks alluding to a vague moral dismissal on the artist's part, which left the pair of them none the wiser.

'Come on. I've got to stop Prince Charming and Ebenezer Scrooge from ripping each other apart, or we'll never get out of here,' the old artist said, earning a small chuckle from Tak-hing, as he, and his son, made their way onto the boat.

'He's still the same old Viktor, isn't he?' Tak-hing said reverently, despite his old friend's crude behaviour.

'The older he gets, the worse he gets!' Knox said with a gravelly titter, mitigating the constricting pressure surrounding them and making all of them let out a short laugh, as he loosened the mooring line in preparation to move off.

As he coiled up the rope, Aria and Marcus sprang over the narrow plank of wood to deposit their sodden bags beneath the shelter of the canopy. McRae was the last to make it onto the boat, and as he and Marcus dragged the plank aboard, the prince settled into a chair by the driving console and prepared to leave.

With the engine running, the potential bomb of Hugo and Viktor's disagreement momentarily diffused, and the adrenaline that had fuelled him now fading into the ether, Marcus felt ruined. He was sat near the back of the boat, slumped against one of the chrome uprights that supported the canopy, staring out at Stockholm as it retreated into the distance. The rain had finally stopped and the pillar of flames was now even more visible on the bridge, its wicked tongues spitting acrid black smoke high into the air, and somewhere the almost indeterminable, but equally unmistakable, wail of sirens could be heard heading towards the scene.

Marcus took in the sounds and smells of the ocean, the boat, the sweat and the fear that clung to his clothes, and watched the dancing reflections of the orange fire as they mingled with the first yellow rays of the dawn, wondering unremittingly, just how much more of the madness he'd have to endure.

Chapter XII

Although it hadn't shed a single globular tear since the downpour that morning, the sky above their small boat was still peppered with supple, mellifluous clouds. Devoid of any dark, unspent rain, however, their white forms hung in the air like the suspended thoughts of some magnanimous God, casting areas of the dazzling sapphire sea into deep shadows. It was glorious to behold, and Marcus couldn't help but envision the undulating waves as a painting in his mind's eye, like a dappled mantle of radiant azure and Prussian midnight.

He was still sat close to the back of boat, considering moving as a rather purposeless endeavour, as there was almost nowhere to move to. The vessel they'd taken may have had the most voluminous fuel tank, but it was hardly large enough to accommodate two people, which made fitting a party of seven onboard nothing short of a logistical nightmare.

Tak-hing was resting below deck in the cramped living space, where Cyril, despite suffering with his own illness, kept a lovingly attentive eye on his father. Knox and Viktor were crouched at the prow, leaning on the shiny, silver railing for support as the boat sloshed its way over the surf.

They reminded Marcus of two rapacious gulls, looking out across the vast sea in search of their next meal, and trading stories in their stridulous caws. Only a few feet behind the older men Prince Hugo was visible in the raised area of the cockpit, directing them towards Russia and, judging by the obstreperous racket coming from the engine, pushing the tiny boat to its limits.

Marcus watched the soft foam of the boat's wake as it traced a line into the distance, like a transient story of their journey away from the perils of the En Röst, and the now scarcely visible Swedish coastline. Losing himself in the waves had a palliative effect on his mind, removing him from the harsh language and close contiguity of his friends, but there was still something nagging at him. He leaned forward and glanced around the cockpit's step to where Aria had arranged some of their luggage into an improvised bed.

She was slouched over the bags in a similar way to how she had been in the ambulance, but strangely, she wasn't asleep this time. Instead, she stared out at the faraway landmass to their left, which Hugo had told them was Finland, with a glassy, unblinking gaze that gave her an almost lifeless portrayal. Aria had hardly uttered a word since they'd left, and it disturbed Marcus to see her so desolate, as though the primordial flame in her heart had been snuffed out; leaving her an empty, corporeal husk.

Listless as she was though, with her rain frizzed hair and tattered clothes, she still stirred a nebulous passion in Marcus that he couldn't quite comprehend. Her beauty was nothing new; he'd accepted it a long time ago as a plain fact of life, but there was more to that notion now, something more personal. Whatever those indistinct feelings were though, they were enlarging by the day, and as he watched her it fascinated him that something so simple as ocean spray on a tanned limb, could fill him with such an ingratiating longing for closeness.

Constrained by those strange emotions and filled with a desire to see if she was alright, Marcus chose to approach her. He was, however, under no illusions as to how fruitless an enquiry into her mental state would likely be; he'd been acquainted with her long enough to know that she guarded her feelings with stringent fervour. Fortune favoured the brave though, and even if she did toss him overboard for his well-intended transgression, he could at least derive some comfort from that.

Using the metal upright to leverage himself to his feet, Marcus took a deep breath and made his way to her Aria's crude lodgings to badger her.

'Found anything interesting out there?' he asked, plonking himself down next to her on the floor.

'What do you mean?' Aria replied, blinking her dry eyes, but not turning to face him.

'You've been staring out at the sea for ages, I just wondered what you were looking at?'

'I'm just thinking that's all.'

'I gathered that, dipstick, what about?' he joked, knowing that this was the pivotal question that would either see the book of her mind opened to him, or slammed shut in his face.

'Sweden.'

'What about it, Ari?'

'Last night.'

'It was horrible, wasn't it?

'Vile,' she said, leaving Marcus with only the tiniest crumb of the conversational loaf. He paused for moment, seeing if she would elaborate further; but she seemed fairly content to remain quiet.

'I feel like there's more going on in that head of yours, do you want to–'

'It was our fault, Marcus!' she interposed, suddenly blurting out her inner strife.

'What are you talking about?' questioned Marcus in bewilderment.

'Think about it. All the anger in those people, those protesters that Viktor almost beat to death, the fire on the bridge, the couple we stole the boat from and that poor, misguided person that's probably dying on the cobbles because we ran them over … they're all consequences of our actions. This whole mess, *our mess*, that the king is now going to have to clean up on *our* behalf, is *our* fault and it makes me feel sick!' she said, disclosing her internal tragedy with a pained expression and a crack in her voice.

Marcus was stunned by her perspective and as such, had no inkling as to how he might reply without plunging her further into the pit of self-deprecation she was digging. Fortunately for him though, she wasn't finished.

'I thought we'd come on this, I don't know, *mission*, to uncover some of the truth behind the virus and do some good with it. So far all we've done is cause more harm and if we'd never have gone to Stockholm at all, none of this would've happened,' Aria trailed off, her words becoming a tangled in a knot of anger.

'We didn't force those En Röst members to act like that,' Marcus said, hoping to direct her blame elsewhere.

'We didn't, you're right, but they're just fighting for what they think is right, which is exactly what we're doing. They're on the streets of their cities trying to protect their country; we left ours to do the same thing, so who's right in all of this?'

'Ari, you're burrowing your way to hell here, what's with all this moral postulating?' Marcus reproved lightly, trying to buy himself some time, when something Tak-hing had said to him provided him with an idea. 'We made our decisions, they made theirs; regardless of how just or unjust you think the motives behind those choices are, it's still not right for you to take responsibility for all of them.'

'How? Our actions directly influenced theirs, that makes it our fault, doesn't it?' she said, articulating the cyclical nature of the dilemma through her confounded questions.

'Listen to me,' Marcus said in a tone that made her, at last, turn her eyes away from the waves. 'You are one absolutely minute, person-shaped fragment of a seven-billion-piece puzzle, and you have no control over any of those other pieces. The only one you can move is yourself.'

'And what's that supposed to mean?'

'It means that the only thing you are responsible for, and the only thing you can control, is yourself. So why are you worrying so much and blaming the deeds of others, which you can't control, on yourself?'

'Piss off with your clever sayings. That just sounds like excuses to me; you have such a detached way of looking at things sometimes,' she argued, unwilling to allow Marcus's aphorising to free her from her moral quandary.

'No, it's not. It's a way of keeping yourself sane when even your best intentions, somehow, end up hurting others,' he huffed in response, becoming irritated by her aversion to rationality.

'Oh really?'

'Those people were trying kill us last night, Aria, for doing nothing more than having a meeting. When was the last time we tried to kill anyone, hmm?'

She remained silent.

'Precisely, never. Nor has that ever been our intention, so just take a second next time you start sympathising with a bunch of crazed rioters, will you? They wanted blood, we wanted answers, there's a difference,' Marcus said, annoyed at just how convoluted their conversation had become, and how impenetrable the castle walls around Aria's opinions seemed to be.

'I just don't think we're innocent in all this, that's all.'

'I can understand that. I know this situation is getting messier by the day, *but* there's no reason to sit here and beat yourself up over it. We're the good guys,' he consoled, shifting tack.

'Are you so sure about that?' Aria said, thwarting his conciliatory intent with the ramparts of her obstinacy.

This time, it was Marcus's turn to be silent.

'Whatever, Marcus.'

'I'm only trying to offer you a different way of looking at the same picture.'

'Just leave me alone.'

'Fine, when you're ready to see reason, let me know,' he retorted, revoking his empathy in a childish bid to inflict upon her, the same irritation that she had caused him.

'Oh, fuck off, Merda,' Aria scolded indignantly, turning her back to him.

Marcus felt no jubilation at the success of his jibe as he rose brusquely and marched the few, short steps, back to the other side of the boat. Rather, he discovered that he was filled with a searing sense of regret at not being able to help his friend and, arguably even more damnable, he'd fallen victim to the very same desire to control external factors that he'd been advising Aria not to indulge in.

Wrestling with his own double standardising and preparing to instigate a severe, internal discourse around the topic of hypocrisy in relation to humanity at large, Marcus wilted back onto the deck. He glowered at the ocean as he set about his brooding ruminations, turning the bejewelled depths into a stagnant, black murk to reflect his foetid mood.

There was something amiss in the sea, however, something prominent enough to stop him from fully realising his embitterment, and that was the vessel's foaming wake. He knew from overhearing a somewhat clipped conversation between Viktor and Hugo, that St Petersburg was, more or less, a dead straight line across that stretch of the Baltic; and yet their route had veered noticeably to their starboard side.

'Hugo … why are we changing course?' came Knox's uncannily timed question to the prince.

'We have a problem,' he said seriously.

'And what might that be?' Viktor added coarsely.

'We don't have enough fuel to make it to St Petersburg,' the prince said, the certainty in his tone leaving no room for doubt.

'I thought you said this boat had the biggest fuel tank – isn't that why we picked it over the others?' McRae enquired, sounding concerned, as he and Viktor made their way to the cockpit.

'It does have the largest tank, just let me explain. The journey from Stockholm to St Petersburg is roughly four hundred and twenty-nine miles; this boat has an eighty gallon fuel tank, and should average around six miles per gallon, even with me pushing the engine. Are you with me so far?'

'Go on, Pythagoras, let's hear your equation,' mocked Viktor.

'That means that although it would take us over ten hours on a full tank of fuel, we could easily do four hundred and eighty miles.'

'So, what's the issue then?' asked Knox.

'The tank wasn't full,' said the Prince, showing a hint of embarrassment, as Viktor let out a patronising chuckle.

'So, what's your back up plan?' the old Russian chided through his rattling laugh.

'Aim for the nearest landmass which, judging by how far we've come, should be Estonia,' Hugo answered, regaining his equanimity. 'In fact, I think that might even be Tallinn's Old City Harbour,' he said, squinting his eyes and pointing to a vague, greyish blotch that bisected the cliffs on the horizon.

'What? How are we going to get through Estonia – surely they'll turn us away at the port?' Marcus cut in anxiously, as his brain exaggerated the information and spun it into the worst narrative he could fathom.

He tuned out as Hugo and Knox spoke, instead imagining a disastrous confrontation with the Estonian border control where they were forced to return to the open water, and drift around hopelessly until they died of thirst, or starvation. It was Viktor who jerked him from his grim visualisation in the end, with an unusually relaxed smile that didn't suit his baneful face.

'We'll get through Tallinn just fine,' he said with conviction.

'What makes you so sure?' McRae asked with an air of suspicion.

'Estonia is,' he paused until he landed on the right phrase. 'Under Russian *control* for the time being. We won't have any problems passing through.'

'Since when?'

'Since we needed somewhere to transport our refugees to,' Viktor smirked darkly.

'I've heard nothing of this,' Hugo stated in disbelief.

'Haven't we already established that your father doesn't tell you *everything*?'

'Is it really that bad in Russia?' Marcus interjected in horror, curtailing another inevitable argument between the prince and his older rival.

'You will see when we get there,' Viktor declared, locking his eyes onto the younger man with a sniper's gaze.

Marcus looked back, spellbound by the deleterious quality of the Russian's crushing voice, and appraised him properly for the first time.

Viktor Stefanovich's face was the complete antithesis of benevolence. It was hard in the same way that McRae's was, but even Knox's had a few faint lines engrained into its cliffs from decades of occasional smiling. Viktor's, however, did not; his aspect was as punishing as a Siberian Winter, and twice as bitter.

His flat nose was grotesque, the curvilinear mouth beneath it was locked into a downward spike that was reminiscent of a shark's predatory maw, giving him a carnivorous appearance. That was further accentuated by a swooping scar which ran around his left eye, and wormed its way over his forehead in an angry, serriform line. Whatever atrocity had caused it, Marcus could scarcely imagine, but the ghost of that wound framed his murky grey eyes perfectly; eyes which spoke of torment and loss, eyes which had lived through too much anguish to voice.

As he turned his attention back to Hugo, Marcus shuddered, and suddenly understood why Knox was so keen to maintain his friendship with the Russian. Falling out of Viktor's favour, it seemed, could easily prove fatal and Marcus doubted that there were worse ways to die, than at the hands of that weathered butcher.

'How long to Tallinn then?' Aria asked, speaking for the first time since her tetchy conversation with Marcus.

'Maybe …' Hugo drawled, considering his answer as he scrutinised the distant bluffs. 'Two hours, I'd say.'

'I'll go let Tak-hing and Cyril know what's going on,' Knox said, leaving the cockpit and heading for the ladder to the lower deck. 'Marcus, Aria, make sure everything's packed and ready to go for when we dock in Estonia. The quicker we get to Russia the better.'

'Agreed,' concluded Viktor with a scowl, as he too left, and set about cleaning his antiquated pistol with a cloth from his trouser pocket.

Aria returned to her mound of bags and began assembling them into some sort of order; meanwhile Marcus extracted the camera from his bag, and took a few photographs of their crossing of the Baltic. After reviewing the images and snagging a couple of discreet shots of his fellow crew members, Marcus retired the camera and perched, once again, on the back of the boat. There was nothing else to do for the moment except watch the world go by.

Thankfully though, Hugo's estimations were correct, his impressive nautical abilities again proving themselves useful, and their overcrowded vessel neared the port in just over two hours. The journey had been hideously boring, however, and with nothing but the infinite rolling of the sea to occupy him, Marcus had become drowsy and fretful. It wasn't until the beautifully wooded island of Naissaar came into view, indicating that they had nearly reached Tallinn, that he found himself with the energy to move.

With a yawn and a stretch, he clambered to his feet, shifting his uncomfortable limbs as he turned to his left, and watched the spindly lighthouse at the northern tip of the isle emerge from the chartreuse treeline. It was the only sign of human life on the island, all else was concealed behind the lush verdure of the vegetation that lined its thin beaches; like a protective crust of emerald spruce. It was a joy to see something disrupt the endless blue of the ocean, and as they continued past Naissaar the clouds parted, showering the terracotta roofs of Tallinn's now visible Old Town, in an effulgent, magical light.

The harbour itself, once a bustling haven of both tourist laden cruise ships and overburdened cargo freighters, was eerily quiet in the wake of recent events. As the mammoth stone arm of the port's northern quay drew them in towards Estonia's welcoming bosom, only a small array of local fishing boats and military craft appeared to be docked in the port; which meant their anomalous vessel would stand out like a bloodstain on a white shirt.

Even with the heartening countenance of Tallinn's radiant appearance, and Viktor's substantiating comments that the country would be of a friendly disposition, they were still exposing themselves by entering the city so blatantly. Marcus, and the rest of his cohort for that matter, had no choice but to trust in the Russian militant and if the situation did go awry, hopefully his penchant for intimidation and brutality would defend them.

Hugo steered their now labouring boat straight through the centre of the harbour, to a tighter passage, which emerged into a square recess of very still water. That enclave was the most inland they could get without going ashore, and it came as no surprise that it was under heavy surveillance from both Russian and Estonian forces.

As Knox and Marcus abandoned the boat and jumped onto the slender jetty to secure the mooring line, a distorted voice boomed its way through a megaphone in a foreign language.

Marcus looked at McRae apprehensively, but the Scotsman went about his business as if he hadn't heard it.

'Let Viktor handle this one, lad, it'll be fine,' he told Marcus with an unhurried nonchalance, as he proceeded to tie a knot around the mooring post.

Unconvinced by the old artist's words, Marcus glanced around the surrounding area in search of the voice's origin, hoping to acquire a measure of its hostility. However, it wasn't until the misshapen sound rang out across the dock a second time, that Marcus was able to identify its location.

Just over the road from their boat, no more than thirty metres away, was a sizable white tent in the shadow of a towering crane. It wore a double eagled insignia on its flank, coloured in a garish yellow and red theme, and there was a Russian flag at its apex that billowed as the light sea breeze tousled its crisp edges.

From that tarpaulin-clad marquee, three people emerged, all donning the same swamp green camouflaged uniform, and armed to the teeth with a staggering array of guns, knives, and explosives. They moved towards the water in an inverted arrow-like formation, the two people at the front, who Marcus could now see were women, pressed forward in a rhythmic march with their rifles directed towards the boat. The man slightly behind them in the centre of their small squadron, who was also the one in possession of the megaphone, held a smaller firearm at his side, and continued to speak as they advanced.

There was no real threat in his tone, only a vital dominance, and it didn't require a great amount of perspicacity to figure out that he was delivering instructions to them. Unsure how to react, Marcus followed Knox's lead and finished fastening his strand of rope to the jetty before standing upright and remaining still; his body tense as they waited for Viktor to explain their situation to the local combatants.

The three, presumably Russian, army personnel circled around the perimeter of the bay, until they reached the point where the small pier that Marcus and Knox were stood on exited onto the road. With a row of emotionless gun barrels ahead, and nothing but the cold embrace of the Baltic Sea behind them, their chances of escaping if the situation became inimical dwindled down to almost nothing. Gratefully though, it seemed that Viktor had spoken the truth, for when he strode off the boat and addressed his countrymen; they lowered their guns to salute him.

'What the hell?' Marcus muttered with incredulity.

'I told you he'd handle it. Apparently being a former *Colonel General* carriers some weight,' McRae snorted, in a show of simultaneous admiration and displeasure.

Viktor made his way to the triage on the road without any further issues, and began to converse with them in a formal, yet animated manner. After several minutes of aggressive gesticulation and rapid-fire bouts of Russian speech, Viktor waved to the group, signalling that it was safe for them to leave the boat.

Aria walked past Marcus and dropped his bag at his feet, without so much as a second glance, as she ascended the inclining jetty. Hugo and Knox followed her, and all appeared well, but when Tak-hing and Cyril left the boat and entered the eyeline of soldiers at Viktor's side, their circumstances vitiated instantly.

The male officer exploded into a babble of outrage, as he and his female guards forced Viktor behind them in a protective stance, and pointed their weapons at the two Eastern men in a blur of viscous metal.

Everyone became a statue then, unblinking and inert; they stared hopelessly up at the Russians trying to pacify them with their eyes, as a host of unintelligible expletives ripped the air apart. Viktor was clearly trying to regain control of the situation before it escalated, but his words rebounded off the soldiers' armour plating with little success.

The fuse attached to the old Colonel General's temper ignited then with an almost audible fizz, his wick continuing to burn down, as the pressure between the two groups became devastating. Realising that words had failed him Viktor set ablaze, and the landmine of bellicosity in his chest exploded, leaving him with only one possible mode of communication.

Force.

With a wicked glint in his eye, he delivered a spiteful kick to the back of the knee of the female solider on his left, making her shriek in pain as she fell to the floor. Then, before her squad mates could even turn to face her, Viktor grabbed each of their ankles, bent low, and yanked them backwards with all his strength; leaving them face down on the concrete.

Marcus couldn't understand what he was saying, but there was so much menace on Viktor's face, that it didn't take much to determine his sentiments. It was then, as he plucked his gaze away from the events unfolding before him, that Marcus realised he was scared of Viktor; and his body trembled faintly at the thought of what the madman might be capable of.

'Forgive my *friends*, they're not used to having visitors and it seems their hospitality is a little rusty,' Viktor scoffed, belittling the soldiers as they rose to their feet and brushed themselves off. 'Trust me when I tell you that they are very sorry. In fact, by way of an apology, they've kindly offered to escort us to the checkpoint around the corner where, I'm told, there may even be a transport for us,' he finished with a disdainful grin.

With that, the soldiers gave a curt nod to the group, their fear of Viktor's wrath unable to keep the hateful look from their eyes, before they shouldered their weapons and moved off. A communal sigh of relief escaped from them all then, as their unlikely collective regrouped on the road.

'Please excuse them, Tak-hing, they mistook you and your son for the enemy. We are on the brink of a war after all,' said Viktor, with a genuine look of regret.

'I do look like the enemy, you should reward them for their skills of observation,' Tak-hing replied with a wry smile.

'Hah, I should have them lashed for disobeying my orders, you mean,' he retorted, putting on that predatory smirk that he wore so well. 'Anyway, I think it's best if we keep you both, perhaps even all of you, disguised where possible between here and Moscow, or I'll be shooting my own soldiers by the end of the day. We'll find something for you to wear at the outpost.'

'Show us the way, my friend,' said Tak-hing, motioning for Viktor to lead them in the direction of the soldiers, which he did so with a gracious, if small, bow.

It was bizarre to see Viktor act so respectfully towards another human being. Given what he'd seen of the man so far, Marcus was dubious as to his capacity for anything more than antagonism and intolerance, and yet, there he was, treating the Chinese Defence Minister as though he were an object of veneration. That small act, however, did little to nullify his adverse perceptions of the Russian General, and it would take more than a bow and a regretful tone, to unravel the coil of fear he'd shackled around Marcus's mind.

Pondering the matter, and the issue of resolving his misfortunate talk with Aria, Marcus, accompanied the rest of his cohort as they left the dock behind, and moved further into the Estonian Capital.

They followed the soldiers through the immense, industrial jungle of the shipping yard, kicking up dust from the gritty floor as they meandered between the soaring cranes, rusted storage containers and dormant mechanisms, to a small alley that intersected a collection of tourist amenities.

The shops and restaurants themselves were closed, but Tallinn wasn't entirely devoid of life, and there were a few signs of human habitation in the neighbouring buildings. As if to punctuate the point that the city was indeed still alive, a tram, in dire need of some maintenance if its brakes were indicative of its health, screeched to a stop somewhere beyond their position as they came through the passage.

Once out of the alley they emerged into flat, expansive space just over the road from the hill upon which the Old Town perched. It must once have been a carpark, Marcus thought, likely catering for the massive amount of tourists which would typically populate the area, but now it had been transformed into a fortified military outpost.

It consisted of a multitude of shelters, similar to the one that formed the guard post by the dock, which were arranged in a grid-like formation around a much larger tent that occupied the centre of the camp. Marcus's eyes roved around, taking in the rugged details of military life with an intrigued wariness as they trailed their unwilling guides and progressed towards the dominating, if temporary, structure at the camp's heart.

To their right was an adjacent area cordoned off by a wall of dusty sandbags and guarded by sentries, where a selection of military vehicles were being stored. They ranged from small, two-man ATVs with preposterously large machine guns mounted to their front decks, all the way up to armoured troop transport vehicles, complete with excessively huge tank tracks and room to accommodate twenty soldiers or more. Marcus wondered redundantly what it would be like to ride in such a vehicle, and a juvenile part of him hoped that he'd be granted the opportunity to find out on their journey to St Petersburg.

Returning his concentration to their current task, he discovered they were now only a few steps away from their destination, but with the late summer sun still beating down from above, the mass of white tents that enclosed them had become almost blinding. He had to squint against the unrelenting brightness as he followed Knox's kinked frame towards the open flap of the command post, and into the soothing shade of its innards.

The interior of the tent was surprisingly cavernous, but its alluring promise of cool shelter was a deceptive one. The atmosphere within those glowing walls was not only hotter and denser, but far more pungent too, carrying a nostril-clogging aroma of odorous sweat and synthetic materials which had ripened with the heat, making it insufferable.

Marcus's squint became a wince as the scent permeated his defenceless nose, triggering a memory from his youth, where his older brother had once told him that it only took thirteen seconds for one's nose to adjust to a smell. The likelihood of that statement being true was extremely improbable, and yet it was one of those obscure assertions from someone he admired as a child, which had imprinted itself on his mind so vividly, that even the inexhaustible protraction of time couldn't wash it away.

Thus, he started counting and, doing his best to ignore the melancholy stab of nostalgia that penetrated him at the thought of his brother, Marcus followed the rest of the group as they manoeuvred through the tent.

They wound their way around a jumble of desks, wires, storage containers and other forms of military flotsam that were strewn around the place, to eventually stop by a broad desk covered in papers and topographical maps. That seemed to be the epicentre of the Russian operations in Tallinn's harbour, and as their three unenthusiastic guides began to converse with what was presumed to be the officer in charge, Marcus became aware of just how many pairs of eyes were scrutinising them.

If the circumstances were of less consequence, the staring may have been merely uncomfortable, but as it stood, at a time when being out of one's home was unacceptable and being out of one's country was punishable by law, the astringency of those glares felt vindictive. Never before had Marcus felt so out of place. Their very presence there felt irreverent beneath the glower of those judgemental eyes, and he wondered if Viktor's rank would be enough to keep them from harm, or if their journey was about to come to an abrupt and grisly end.

It wasn't a notion that he really wanted to consider; Marcus just knew that the sooner they shed their foreign skins and began to blend in with the locals, the better.

Chapter XIII

Around the age of eight or nine, Marcus had been obsessed with the prospect of joining the army. He and his friends had waged a thousand imaginary battles, slaughtered countless hordes of illusory enemies in the blithe, innocuous way that only children can, and shrugged off life threatening, fictional wounds with casual heroism.

Those were days that he always looked back on with fondness and, despite his creative talents and infatuation with painting, a career in the military had always beguiled him. Indeed, if he hadn't have had so much success in monetising his art, Marcus's life would've likely taken him down a very different road and yet, quite remarkably, he'd still found his way to a war.

Maybe it was destiny, or perhaps it was nothing more than sheer coincidence? Regardless of the forces that had marshalled to place him in that exact spot, at that precise moment, the eight year old boy inside him was still ecstatic to be wearing a soldier's uniform.

The outfit, which he and the rest of the group were now wearing, was typical of those donned by the 51st Logistics Brigade of the 6th Army, whose camp they had been led to and subsequently whose supply tent they were currently stood in. They'd each been sized up by a young private and given a bundle of clothes to put on, which they did so individually, behind a great sheet of canvas that hung from a rail in the far corner of the room.

Pleasantly, the trousers and jacket were much more flexible than they appeared and the folds of their green, patina cotton featured enough pockets to lose the entirety of one's worldly possessions in. The black standard issue boots again, were far more comfortable than they had any right to be for such a high laced, breeze block of a shoe; and the only real issue brought about by wearing the military outfits was the heat.

As stifling as the uniforms were, however, it was a meagre price to pay for the ability to be almost invisible. Tak-hing and Cyril had also been given a high snood made from a lightweight, breathable material that along with their helmets, did a superb job of disguising their Eastern features. Everyone else excluding Viktor, who unlike them, actually benefited from being noticed, also wore a camouflaged helmet to complete the image.

Now substantially less conspicuous, and far more suitably equipped for the next leg of their journey, they made their way out of the supply area, back through the astonishingly bright rows of tents, and headed in the direction of the vehicles that Marcus had seen earlier.

Along the way they ducked into a longer, thinner tent which looked to be a mess hall of some description. There were a series of long veneer coated tables running through its centre, with rows of simple plastic chairs tucked away beneath them and, butted up against one wall, a stack of boxes labelled "ratsion". Those carboard punnets seemed to be the reason for their visit, and as the soldier tasked with leading them through the camp unlidded the top-most one, Marcus's inklings regarding their contents were confirmed.

"Ratsion", it appeared, translated to "ration", and as the soldier offered a number of silver packages to Viktor, who in turn divvied them out between the group, Marcus was overpowered by hunger. Supressed by more demanding issues, such as fleeing a horde of demented Swedish Nationalists, his typically ravenous appetite had been relegated to a lower league of importance. Now though, reawakened by Viktor slapping the parcel into his eager hands, Marcus had to resist the temptation to tear into it straightaway, and fought to place it in his bag for later as his companions had.

With nothing else to do now but get themselves into a transport, they zipped up their bags, and walked the short distance from their current location over to the carpark. After a lengthy conversation between Viktor and the site's commanding officers, the rough shape of a plan had materialised which would hopefully see them over the Russian border that very night.

Rather conveniently, the 51st were actually based in St Petersburg, and had been tasked with overseeing the evacuation of Russian refugees into the Estonian countryside. That meant that transports frequently moved provisions, materials and even people across the country; all they had to do was join the next convoy.

It was a cause of consternation for Marcus, that they were deliberately heading towards something so formidable, that it was deemed worthy of evacuating the native civilians over. Given his and Aria's comparatively trivial experiences of the virus, as life altering as they'd been, it was difficult to comprehend a situation so volatile, that the rulers of the country were willing to displace entire cities' worth of their population in order to prevent them from dying. It was a preposterous concept, and Marcus didn't know if he possessed the stomach for what they'd find in Russia. He just prayed Viktor would be true to his word and find them a way home.

However, amidst the fear of the virus that was now stalking the periphery of his mind like some reprehensible phantom, there was also another force at work inside his head; a form of excitement. Its origins were founded, almost contradictorily so, in the very same idea that was causing his trepidation. Russia had always been a source of fascination for Marcus, and to be visiting that land of mystery and madness, irrespective of the circumstances, was still a tremendous cause for delight.

That ethically questionable sense of joy kept the spectral apparition of his dread at bay for a time, shining a hallowed light upon it, and driving it back into the shadows. Happily for Marcus though, his attention was returned to the material world, and the duel between those two conflicting feelings was cut short, when their cohort stopped walking, and was presented with the vehicle they'd be travelling to St Petersburg in.

'Here we are then,' said Viktor, placing a hand on the high bonnet as though he were stroking a horse's muzzle.

'Bloody hell, it looks a cab that someone's overfed,' Aria stated in reply, mildly amused to see that the company that made quaint, little vans for cab drivers and delivery men in the UK, were also responsible for that monstrosity.

It stood high off the ground on a set of chunky, black tyres, which complemented the equally dark armour plating encasing the lower half of the transport's wings and bumper. The rest of the body was coated in a matte, khaki green paint which made it appear extremely flat and somehow aggressive. A look that was completed by the addition of a huge set of bull-bars that snaked around the face of the beast like an iron muzzle.

'Definitely looks like it'll eat your children,' Marcus agreed, impressed by its stature, and only faintly disappointed that it wasn't one of the heavy, tank tracked transports he'd fantasised over earlier that day. 'I think I'd quite like a steroid taxi of my own,' he joked, with a raise of his eyebrows and a crooked smile, hoping his paltry comment would break the ice between himself and Aria. A faint giggle escaped her full lips as they studied the van, which was just enough to appease him.

'Might I ask who will be driving?' Cyril enquired with a pensive look. 'I would much prefer it if it were someone other than Mr McRae.'

'What's that supposed to mean?' the old artist hit back, feigning abashment.

'He does have a point, Knox,' Aria added.

'I hate to jump on the bandwagon here, but I'm with these two.' Marcus shrugged.

'*You ungrateful little nyaffs,*' McRae reproached. 'Next time, you can walk yourselves to Scotland.'

'It sounds as though you're not the chauffer of choice, Knox,' Tak-hing said with a smile, enjoying the ridicule of his old friend.

'Not a chance, I have to drive,' Knox insisted, addressing the group with a rasping arrogance. 'Viktor can't be seen by the soldiers to be driving a lowly transport, Hugo needs a rest after last night, Tak-hing's almost blind and I wouldn't trust any of you to drive a push bike, let alone a military people carrier.'

That silenced all of them for a moment, other than Tak-hing who was chuckling softly, but Marcus could already see Aria reloading, readying herself to launch an insult in return.

He waited for the fireworks to go off, enjoying the ordinariness of the conversation and the lighter atmosphere it was ushering in; however, Viktor beat her to the punch.

'It's nice to see that you're finally accepting your place beneath me, Knox!' he jibed savagely. 'And you're right, driving a simple truck like this *is* beneath me but for *you*, I'm sure it will be an honour. Now come on, let's move.' He finished with a scything laugh, as he opened the door of the front cab and hopped into the passenger seat.

'Wonderful,' McRae mumbled, walking around the hulking machine to enter the other door; which he then slammed shut.

'Great, now Viktor's wound him up he's going to drive like even more of a maniac,' Aria huffed with a hyperbolic roll of her eyes.

'Don't worry, he's got to drive as part of the convoy so there's no way he's going to be able to race off. We'll be fine,' said Hugo reassuringly.

'What a relief, I am not sure I would survive a sea crossing *and* a car journey with Mr McRae in the same day,' Cyril replied with a weary smile.

'Are you going to stand there yapping all day, or do you think you'd be able to kick your brains into gear and figure out how a door handle works?' Knox yowled, sticking his head out of the window of the cabin.

That sent the three young companions scrambling towards the cargo bay to load their bags. Hugo, however, older and less daunted by the Scotsman, and Tak-hing, who seemed to find McRae's idiomatic rage thoroughly entertaining, calmly opened the door and climbed in.

The seating arrangement featured two rows of double benches, the first of which Hugo commandeered whilst Takhing claimed the second, sliding gracefully towards the window to allow room for his son. Cyril trod lightly over the bare metal floor, scarcely making a sound as he settled down beside his father; meanwhile, Marcus and Aria rushed past noisily, to the furthest row of seats which stretched across the entire vehicle in a three-seater pew.

Aria's still matted hair wafted out behind her as she flung herself into the soft embrace of the fabric, taking up the majority of the space for herself, and leaving Marcus with little more than a sliver on which to sit. He wormed his way into the corner beside her with a complicit sigh and glanced out of the lightly tinted window to see a technician of some kind, giving the truck a last minute check.

The stout man's somewhat perfunctory inspection involved a senseless poking of various panels, a fleeting examination of the tyres and an almost convincing, but still clearly uninterested, analysis of the engine fluids. Judging by the pervasive artificial smell of the van's interior, it was likely a very new vehicle that didn't need an inspection at all. Still, the man had unwittingly offended Marcus with his lack of automotive respect and he found himself staring after him as Knox drove them out of the carpark, and he waddled back into the encampment.

Their convoy was only a small one, and as McRae pulled out onto the wide road, the drivers arranged their automobiles into a tightly packed column. There were two more small transports similar to their own ahead of them, a much bigger wagon behind which was full of medical supplies that had recently been sent from Finland, and an armoured assault jeep which piloted the operation.

Marcus felt somnolent now he'd sat down. The events of their final night in Sweden, paired with a baffling morning in a country he hardly knew a thing about, trying to interpret a language he didn't understand, had completely sapped his energy. He slumped in the chair and assessed through his hazy vison a series of shallow grazes on his right hand that had, up until that point, gone unnoticed; when Aria tapped him on the shoulder.

'Marcus, look!' she said, pointing past his head and through the window.

'What is it?' he asked in a sleep-clouded voice, jerking himself awake.

'Tallinn, it's gorgeous,' Aria responded, prompting him to turn his head and follow her gaze to a view which was nothing short of rapturous. The historical region of Tallinn spilled down the hill to their right in a voracious avalanche of colour, like a glistening tide of scrumptious, melted sorbet. Rivulets of blue, yellow, red, orange and white, tumbled across the landscape in an almost indivisible swathe of jubilant chromaticity, merging with the green trees as they fell. The sight of it ensorcelled Marcus, and when his astute, painter's eye began to pick out details in the bright streams, the beauty of the scene multiplied.

Several fairy tale turrets sprang up from the ground, their cylindrical stone forms topped with cones of burnished orange tiles, which were set ablaze by the sun. An abundance of other medieval style buildings also appeared between them, like colossal marble cakes, full of character, elation and the untold stories of Estonia's lost generations. Most extraordinary of all though, were the churches and cathedrals.

Those monuments to the human need to for a higher power, stretched their religious spires high into the sky, and looked down over the land with reverent loftiness. Hewn from a splendid white stone and topped with a breath-taking array of ornate black domes, decorative spikes and shining gold crosses, it was hard to believe they'd been crafted by human hands at all.

Gawping at the splendour of the scene, Marcus tried to forget about the disastrous state of their planet and just revel in the unblemished wonder of the then and now. How could a race responsible for creating things that exquisite, be riddled with such a rotten need to destroy one another?

It was of course an impossible question to answer and for the meantime, one best left alone, so in order not to spoil the moment he turned back to Aria as the view slipped out of sight.

'Yesterday I didn't even know this place existed, now I feel like I don't want to leave,' she said with a vaguely sad smile, as he twisted in his seat to face her.

'I know, what a hidden gem. I would've loved to take a walk around those churches, I can't imagine how incredible they must be inside,' he answered wistfully.

'Maybe one day we can come back and explore them properly?'

'Surely you wouldn't actually agree to go anywhere with me again?'

'I mean, this hasn't been the *best* holiday I've ever had,' Aria joked, but Marcus knew there was an undercurrent of honesty in her statement, and with it, came that inescapable feeling of being drawn towards his doom again.

It seemed that no matter where his thoughts lingered lately, that ubiquitous pull of the present always found him, and yanked at his senses, dragging him away from any shred of happiness he found with an iron fist; and a chain around his neck. There was only one voice capable of hauling him back, and fortunately for Marcus, it was speaking now.

'I'm sorry about earlier,' said Aria in a shy, quiet tone.

'Pardon?'

'Don't make me repeat it, Marcus,' she huffed.

'What? I genuinely didn't hear what you said?'

'I *said*, I'm sorry about earlier.'

'Oh! Don't worry about it, Ari,' he tutted, assuming nonchalance, whilst secretly appreciating her apology.

'I know you were trying to help but this morning it all just felt so raw. I just couldn't get my head around it, I mean, I still can't really but it's happened now so I guess I've just got to accept it.'

'I get it, of course I do, I just didn't want you to sit there brewing all day and blaming yourself for decisions that weren't yours. As I'm sure you experienced, that's a one way ticket to a mental breakdown; luckily for you though we stopped in Tallinn before you got there,' he said lightly, pinching her arm softly and smiling.

'Get lost, loser.' Aria giggled, retracting her arm from his fingers. 'Some days I think I'd rather have a mental breakdown than admit you're right.'

'Wow, someone's got their claws out,' Marcus retorted, adding a poor imitation of a cat meowing for good measure. 'I'd probably take the breakdown too if I'm honest. Can you imagine how much of an arse I'd be if people started *admitting* I was right rather than just *thinking* it?'

'I pray we never have to find out,' she replied with an expression of spurious harshness, which quickly morphed into a bout of laughter when Marcus grinned at her.

As their merriment petered out, both of them returned their attention to the view outside, quickly becoming absorbed in the urban maze of the Lasnamäe region of Tallinn. It was a far cry from the decadent, architectural sundae of the city's Old Town and in comparison to that pinnacle of charm, the new area seemed drab.

The highway their convoy was on divided the north and south sides of the district like a wide artery separating two vast muscles. There was a lattice work of bridges at regular intervals, that crossed over the top of the multi-laned road, allowing traffic to pass from one section to the other without disrupting the flow of cars beneath.

Beyond the road, the landscape was dotted with high, flat buildings in various shades of carmine, off white and a whole host of noncommittal beige tones that were barely worth mentioning. Scattered amongst the generic blocks of concrete and steel, were patches of green vegetation, which did a wonderful job of breaking up the monotonous wall of buildings. The occasional glass fronted office block also popped into their lines of light briefly on the south side of the highway, and it became apparent then, that Lasnamäe was probably Tallinn's industrial region.

Marcus considered the lives of the hundreds of thousands of people who lived and worked in that quaint, little city then, and wondered just how much their lives had changed. He imagined they felt a lot like he and his companions did. Some were likely to be angry, others confused, and a select few would've probably just have accepted it; resigning themselves to ride out the storm to its unknowable end.

It was possible that a minority would be grieving, maybe they'd lost people to the virus, perhaps a portion of them had had to watch businesses they'd spent their entire lives nurturing, crumble around them due to forced closures. There would be pockets of suspicion, a handful of misguided blame and an entire spectrum of other emotions, and thoughts, that occupied the space between the extremes of hope and despair.

Marcus felt the weight of all those diminishing souls press down on him then, his painful contemplations sequestering him from the small scrap of optimism he still possessed. Passing out of the city, however, lessened that feeling of compression, and he took a deep breath to relax himself as he watched the verdant Estonian hills roll into view.

Knox's driving had been rejoicefully considerate thus far, no doubt a result of the vans ahead keeping him in check, and in comparison to his previous escapades, the drive through that bucolic expanse of Northern Europe had been drastically more tolerable. There was still one irksome factor though, and that was the noise.

Every time the truck switched lanes or rode over a particularly prominent anomaly in the road surface, a rumbling, sucking sound garbled through the transport's interior. The longer the journey continued, the more frequent it became, until it was almost a permanent part of the ambience. It gave the impression that it was coming from somewhere near the front axle, or possibly the right-hand door, but when Marcus raised himself slightly and peered over the seats, he found that the source of the din was in fact Hugo.

The crown of his head, with its surge of thick, Nordic hair was just visible on the edge of the seat closet to the aisle. His muscular body had slackened and was now contorted into a shape half its normal size, made loose by the comportment of a much needed slumber.

For some reason seeing the prince, a man normally so straight backed, large and unassumingly dominant, curled up like a child, amused Marcus greatly. He let out a small chuckle and moved his arm to poke Aria, and alert her of his hilarious discovery, but as he altered his position on the seat she fell into his lap with an unflattering thud.

'You've got to be kidding me, not you too?' he said out loud, but there was no response from the sleeping girl. 'So now I've got to spend the rest of the journey like this? Great ... The things I do for you, Bianchi,' he muttered, shaking his head as he tried to get comfortable.

His fidgeting didn't quite have the desired effect though, and every time he moved, so did she. By the time Marcus had given up the endeavour as a bad job, Aria's head, shoulders and most of her torso were now pinning his thighs down.

He looked at her peaceful, delicate form, unusually garbed in the army uniform of the Russian Federation, and found his heart suddenly drowning in yearning. There was more, however, than humble longing flowing through him then; it was something more infinite and undeterminable, a feeling that could not be defined so simply.

As his eyes met her supple, olive skin and his hand unconsciously reached down to brush a stray strand of hair away from her face, Marcus was hit with a memory. He was slung back through time, six or seven years, to the end of a rather terrific night out somewhere in the north of England. They'd been visiting a friend for his birthday in the city where he was attending university, Marcus couldn't remember precisely which one it was, but he and Aria had ended up in an almost identical situation.

His recollection of that moment was vivid and to him at least, remained untainted by time's cruel hand, as most memories are. The way he stroked her hair, the look on his face as he stared down at hers, it was uncannily similar, and if one were to change the clothes and the context, Marcus suspected there'd be no differences at all.

The aspect that struck him most powerfully though, was the feeling that lingered in him from that night. It was branded on his mind, scorched into his very fibres for him to introspect upon for all eternity, and there was no denying that it was the same one he was experiencing at that precise moment, somewhere on the Estonian highway.

What's more, was that as Marcus foraged through his history, he realised there were several instances where that feeling had manifested itself. They stretched back into his past like a series of luminary dots, bobbing in the immeasurable deep of the memories he could never remember. Frantic now, he followed the trail, scrutinising each and every event along the path until he arrived back at its source; some nineteen years ago.

It was, of course, Aria.

Everywhere he found that inimitable stirring of emotion, he found her, but what was it? That labyrinthine, implacably beautiful protuberance of his heart was a law unto itself, and it was like nothing else in existence.

Vile and sublime, crushing and uplifting, it was like being burned by ice or finding oneself being drowned in air. It threatened to force him to his knees with want, only to make him run away in fear or to drop him from a perilous height, just to catch him before he hit the floor. Something and nothing, as contradictory as human nature itself and as old as time; it was *everything*. Which meant it could only be one thing.

Love.

'When are you going to tell her how you feel, Marcus?' said a voice, its unexpected sound rattling him from his own mind with an earthquake's shake.

'I don't know what you're talking about,' Marcus stated, swiftly withdrawing his hand from Aria's cheek.

Utterly mortified to have been caught caressing her face in such an amorous way, he glanced up curiously to see who'd invaded his private moment, to find that it was Cyril.

'You are a terrible liar – has anyone ever told you that?' He smiled.

'Almost everyone I know, including your father actually.'

'Then it must be true.'

'Where are you going with this, Cyril?' Marcus asked defensively, but there was something so disarming about his friend's aquiline features, that he was unable to stop the flicker of a smile warming his face.

'You used to tell me stories about Aria all the time when we would work together in London, and even when she had annoyed you, or you had fallen out, you always spoke about her so passionately.'

'Did I?'

'Yes, all the time, and now I can see why.' Cyril grinned through the gap between the seats.

'Go on?' Marcus said, growing uncomfortable.

'You love her.'

'Bollocks,' he replied in instant dismissal, refuting everything he'd just admitted to himself only seconds ago.

'Please, every time you see her, you glow. You ogle at her as though she were the most precious thing you have ever witnessed.'

'I'm sorry, but I'm going to have to disagree with you there,' Marcus disputed, hoping his affections for her weren't as obvious as Cyril was proposing.

'I have no idea why you feel the need to hide your emotions, but you cannot deny them forever, Marcus.'

'Of course I can.'

'So, there is something to be denied?'

'No, I …'

'Just admit it.' Cyril laughed quietly, watching Marcus tie himself up in a knot.

'I … Can't.' Marcus faltered.

'But why?'

'Because, if I admit it, then it exists.'

'And what is wrong with that?'

'Everything!' Marcus whispered, with a kind of wide eyed desperation. 'Whilst this senseless little fantasy is just in my head, it's not physical, it doesn't matter, and it can't have an impact on anything in the real world.'

'What if she feels the same though?' Cyril persisted.

'I know she doesn't.'

'How? You have never asked her.'

'I just … do, alright.'

'No, not alright. Knowing is suggestive of certainty, and you would need some sort of evidence to support that, but you don't have any at all. What you do have, is an image in your mind that you're projecting onto Aria because it suits the story that you're telling yourself.'

'Fine then, Mr psychoanalyst, I don't *know* and it's likely that you're right, but I can't take the risk of telling her,' Marcus said defiantly, hoping to bring their conversation to a close.

'Enlighten me, what is this risk?' the young Chinese man continued gaily, pretending to be oblivious to Marcus's unease.

'Ok, listen. Me and Aria have a long history, we've been close friends for pretty much as long as my life's been worth remembering. If I tell her that I *care* about her–' Marcus said, gesturing an inverted comma with his right hand. 'And she doesn't feel the same, she'll look at me differently and our friendship will end, probably immediately knowing her. On the other hand, let's say she does feel the same, and we somehow end up in a romantic relationship–'

'Yes?' Cyril interjected, listening intently.

'Then it ends.'

'What?'

'Then I've lost my best friend, and a lover, all in one go! My life is empty and will continue to remain empty, because we both know I love to agonise over *everything* that's ever happened to me. I'll still retain feelings for her, potentially forever, and die alone under a mountain of paintings dedicated to her memory,' he blethered effusively.

'And you do not think you might, perhaps, be jumping the gun there?' Cyril replied facetiously.

'Absolutely not. You wanted to know the risk, well that's it. I would lose everything me and Aria have now and gain nothing, therefore there's no way to win, and silence is the best option.'

'What about the third option, where she reciprocates your feelings, and it *does not* end?'

'Nonsense, it could never happen,' Marcus resolved insolently. 'Why are we talking about love anyway, at a time like this?

'During times like these, Marcus, love becomes more important than ever,' Tak-hing intoned, weighing in on their discussion, but still looking forwards.

'Then maybe I'll tell her *someday*,' breathed Marcus hastily, beginning to feel trapped and violated by their prying enquires into his inner world.

'You talk as though you will live forever,' the older man said in reply.

'I don't understand what you mean, Tak-hing.'

'Then allow me to explain,' he crooned, clearing his throat with a prudent cough, before proceeding in his magnetic, accented voice. '*Someday* does not feature in any genuine timeline, and therefore it has no specific chronology. It is merely a term used as a means to delay, or reference, a vague point in the future. By using that term, you naturally assume that you have a future, which I concur is a reasonable prospect. However, the length of that future is indeterminable, and could range from five minutes to fifty years, or perhaps, should you be so lucky, even longer.'

'I'm still not sure of the case you're making?' Marcus remarked, reminding himself to be respectful.

'My case is that we are transitory, all things are, which is why something so crucial as a future should not be taken for granted. Have you ever said to yourself, or another, that you feel as though time is running out?'

'Yeah, plenty of times.'

'Good, but that's a flawed statement. If our greatest physicists are to be believed then time is not, has not, and will never be running out, Marcus, because it is infinite. What is running out, is you,' Tak-hing said profoundly, his expression heavy in the teal light shining through the tinted windows. 'All those grains of sand mounted in the hour glass are not made from dust and rock, they are fragments of flesh and blood, and as the minutes pass and the pieces fall, we lose a bit more of ourselves to the abyss every day. The tragedy is that none of us know how many we have left, so if you do love her, Marcus, give her a piece of yourself now before there are none left to offer.'

Finished with his pontifications, Tak-hing became quiet once more, and with a self-satisfied look that was tantamount to the phrase "I told you so", Cyril turned away too.

Their words loitered in his head though, harassing him with an all engulfing, portentous sense that he might have much less time left than he'd thought.

Chapter XIV

Held hostage by his disgruntled thoughts, Marcus found himself exhausted but unable to rest, as the convoy powered through the Estonian countryside. They'd been on the same serpentine road, the E20 he'd assumed it was called from the frequent signs dotted along its edge, for the entire journey and his sleep deprived brain was growing unappreciative of the tedium.

The monotony was augmented by the unchanging nature of the terrain, and climate, that pervaded over that specific part of Northern Europe during the late summer weeks. Over fifty percent of the country, he'd been told by Hugo once the prince had resurfaced from his dreams, was covered in forests and judging by the view from the window, Marcus was inclined to believe him. Even when the road had veered off towards the coast some time before, briefly reintroducing them to berylline depths of the sea, that tenacious line of trees on their inland side had not once abated.

Graciously, however, after almost three hours of travelling had passed, a statistic Marcus knew to be accurate as he'd foolishly insisted on checking his watch every five minutes or so, the vegetation began to fade. The verdurous landscape gave way to a flat, barren looking plateau, covered in a sparse array of ugly tower blocks, bulky industrial units and residential suburbs. It became clear though, as the density of the urban areas increased and their caravan neared the Russian border, that things were not quite as they should have been.

The clues were subtle at first, barely tickling the far reaches of Marcus's cognition, but the closer to the Soviet state they got the more aberrant the view became. Naturally, he'd never visited the region before, so he had no accurate measure by which to arbitrate his surroundings, but even to his uneducated self the wrongness of the place was unambiguous.

Marcus shuffled in his seat, trying not to disturb the still slumbering Aria, as he moved his face closer to the glass to scan the somewhat decrepit congregation of houses to his right. Each one was unique and detached from the rest, making them look more like faces in a crowd, than places to live. They stared back at him from the roadside as the transport rolled by, or they would've done if their eyes hadn't been sealed shut with wooden planks and sordid nails. Maybe they would've screamed too, if their vocal cords hadn't been locked away behind riveted steel plates, and yet more of those repulsive plywood boards.

There wasn't a single, crooked house that hadn't been sealed. Every available window and door had been barred and that trend continued, becoming even more prevalent, as they moved towards the Russian boundary.

What concerned Marcus the most though, was that he couldn't discern whether those boards had been so hastily erected in order to keep something out; or to trap something in. With that idea came a horrible vision of local authorities confining infected people in their homes, and leaving them to die. Becoming inescapably invasive, that thought bled out into his consciousness like a weeping stain, painting the world with a brush that Marcus did not wish to accept, and yet, its strokes refused to be washed away.

Between the buildings makeshift shelters were now starting to appear, making the semi-rural outskirts of Estonia start to look like a shanty town. The slum-like shelters were constructed from a variety of discarded materials, and then propped up against the walls of existing houses, or in some cases, lashed together to form great piles of barely habitable waste. Everything from chunks of old stone, cardboard, sheets of plastic, wood and, in one exceptionally large mass, even the shell of a car had been used.

'Viktor what's happening here?' Tak-hing asked in an austere nuance, as he and Cyril gazed out at the squalor.

'What you are seeing, my friend, is the full effect of whatever the Chinese have unleashed into the world,' the Russian replied with an air of decaying grandiosity. 'We had to move our people out of Russia as quickly as possible, even though we had nowhere for them to go, and this is the result.'

'Why is it so concentrated here though, or is the rest of Russia like this too?' Cyril questioned, echoing Marcus's own thoughts.

'St Petersburg was an easy target. It's our most commercial city, and one of the main trading outlets for the country, so when several hundred Chinese tourists turned up, no one batted an eyelid. Those same tourists, oblivious to the havoc they were silently wreaking, spread the virus throughout the city like wildfire.'

'So, all these people are now homeless?' Marcus chimed in, sounding far more accusatory than he'd meant to.

'Better homeless, than dead, boy.' Viktor growled, but as Marcus glanced about at the frail structures which now housed the displaced population of Russia's Western fringe, he wasn't sure he agreed with that statement.

'And how do you know the ones you're letting into Estonia aren't infected themselves?' Hugo probed, with a trace of alarm ringing through his musical voice, as he too took stock of the scenes beyond the road.

'The border control point is only about a mile from here, at the Narva River; when we reach it you can see for yourselves,' said Viktor, leaving them all hanging from the cliffs of his words.

Outside the situation grew increasingly dire as they progressed through the municipality of Narva, and the streets were becoming clotted with great masses of the shambling, tumble-down shacks which barely passed for salvageable garbage; let alone homes.

They swashed up against apartment blocks, leaked out across parklands in enormous, viscous pools and clogged every conceivable space that Marcus could see. The way that reservoir of filth had developed made it seem alive, like it was some sentient creature about to gorge itself on the city, and its inhabitants, alike. Maybe that was why they hadn't seen any signs of life, Marcus pondered worriedly, perhaps they'd already been consumed by that cankerous mire?

As that thought floated around his head, their convoy skirted the outer lane of a gigantic roundabout and then stopped quite suddenly, only a few metres past it.

'Passports,' Viktor barked from the front, making Marcus tense. 'Make sure they're fake, we need to keep a low profile here. The fewer people who know you're not Russian, the better.'

'Ari, wake up,' said Marcus softly, trying to keep the urgency out of his voice.

'What, why?' she mumbled, sitting up in a daze.

'We're at the Russian border, we need those passports that Cyril gave us.'

'Mine are in the front of my bag, jump over the back seat and you'll be able to grab it,' Aria said as she scraped at her hazy eyes.

Under any other context, Marcus would've likely wound Aria up and made her get it herself, but there was something scarily insistent about Viktor's tone. With that in mind he dragged himself over his seat, his trailing foot narrowly missing a collision with Aria's head; and fumbled around for the passports.

'Cyril, do you need yours?' Marcus asked, as he retrieved Aria's and then his own.

'We have got different papers, my father and I couldn't risk having our faces on the documents,' he answered placidly, in stark contrast to Marcus's panicky tenor.

'That's some pretty serious foresight,' Marcus said in puzzlement, remembering then, that his friend had known all along about McRae's plans to push on to Moscow.

'Knox?'

'Got it, lad. Grab a wad of those rubles though, Marcus, money goes a long way with this lot,' the Scotsman ordered, his remark prising a short laugh from Viktor's toothy mouth.

He did as he was told, grabbing a handful of notes from his pack, as well as his camera which he kept hidden inside his jacket, before climbing back over the seat to resume his position.

'What have I missed then?' Aria enquired intensely, noting the stiffness of the atmosphere inside the transport.

'Take a look outside,' replied Marcus, pointing to the window on her left, where a vigorous wave of black plastic was rippling like a taut slice of skin.

'Holy sh—' she began, but her words were cut off by a heavy beating on the side of the truck. Marcus jumped at the sound, the tension he felt shattering like glass inside him. The prince hardened too, the thick muscles around his neck contracting into armour as his face took on a warrior's front. Cyril and Tak-hing, unsure of what was about to transpire, pulled their snoods up around their faces so only their eyes were visible.

One of the doors to the front cabin opened then, allowing bright beams of sunlight to streak in and illuminate the space. Viktor's thick, congealed voice could be heard conversing in his native tongue with an unseen character on the road. It was a short exchange with little inflection from either man, which gave Marcus no clue as to what was about to happen. So, when the door ahead of them was flung open, and a tough looking Russian solider leapt into the cramped space, he very nearly let out a cry of shock.

The man, somewhere in his mid-thirties Marcus estimated, looked haggard. His chiselled face was coated in scruffy stubble, the purple tinged rings beneath his eyes suggested he hadn't slept for days, and the trenches in his forehead were so deep that his brow looked like it may never unclench again.

There was something odd about his granite demeanour though. It didn't seem to be inherent, and there was a softness hidden underneath his gravelly carapace that gave him away.

As he moved into the centre of the transport, Marcus caught his eyes and, noting the sheen of fear coating them like a waxy glaze, suddenly understood.

'Propuska,' the soldier stated roughly, opening his palm.

Hugo nodded and fished a battered, red passport out of the pocket on his right arm. He flicked through the curled pages, eventually landing on the one which displayed his picture and identification, then handed it over.

Marcus reached for his own passport, as the soldier surveyed Hugo's, and when he saw that the one that he'd retrieved didn't possess an insignia that matched the prince's, he was hit with an awful notion that he'd done something very wrong.

'Hey,' he whispered tightly to Aria. 'My passport's in English, won't it give the game away?'

'Cyril gave us three, remember? One of them is Russian, or what looks like it at least. Here look,' she replied heatedly, flicking her own open and showing him the foreign characters.

Fuck! I've picked up the wrong one,' he hissed through gritted teeth, as he spun around and reached through the gap between his and Aria's seat for his bag.

'Hurry up, Marcus.' Aria breathed, pursing her lips and squeezing the words out of the side of her mouth.

The unnamed border guard had dealt with Hugo and was now assessing the mysterious documents that Tak-hing had handed him. Marcus still had his head and arm pushed through the seats, but the pressure around them had become so palpable that he could practically taste it.

After what felt like an eon of detailed examination, the solider gave the papers back to the disguised sage with a curt nod. Then, having already scanned over Cyril's papers, he stepped towards the back row and raised his gaze, just as Marcus flipped around with the Russian passport in hand.

'Propuska, seychas zhe,' he said, snatching the red and gold booklet from him.

That close, Marcus could smell the reek of stale cigarettes emanating from the man, and he bit down on his tongue to hide his distaste. He threw the passport back at Marcus without another word, and turned his focus to Aria, where his eyes snagged on her features and lingered with revolting intent.

He took a step nearer to her, blocking the light as he flicked over her passport, and adopted an intimidating stance with his crotch less than a foot from her face. Aria kept her composure as the brute leered at her through smoke stained teeth, but Marcus's fury was beginning to rise.

'Kak vas zovut?' the man said, his pronunciation making it clear that it was a question, although none of them understood what exactly he'd asked.

When she didn't reply, he repeated himself more vigorously, pressing his legs against hers as the vapours of his foul breath sunk into their clothes.

The soundlessness of the void where her reply should've been filled the rear of the transport, becoming awkward, and undoubtedly steering them towards trouble. Marcus didn't dare react for fear of jeopardising their crossing, but he knew that if that repulsive soldier laid a hand on her, the chances of him restraining himself would be non-existent. Luckily for him, the former Colonel General intervened.

The older man shouted something harsh through the cabin, seizing the border guard's awareness but not his eyes, which remained glued to the sun-kissed girl before him. Whatever Viktor had said though it hadn't been well received by the soldier, and a series of phonetic mortars were launched from both sides, smattering the walls with verbal shrapnel as the men argued.

It was a frenetic, if disorientating, altercation which gave little away. After the first few shots, the solider turned from Aria and marched towards the front of van, where more words were had. It still wasn't clear who was winning, until Viktor's biting voice grew so loud and murderous that eventually the man flinched back, ceasing his assault. He dropped Aria's passport on the floor in a rush and fled the transport without looking back, as Viktor wound down his window and hurled one last cursory shell in the man's direction.

'Ubiraysya otsyuda, pridurok!' he roared, shaking his fist in the air, before closing the window and mumbling something under his breath.

'Are you alright?' Marcus asked Aria tentatively.

'More confused than anything,' she huffed, alleviating some of Marcus's worry with her smile, as Cyril left his seat to collect the passport from the floor. He returned it to Aria with his soft, gliding steps and then sat down once again beside his father.

'My Russian is far from comprehensive, but from what I gathered, there was a lot of swearing,' he said, glancing through the seats with an expression that amalgamated an affronted grimace, with a regaled simper.

'Yeah, I think we all got the gist.' Marcus laughed, before exhaling deeply. 'I just hope that's the last of the trouble for today.'

'Unlikely. Hugo, flip the catches on the doors in the back, and the rest of you, make sure your windows are locked too,' Viktor instructed in his bone saw voice. 'You'll need to put one of these on as well, we're about to cross the river,' the grizzled Russian continued, dropping a faded cardboard box over his shoulder into the rear area of the transport; just as its wheels began to turn once more.

'Gas masks?' the prince enquired, grabbing the box and exploring its contents.

'Life across the border is no longer safe without one, and as surgical masks are like gold dust these days, we've had to resort to these,' answered Viktor.

'They just seem, excessive, that's all.'

'Reserve your judgements until you have seen what lies ahead. The truth may … startle you,' Viktor finished, pulling a mask over his head and wriggling it into position.

Hugo, once he'd removed one for himself, placed the box on the floor and pushed it down the aisle towards Cyril and Tak-hing with a satisfying whooshing sound. The strength of the prince's arm impelled the box all the way to the very rear of the truck, where it landed at Aria's feet, meaning both she and Marcus could also reach it. She pulled out two of the gummy, rubber face protectors and tossed one to Marcus, which he managed to catch as it bounced off his chest. He placed it in his lap and scrutinised it with diligence, trying to figure out which way around it went and more crucially, how to put it on.

It was made from a combination of thick, black rubber and a material that looked like plastic, but felt significantly denser and was presumably more resistant. Marcus realised quickly that he was holding it face down, and briefly observed that there were a total of five adjustable straps across the sides and top of the mask, before turning it over. He stared down into the empty oval eyes of the contraption, wishing it didn't look so sinister, and studied his scruffy reflection in the lenses.

Placing it over his face, Marcus tightened the straps and breathed in, feeling a small panic bubble within him as the suction tugged at his skin, and he had to try his best not to picture it as some disturbing parasite that was gripping his face in its maw.

'You look quite fetching in a gas mask,' he joked, looking into Aria's icy blue eyes through the drooping lenses of her mask.

'I'm glad you think *not* being able to see my face is an improvement; you always were great with compliments, Merda,' she quipped in sarcastic retort.

'Look, you can't teach charm, you've either got it or you haven't.' Marcus chuckled, noticing the alteration in his voice as it moved through the plastic mouthpiece.

'I know. That's why you haven't got any.'

'Touché,' he said, smirking beneath his mask, and lampooning her with an exaggerated display of clapping.

She reached out and smacked his leg then, leaving a stinging imprint of her fingers on his thigh, which caused them both great hilarity. Their laughter was fleeting though and sounded eerily like the crackling bursts of white noise from an untuned television, due to the masks. Nevertheless, those short seconds acted as a small slice of sanctuary for them and were to be devoured; and savoured.

As they watched the transport ahead of them being swallowed by the great, iron barred gates of the crossing, Marcus found himself amazed that they were able to laugh at all in light of all they'd seen and heard, and yet they did, over and over again. A fact that comforted him in the present, for if Viktor's prognosis was to be believed, there would be little to find any exuberance in once they crossed into Russia.

Struggling not to allow that thought to supplant any positivity he still retained, Marcus watched out of the window as their own vehicle started to move through the enormous gates, and out onto the concrete bridge.

The span they had to cover was itself fairly short, and should've proved uneventful, with the serene waters of the Narva river below quite obviously in no hurry to reach the Baltic Sea to which they led. However, as they crossed to the other side, a series of weak jetties and rickety platforms came into view, emerging from the depths below.

Their disconnected, incomplete forms appeared to rise from the water in random arrangements, but when Marcus followed their vague patterns he realised they originated from the Russian bank. What's more, as he looked deeper, it became apparent that that each section had once been attached; and together they would have formed a bridge.

Building up a mental image of what the fragmented crossing would've looked like whole, he concentrated on the missing portions, and soon discerned that they must've been broken, and recently too. Allowing his eyes to wander the banks, a number of other disunited appendages could be seen stretching up and down the river, all of which shared the same sorry fate of dismemberment. He shifted his gaze to the area below the closest one once more, noticing for the first time the debris hiding amongst the blue currents, and something else far more disturbing lurking in the shadows too.

In a tangle of ropes and splintered wood, which had become caught on one of the stilted legs of the structure, the remnants of a human arm could be seen poking out. It was horribly scarred and bloated from its time in the river, but what distressed Marcus more was just how inhuman the limb looked, now it had been severed from the body to which it belonged.

Wavering between the two poles of disgust and fascination, he rambled through the floating rubble with his eyes, coming across more hunks of human wreckage as he did so. Feeling the bile in him begin to simmer and rise up his throat as he scanned the irreparable bodies, Marcus averted his eyes; worrying he might vomit. But the harrowing sight consumed his mind, and as Knox applied the brakes to stop their truck, he couldn't help but wonder what kind of life-snatching disaster had played out there.

'Aria, did you look at the river as we came across?' he asked sheepishly.

'Yeah…' she replied, in an almost inaudible tone.

'You saw them then?' Marcus probed, feeling the gooseflesh climb up his arms.

'There were *so many* … I think they were running from something,' Aria said with a terrible allusion.

But Marcus never got the chance to ask her what she thought they were running from, as the grinding sound of metal gouging through stone rang out ahead, indicating that the entrance to the former Soviet Union was now open. He gulped as McRae put the transport back in gear and proceeded through the opening.

After driving through a very short tunnel, they entered a courtyard, which was lined on all sides by imposing slabs of gabion walling. The cages of stones that comprised the wall looked to be well over a metre deep and were topped with a swirling reem of barbed wire, turning what had once been a simple border crossing point, into an armoured bastion.

The compound, along with the concrete tunnel they had come through only moments before, seemed to have been built only a short time ago; most likely as a reactionary means of controlling the virus. On their right hand side, the grass verge which led from the river bank to the road had been cleared as a type of drop off spot. The supply truck that had brought up the rear of their convoy was being signalled to by two soldiers on the ground, and it veered off towards the slanting, green cargo bay to be unloaded.

Meanwhile, the vehicles ahead of them turned to their left, where the somewhat charred remnants of the customs office now formed part of the outer wall. The jeep and two transports wheeled around to position themselves in front of the building's entrance, looking as though they were waiting for something.

'We're going on alone then?' the prince queried, sounding pensive, as he looked past Viktor's shoulder. Everyone was so engrossed in the happenings outside though, that his question, whether rhetorical or not, did not receive an answer.

The transports that led them had stopped in such a way that Marcus and Aria could still see the burnt outline of the doorway between their bumpers, and the two of them stared into the orifice with anticipatory frowns. What surfaced from that ghastly cavity was a jittery group of emaciated, rag clothed people, who made their way towards the army vehicles with wide, petrified eyes.

Marcus counted nine adults and three children before they were herded into the green trucks, and he felt a spear of sympathy jab at his core, as he watched their frail frames struggle aboard. It was sickening to imagine the ordeals they must have survived to get them to that point. To consider a life where homelessness in a foreign country was the best option, was incomprehensible, and it forced him to question what could possibly be on the other side of that stone wall. Did he even want to know?

The choice was not for him to make and as a single, ear splitting bleat of a siren tore through the air, he felt the truth rushing to meet him. The noise had been created by an alarm on the compound's exit, which had just turned from a cloying shade of red, to a burning green colour, as two guards began pushing open the heavy, metal plated gate for them.

'Be ready,' Viktor commanded, as Knox manoeuvred past the soldiers and through the exit.

'For what exactly? Why are you being cryptic?' McRae pushed, clearly tense, his rasping voice sounding like sand hitting a fan blade through his gas mask.

But as the soldiers charged to slam the gate shut behind them, Viktor's mouth did so too, the immovable lock of his jaw securing the secrets within.

Once through, they found themselves walled inside another courtyard, but in contrast to the previous one's clean, strong appearance, the new area was crumbling to dust. The same immense gabion cages which had once looked so impenetrable, now laid on their sides in defeat, their stone entrails leaking across the trampled ground from a series of rending wounds.

To their sides, two wooden carcasses could be seen lining the road too. The size of them suggested that they had likely been buildings in a former life, but now they were reduced to little more than piles of unrecognisable waste. Amongst the blasted wood of the left most heap was a red and white sign that had a statement written in three languages on its blackened surface; the English read "Virus Testing Centre".

As McRae edged the van slowly onwards, examining the chaos himself, Marcus became curious as to what motive could have possibly driven the Russian people to destroy something that could potentially help them? Not only that, but how had they succeeded in obliterating everything so thoroughly, if they were just civilians? The questions perplexed him, but as he pondered over the post-mortem of the defences, the pummelled remains of more metal gates came into view.

Their warped shapes, although alarming in themselves, paled into insignificance, as their first true glimpse of the new Russia came into view, and they saw exactly why Viktor had never elaborated on what they'd find at the border. There was no honest way of describing a scene so appalling and to try, would be spirit breaking; even for a man as adamantine as Viktor Stefanovich.

In spite of the late afternoon sun, Marcus's blood turned cold, as he stared out at the horizon wide devastation that was unfolding before them.

'What is this place?' Knox asked, with more than just a trace of fear entwined around the husk of his usual, discordant voice.

'Welcome to the Trushchob Smerti, the *Death Slum*, where even the Devil himself would not dare tread,' Viktor replied solemnly. 'We shouldn't linger here, it's not safe,' he added, noticing that McRae had slowed almost to a complete halt, as he gawped at the withered landscape.

The town of Ivangorod, which occupied the Russian side of the river, had been overrun by the same pestilent scourge which had swamped its Estonian counterpart. Everywhere they looked the houses, shops, streets and buildings, were being choked by masses of the soiled shelters which had become so dominant throughout Narva.

On the Russian side though, their growth had been rampant, and the shelters stretched out as far as the eye could see, casting a dreary shadow over everything they touched.

'It's so, so *big;* how many people are here?' Hugo enquired, his adagio tone betraying the incredulity he felt.

'Millions. All of them infected, that's why they're here and not across the border,' Viktor answered shortly, evidently not wanting to say any more than was necessary.

'What are all those fires?' asked Cyril, his inquisitive eyes drawing everyone's gaze towards the plumes of smoke that were being belched into the air around them.

'Bodies.'

'What?' Marcus cut in, tearing himself away from the window which he was taking photographs out of, his face a picture of shock behind the mask.

'They worry that the virus lives on even after its host has died, so they burn the dead,' the older Russian stated with grim simplicity.

'But those fires are gigantic,' he balked, unwilling to believe Viktor's words.

'There are a lot of bodies.'

'This can't be the way, surely there is more to be done to help these people?' Hugo said, raising his voice to a crescendo. 'Look at this mess! How can you trap your own people in such an awful place and just leave them to rot?'

'Watch yourself, Hugo.'

'No, this is wrong! If the virus doesn't kill these people, the conditions *your* government has put them in, will. Where is your conscience?' the prince asserted.

'You'd dare to speak to me of conscience? Do not judge what you cannot comprehend, child!' Viktor shouted, his temper detonating. 'How can you be so naïve? If we let the infected run free across the rest of Europe, the virus spreads. If we allow them to move further into Russia, the same thing happens. The most effective option is to contain them as best we can.'

'Like this?' snapped Hugo, gesturing out of the windows at the dirty hovels, piles of excrement and smog filled sky. 'You've herded them here like cattle, and now you're just watching them die in this hell; it's genocide!'

'It is rational! Are you fucking blind? You're looking but you're not seeing, death lies in every direction, the only variable is the amount of lives we lose. The uninfected are being moved to Estonia, the remainder are being treated here and–'

But Marcus had tuned out of their argument, knowing that it wouldn't reach a resolution any time soon, and instead retreated inside himself. Sealed within the sepulchre of his extroversion, Marcus's world became quiet and still, untainted and immune to the external influences of the realities that encompassed him. It was peaceful in a way, despite the carnage outside, or it was, until a pair of eyes by the roadside pierced his own and hauled him away from his refuge.

They belonged to a cadaverous little girl, who sat hunched by a scrap of debased fabric and plastic sheeting, her gaunt cheeks heaving as she coughed. That guttural croak, although muted by the plating that coated their vehicle, was the undeniable sound of her tiny lungs being torn apart by the virus.

He'd never seen, or heard, of anyone so young to be afflicted that badly. In fact, many reports had stated that it was nigh on impossible for children to catch it; and yet there she was, a grim reminder of just how much information had been kept from the public.

Knox was still driving so slowly that Marcus had time to take in every agonising detail of her, from the listless stuffed dog in her hands, to the muddy, diamond patterned dress she wore. He looked deeper and deeper into her, seeing the pain written in her stiff, corpse like features and wished with all the will he could muster, that he could take it away.

As if she'd heard his silent plea, the girl smiled, releasing a stream of blood and spittle from her tiny mouth, that trailed over her skeletal chin like a crimson waterfall. The poor thing looked demonic, making Marcus want to pull away from the window, but instead, the sorrow in him pulled his hand to the glass to wave at her.

She coughed again, spraying rivulets of blood across her dress, as she waved back at him. With every delicate pluck of the air her fingers made, a piece of Marcus's heart broke off, and was crushed by the atrocious weight of history's negligent boot. So many lives would be trodden into nothingness in that camp, forgotten by the world and stripped of their chance to be. But not her; she would haunt the ruins of Marcus's heart until the day it stopped beating.

Chapter XV

If knowledge is considered to be power, then why, Marcus asked himself, did he feel weaker and more helpless, with every new truth he unearthed? Did he still know too little? And, if the state of ignorance is widely regarded as one of bliss, why did he find no solace in it when he was blind to the world and its ills?

The mystery of those questions made him feel trapped. On the one side, the chagrining push of knowledge railed against him, and on the other, the perpetual disappointment of ignorance pressed in. His only chance of salvation was the shining rope of logic and reason that dangled before him, offering him a way out of the snare; but even that could form a noose if he wasn't careful with it.

Seizing that cogent chord, Marcus started to climb, one slow, deliberating hand at a time, until his cerebral tribulations receded and were burnt to cinders by an epiphanic stirring within him. He didn't know too little, he knew too much, far more than he'd ever anticipated he might and now, he'd needed a way to share it.

Despite not knowing how to do so, that thought still generated a glimmer of hope and Marcus snatched at it, nourishing its weak glow with promises; causing it to mature into a lustrous orb of conviction. That very same orb, which was now illuminating his mind, seemed to be reflected in the sky above St Petersburg, taking on the form of an iridescent sun.

Although the hour was growing late, and the sparse streets of the city's Southern Krasnoselsky district were already tinged with the raisin-wine hue of dusk, the sun still burned in a bright solar yellow. It sat low on the skyline, still clinging onto the day, and shooting its triumphant rays upwards like the resplendent spray of some enormous, elemental fountain. The sight of those incandescent streamers chasing the grey clouds up into the ether was splendorous, and by far the most exciting thing to be seen in the suburbs.

Marcus used that quiet portion of the journey to tuck into the rations he'd been given back in the Estonian encampment, and although his hunger had been somewhat curbed by the events at the border, he knew his body required it. Using the last of the sun's fading glow to examine the contents of his pack, Marcus fished through it until he found the shining parcel tucked away to one side.

Food in hand, he removed his gas mask tentatively, not knowing if it was entirely safe, but when he noticed that Takhing and Hugo were no longer wearing theirs either, his caution subsided. He examined the silver package for an obvious entry point, and after finding none, Marcus decided that the best course of action was to prise it open with his teeth; which he did so with a cumbersome ripping motion.

Through the untidy hole he'd made, a number of smaller packets were now visible inside, all of which were labelled in Russian and therefore unhelpful. Knowing his linguistics had failed him, he attempted to identify what was in each of the varyingly sized packs by squeezing, prodding and poking them, as a toddler might inspect a birthday present. Eventually

Marcus settled on one of the larger bags made from a thick white plastic and, not knowing if he was about to find a fish finger or a flambé, tore open the oblong bag with vigour.

He was pleasantly surprised to find a combination of sausages and potatoes lurking within, along with some deliciously fragrant sauce, and a blunted wooden fork to eat it with. Rather impressed by the military fare, he offered the packet to Aria who, after a fleeting visual inspection and a sniff, declined with an apathetic expression.

Marcus finished the meal quickly, enjoying it thoroughly, despite its lukewarm temperature, and was grateful for the distraction it had afforded him. He washed the food down with a small bottle of mineral water which he'd also found inside the ration pack, before returning the gasmask to his face. With his appetite satiated and the sun now entirely absent from the mauve sky, Marcus resettled himself, and surveyed St Petersburg from the window.

Viktor issued directions to McRae, who in turn followed them with precision, driving them onwards through the slightly more abundant Kirovsky district, and then into the industrial density of the Admiralteysky area. Here the city overtook the sunset in levels of intrigue. Most notably because it was so empty.

With its entire populace now either deceased or displaced, St Petersburg was home only to creeping vermin, cawing gulls and a scant few military personnel. Coupled with the frightful silence which had been left in the wake of Viktor and Hugo's moral disputation as they'd crossed the border, the vacant streets seemed malevolent. Almost as though they were concealing something; or waiting to pounce. A feeling that was all the more perceptible in the more central regions of the city, due to how hectic they would've usually been during more peaceful times.

That fact was made apparent by the signs of life that had been discarded, and cast to the wind, as the inhabitants had been evacuated. Scores of neglected vehicles could be seen abandoned on pavements and in carparks, traffic lights gave instruction to people who were no longer there, and the streetlights shone down onto the dusty ground, lighting the way for nothing but roaches.

'How long has St Petersburg been empty, Viktor?' enquired Tak-hing, as he examined the layers of dust which had accumulated outside.

'Since January, so around seven months,' he replied.'The very beginning then … And the soldiers still present in the city, what is their purpose?'

'Initially they were here to round up any stragglers and take them to the Estonian border. Now they're here to sanitise everything, in the hopes that we can make St Petersburg safe to return to,' the Russian said, his voice hard and defensive, no doubt waiting for another challenge from Hugo.

'How are they disinfecting an entire city?' Cyril asked warily, taking heed of the warning in the older man's tone.

'You see that?' Viktor said by way of reply, pointing everyone's attention to what looked like an army specification fire engine on the road ahead. Marcus examined its squat haunches as they drove past, wondering how long the black coil of intestinal hosing was when full outstretched.

'Five of those engines have been assigned to each of the city's eighteen districts, and instead of carrying water, they are filled with a highly concentrated antibacterial fluid.'

'So, they are literally hosing the streets down?' continued Cyril, his curiosity ignited.

'Not exactly. The liquid comes out as a fine mist, and it'll be sprayed onto everything, both indoors and out.'

'Something bothers me about all this, Viktor,' Knox stated, the gears in his mind clearly at work.

'Is it the sound of your own voice, McRae?' he asked, his humour sounding spiteful.

'No, and, *shut up*. What I can't figure out is why your officials moved the entire population of St Petersburg over a hundred miles to Ivangorod. If they wanted to contain the virus, why not just lock the city down? It's worked in other countries?' the Scotsman debated earnestly.

'When we evacuated the civilians we had no idea what we were dealing with, we were a little hasty in our decision making,' said Viktor, his self-assuredness faltering slightly for the first time. 'No one knew that the virus was airborne, we had no ideas as to its origins at all. Our scientists assumed it was localised at the time and that it was something in the city itself.'

'That still doesn't explain why you moved everyone?' McRae rasped.

'We moved everyone because we lost so many people in those first three weeks, that the government wanted to level the entire city. Evacuation seemed more humane, wouldn't you agree?' Viktor intoned unempathetically.

'But the virus wasn't in the bricks of the city, it was in the people all along, so all you've done is move the concentration of the virus elsewhere; you haven't contained it at all,' Knox pushed, slating the approach the Russians had taken to the crisis.

'You and the prince are the same, McRae, I expected more from you,' sighed Viktor. 'St Petersburg lost more people in three weeks, than Britain has in six months; and more than Sweden ever will. The government wanted to fire a nuclear warhead at, wiping out the virus, the structures, the *people* and everything in between unless we could find an alternative. Mass migration was never our first choice, it was the only one we had left.'

'Christ. So that's why the infection rate is so high at the border – you had no way of knowing they were already carrying the virus, did you?' Knox's voice rattled from within his mask, as he pieced together the events that had befallen the dead city they were now traversing.

'We did not … No man in his right mind would knowingly create a place like that,' snarled Viktor, the anguish he felt for the fate of his countrymen rumbling through his chest.

'I just wished you'd told us more, you could–'

'And how would you have described that atrocity, ah? What's the point in knowing who holds the strings if you can't see the puppets, Knox? Tak-hing and Oliver gave you the answers you so sorely wanted, but to see the true depth of the depravity this virus is responsible for, you knew you had to come here and see it for yourself. It is no fault of mine, that you're too soft to cope with what you found,' said Viktor, denouncing his old friend's grit and wisdom.

'Oh fuck off, V–'

'That's enough,' Tak-hing hissed, the keenness of his voice sharper than any blade, though it barely rose above a whisper. 'How many times must I tell you? Wise men do not need to prove their point; and men who need to prove their point are not wise. Arguing is merely an exercise in stupidity, there is no place for it here,' he finished, his apothegm quashing the disagreement taking place in the front of the truck, with a nearly tangible finality.

The ability of the elderly Oriental man to reduce the unimpressionable Knox, and the positively recalcitrant Viktor to mere children with no more than a witticism, was astounding. For men such as them, who were typically so forthright and changeless, to act with such open consideration for the views of another, demonstrated just how much they respected Tak-hing. Marcus supposed that the two of them viewed the numinous Chinese Defence Minister, in the same way that he saw McRae: as a stable body in a world full of flux, and perhaps, even a stick to measure one's worth against.

Sadly though, none of those realisations did much to redeem the maladroit silence which had descended over them in the absence of the bickering between the older men. What did break it though, was a weighty sigh from Hugo, which was swiftly followed by a question.

'So how are we getting to Moscow then, Viktor? We're right in the heart of city here, which doesn't leave us many options.' The prince's tone open and musical, clearly showing he wasn't looking for a fight.

'There are still trains running from St Petersburg to the capital, mostly for supplies and equipment to help with the cleansing. But some do take soldiers too,' replied Viktor, his voice retaining its frosty edge.

'How are we going to explain our reasons for going to Moscow though – isn't it under quarantine now?' Knox enquired, attempting to dissolve the tension between himself and his old friend.

'Indeed. You'll find Moscow a lot like London, just more heavily armed. However, I was, up until a few years ago, the Colonel General of Moscow's military district so I shouldn't have too much trouble getting around,' he answered, the abrasive ice in his tone melting fractionally.

'And the rest of us?' Hugo added.

'I'll see what I can do,' Viktor said, grinning into the rear-view mirror, the sentiment of his expression split between contempt and goodwill. 'We're not far from the train station now, but we'll have to take a detour. Normally we'd take the next right, onto Zagorodnyy Prospekt, but the street was undergoing repairs when the virus hit and the machinery is still blocking the road.'

'So where do you want me to go?' Knox said, surveying the route ahead and searching for another chance to turn right.

'Keep going straight. We'll head over the Obukhov bridge, circle around the northern part of the district, and then make our way towards the Station via the Anichkov bridge,' Viktor responded, talking to the old artist as though he was a local.

'Viktor, I've been here twice, do you really think I have any idea what you're talking about?'

'It wouldn't matter if you'd been here a hundred times, you've got a brain like a sieve, McRae!' jostled the Russian with a throaty chuckle. 'Just keep driving, I'll tell you where to go.'

'That's more like it,' said McRae, rewarding Viktor's petty joke with a sarcastic smile as he put his foot down, imploring the engine to carry them onwards.

Being forced to take a more scenic route through the regimented streets of St Petersburg was both a blessing, and a curse. The city presented a pulchritudinous blend of dainty baroque styling, impervious Soviet architecture, and quaint, somewhat over embellished, traces of the Style Moderne. The architecture did carry a flavour of Northern Europe, but what made it so distinct, unique even, was the feeling of supremacy that emanated from every surface.

Like its people, St Petersburg was hard, beautiful and gloriously powerful. Even wearing the black dress of night, deep in mourning for the loss of her people, she still shook the prideful, gothic fists of her gleaming spires at the tyrannous stars; asking them where they'd found the audacity to challenge *her*.

The contours of her dress were like a shard of deep onyx, its surface veined with a blackish blue network of canals and rivers that criss-crossed her finery and sprinkled with orange glints, where the streetlights hung their sallow heads.

Away from any disinfectant patrols, in the eerie quiet to the north of the Fontanka River, the ghosts of the tragedy played in the sable skirts of their mother city. But only from the corner of one's eye could they be seen, like translucent spiders, they spun out the webs of the lives they should've lived; only to disappear if one then faced them head on. It was spellbinding, and only made more otherworldly when some of St Petersburg's most impressive sights came into focus.

As Knox turned to the right once more, Marcus caught a brief glance of perhaps the most exquisite church he'd ever seen. Its tall, mosaiced walls blossomed into several brightly coloured domes which shone green, gold and turquoise, like the shimmering petals of a stupendous summer orchid. He spun around as its heavily patterned walls disappeared from view, desperately trying to catch another glimpse of it, but found his eyeline impeded by the interior of the cargo bay's smooth, metal door.

'Were you looking at the church?' Cyril enquired, as Marcus turned back around.

'Yeah. I've never seen anything like it,' he answered.

'It is special, I remember reacting the same way the I first time came to St Petersburg.'

'What's it called, it must be pretty famous?' Aria added, evidently interested herself.

'That is where it gets a bit strange,' he said with a smile. 'It is called the Church of the Savior on Spilled Blood; please do not ask me why though.'

'Catchy!' Marcus said, raising his eyebrows.

'That is weird, but regardless, it really did look incredible,' said Aria. 'I can't believe how pretty this part of the world is, I'd never once considered that Russia could be anything but hostile.' She trailed off, sounding a little embarrassed by her own short-sightedness.

'My country has a chequered past, as does every great nation, but the portrait the West has painted of us is not accurate,' Viktor remarked, having overheard their conversation. 'We are resilient because we have to be, and dangerous when we need to be, but for the most part at least, we aren't the uncultured savages the rest of the globe likes to write us as. Read our literature, then you'll see the true artistry of the Soviet spirit,' he concluded in an ardent show of patriotism, hinting that there might be more to the man than they'd seen thus far.

'Where am I going now, Viktor?' Knox interrupted, as they drove over the second of the bridges that he'd mentioned earlier.

'It's a straight line from here; when you the reach the Leningrad Hero Obelisk, the station will be on our right,'

Viktor instructed, leaning forwards in his seat to point towards a tall, brightly lit monument in the distance.

With the streets empty and the way ahead perfectly straight, they travelled quickly, arriving at their destination in only a few minutes. The road itself seemed to widen as they progressed, its girth multiplying until it was a massive five lanes abreast. As they neared the Obelisk, which sat proudly in the middle of a hedge rimmed roundabout, several of the lanes snaked off to their right, eventually crossing another three at an obscure angle; and bisecting a few more before they finally led around the opposing side of the central structure.

It was a preposterously confusing intersection, and one that would have undoubtedly been a tortuous thing to navigate during a rush hour. But of course; those did not exist anymore. Marcus journeyed down the many avenues with his eyes, surveying the tall structures that encircled them, exploring each and every intricacy of their decorative walls and dazzling neon lights.

To the left of the road they had entered on he noticed a round building, an uncommon sight in the predominantly straight edged St Petersburg, that displayed a wonderful array of columns around its upper level. Straight ahead of them the landmark Obelisk sprouted from a polished base, its carved form holding a metallic gold star at its pinnacle, thrusting the icon skywards in a futile attempt to reunite it with its cosmic brethren.

To the right of the centrepiece, just as Viktor has described, the rather compelling Moscow Station stood, its staunch posture exuding a dominative quality. It was a gargantuan sprawl of Renaissance lines, dotted with pilasters and pediments which adorned its apricot coloured face, and stretched all the way to the clocktower, which rested like a crown atop its tiled head. Illuminated by the ginger root glow of the streetlights, and obumbrated by the phthalo blue of the moonlit evening, the station looked magnificent.

Knox, ignoring the unintelligible road markings, cut across four lanes and brought them into the narrow carpark located at the front of the building. It was littered with clues of human activity. How recent that activity may have been remained a mystery, however, until Tak-Hing directed their attentions towards two still steaming cups set down on a crate by the entrance.

How one was supposed to drink anything, let alone a hot beverage, through a gas mask Marcus didn't know, but their presence by the door came as no real surprise. Moscow Station was one of the city's main hubs of transportation and, given that no one besides the military were supposed to be travelling to or from St Petersburg, it made sense for it to be monitored. He just prayed they'd make it through unhindered; and alive.

'I'll lead the way in and see if I can talk us into a free ride, with any luck there won't be too many of them inside and we'll make it through without a problem,' Viktor said, addressing them all, whilst Knox pulled up alongside one of the huge Venetian windows, and promptly cut the engine. 'In fact,' he continued, glancing towards the doors, 'let me go in alone, you can unload the bags and get yourselves ready. Don't come in unless I come out to get you.'

'Are you sure that's a good idea? Almost every conversation you have ends with a gunshot,' Hugo said, chastising the older man's aptitude for intimidation, as he recalled the incident with the boat.

'A firearm is a tool of communication when used correctly, and as I've proved, having one means you usually get your way,' replied Viktor, narrowing his eyes condescendingly through the goggles of his mask, as he opened the van door and strode off towards the station.

'There's not much point arguing with him, lad,' McRae told Hugo in a conciliatory tone. 'As we both learned on the way here, he's crabby enough to win a staring contest with Medusa. Just let him go, and hope for the best.'

'I did warn you,' Tak-hing laughed softly, knowing the Scotsman's words were true.

'Aye, you did. I suppose that means he's not the only stubborn one around here.' Knox shrugged, as he readjusted his mask and opened his own door to leave the cabin.

The rest of them followed suit. First ensuring their gas masks were on correctly then, with a circumspective attitude towards the quality of the air, left the confines of the transport to gather their belongings. By the time Marcus and Aria had made their way around the truck, Knox, with a bit of help from Hugo, had already unloaded their packs onto the floor. Marcus passed Aria's still laughably huge bag over to her, before stooping down to collect his own, feeling the chill night air brush against his bare hands and neck as he did so.

Having been inside the transport for hours on end, Marcus hadn't really considered that the temperature might change as they headed north into Russia; but it certainly had. The lack of heat was made all the more salient by a blustering gale, that gusted around the circular plaza like the massive wing beats of an invisible, avian creature. He turned his face down and shivered slightly as the wind redoubled its efforts, suddenly glad to be wrapped within the layers of the army uniform, making him forget the previous discomfort it had caused him during the day.

The torrents proceeded to whoosh around them, remaining insistent, and whistling through their gas masks as they waited for Viktor to re-emerge from the station. By the time he did, the howling in their ears had become almost deafening, and they rushed towards the open door where he stood beckoning them with a wave of his arm.

'What's wrong with you all?' Viktor scoffed peremptorily, if somewhat quietly, as he closed the door behind them and escorted them up a small set of stone stairs. 'Can't you handle a little Siberian breeze?'

'Your Siberian breeze is still warmer than a Scottish summer, so you can wind your neck in, *Colonel*. What's our situation?' McRae sneered, matching the trenchant tone of his old friend.

'Keep your voice down, we don't want to get caught speaking in English here,' warned Viktor, the rubber of his mask squirming as he furrowed his brow.

Knox nodded in apology, and although he hadn't spoken above a normal volume, the expansive room in which they were now stood amplified his voice, and fired it in all directions. As the echo of McRae's comeback ricocheted around them, Marcus surveyed the space, looking for any signs of bemused Russian soldiers heading their way.

They waited silently, but when no one appeared and no footsteps were heard, their group let out a communal sigh of relief, before turning their tired eyes back to Viktor.

'As I said, keep your voices *down*,' the Russian said, his words sliding out from between his gritted teeth, like paper from a shredder. 'Now, we do appear to have had some luck.

There's only four soldiers down there; the rest of their platoon is scattered around the area on disinfectant duty, so negotiations went well.'

'How big is a platoon?' Marcus asked, for no other reason other than to satisfy his mental acquisitiveness.

'Four squads, around forty men,' Viktor responded, somewhat taken aback by the question.

'So, when you say negotiations went well, is it fair to presume that that means you've got us a train?' Knox whispered in a low, deliberate way.

'You presume correctly, with a few rubles passed over to ease the process … *However*–'

'Oh, this should be good,' Hugo interjected, folding his arms in pre-emptive remonstration.

'It's a freight train,' Viktor finished.

'Meaning?'

'Meaning that the seating arrangement is going to be less than comfortable, Hugo, and if you keep looking at me like that, I'll strap you to the fucking tracks. How does that sound?' the older man said, puffing up his chest confrontationally as he spoke to the younger Swede.

'Better than being stuck in a boxcar with you for however long it takes to get to Moscow,' the prince contested defiantly.

'Even with the lines quieter than usual, freighters are slow, so how does six hours sound?'

'Terrific,' Hugo said, punctuating his statement with a sarcastic exhalation which, much to everyone's surprise, resulted in both of them laughing.

'Maybe your father managed to raise more than just a little *Suka* after all, ah? There might be hope for you yet,' Viktor mocked. But despite his intrinsic nature to patronise, hurt, and belittle the people around him, there was a twinkle of something else in his mannerisms too. Something close to a blunted sense of affection maybe.

'And where is this freight train then?' Tak-hing asked, entering the conversation with his appeasing, Eastern voice.

'Platform four, it's the only train in here from what I gather, so it shouldn't be hard to find. We just need to find a boxcar with enough room for all of us,' Viktor responded, his shell of seriousness reforming, as the rest of the cohort looked at him expectantly. 'Follow me,' he said, turning a hundred and eighty degrees and heading off.

As they moved through the entrance hall with its slew of vending machines and ticket offices, the station became an indubitable feast for the eyes, and in places it looked more like a stately home than a place of public transport. Before they reached another set of stairs, which this time led down to a vaulted hall where a row of security scanners were located, Marcus took stock of his surroundings.

The space was dripping in iron chandeliers, carved stone accents ran up the walls, and the mural that garnished the main section of the ceiling was a centuries-old masterpiece. Coupled with a multitude of heavy oak benches, worn smooth by the bodies of innumerable travellers, and the curvaceous stone arches; the building felt noble.

Beyond the security systems, the interior of St Petersburg's Moscow Station underwent a dramatic, modern change, however. The newer, more contemporary hall offered all the niceties one would commonly associate with twenty-first century travel. Gone were the ornamental stone walls and columns, usurped now by glass fronted shops and fast-food restaurants, their headily coloured signage displaying things like "pizza" and "coffee".

The ceilings too had been transformed. The painted characters from the more archaic areas were nowhere to be seen, and instead had been replaced by a white, sculpted surface that resembled a bland form of square honeycomb. It was still a spectacle, but it lacked the richness of the older rooms, and Marcus found the contrast disappointing.

What did snare his attention though, as the group marched across the vacant hall, was a complex diagram of the Moscow and St Petersburg railway lines. It reminded him of the pictogram which he'd so often seen on British trains as he crossed from his home town in the Midlands, to London, during his frequent visits to McRae's studio.

But where the map of the United Kingdom portrayed a muddled network of small scale routes, the Russian equivalent was a scrupulously straight-lined schematic, festooned in bold, black lettering. That made it no less baffling though, and even if Marcus could read Russian, he thought it would take more than an understanding of the language to make sense of it.

Passing a bronze bust of Peter the Great, the eighteenth-century founder of the city, they made their way through the exit and onto the platforms of Moscow Station. The wind was still strong outside, berating them as they moved with its ghostly elegy, blowing loudly around the metal struts and beams of the canopies above.

The now torch-wielding soldiers who Viktor had conversed with could be seen further down the platform, opening, checking, and then closing the sliding metal doors of the freighter's numerous carriages. The former Colonel General walked in their direction, cohort in toe, and began talking to the closest one as he slammed a metallic door shut and tested its seal.

As was becoming quite common, the lightning fast flow of Russian, not helped by the roaring wind in that particular instance, was completely undecipherable. Thankfully, body language was a relatively universal mode of communication and, as the soldier stepped back from the silver door, signalling with his hand to a coach further down the tracks, its ability to transcend the spoken word was displayed once again.

Using Viktor's behaviour as a guideline, each of them nodded their thanks to the solider as he resumed his checks, before carrying on towards the denoted carriage. The train was immensely long, and painted in a simple grey design, with horizontal red stripes running along its lower aspects. What surprised Marcus the most though, was that it didn't look like a traditional cargo train, at least in the English sense.

He'd expected something loaded with cart after cart of open topped troughs, laden to their brims with coal or some other commodity. Instead, they'd been greeted by something that wasn't massively dissimilar from a standard passenger train, other than the lack of windows lining the coaches, and he found himself relieved to see that he wouldn't have to spend the next six hours sat in a pile of unburned fossil fuel.

Reaching their designated carriage, Viktor flipped the rusted, metal latch on the door's right-hand side, and opened it to reveal a very dark space within. It was no wonder the soldiers required torches to see what they held, Marcus thought, but it was still preferable to any alternative they currently had. If anything, the arguably uncouth freighter seemed fitting, when compared with the other obscure modes of transport they had experienced over the past few days.

Marcus couldn't help but smile at the absurdity of it all then, as he considered everything they'd been through to get where they were, and watched the unusual, eclectic and otherwise incompatible group of people he now called friends, make their way into the black mouth of the carriage. They were almost there now, almost on their way home; the final roll of the dice was at last, in play.

Chapter XVI

'I can't believe we've been sat in the dark all this time, and you've had *that* in your bag all along!' Aria moaned, directing her angst towards Marcus, who'd last been seen somewhere in the gloom to her left.

'It slipped my mind! What does it matter anyway, we've all been asleep?' he blurted out in response, fondling an object in his hand, when a beam of light suddenly burst from its end. 'Ah ha!'

'Christ, lad! Would you mind shining that somewhere else? If I want my corneas burning out, *I'll ask*,' Knox yelled, rushing to cover his eyes with his long, spindly fingers.

'Shit, sorry,' Marcus said, redirecting the beam of the thin, plastic torch up towards the ceiling of the boxcar in an effort to illuminate it.

His tactic worked rather well, with the light diffusing into what could've been an almost cosy ambience as it hit the dull, but still partially reflective, metal surface above. Looking around at the roughly circular arrangement of his companions though, Marcus realised that the bluish hue of the modern LED was more sterile, than snuggly. They'd taken their gas masks off not long after the train had left St Petersburg and as Marcus scrutinised the harshly shadowed faces surrounding him, he thought of gargoyles.

There was nothing inviting about the angular peaks of Hugo's cheekbones, no comfort to be derived from McRae's batholithic features, and even Cyril's usually elegant aspect was distorted by the high contrast of the torch light. Marcus couldn't help but wonder what he looked like too, in that most unusual setting, with his bedraggled hair and patchy stubble, his limbs scrunched around his open bag. There was no doubt that he must've appeared as grim as the rest of his cohort, and although he knew that vanity had no place in that environment; an irredeemable twang of self-consciousness shot through Marcus as he felt Aria's gaze land on him.

'So why have you got a torch anyway?' she asked, in a tone that insinuated she was both pleased by his preparedness, and oddly irritated by it.

'It just seemed like a useful thing to have. You know I like to be prepared for, well, everything,' replied Marcus, as he placed the torch upright in his bag, zipping it in place so he didn't have to hold it.

'In all fairness you've always been like that. Your pencil case was like a treasure chest at school; in fact, I'm pretty sure that's how we became friends actually,' Aria said, throwing her mind back nearly two decades.

'You're not wrong; you asked me if you could borrow a pen in maths!' he said, as the faded memory of him handing her a black ballpoint suddenly rushed back to him. 'I'm still waiting for you to give it back.'

'Get lost, it didn't work anyway!' Aria snorted. 'Speaking of how people met though, that reminds me of something,' she continued, turning her barely lit face towards Cyril.

'I have a feeling this involves me, somehow?' he said in his wonderfully prudish way, with a catlike tilt of his head.

'I asked you when we were on the way to Scotland, how you'd ended up in England, but you never told me?' she queried, the crease in her inquisitive brow becoming all the more prominent in the boxcar's divergent lighting.

'From what I remember, Aria, you asked me about three hundred questions on that journey,' he quipped, smiling broadly at the recollection of their first meeting.

'Yeah, you're probably right but regardless, you never did tell us the story.'

'Go on, Cyril, we've still got an hour or so to kill, at the very least it'll be a nice distraction,' Marcus said, trying to entice his friend into spilling the proverbial beans.

Cyril, however, who was sat opposite the corner which Marcus and Aria were squished into, seemed unwilling to share his tale for some unknown reason. He leant against the crates of what they had generally assumed to be fruits, judging by the market stall-like odour that saturated the carriage, and glanced quickly between his father and McRae. That somewhat abrupt show of unease, from a person so habitually composed, was almost laughable and the longer the moment before he answered stretched out, the more intense the strangeness of it became.

'Perhaps *I* should tell you the story?' Tak-hing said, coming to his son's aid with a wry smile and a short chuckle, that sent his wispy moustache fluttering.

'Ok?' Aria drawled, unsure exactly what she'd just instigated, but committed to hearing its outcome nonetheless.

'Are you both familiar with China's One Child Policy?' the old man asked, his disposition serious.

'Yes?' Marcus and Aria answered in tandem, unsure what relevance it bore.

'Good. That policy is, in essence, what brought my son to England.'

'How? Why?' The two of them questioned insistently.

'You'd better tell them plainly, Tak-hing, or this pair will ask you so many questions you'll want to tear your ear drums out,' Knox interposed with a weary expression.

'For your sake then, Knox, I'll be sure to go into as little detail as possible.' The man of the Orient winked, always glad for the opportunity to make a light joke at McRae's expense. 'Now, I was married once, between 1975 and, let me see.' He paused thoughtfully. '1993, I think. However, it was not a marriage born of love; we were both forced into the predicament by our families.'

'Why were you forced into it, is there some sort of arranged marriage system in China?' Aria interrupted, her proficiency for nosiness eliciting an amused huff from McRae.

'Not quite, but you're close. There was a time, up until the 1950s in fact, when arranged marriage was not only legal in my country, but also common too. Now, although those laws shouldn't have affected me directly, having been abolished some decades before I was wed, they still did. A law can be changed in a day you see, but a culture, and the minds it inhabits, they take far longer to come around,' Tak-hing said, pausing for breath and flicking his eyes around the faces of his rapt audience. 'Even today there is a stigma attached to the age at which one marries. If a man is over twenty-five with no wife, or a woman finds herself over twenty-three with no husband, they are widely regarded amongst their communities as "*leftover people*". It's a terribly disparaging term, and thankfully one that is dying out now, but back in 1975, to be a single man who'd almost reached the ripe age of twenty-six, was not enjoyable.'

'So how does your less than ideal marriage fit in with Cyril coming to England?' Marcus enquired, his own curiosity now on the verge of surpassing Aria's.

'I was not faithful to my wife, I am ashamed to admit, and Cōng-ming is the fruit of a different womb,' he replied plainly, the sincerity of his words striking Marcus and Aria, with enough ardency to challenge their conceptions of him.

For Marcus, the blow was especially keen. The commitment of such a base act by a person he'd previously considered to be the archetypal wise, omniscient and all round benevolent old man, was a gut wrenching thing to accept.

'Right, ok, so you had a baby with your mistress; how does that tie in with the One Child Policy?' Aria probed, pursuing more truths as Marcus swept the debris of Tak-hing's fallen pedestal from his mind.

'I am right here you know?' Cyril said flatly, attempting to remind Aria that he was more than just the product of an illegitimate relationship.

'Bollocks, I'm sorry, Cyril, I didn't mean it like that!'

'You've landed yourself in it now, lass, would you like a shovel, or is the hole already deep enough?' Knox mocked with a gruff laugh.

'Well.' Tak-hing sighed. 'At the time when Cōng-ming was born, I already had a daughter with my wife, despite our loveless relationship and, as I'm sure you can discern from the title of the *One Child Policy*, having two was against the law. So,' he proceeded, holding a short, slender finger up to silence Aria before she could interpose. 'For seven years, I sustained a very precarious balancing act between both families, the details of which aren't important, but the collapse of that situation ultimately led to my son being raised in London.'

'Let me guess, one of the women found about the other? But either way, how did you manage to steal a seven year old boy from his mother *and* ship him to the other side of the world?' pressed Aria, with a wolfish hunger for answers glinting in her ice pond eyes.

'You really are insatiable, aren't you?' Tak-hing said, analysing the girl's appetite to know things before he continued. 'In part you are right, yes. Cōng-ming's mother gave me an ultimatum. I was to leave my wife and daughter behind, in favour of her, or she threatened to expose me to the authorities and have me ejected from the government. I was not prepared to make that choice but– and to call this fortunate would be distasteful but it was certainly *practical* – she was also a severe alcoholic and coincidently, Cōng-ming was taken from her by China's equivalent of your social services, before she had the chance to make good on her promise. I took him to London at the earliest opportunity, and Knox has looked after him ever since. All her accusations fell on deaf ears once there was no child to prove her claims.'

'Bloody hell, talk about heinous. I can't believe you did that?' Aria berated in slack jawed disbelief, her tone making Marcus rouge with embarrassment.

She was, after all, indirectly accusing the Defence Minister of China of being a misogynist; and to his face no less.

'I cannot pardon what I've done, nor will I try, but I do believe that my son has had a better life as a result of my actions,' Tak-hing said placidly, the twin notes of regret and acceptance resonating in his Eastern cadence, as he placed a hand on Cyril's shoulder.

'And how do you feel about it, Cyril?' asked Aria, her voice rife with the heat of challenge, clearly wanting him to rebuke his father's debauchery.

'It is not an easy thing to summarise, but I do not believe a man's character should be judged on one or two actions. In my opinion, he should be defined by his consistencies, not his anomalies,' he replied with scholarly pragmatism. 'There is no dispute to be had in regards to the wrongness of my father's actions, and although I do not agree with infidelity, how he chose to treat *me* is, at least a little redemptive, don't you think? He could have easily disowned me and my mother, or worse, he could have had us killed to cover up the secret. Instead, he provided for both of us, visited me regularly when I was very young, and ultimately saved me from a life spent in lower class Beijing with an alcoholic parent.'

'I suppose from that perspective, the picture's a bit less black and white isn't it?' Aria said, the objectiveness of Cyril's words cooling the lava in her own to form a base of igneous thought, upon which the seeds of new ideas could be sown.

'Very,' he concurred, with an easy smile tickling the lips of his dollish face. 'Black is just one tiny sliver of colour, white its equally minute opposite, and together they only make up a fraction of what we perceive. Now consider how silly it would be to view the world in that limited way, think of all we would miss, when there is a sea of grey between those two poles. That is why the greyness of a person is what they should be assessed on; it is the true colour of life.'

'Very poetic, young man but I'm fairly sure you'll all agree that some things are indeed only black *or* white. Take my soul, for example, a superb example of the former,' Viktor remarked, offering them a brief glance at his jovial side.

'I can't argue with that,' Hugo said, raising his voice mid-sentence, to be heard over the unexpected squealing of the train's brakes.

'Me neither,' seconded McRae with a croaking laugh. 'Now enough of all that, I want to know how we're getting out of here. You obviously bribed the soldiers in St Petersburg to let us on the train, but how are we going to explain our presence to soldiers at *this* end?'

'We're not going to, it's too risky here,' Viktor said matter-of-factly, as though it was obvious.

'What are we going to do then, sneak out of the station?' grumbled Hugo sarcastically, as the train slowed down even more.

'That's exactly what we're going to do, actually.' Viktor grinned invectively, showing his shark like teeth. 'If we can get away from the train, and into the station proper without being seen, we won't have any issues. Dressed like soldiers ourselves we'll be able to move freely around the city too; we just need to get off the platform unnoticed first.'

'And if we get caught?' Marcus questioned, his anxiety creeping out of its dark hole once more.

'Then we use you as bait whilst the rest of us escape,' the Russian leered, his deep blue eyes glowing like moons in the torchlight, their celestial bodies refusing to fall out of the sky; even when the train rocked violently as it came to a complete stop.

With the squeaking of the dusty brakes now dissipating, and the freighter at a standstill, everyone turned to Viktor. Their expectant faces were met, however, with only silence, as the former Colonel General shuffled closer to the door and listened intently.

From beyond the steel walls of the boxcar, a surfeit of noises could be heard now that they were stationary. A variety of claxons and buzzers rang out from different directions, their precise meanings impossible to know, but the mingling of them produced a gelatinous mix of sound that muddied everything else.

Viktor unhooked the latch on the inside of the carriage door and pushed it open marginally, trusting that the unmelodious rabble outside would disguise the creaking of its hinges. Through the brightly lit gap, which was hardly even the width of his face, he scanned the platform to his left at length. Not bothering to voice what he'd seen, the first indication that their path was at least reasonably clear, came when he stuck his entire head out of the boxcar to glance in the opposite direction.

'Right, masks on,' he ordered, as he returned his head and shoulders to the inside of the carriage, closing the door behind him. 'There's three men near the front of the train, and they're heading this way. From what I could see, it looks like they're checking and disinfecting each carriage, which leaves them four more before they get to us.'

'How are we going to get past them?' the prince asked, his prejudiced scepticism of Viktor's answer clear on his face.

'Not past, *around*. This is the only train here, which means the other platforms should be clear of soldiers. So, when the car before the one we're in is being searched, we're going to slip out onto the tracks, and enter the station via the adjacent platform. As the freighter is windowless, it should keep us hidden from view and, providing we're quiet, we shouldn't have any problems.'

'That sounds a bit complex; are you sure you wouldn't rather just run around waving your pistol – I thought that was your answer for everything?' Hugo bantered.

'Very funny. You know, there's still time to tie you to the tracks, Hugo, I wonder how cheeky you'd be then?' Viktor snorted through his mask, making his quick laugh sound like the exhalation of some rampant boar. 'Now, turn that torch off and make sure you have everything you came with. We need to be ready to move.'

Marcus ensured his companions had their belongings before obediently switching off the light and placing it back into his pack. Then the waiting commenced. Nothing seemed to be happening at first, and Marcus began to question Viktor's eyesight; he was in his middle sixties after all. But as the dark interior of the carriage dragged the seconds out into callous minutes, the clomping of booted footsteps, first on concrete and then on metal, became noticeable somewhere to the left of their position.

When the scuffling stomps stopped, Viktor moved to the door once more, eking it open in an attempt to locate the soldiers who were searching the cars. This time though, he did not dither, instead retreating back into the gloom as fast as he'd left it.

'They're only one carriage away now; when you hear the next door open, we go,' he whispered, and even though it was pitch black without the torch, Marcus uselessly nodded his understanding anyway. They didn't have to wait long this time, however, and as the unoiled door to the preceding carriage was prised open with an unyielding metallic grind, Viktor led them out.

Sneaking to their right, they followed his painstaking steps around the corner of the boxcar, and watched with racing hearts, as he slipped down onto the tracks. The reason he'd chosen that point became clear when Marcus realised just how small the space was between the train and the platform edge was; even Cyril, with his nimble predisposition, wouldn't be able to squeeze through it. Conversely, where the carriages were joined, the room in which to manoeuvre was more than doubled.

The Russian moved like a man half his age as he dropped into a crouch and crawled beneath the coupler, placing his hands and feet with fastidious accuracy, to avoid the dusty ballast. Once he emerged on the other side he turned back to the others, still waiting nervously where he'd left them, and beckoned them forwards with his left hand, whilst making a "shushing" gesture with his right.

Tak-hing and Cyril were the first in the line, both of whom followed Viktor's example effortlessly, and joined him as he began to make his away over the track to the adjacent platform. Hugo, in spite of his bulk, also ducked under the coupler without any hinderances, closely shadowed by the gangly, rakish form of McRae. By the time Aria had lowered herself down, Viktor and the others had already reached the other side and were helping one another up from the railway line.

She waited with her arms spread as Marcus passed their bags down to her, which she then rolled under the rusted mechanism that bound boxcars together, before slinking after them herself. Marcus was the last one to venture down onto the tracks and, if he hadn't gotten distracted by Aria banging her head on a protuberant chunk of the locomotive, may have done so without a fuss. As it was though, his lack of concentration caused him to misplace his foot and fall onto the tracks with a resounding twang, as the steel under him vibrated.

The noise was startling, prompting Aria to spin around with wide eyes, and the remainder of the group on the opposing platform to flap their arms in dismay and annoyance. McRae started to pace, looking for any signs of the soldiers rushing to the sound, but in some wildly implausible twist of fate, they appeared not to have heard it.

It was then that Marcus and Aria, still close to the freighter, heard three pairs of heavy footsteps almost directly above them. Staring at each other with tense, frightened eyes, they grasped that the soldiers must've entered the carriage they'd arrived in at the exact time that Marcus had fell, therefore masking the sound. In that knowledge, understanding that all wasn't quite lost, they scrambled the rest of way over the sleepers with the unhuman speed that only fear can provide.

'Christ, lad, do you have to be so fucking dim witted?' Knox reprimanded, as he hauled Marcus up from the tracks.

'I told you he'd be better as bait,' Viktor chided, the curl of his dreadful smile shaping his words under his mask.

'I know, I know, sorry,' Marcus mumbled, as he turned around to offer Aria a hand, only to realise Hugo and Cyril had already flung her up.

'No more mishaps and no more English where we can be overheard. Now come on, we need to get to the Metro,' commanded Viktor, addressing the whole group, but keeping his gaze fixed on Marcus before stalking off towards the exit.

Moscow's Leningradsky Railway Station was an almost identical, if slightly less extravagant, copy of the terminal they had left behind in St Petersburg. The layout became immediately familiar as Viktor, the military leader turned expatriate cicerone, guided them up into its firstly modern and then rustic halls, down a short flight of stone steps to the doors, and then finally out onto the street.

They'd been lucky to have made it away from the freight train without being discovered, and now, dressed as they were in the swamp green attire of the Russian military, they'd be free to roam the city will little interference. Marcus spun briefly to take one last look at the terminal as they absconded it, noting the white face of the clock on the main tower, whose gold plated hands informed him it was roughly 7 AM.

As they were led over two broad, multi-laned roads, separated at their centre by a wedge of leafy trees, well attended lawns and a statue crested monument, Marcus began to see why Viktor had been so eager to secure the uniforms. There were soldiers everywhere, even that early in the day, and what better way to hide than in plain sight?

Marcus gawked at their sheer numbers, his gas mask doing a fine job of disguising his awe-stricken expression as he observed their movements. Although he had no way of knowing what the difference in uniform colouration meant, or what rank the golden emblems worn by certain soldiers denoted, their collaborative purpose was, nonetheless, easy to determine.

They were, for lack of a better term, fortifying the area which, from the smidgen of information Viktor had given them, Marcus knew was a vital part of Moscow's transportation system as it held three of the nine railways stations on its single boulevard. The severity of the heavy military presence, tent like operations centres and temporary armoured ramparts which now peppered the streets around that crucial artery, was disquieting.

Trying to brush his intuitive thoughts under the cognitive rug, Marcus set his eyes forwards, as their small group left the road and approached one of the most colossal buildings he had ever seen. The edifice in question was the Kazansky Railway Station, where several hundred thousand tonnes of masonry had been meticulously carved into an Art Nouveau masterwork, of imperial proportions.

Its multi-faceted archways, assorted roofs and prominent square spire were all incredible displays of construction, and yet, it wasn't any of those features that left the deepest impression on his mind. Nor was it the spectacular sight of the enormous windows, or the way the ivory coloured exterior perfectly reflected the shade of the clouds that day. In fact, the entire memory of the walk to that rice-white station was eclipsed by the sight of a hardnosed, battle worn tank, which came rumbling around the corner to their right.

The appearance of such a machine, with its dark olive, beetle like skin, was both glorious and terrible, and as Marcus stared down the flagitious barrel of its armament all the hidden dust motes of thought that had coagulated beneath the aforementioned mental carpet, broke free. There could be no doubt now that war was indeed coming to Russia, just as Viktor had foretold, and Moscow, it seemed, would be waiting for it with open arms.

Chilled by the outrageously large implications of that notion, Marcus battled with the urge to run for his life, and searched for a distraction as the world suddenly felt far too big, and he became horribly, inconsequentially small by comparison.

Taking one final glance at the tank as they pushed through the polished, wooden doors of Kazansky Station, Marcus found refuge from his mental plight in the stunning design of the ceiling. He knew there were far more ostentatiously modelled stops along Moscow's railway, particularly below ground in the serpentine tunnels of the Metro, but there was something soothing about the simplicity of the hall they were now traversing that he found irresistible in that moment of internal turmoil.

Ignoring the trivial, modern additions to the room, such as the garish arcade games, travel boards and overly lit shopfronts, the long atrium featured a curved roof which had a series of protruding sections set at regular intervals along its length. Walking through that room behind the slender knurl of McRae, with the shining floor underfoot and the huge stone ribs above, Marcus felt like he was being sucked down the gullet of a giant sandstone whale. A feeling that was augmented further when they left the upper floor and descended into the bowels of the city.

The train, rather conveniently, had just arrived as their group emerged from the staircase and onto the platform. As they moved closer, with Viktor still leading the way, Marcus was surprised to see that there were civilians, as well as the now typical array of soldiers, seated within the carriages. All of them were wearing some form of face covering; in some extreme cases Marcus also noticed people donning helmet like visors too; similar to those a welder might use, if slightly less industrial in appearance.

Compared with the black, rubber skinned gas masks that he, and every other military operator they'd encountered were clad in, however, the precautions made by the public seemed somewhat mundane. It was promising though to see the Muscovites going about their days with relative normality and autonomy; unlike the British, who had ground to a painful halt some months ago.

It seemed shameful to him then, that the people of a country with such a catastrophic death toll, in the midst of preparing to fight a war, were still going about their business; whilst the UK put its population on house arrest and waited for the storm to pass. How low had the once mighty empire fallen, he wondered? Had Britain ever truly been *great* at all, or had it always been a nation of cowardice, the flaws of its civilisation buried behind endless tomes of one sided, historical lies?

It was a genuinely profound prospect, but one that he did not have the mental capacity for at that time. Storing it instead for later rumination, he boarded the train with his companions and listened intently to an automated Russian announcement that he had no hope of comprehending.

Some fifteen minutes later, they were eructed out of the Metro's dark tunnels, and into the gleaming galleries of Okhotnyy ryad Station. Leaving the train, they walked through a set of wonderfully crafted marble arches and boarded the escalators which would take them up towards the surface, all the while being mindful to keep their distance from other commuters.

As they reached the upper levels of the station, and Viktor steered them in the direction of the street, Marcus studied the pattern of perfectly square, concave studs which adorned the curvature of the vanilla ceiling. Paired with the black and white chequered floor, which was polished to a high sheen, and the pale stratums of the now perennial marble walls, the building enfolded them in a drapery of monochromatic beauty.

To the architects of Moscow, it appeared that even the creation of something as humble as a Metro stop, could be expounded, and utilised as an opportunity to make the dreary, delightful.

That newfound respect for the edaciously creative minds that had shaped Russia's capital into the superlative feat of artistry that it was, stayed with Marcus as they withdrew from the station. Then, as he caught his first proper glimpse of the city's pulsating, metonymical heart peeking out from the top of the station's exiting stair, that respect began to grow, boil, and then finally explode, transforming it into a blaze of outright admiration.

The trudge of his heavy, booted feet became a light footed skip at the sight of the wonders above, and as Marcus climbed the last of the concrete steps out of the Metro, he was greeted by one of the most tremendous spectacles he'd ever laid eyes on.

Straight ahead of them, the State History Museum rose from its piazza like a mountainous ruby. Its strawberry brickwork was radiant in the bright, albeit sunless day, and the white tips of its accents trickled down the structure like lovingly poured cream. To their left, a behemothic hotel stood, the density of its imposing bulk generating an almost palpable sense of weight and, on their right, was the Kremlin.

The somewhat infamous strategic, economic and political epicentre of Russia hunkered down in middle of Red Square, as a dragon may lay upon on its horde of treasured jewels. It wasn't the tallest building in Moscow – that accolade belonged to the significantly more modern Federation Tower; nor was it the most iconic – Saint Basil's Cathedral surely held that position; but it was perhaps the most crucial. A notion that bled from its rubicund walls and out into the surrounding streets, where it soaked through the ground, imbuing Moscow's very foundations with an inherent feeling of power and pugnacity.

No wonder the soldiers there felt such a sense of nationalism, he thought, as they walked by a huge collection of them who had gathered around a domed monument on the fringe of the Kremlin's gardens. At a pass, they looked to be watching something taking place at the base of it, but the congregation was so deep that Marcus couldn't see a thing through their ranks. Some hardly perceivable instinct, however, alerted him to the fact that it was unlikely to be anything good; an inkling bulwarked by the choleric bleating of the crowd.

The ominous atmosphere became thicker as their cohort moved past the throng, and when a sliver of the events transpiring became visible through a channel of arms and legs, Marcus found out exactly why. The splatter of blood on the cobbles arrested him, and the sight of the man it belonged to lying on the ground stopped him dead in his tracks, even as the rest of his companions strolled on.

Chapter XVII

The body was so limp, so lifeless, that when a boot from a passing solider struck its chest, it wobbled and rippled like water in a bucket. Marcus couldn't take his eyes from the scene; he watched every sinuous twitch of dead muscle as more feet struck out at the wilted form which had, perhaps only moments ago, held the hopes, dreams and soul of a man.

He had no concept of what that man might have been like, good or evil, loving, caring, misogynistic, or hateful, Marcus would never know; but, regardless, he sincerely doubted anyone could deserve such violent desecration.

As the swarming militants jostled to get closer to the dome, which he now noticed was the centrepiece of a fountain, no doubt hungering for blood themselves; their bodies parted, creating new windows through their masses. Those shifting panes of visibility revealed, to Marcus's horror, yet more dead men, and even a few women, lying on the stone floor. He couldn't stand to watch it, nor could he turn away though, and he observed with a growing sense of revulsion, as the Russian soldiers continued their ruthless onslaught.

He had no context of the situation, Marcus told himself, trying to explain away the barbarity taking place before him. But an explanation, even though there had to be one somewhere, could never be equivalent to justification; of which he could find none for such unhuman actions. That thought kindled an anger in him, hot and decisive, which overrode his rationality and forced on him a compulsion to fight.

Disregarding the fact that he could not speak Russian, that he would be drastically outnumbered, and that he may never make it home if his identity were to be discovered, Marcus started to march over the brickwork towards the crowd. Part of his mind screamed at him to be reasonable, to stop and reconsider, but those platitudinous cries could not outweigh the sense of regret he'd feel if he stood idle.

Approaching the outskirts of the crowd, he reached out to grab the first man's shoulder and yank him out of the way, but as he did so Marcus's own arm was almost ripped from its socket by Viktor's vice like claw.

'What are you *doing*?' the Russian growled, bringing his face so close to Marcus's that he could see the network of blood vessels in the older man's azure eyes.

'Putting an end to this madness,' Marcus replied angrily, feeling somewhat incensed to have been stopped.

'You have no idea what you're dealing with, Marcus; forget whatever you've seen, we need to keep going,' insisted Viktor, his voice low as it scraped through his mask.

'Forget it? Those people, those civilians, have been beaten to death by *your* soldiers, and you're condemning *me* for trying to stop it. Are you out of your mind? You should be helping me!' He bristled, unsure of where he was finding the courage to talk to Viktor in such a way.

'You can't save them, you fool, they're already dead, now come on!'

'They might be, but what about those ones?' Marcus said heatedly, pointing over Viktor's shoulder, to where a group of petrified looking people were being shepherded towards the monument through an opening in the mob.

As Viktor twisted his head to follow Marcus's finger though, the faces and shapes of the of the new group became more distinct and, as he was plunged into a vat of acrid despair, as the true nature of the brutal scenario dawned on him. Every single one of those individuals, both those still alive and fighting their captors, and the ones scattered across the crimson ground, were Chinese.

'What the fuck is going on here, Viktor?' asked Marcus, his tone frigid with mounting dread but still smouldering with intense rage. 'Tell me this isn't what it looks like.'

'We need to leave, now!' he responded, refusing to address the question, as the soldiers behind them grew louder and more animated.

'You knew, didn't you?'

'I've had enough of your bullshit, boy.'

'You knew who they were all along and you didn't care, did you?'

'Marcus!'

But the younger man was enraged now and, desperate to intervene, wrestled to regain possession of his arm. Viktor clung onto him though, his impossibly strong grip making Marcus flail like a hooked fish. He fought on nonetheless, and succeeded in pushing the former general back a few paces, which is when he saw that the people had been forced to their knees before the rim of dome. When several rifles were then raised in their direction, and the Chinese civilians were ordered to put their hands on their heads, the nauseating realisation that he was about to witness a public execution drove Marcus to launch his fist into Viktor's gut.

Crumpling slightly, the older man emitted a hoarse grunt as the air left his lungs and the shock of the blow loosened his grip on Marcus's arm; allowing him to slip away. He scrambled past Viktor, barrelling into the back of the soldier obstructing his path and knocking him to the floor, just in time to see the head of the closest woman explode into a cloud of gore.

The sound was deafening, the smell of gunpowder putrid, and the sight of it all was beyond appalling. Seven Chinese men and women who, up until ten seconds ago had been living, breathing workers, family members and loved ones, now lay cold and dead in Moscow's Red Square.

Watching them die had rendered Marcus entirely useless in the moment, and far worse than that, it had obliterated his innocence. The exhalations of their last breath had extinguished the fires of hope burning in his chest and, without the fury to fuel him, his taut body softened to mush as he glared out at the human mess in front of him.

Before he could sag to his knees in delirium, however, he was snatched from behind by Viktor, who all but dragged Marcus away from the gruesome tableau and off towards a side street; where the remainder of their companions were waiting.

'What the hell happened over there?' McRae asked, concern resonating in his Scottish burr, as Viktor released Marcus from his grip and hurled him into the folds of the cohort.

'Your *apprentice* fancied himself a hero, that's what happened. What did I tell you about bringing children into this, Knox, ah?' Viktor snarled; frustration written in every creased wrinkle that was still on display through the lenses of his mask.

'What are you talking about? I was trying to save those people ... those innocent people who were being murdered in cold blood, whilst you were content to walk on by as if nothing was happening. Were you hoping that none of us would notice?' Marcus retorted, suddenly exhausted, but unwilling to let the injustice of what he'd seen go untold. 'It doesn't matter now anyway because I *did* notice, I saw everything.'

'What's he talking about, Viktor, is that what those shots were?' Hugo said, with a shade of disbelief colouring his voice.

'He doesn't know what he's talking about, that's the problem.'

'You're a liar!' said Marcus, the resurgence of his anger causing his voice to rise. 'Go on, tell them. Let everyone know that your soldiers are rounding up Chinese civilians like pigs to the slaughter, and fucking lobotomising them as though it were some sort of sick game. It's fairly obvious now that China and Russia are at war, but that doesn't mean you can cull the entire race based on the decisions of its leaders ... You massacring, Fascist, piece of shit!'

'Why are you accusing me of making those orders? Do you really think I agree with what you just saw?' Viktor fired back, changing tack, and taking Marcus by surprise when he didn't rise to the insult.

'Well, you didn't help them, and you stopped me from trying too?'

'And did you ever, once, slow down to consider why I did that?' the Russian said, punctuating his words by repeatedly thrusting a finger into Marcus's chest, until he had him backed against the cold stone of the building behind him. 'No, you didn't, you were too busy wallowing in your emotions to even think that I might have been doing it to protect *you*.'

'That doesn't make any sense,' Marcus replied, his bewilderment at such a notion making his voice quiver.

'Do you have any idea what they would've done to you if you'd rushed in there to defend them?' He paused, waiting to see if Marcus would respond. 'No? Well, let me explain to you then, that if I'd let you run into that mob, they would've beaten you to nothing with the others, and you'd be little more than stain by now, you *Glupyy mal'chik.*'

'But ...'

'No fucking buts this time! You think because I'm Russian, and because I have a history with the military, that I must think and feel what every other solider in the nation does? I do not condone what they've done, and should I get the opportunity to do something about it, they will be *dealt with.* But you.' He shook his head angrily. 'You criticise me and my *race*, for damning the entirety of another based on the behaviour of a few, and yet you've lumped me together with all those murderous bastards? Quite the hypocrite, aren't you?' Viktor scorned, the acid in his voice like white hot flames.

'How was I to–'

'Not another word, you fucking child,' spat Viktor, as he stepped towards Marcus, leaving only a few inches between their faces. 'That little cushy bubble you live in, in the British countryside – oh yes, Knox told me all about that – that's not the real world, Marcus, *this is,*' he said, gesturing to the surrounding streets. 'I don't know what you were hoping to find when you left home, but what you've stumbled upon is the true nature of things. We inhabit an endless cycle of contradictions, war and loss. It is happening all across the globe, in a thousand communities, a million struggles are taking place right now and not one of them will end well. So, listen to me now, life is not fair, life is not just, and life is not good. Don't delude yourself with thoughts of grandeur, just pray that death is easier than this.'

Marcus wished then, as the feelings of shame and denigration came to claim him with their awful hands, that the street would split and swallow him whole. Viktor's diatribe had exposed in him every unvirtuous quality he thought he possessed, and to be castigated so perfectly in front of everyone else, made Marcus want to evaporate.

'I think you've made your point,' Knox said with a hint of constrained irritation, as he broke the silence which had fallen in the wake of Viktor's reprimanding words.

'Indeed.' He sighed in reply, the gas mask warping the sound. 'The sooner you're gone the better.'

'I couldn't agree more, but go easy on the lad, will you? He was obviously trying to do the right thing for the poor buggers,' the old artist implored, defending Marcus's motives.

'There's nothing noble about a failed martyrdom, Knox, you know that as well as I do,' Viktor rebutted; his opinion unmoving.

'Christ, and what would you have done in his position?' the Scotsman argued back.

'That is irrelevant! He made an uninformed, misguided, reckless decision that nearly got us both stranded in a very deep pile of shit.'

'He's not a bloody soldier, Viktor!'

'Which is exactly why he shouldn't be here!' the Russian practically shouted through his clenched jaw, the noise becoming shrill, as he and his old friend traded shots.

They stared at one another then, long and hard, and panted lightly, like two stags sizing up their opposition before locking horns. Neither one of them blinked, or moved, refusing to concede to the other's dominance; and the resulting stalemate slowed the passage of time to a miserly crawl.

Marcus glanced from one grizzled man to the other, hoping one of them would submit, as the pressure mounting in the space between them became dense enough to cut, and hot enough to boil. As the hostility swelled, and the probability of either of them acquiescing to the other's whims became virtually naught, he edged away along the wall. However, just when it seemed as though the impasse might indeed stretch on for eternity, the ever ratiocinating voice of Tak-hing ended their soundless quarrel with the introduction of a more serious matter.

'Gentlemen, we appear to have garnered some attention,' the elderly man said coolly, motioning discreetly to a group of soldiers on the other pavement.

'From where?' asked Viktor seriously, pulling his eyes away from Knox's with an almost audible rip.

'Over the road, there's only three of them but I think they've noticed our *unusual* behaviour,' Tak-hing said.

'Let's leave this place then, my apartment isn't far from here, we can gather ourselves there and discuss how best to get you out of here. I only hope the events in Sweden haven't thrown a spanner in the works.'

'We'll have to see, I suppose,' the prince huffed. 'I need to try to contact my father and find out what happened with the En Röst when we left.'

'You can do that from my home. I'm hoping he's regained control of the situation; that way we can go along with our original plan. Now move it, we're going right out of here,' their guide said, stepping back towards the main road which ran past the bastion walls of the Kremlin.

'And how, exactly, are we getting home?' Aria questioned irksomely, the confounding experiences of Moscow so far and the upbraiding of her closest friend, beginning to trigger her irascibility.

'Viktor has a small aircraft which we intend to travel back to Stockholm in. After refuelling there, Hugo will fly the four of us back to England. I know of a secluded aircraft graveyard in the Midlands, before you go asking me questions about where we're landing. Then he'll return home to Sweden,' McRae explained quickly, his voice low, as they moved down the street.

'Four of us? What about you, Tak-hing?' the dark haired girl asked, as she turned to watch him pass beneath a streetlamp.

'I am to stay in Moscow with Viktor. There's no way I can return home now, and from here I can aid Russia in holding off the Chinese assault,' he responded with sobriety.

'It's all hinging on my father then really, and whether or not we can safely re-enter Sweden,' concluded Hugo.

'Aye, I suppose it is,' McRae remarked, looking to another band of soldiers who appeared to be watching them from across the road. 'Now, I feel like we should probably shut up before we draw any more attention to ourselves. The more blabbing we do in English, the more suspicious we look.'

'That's the first good idea you've had since I met you in Sweden,' Viktor said, his accented tone too grave for the statement to be considered a joke. 'Let's keep moving then, and remember, no stopping this time.'

Marcus knew the words were for him, and each of them stung his pride like a hot poker branding flesh. He was still shaken by what he'd seen at the domed fountain and his mind replayed the events incessantly as he walked; like a film reel of blood-spattered slides shown in an endless, recurring loop. The vividness of those images was so poignant that Marcus scarcely noticed the city passing by, as he dragged his feet along behind the bulky slab of Hugo's muscled back.

Countless structures of barely fathomable size and beauty came and went as Viktor proceeded to lead them through the capital's centre, but Marcus's disenchantment with life at large made them appear banal now. There wasn't a cornice pretty enough, an oculus of sufficient elegance, or a pediment so ravishing that it could wake him from his stupor; and the further they went, the more severe it became.

Maybe it was the shock of witnessing first hand, the wanton, life ending cruelty wrought by that pack of rogue soldiers which was chilling him? After all, Marcus thought, as he splayed and then retracted his clammy hands, the thought of ever seeing such an abysmal event taking place in front of him was hardly conceivable. Yet, it had happened of course, the replayed image of it still pummelled his senses relentlessly, refusing to let him disengage from that very fact.

However, there was more too, contributing to the emotional frost that had started to ensconce him. The killing itself, despite the indelibly terrible motives behind it, did not trouble Marcus anywhere near as much as his guilt did. He knew that he could not hold himself culpable for the assassinations, but that scrap of rationality still couldn't stop him from blaming himself for not doing more to prevent them.

He toiled over that issue for the next couple of blocks as they marched on, continuing to head down Mokhovaya Street, until they arrived at another one of the city's complicated, vehicular intersections. He didn't pay much attention to the passing cars, or army transports that sped around the sweeping bend to their left. Nor did he acknowledge any of the commuters or military personnel, as their cohort crossed the road and moved onto Ulitsa Volkhonka. Instead, Marcus kept his gaze pinned firmly on his feet, watching each marked, black boot stride out before the other with an odd sense of detachment.

So often one likes to picture oneself as a complete product, like a Rubik's cube with each of its six sides showing a perfectly uniform plane of colour. All it takes, however, is a single intellection altering experience to expose the hubris that allows the formulation of such views, and to therefore reveal that there is indeed still a splodge of orange in the blue; or a dash of red in the green. Once that realisation takes place, it cannot be undone, and so a person has no choice but to rearrange one's cube to accommodate the abnormality.

For Marcus, the influx of perception bending information had been prolific since he'd left the UK, and he struggled to keep up with the demands the world made of him to understand it all. His cube was still whirring around, the failure to readjust himself quick enough before the next hit only prolonged the growing pains, which in turn brought about a renewed mood of inadequacy.

What had Aria said to him when they'd been sat on that bench by the river? "You're just an artist and I sell insurance policies," she'd told him, "we're just ordinary people."

She'd been right, of course, as she so often was, and now they were two ordinary people out of place and out of their depth, three thousand leagues beneath a sea of violence, politics and global unrest.

Peeling his eyes away from his leather clad feet, Marcus glanced up then, looking at Aria as she walked alongside him. Her slightly too large uniform flapped around her small waist, and a wayward curl of her brunette hair had fallen from her helmet, which shook a little bit every time her boot hit the pavement. He wondered how she felt and questioned whether she, too, might be transforming in light of what they'd been through.

Feeling his eyes on her, Aria returned his gaze, and the two of them unknowingly gravitated towards one another until their elbows were almost brushing. The closeness of her melted some of the coldness he felt, allowing Marcus to shake off a portion of his emotional inertia. Neither of them dared speak out loud, concerned that being overheard would attract unwanted attention, but their nearness gave them both a source of strength to cling to. He inhaled deeply, which sounded like the sucking of a vacuum cleaner through his mask, to cleanse his mind of worry and watched as a series of golden domes appeared above the buildings behind Aria.

There was something indistinctly hopeful about the shining of those onion shaped baubles, and an almost metaphorical beauty to the timeliness of their manifestation. When the structure upon which they sat came into full view, Marcus felt more of his glacial sheath begin to dissipate.

The Cathedral of Christ the Saviour stood pristine on the bank of the Moskva river, its walls the colour of soft daisy petals, were bright enough to cause him to squint; but he refused to turn away. Marcus committed as much of that scene to memory as he could, before Viktor steered them right down the next road, taking them away from the river and towards the peripheral areas of the Arbat District.

Marcus couldn't help but chuckle dourly to himself then, as he saw just how fickle his own mind was. One moment, he was belaboured by the perceived guilt of letting people die, the next, he found inspiration in petty glittering stone and the closeness of someone he cared for. His passions swung like a kite in an unpredictable wind, taking him from heart-breaking lows to unreachable highs and back again faster than a human eye could blink; and always the catalyst was something external.

What a ridiculous concept it was, he pondered, to be constantly at the mercy of something so much larger than oneself. Life, it seemed, was quite the game. One where the universe is a constant and inexhaustible opponent, a rival whose reach and power extended far beyond the human, and whose plays could unstitch and re-hem the tapestry of existence with ease. So, did one ever really have a choice? Or was the course of one's life merely a series of reactions, a sequence of move matching, until the passage of time and the flow of matter eventually arrived at some preordained terminus?

He didn't have time to deliberate over the answer, as he was pulled from his sojourn down that fatalistic worm hole, by the collision of his face and Hugo's wide back. Marcus's nose was scrunched against his face at an awkward angle in the process, making his apology to Hugo sound like the nasal ring of a supermarket cashier. The prince, although briefly surprised, waved off the appeasing statement, and raised his chin into the air to examine the building that Viktor had stopped them outside of.

It was a five-storey apartment block with an ornately styled exterior, built on the corner of a fairly busy offshoot of the main road. In comparison to the much uglier residential towers around it, which were clearly erected in the vein of socialist classicism, the sandy colour stonework of Viktor's home was actually quite impressive.

Their guide, still refusing to speak in spite of the emptiness of the neighbouring streets, made his way into the portico and entered a code on the panel by the door. It was an oddly modern thing to see attached to such an old building, and the apposition of dated architecture and contemporary technologies only increased when the buzzer hummed, allowing them entry.

Viktor grabbed the thick, brass handle on the wooden door and opened it, making its considerable heft appear insubstantial as he sauntered in. Knox followed him, holding the door for Tak-hing and Cyril, who in turn kept it open for the rest of them before closing it. As the door clicked into place, reconnecting the magnetic locks built into its frame, Marcus cast his eyes around the mahogany and marble foyer, watching Viktor as he began to ascend a set of stairs with embellished, bronze coloured spindles and florets carved into its handrail.

By the time they'd reached the fourth floor, which was where Viktor's apartment was located, Marcus had deduced that the former Colonel General must be rather wealthy. The sumptuously piled carpet that was swallowing both his, and the rest of his companions' feet as they waited for the Muscovite to open his front door, was just one of many indicators that supported that fact.

Once inside, Viktor shut them in, ripped the gas mask from his face and let out a long, lung filling sigh as he proceeded into the gigantic open plan living space.

'I hate these things,' he said, throwing the mask onto a chocolatey leather armchair that looked more like a seat to rule an empire from, than a place to read a book or watch television. 'It's good to be home.'

'I'll bet it is,' McRae scoffed, taking in the luxury of the room as he removed his own mask. 'I think someone's been paying you too much.'

'It's only a *small* upgrade from my apartment in the suburbs, and besides, you're one to talk! I've seen how much your crappy paintings sell for, Knox, you're hardly a pauper,' Viktor reprimanded with a sly curl of his lip, prompting another balk from the Scotsman, who, along with Tak-hing, had positioned himself on a tan couch near the far window.

The rest of them also took off and discarded their masks then, placing them in a neat line in order to remember which one belonged to whom, on one of the kitchen's expansive marble worktops. Depositing his rubbery gas mask next to Marcus's, Cyril made his light footed way around the pillar which propped up the ceiling between the kitchen and living areas, to take a seat near McRae in another of the fudge coloured armchairs. Meanwhile, Aria and Marcus, who were both rather sheepish, examined the peculiarly opulent home of the former Colonel General, as the man himself rummaged through his cherry wood furniture in search of something.

Viktor crossed the living room several times, checking two sideboards, one of which had a fantastic crystal decanter and tumbler set resting atop it, a score of cupboards, several of them having decorative glass doors, and let out a groan of frustration when he realised none of them held what he was looking for. Closing the low cabinet he'd just sifted through, Viktor stood up and paced a rectangle around the florally patterned rug, a contemplative expression bedecking his rough face. Quite obviously lost in thought, he began to rub his chin quite harshly, slowly reddening it as he patrolled the room.

None of them made a sound whilst Viktor scoured through his memory for the location of whatever it was he was so eager to find; instead, they simply watched him. Or, in the case of Marcus, Aria and Hugo, who were still stood in the kitchen for fear of disrupting the Russian's intense thought process, explored the apartment with their eyes.

The majority of the walls were adorned with at least one oil painting, all of them presented in chunky, gilt frames. On their right side, Marcus noticed a hallway that led to another room, the entrance of which was tucked away beside a polished, wooden drinks cabinet, which contained an extensive collection of whisky and vodka. To their left, behind the seat which Viktor had thrown his mask onto, was a dining table with six chairs, lit from above by an intricately designed, filigree chandelier and beyond that, was another spot-lit corridor which housed two more doors.

Marcus realised then that the reason they'd only seen one entrance on the fourth floor, was because Viktor owned the entire thing. That fact made him consider Knox's comment, and although he had no clue as to how much housing cost in Moscow, especially that close to the city centre, he wagered it would be an eye watering amount.

For Viktor to live in such luxury and still possess such a dark outlook seemed strange to Marcus. Of course, he had served nearly forty years in the military and one could only imagine the evils he would've seen, but still, something didn't quite add up and Marcus was struck with a sudden, burning desire to find the missing link.

At the same time that Marcus was trying to extricate the strands of Viktor's personality, the former Colonel himself, appeared to have finally remembered where he'd left the elusive item he'd been trying to find. Still with a degree of uncertainty in his expression, but moving with decisiveness nonetheless, Viktor strode past the kitchen and disappeared into the room by the drinks cabinet. When he came back, after a short period of banging and hushed expletives, their host had in his hands an antediluvian communications radio.

'Finally!' he said, the exultation undisguised in his gruff voice, as he showed the object to the group. 'Now we can contact your father, Hugo.'

'With that?' the prince replied, sounding astonished. 'It must be older than you.'

'And what does that have to do with whether or not it works, ah? All your fancy modern technology is rubbish. It's unreliable, it's easy to trace and it's confusing, but this–' Viktor said ogling the greyish box, with its many dials and knobs, as though it were a priceless artefact. 'This has never let me down. Why do you think your father still uses one?'

'Does he?'

'Actually, we all do,' Tak-hing admitted, a droll smile tickling his thin lips, giving the impression that he'd just revealed an untellable scandal.

'Well, the more you know,' Hugo responded, twiddling a curl of his beard as he conjured up images of the four older men talking and joking like dinosaurs from a bygone era. The thought made him laugh.

'Aye, lad, every day's a school day, as the saying goes,' McRae added, chuckling himself, before placing his hands on his knobbly knees and getting to his feet. 'Right then, shall we make this call, Viktor?'

'Yes, come with me to the library, you too Hugo, we'll transmit better by the balcony,' he told them, turning to head back towards the door nearest the kitchen. 'Tak-hing, will you be joining us? I'm sure Oliver will be keen to hear your version of events,' said Viktor, pausing briefly as he waited for his elderly friend to rise.

'Certainly, I'm interested to hear what happened in Sweden after our unexpected departure,' remarked Tak-hing, with genuine curiosity in his soft voice.

As the four of them departed the living room and entered what had been revealed as the library, Marcus and Aria looked first to each other, and then to Cyril, finding the same expression of dissatisfaction knotting the others' features.

'Anyone else feel like an afterthought?' Marcus grumbled, showing a kind of amused disappointment not to be included in the radio call to King Oliver.

'Yeah, you could say that,' Aria agreed, folding her arms moodily.

'On the plus side, at least now we will have a chance to be nosey,' said Cyril, with an opportunist's shrug and a mischievous grin.

'Cyril! I'm shocked.' Aria giggled, making gestures of mock indignation, clearly very pleased to see him suggest that he might be willing to veer away from the straight and narrow.

'Yeah, and me. I guess it really is the quiet ones you need to keep an eye on, isn't it?' added Marcus as a smile lit up his face. 'Where shall we start?'

But Aria had already commenced her scrutiny of the paintings and study of the ornaments, looking for clues that might unearth the origins of Viktor's quarrelsome character. Cyril too had begun his search, the adventurous part of his mind clearly taking control, and persuading the more obsequious faction to go along for the ride.

Marcus remained in the kitchen, appraising the items and utensils which, in spite of the dust gathered on them from lack of use, were organised neatly. Every so often though, he found himself glancing towards the other corridor with its alluring, secret concealing doors, but he disregarded his temptations; knowing that if Viktor caught him snooping through his home without permission, he was liable to kill him on the spot.

Thankfully, however, there were still things to be learned where he was, and as Marcus ran his fingers over the engraved motifs in the cupboard doors, and observed the profusion of floriated designs on the china cups, he realised just how feminine it all was. Rotating to face the living area again, with his newly adjusted sight, he picked up more and more of those distinctly female stylistic features, which were now evident throughout. The colour of the tablecloth with its crocheted edges, the flower like doilies under the decanter, even the smoothness of the paintings all clashed with Viktor's surly, ruler straight masculinity. But what did that mean?

'Marcus, Cyril, I think I've found something,' Aria whispered loudly and ambiguously, her voice carrying a degree of uncertainty. 'You won't believe this.'

'I think I might,' replied Marcus, starting to piece the evidence together.

'Check this out,' she said, turning away from the sideboard where she was standing, and offering them both a look at the framed photograph she was holding. Marcus and Cyril peered down at the aged picture, its slightly hazy, yellow tinge making the image difficult to see, but there was still no mistaking what it was.

'You do not think that is–' Cyril began.

'Viktor's wife, it has to be! I knew it, look at all the feminine touches around the place, there's no way he would've chosen this stuff by himself,' Marcus interrupted loquaciously.

'I think you're right, Christ, he's even smiling in the picture,' Aria joked.

'Where is she now though I wonder … Where did you find this, Aria?' asked Cyril thoughtfully.

'Over here, by this little clay jar,' she answered, moving out of the way so the two of them could see it. 'Wait though, it feels like there's something etched on the back of it,' Aria said, as she flipped the golden frame over and examined the insert on its rear.

'Let's have a look,' Marcus said as he came to her side, greedy to know more.

'It looks like writing but it's all in Russian, I can't read it.'

'May I see?' queried Cyril as he reached for the picture. Aria passed it to him without question, looking to him enthusiastically as he studied the writing with his intense, black eyes.

'This is a name, look,' he told them, turning the rectangular image back to his friends. 'Annika Stefanovich, and here, I think these two lines are dates.'

'What do they say?' Marcus enquired, utterly entranced by the discovery.

'The first one says March seventh, 1963 and the second says …' He hesitated, confusion registering on his face. 'June twenty-third this year.'

'That's only two months ago though, surely that can't mean what I think it does?' Aria said, wanting to dissever her opinion from the facts.

'I think it does, Ari, I think she's dead and judging by the second date, I'd go as far as to presume it was the virus that killed her,' Marcus remarked earnestly, flicking his eyes to the jar where Aria had found the photo, grasping then that it was most likely an urn.

'Fuck, no wonder he's such an arse all the time, that's bloody awful. The poor bastard.' Aria breathed, the recurrent swearing, Marcus knew, was her inimitable way of showing the depth of the grief she felt for Viktor.

'That is terrible, I understand now why he is such a bitter man, I think I would be too after such a loss,' said Cyril quietly.

Marcus said nothing, choosing instead to contemplate the woeful revelation privately. Sadly, there was little time to truly mull over that new knowledge, and its many implications, as the door behind them was thrown open unexpectedly. The three of them flinched in surprise at the sound of their older companions returning, and as Cyril quickly placed the frame back onto the sideboard, Marcus and Aria separated, doing their best not to look suspicious. Something which apparently, none of them were particularly good at.

'Why do you three miscreants look so shifty?' Viktor asked, his face like a saw blade.

'It doesn't matter!' McRae said, brushing the comment off with his oddly delighted tone. 'We have good news at last: it looks like we're going to make it home after all.'

'What, when?' Marcus asked, his own voice imbued with relief.

'Tomorrow.'

Chapter XVIII

Coltish pink light streamed in through the tall windows of the apartment, infusing the living room with a syrupy, candy floss glow. It was a colour seldom seen, one that the cosmos reserved only for that exceptional moment when dawn becomes day, and Marcus took great pleasure from basking in the warmth of those shining, thulian beams as he tucked into his breakfast.

He was sat alone at the head of the long dining table, watching the sun hunt and consume the last of the straggling, mulberry shadows outside, as he himself munched his way through a mountain of scrambled eggs.

Denounced as unworthy of consumption by everyone else as a result of their questionable age, they were, after all, coming up to being four weeks old, all eight of the eggs had found themselves on Marcus's plate. However, aside from the infrequent appearance of a greenish yolk and, according to Aria's hound like sense of smell, an odour akin to that of a "wet dog's fart", Marcus could see no issues with them; and he gobbled them down accordingly.

The rest of his companions had opted for a safer alternative of dry crackers and hard cheese, which were the last remnants of the grocery shop that Viktor had undertaken a month prior, before he'd left to meet King Oliver in Stockholm. Driven away by the malicious stink of Marcus's meal, they had taken up seats on the sofa and armchairs furthest away from him, quite blatantly hoping the open window would diffuse some of its potency.

As Marcus came to the bottom of his eggy hillock, feeling far fuller than he was willing to admit – he did have a reputation of insatiability to uphold after all – he slid his chair back with a creak and rose to take his plate to the sink. After depositing it next to a pan, he returned to the living room to collect the tableware from his companions. Manoeuvring around the circle of his friends, Marcus stacked the plates on top of one another as he went; until he'd created a somewhat perilous pile of wobbling crockery.

Rattling with each step, he headed back towards the kitchen with a look of concentration ruffling his eyebrows, as he reached out to take the cheese knife from Cyril on his way past. Acting of its own volition, his tongue poked out of the corner of his mouth as he balanced the plates in one hand and extended the other, but just as he clasped the handle, a burst of static from Viktor's radio startled him. Shocked by the abruptness of the noise, Marcus's arm jerked slightly, sending the knife hurtling into the air.

Hampered as he was by his ceramic load, Marcus knew that there was no hope of him catching it, and although dropping a single piece of cutlery would be frivolous in any other context, he was loath to make another wrong move in front of Viktor; no matter how trivial. Fortunately, as the blade started its descent, sending glimmering rays of amaranth light bouncing off its serrated edge, a deft hand shot out to filch it from the air.

Moving with all the dexterity and speed of a hummingbird in flight, Cyril had captured the knife between his thumb and forefinger, rescuing Marcus from the inevitable reprehension he would've suffered, if it had indeed clattered to the floor. Knowing he had been saved, he sagged with relief as Cyril, wearing an infantilely triumphant smile, gently put the knife on the top of the plates in his hand. Mouthing a silent thank you to his saviour, Marcus rushed in the direction of the sink once again, loading the items into the washing up bowl before any more of them had a chance to escape.

Viktor, for his part, was so engrossed in the tuning of his timeworn radio, that he'd remained oblivious to the entire debacle; even as Knox and Tak-hing had sniggered quietly to each other. The sound of their chuckling had most likely been drowned out by the white noise which was being emitted from the single, circular speaker in the upper right corner of the radio's bland surface. Despite Viktor's best efforts to find a suitable station though, the unpleasant noise persisted, rising to an ostentatious volume, even as he frantically spun dials and twisted switches.

'I thought your prehistoric brick was supposed to be bullet proof, Viktor?' the prince jibed, raising his voice above the crackling din. 'Or is that just the sound they make when they finally die?'

'It's *fine*, alright. She just needs a moment to warm up in the morning, that's all,' Viktor replied, his tone genial and warm, as he personified his cherished possession.

'Mine's never done that,' Knox said bumptiously, running a hand through his wild hair.

'There's nothing wrong with it, ok? She just needs a firm hand!' said Viktor, doing a terrible job of concealing the frustration he felt at McRae's comment, as he brought his fist down on top of the radio.

'Well, that went well for you.' Knox laughed when nothing happened.

'The third time is the charm, my friend, watch this,' Viktor said confidently, this time slamming the palm of his hand onto the machine. The first strike did nothing, but the second, which was so hard that Aria and Hugo winced at the force of it, miraculously transformed the static into a symphony of classical violins.

'A lucky coincidence, nothing more,' the Scotsman balked, dismissing the switch to the harmonious notes as a fluke.

'To be honest, Knox, I don't care what's playing anyway, as long as it is so loud that it stops me from hearing *you*,' Viktor responded, a satisfied grin spreading across the stony features of his face, as he resumed his seat in the largest of the armchairs. 'Hey, servant boy, bring that pot of coffee over here, will you? I need something to wash my victory down with.'

Marcus, who had finished washing the breakfast items and was now drying his hands on a tea towel embroidered with roses, looked to the tray on the worktop nervously. There was, of course, nothing inherently scary about a tray of mugs and a coffee pot, but the mistrust of his own ability to walk across the apartment without spilling anything certainly did incite his anxieties.

Nevertheless, Marcus grabbed the wooden platter by its thick, ridged handles, and made his way back towards his reclining cohort in the living room. By the time he'd crossed the threshold, however, an intense expression of attentiveness had wrinkled his face so thoroughly, that Marcus resembled an equatorial landscape in drought. Setting the tray down on the low table in the centre of them, he let out a sigh and uncrumpled his face, feeling the tension ease around his temples as he did so.

'It's nice to see that you can take orders after all!' Viktor teased, his tone sarcastic, as he portrayed a look of exaggerated amazement.

'Turns out it's a lot easier when the only thing at stake is someone's thirst.' Marcus shrugged as he sat down beside Cyril, already regretting his cheeky retaliation.

'Anyway,' Aria cut in quickly, doing her utmost to interfere with the reignition of the previous day's feud. 'What did King Oliver have to say yesterday – you never told us the full the story?'

'Well, from what I gather,' Hugo began. 'The En Röst have more or less collapsed now. After seeing the carnage they'd left in the streets around the Diamant, and noticing our quite obvious disappearance, my father pulled the surveillance footage from the hotel's security cameras and watched the whole thing back. Then, once he realised that they'd tried to kill us, before essentially running us out of the country, he had them publicly labelled as a terrorist group.'

'Which means?' Aria chimed in, willing Hugo to get to the point.

'Which means, that almost everyone associated with them is now in custody and the other, less extreme supporters have cut their ties. Basically, there is no *En Röst*. So, for the moment at least, it's safe to return,' the prince concluded, at last supplying Aria with the facts for which she yearned.

'And what's more,' McRae interpolated, 'is that because Oliver has detained them, he's also managed to restrict the flow of false news they were spreading using the pictures of us. Let's just hope the ones that were already circulating don't make it back to the UK before we do.'

'So even after all that, we've still pretty much come out on top,' Marcus said, with a whiff of gloating in his tone, as one side of his mouth folded itself into a smile.

'Not entirely,' said Hugo reservedly.

'How so?' asked Marcus, his smile turning downwards into a quizzical look.

'I'm sure you remember my sister, Lilly, the one who greeted us on the first night we arrived at the Diamant? Well, she's been involved in a car accident and by the sounds of it, she's lucky to be alive.'

'When?' Aria pressed unsympathetically, remembering the surreptitious meeting she'd witnessed between the princess and the two disreputable looking men, the day before they'd left.

'The same night we escaped from the hotel. They found her unconscious on one of the bridges, near a set of long skid marks, hence why they think she was hit by a car,' the prince responded, his voice becoming worrisome as he recounted what his father had told him.

'And you still don't think she has any connection with the En Röst? Honestly, lad, even you must see how suspicious it looks? What would she have been doing outside?' the old artist chided, still striving to convince Hugo that his sister was indeed the instigator of the attack.

'Why must you always portray her as the villain? What if she was out there fighting against them, trying to help us to escape, did you ever consider that?' the Swede countered.

'Come off it, you can't make excuses for her forever! I'm sure you'll see her *valiant* attempt to save us when you get back to Stockholm, and check the footage of that night yourself?' Knox rebuked sardonically, the implication that no such event had ever taken place, written evidently in his tone and mannerisms.

'It's unlikely that there'll be any recordings to see, the surveillance cameras only cover part of the bridges, not their entire length,' Hugo said puerilely, his muscular stature and dense beard clashing with the immaturity of his voice, making him appear as a caricature.

'Of course they don't, that's bloody convenient isn't it, lad?' McRae huffed with an overstated roll of his jade green eyes. 'I'll take it up with your father then, the next time I get the chance,' he finished, finally dropping the argument.

'I guess a lot has changed in the past few days then. At least those lunatics are off the streets now though,' Marcus added, looking to extract at least some positivity from Hugo's account.

'Very true,' the prince agreed, but the wind was gone from his sails, and the conversation died in the wake of his laconic reply.

The sounds of the classical music, still playing through the radio's speakers, prevented the situation from becoming awkward, but Marcus still cast his eyes downwards to study the contents of his mug as he thought of something else to say. His frenetic search for a new course of dialogue wasn't necessary, however, as Aria, whose plainspokenness bordered on cutthroat, was already on the case.

'So, when are leaving then?' Aria said curtly, her impatience to get home making her voice much harsher than she'd intended it to be.

'If the slave child has washed the dishes and completed his chores, we can go now,' Viktor said, unable to refuse another opportunity to debase Marcus. 'My plane is stored at a private airfield just outside the city; it's about an hour's drive.'

'And how are we going to—' Aria began, only to snap her mouth shut again as a sudden spurt of fizzing, angry static from the radio made her jump.

'I thought you'd sorted that out?' Knox shouted, struggling to make his voice heard above the strident squeal of an alarm that was now ripping out of the speaker.

'Quiet!' Viktor roared, the look in his eyes making it clear to all of them, that the time for joking was over.

Unnerved by the terrible noise, and disturbed by Viktor's flippant change in attitude, each of them glanced nervously from their host, to the radio, and back again. Eventually the siren cut out, just as abruptly as it had started, and was replaced by the stern orations of a deep, male voice. His words were clear, his annunciation crisp, but they were still in Russian, which meant that despite their best efforts to glean understanding from those disembodied intonations; they were still none the wiser.

With that being said, all they needed to do to grasp the meaning of the bulletin, was look to Viktor, whose eyelids were rapidly retreating into his skull with shock. With each word his face remoulded itself, becoming more ashen, more flummoxed and more irate as the dithyrambic speech went on. By the time it had ended, Viktor's face had disappeared behind a spectral veil of hate and disbelief that was so unsettling that Marcus looked away. Before any of them had the chance to ask what had been said though, his otherworldly lips parted to speak.

'They're here,' he whispered, just as an earth shattering explosion rang out in the distance, shaking the building to its very foundations.

'What are you talking about, Viktor, who's here?' Knox asked briskly, his voice agitated.

'The Chinese,' he answered flatly, as more blasts resonated around them.

Tak-hing sighed quietly at the news, and pinched the bridge of his nose with his hand, as an expression of agonising dismay enveloped his features like a raincloud eclipsing the sun.

'Surely, they wouldn't be brazen enough to attack *Moscow* though, not directly?' Hugo reasoned.

His tone, however, was unconvincing, and despite the logic of his statement, any reassurance he'd hoped to leaven within his companions died when the howling screams of jet engines sounded overhead.

The baleful noise tore the sky asunder, leaving it in tatters, whilst the city below trembled in incredulous fear. Viktor, now woken from his benumbed state, and stirred into action by the beastly ruckus, spun around to face the row of tall windows behind him and leapt onto the sofa to see what was happening. Tak-hing and Knox, who were still seated to either side of him, also turned to follow Viktor's gaze, as the younger members of the cohort rushed forwards in order to snatch a glimpse of the outside world themselves.

Disappointingly though, the other residential blocks surrounding them substantially impaired their view, leaving only the road directly outside and a minimal amount of once pink, now blackened, sky visible. For the former Colonel

General though, that limited field of vision still provided him with enough information to get a handle on the situation.

'Tak-hing, those jets look like Shenyang fighters, but they're carrying AGMs?' Viktor said with the professional candour of a man forged in the military.

'There's very few of those in the fleet, maybe ten or twelve at the most. As I'm sure you're aware, there's very little use for AGMs in modern conflict,' the Defence Minister replied, as he bent his neck back to look upwards, just as another one of the infernal birds flew by.

'What's an AGM?' Aria muttered to Knox, not wanting to distract Viktor.

'It stands for Air-to-Ground. Basically, they're firing missiles from their jets down into the city,' McRae answered in a rasping murmur.

'Fuck, guess that explains the explosions then,' she said more loudly, as the severity of their circumstances became apparent.

'Aye lass, fuck indeed,' he whispered back to her, then, at full volume for everyone to hear. 'We need to get out of here, *right now.*'

'Wait, wait, what's that?' Viktor barked, shushing Knox with his hand and screwing his eyes up, as a series of fine, black dots fell through the clouds towards the burning city below. 'It can't be …'

'It is,' intoned Tak-hing.

'What?' Knox enquired with urgency, unable to make out the shapes in any detail.

'Para-troops.'

'This makes no sense at all,' Viktor scoffed, the temerity of the Chinese siege whirling him into a rage. 'They use needlessly risky techniques, when they could've fired at the city from miles away, and now, they're dropping troops into a warzone they haven't even finished bombing! Something is very wrong here, Tak-hing.'

'I agree, there's definitely something amiss, the attack is too uncoordinated and rash to be of much use. Unless, that's precisely the point?' he responded reflectively.

'How so?'

'Well, China's Airborne Corps only has the capacity to lift roughly eleven thousand troops at a single time, and even if Moscow wasn't as well prepared as it is, that's not enough to conquer the city. It's a suicide mission; therefore, it's most likely a distraction. But from what, I couldn't tell you,' said Tak-hing in a meditative voice, his unique knowledge already proving invaluable.

'If we could see what they are targeting, maybe we could understand their plan more clearly?' Cyril offered, demonstrating once again his predilection for strategy.

'That's a fine idea, lad, but we need to leave before this escalates any further,' McRae said firmly.

'I'm not leaving, Knox, not whilst my city is under attack,' Viktor stated, his tone equally as rigid, leaving no margin for contest.

'Viktor! We don't have time for this argument, and you know it,' the old artist beseeched.

'Fight *with me*, then, instead of always against me.'

'I would, in a heartbeat, but it's not just me I have to worry about. It's them, too,' Knox entreated, sweeping his hand in the direction of Cyril, Marcus and Aria, whose faces portrayed a miasma of apprehension and childlike bravery.

Astounded by the paternal warmth in McRae's voice, Marcus had to stifle a gasp as he stared at the two hard faced men, who were both now on their feet. Like the parallel walls of a rugged canyon, they stood. Indivisible in material, they would always be brothers, and yet the river of providence, chance and destiny that flowed between them would forever preserve their dissidence. It was an abstruse confrontation to observe, and Marcus looked to Viktor in anticipation of his reply, only to have his thoughts wrenched away by an obscure billowing sound, followed by a heavy thump from somewhere above them.

'Looks like you're all fighting now,' Viktor said bitterly, biting off his words. 'Come on, the quicker we get that bastard off the roof, the quicker we can get you out of here.'

'And how do you propose we do that?' Knox queried, following Viktor towards the library.

'You'll see,' the Russian said, as he entered the room, leaving the door ajar for his old friend.

Marcus began to shuffle his feet restlessly whilst they waited, the chafing of his boots on the floorboards wearing his nerves threadbare as the minutes slipped by. The rest of them didn't seem to be faring much better either.

Aria was biting her lip so hard it looked like it might split, Hugo ground his jaws together with such ferocity that the veins on his temple bulged, and even Cyril's enduring ataraxia showed the first signs of cracking. Tak-hing was the only source of stability in the room, his sagely countenance provided some relief from the gathering madness, but it could never fully mask the capriccio of destruction booming outside.

When Knox and Viktor returned to their companions, the anxiety in the living room was like a soupy fog, and their arrival only appeared to increase its opacity. They each had a long barrelled, wooden stocked, Dragunov rifle slung over their shoulders by a thick canvas loop, and between them, they carried a worn munitions box that jangled as they walked.

'What's wrong with your faces?' Viktor mocked derisively, when he saw how distressed Marcus and Aria looked. 'How did you think I was going to get rid of him, ah, by giving him a stern talking to? This is war, children, bullets are the words of conversation now. Which reminds me,' he said, dropping the box onto the rug and lifting the lid. 'You've just been inducted into my squad.' 'Not quite,' McRae elucidated. 'We only need to clear the local area, *if* there's anything to clear at all. Me and Viktor will do all the heavy lifting but Marcus, Cyril, we might need you on overwatch depending on the how bad the situation is.'

'What do you need us to do?' Marcus probed, doing his utmost to sound reliable, and capable.

'Take these,' said Viktor, thrusting a pair of military binoculars into both of their hands. 'You survey the area, locate any targets for us to eliminate, or give us the all-clear. Once the blocks around us are free of these vermin we'll try to leave for the hangar.'

'What about the rest of us?' asked Aria intently.

'We need all of you, unfortunately,' Knox answered in a subdued, regretful croak. 'Our plan is to split into two groups and attack the roof from multiple directions at once. Marcus, Tak-hing and Aria, you're with me. We're going to use the fire exit at the top of the stairs.'

'Won't the tenants on the top floor notice us, or give us away, or something if they come out to see what all the racket's about?' she persisted.

'The rooms on the fifth floor are empty, don't worry, your position won't be given away,' Viktor assured them. 'Now, Cyril, Hugo, you lucky devils get to come with me. We're going to hit the street and make a move on the roof from the external staircase. We can access it in the alley behind the building,' he announced, his orders precise and imperative. 'I don't have enough weapons for all of you though, so keeping you out of harm's way is essential. Hugo, you can have the papasha in the box, I trust your father has taught you how to use one?'

'Of course,' the prince said, kneeling down to take the compact sub machine gun from the metallic trunk. 'I just hope I don't have to use it.'

'And Tak-hing, I'm trusting you with this,' Viktor told him, as he removed the antique pistol from the back of his belt and placed it delicately in the hands of his old friend. 'May she serve you well. Now remember, watch us from the window, Knox, when we make our way around the corner, you go to the fire exit and we should reach the roof at the same time.'

'Done. Shall we?' the Scotsman rumbled, determination coursing through his voice.

'Let's,' concurred Viktor, matching Knox's tone with a guttural snarl of his own.

Beckoning to Cyril and Hugo, and readjusting the heavy weapon on his shoulder, Viktor left the room with the prince close behind. Cyril, however, lingered a moment longer and took his first few steps with his back to the door, before dipping his head in deference to his father and jogging to catch up to Hugo.

The gesture had been almost imperceptible, yet within it, was contained an entire universe of unspoken but immediately comprehensible emotion. It was a goodbye, and the recondited nature of its circumstance made it seem prophetic, the implications of which made Marcus uncomfortable.

Pivoting around to survey the road through the window instantly brought him back to the present though, as he noticed a pair of cars trapped beneath a hunk of rubble, not far from the apartment. The chunk of debris looked to have fallen from the building above, flattening both vehicles into unrecognisable shapes, but there were still people visible through the smashed windows.

'Look, look!' he yelped, pointing to the bloody hands clawing at the misshapen metal. 'There's people in those cars.'

'I know, don't worry, I think Viktor's seen them too, see? He's sending Hugo and Cyril over,' Knox said, as he and Marcus watched the prince dash over and begin prising the door open with a piece of steel he'd found lying close by.

'It seems Viktor's not stopping though?' Tak-hing remarked, sighing at his foolhardiness.

'Shit, you're right. Marcus, help me with this box!' McRae bellowed.

'Wait, I need my camera,' he said, sprinting off towards the guestroom he'd slept in before Knox could object.

'Christ, lad, this isn't the time to be mucking about, there's lives at risk!' his mentor chastised as he returned, setting the camera to record, and tying it tightly around his neck. 'Now move it!'

Marcus and Knox led the way out of the apartment, practically running up the stairs with the ammunitions box clanging around between them. The box itself was lighter now some of its lethal contents had been passed to Hugo, but Marcus still had to labour to keep up with McRae's drastically longer strides; a feat made all the more stressful by the constant groaning and shaking of the building.

The fifth floor came and went in a flash, the plush carpet outside the empty apartment muffling their footsteps as they ran in the direction of a narrow corridor nestled at the end of the landing. The hallway they entered was tatty and unmaintained in comparison to the rest of the lavishly decorated block, and its peeling wallpaper scraped at them as they charged by. Eventually the passage culminated at the foot of a thin, metal staircase, which they ascended one meticulous foot at a time in order create as little noise as possible.

'I still don't understand what my role is supposed to be here?' Aria breathed in the weak light, as they at last reached the building's summit.

'You'll be our munitions runner if things get hectic, lass,' the old artist responded, in an equally susurrant voice as he panted softly. 'You and Tak-hing are to stay in the stairwell out of sight, unless you're needed though, ok. You too, Marcus, don't come out unless we tell you it's safe, alright?'

'Yeah, got it.' Marcus nodded.

'Good. Stay in the shadows, I'll be right back,' Knox said, removing the Dragunov from his shoulder and checking it over, before testing its weight and looking down the iron-sights exploratively. 'Bloody marksman rifle for close quarters combat; honestly, I should've brought the papasha,' he grouched to himself, edging towards the exit.

With a calming breath, Knox burst through the door with his shoulder, leaving no barrier between them and the uproarious sounds of the battle being fought outside. Bullets whistled through the air, their conical bodies ricocheting off metal, puncturing stone and decimating flesh like a swarm of metal jacketed hornets.

Bricks and mortar rained down from structures that had been impacted by the missiles, the fragments plummeting to the streets, and creating rambunctious shockwaves of sound as they hit. Sirens blared, people screamed, and fires crackled in all directions.

It was chaos, and Marcus's self-preservation overwhelmed him with a relentless urge for him to plug his ears; and run away as fast as he possibly could. But when a solider pounced off the roof above the fire exit and landed on Knox's back, the instinct vanished, leaving only the will to protect his mentor in its place.

McRae was caught unawares, and as he floundered, the weight of the man clinging to his back sent the rifle skittering from his hands across the low pitch of the bitumen roof. Marcus knew that Knox's stringy frame was far more durable than it looked, but even so, watching the Chinese soldier squeeze his neck with such crushing violence made his heart hammer.

'We have to help him!' Marcus shouted, as the Scotsman thrashed around, unable to dislodge the choking grip of his assailant.

'Let me go, I'm armed,' Tak-hing said authoritatively, brandishing Viktor's pistol.

It was clear from the way he wielded the weapon that he wasn't familiar with firearms, yet he levelled it at the enemy all the same in a bid to save his friend; and repay the old debt. He shuffled past Marcus and Aria, right to the opening of the doorway, but it was of little use as Knox's bucking form made it nigh on impossible to take a clear shot.

'It's too dangerous, Tak-hing, he's moving too much,' Aria bleated, the stress of the situation making her sound manic.

'I can, I can,' the elderly man replied, tracing McRae's erratic movements with the pistol.

'He'll run out of time, let me g–' Marcus began desperately, only to have his sentence annihilated by the sonorous bang of a gunshot close by.

His breath caught in his chest as Knox sagged to his knees, and he reached out a useless hand, as though he could stop time with only his fingertips. Aria gasped too as the Scotsman fell forwards, letting out a hacking cough as he landed on his palms. The three of them pelted from the stairwell to his side, crouching down to his level to examine him for wounds, and it wasn't until they pushed the flaccid body of the soldier from his back, that they realised it wasn't McRae that had taken the bullet.

'It's just like the good old days ah, Knox? Me saving your ass, time and again.' Viktor laughed, striding over from the staircase he had just scaled to regroup with his companions.

'The swine, I would've had him if he hadn't have got me from behind,' McRae wheezed, fighting for breath in the dust filled air.

'I'm sure you would have,' Viktor agreed insincerely, as he hauled his winded friend to his feet. 'Next time I'll be sure to leave you to it then, if you could've taken him by yourself?'

The joke should've been funny; man's capacity to sustain a sense of humour even in the direst of circumstances, is after all, one if its most ingratiating qualities. But Viktor's words never really had the chance to be absorbed, for no sooner had they been uttered, Tak-hing burst through the pair of them to fire his pistol at another unseen soldier hiding on the roof.

Time ceased as the burning fizz of bullets whizzed around them, but Tak-hing's aim, for all its zeal, was too inaccurate to be deadly, meaning that before a single bullet of his had found its mark, his own body had been ruptured beyond repair.

Reality crashed back into them then, bringing all its sickening truths to bear in a sensory overload of events. In the same instant that the solider toppled, Aria's hands rushed to her face in shock, Marcus let out an involuntary keening sound, and Tak-hing's gurgling body fell between Knox and Viktor; who caught him in their awe struck arms. The Oriental man's dark eyes fluttered and widened with shock as he was lowered onto the ground, where his damaged body wept streams of blood onto the roof.

'I suppose this time, my friends, it was my turn to save you,' he gasped through a crimson smile.

'Don't you die on us, aye, you mad bastard!' wailed McRae, his face white.

'I ... I,' stuttered Tak-hing, trying desperately to form words.

'Come on, man we need you, don't we? You've got a world to save! And besides, who else is going to keep Viktor in check, and make sure Cyril listens to me?' Knox murmured softly, shock hastening his words, as a solitary tear fell from his faded emerald eyes and dropped onto the chest of his dead friend.

'He's gone, Knox,' Viktor said quietly, as he brushed Tak-hing's eyelids closed for the final time.

'I know,' he replied, the agony in his tone unspeakable. 'What the fuck are we going to tell his son?'

'That his father was a beacon of light, even in our darkest hour,' replied Viktor rising to his feet, his face ruinous, as the heartache in him transformed into a scorching anger.

He turned to face the fallen, but still breathing soldier who had so cruelly murdered Tak-hing; and let out a stentorian cry of animalistic pain. In that moment, it sounded as though his entire life's suffering was being expelled and the awful noise echoed in the streets around them, making the mutilated buildings scream back like a crowd of fanatical peasants at a witch trial. Moscow had heard his cry, and it demanded justice.

'First, you poison my people!' Viktor seethed, marching towards the downed man. 'Then, you take my wife!' he continued, collecting his pistol from the floor where it had landed. 'And now, you have the *fucking gall* to take my friend? Well, as a reward,' he said, grabbing the solider by the scruff of his neck, and jamming the barrel of the gun into his throat. 'I will wipe every single one of you *mat' chertovski kusochki der'ma* from the face of this planet, starting with *you*.'

Viktor emptied the entire chamber into the man's skull, leaving nothing but a puddle of viscera where his head had been. But the penance was insufficient, and when the trigger clicked again and nothing happened, Viktor cast it aside and began to beat what little remained of the soldier's face with his fists. Driven by an unquenchable bloodlust, he punched, wailed and screamed incoherent Russian words at the corpse, until Knox ran over to tear him away.

McRae held him against his chest as he shuddered, and Marcus gazed at them with a horde of questions clamouring in his mind. What was worse, he thought, to watch a man die with his entrails strewn across the ground, or to witness the heart rending moment when a spirit breaks? He wasn't sure there could ever be an answer, the world had stopped making sense, and as he stared past the two quaking men to the apocalyptic skyline beyond them, he begged silently for it all to end.

The heavens, it seemed, had heard his call, for no sooner had he conjured the thought, did an enormous piece of avian shrapnel come tumbling out of the sky towards them. Marcus gawked at it hopelessly, wondering if the angel of death really had come to steal his soul, but the dismembered wing struck the building with shattering force a few feet from where he and Aria were standing, narrowly missing the heads of the two older men in the process.

Marcus and Aria looked at one another with terror in their eyes, smiling nauseously at their luck, only to have the ground beneath their feet ripped away as half of the roof collapsed; sending them plummeting into the void below.

Chapter XIX

He couldn't move.

That was the first thing that entered Marcus's mind, as he opened his dust filled eyes and attempted to define his environment. Wherever he was, it was extremely dark, and he blinked profusely against the clouds of floating detritus, trying to adjust his vision to the blackness. When that proved futile, however, and he remained blind, the panic inducing sense of claustrophobia gripped him in its fiendish talons, berating him with thoughts of entrapment.

He made another effort to move from his sitting position, starting tentatively with his neck, he realised that looking upwards and to his right was no issue, but looking to his left caused a searing pain to shoot down his spine all the way to the small of his back. Exhaling through the portcullis of his gritted teeth, and wincing with the shock of the sensation, Marcus stilled his head and began testing his limbs.

Once again, his right side seemed relatively mobile, if a tad stiff, but his left arm and leg even if only moved a fraction, struck him with the same lightning bolt of hurt that moving his neck had.

Pressuring his mind into disregarding that troubling fact for the meantime, Marcus probed the area around him with his right hand and foot, establishing quickly that he was detained in some sort of cavity. Above him, coarse remnants of the fallen roof formed a close, immovable ceiling and in front of him various pieces of rubble boxed him in.

As he scrabbled around with his boot though, some of the debris became loose and fell away, exposing a tiny beam of light ahead of him. Its somewhat symbolic appearance allowed a paltry taste of hope to wet his parched tongue, and although it caused him unimaginable discomfort, Marcus continued to lash out at the crumbling wall. After five or six gut wrenching blows, an entire slab of concrete collapsed, creating an aperture large enough to illuminate the entire space, and giving him a view of the room beyond.

Guarding his face against a fresh plume of brick dust with his hand, Marcus squinted out of the hole he'd made, and found the view instantly recognisable. The light which now afforded him his vision, was cascading in through a window that was almost identical to the one behind the sofa in Viktor's apartment. For a moment he thought it *was* Viktor's apartment, but this one was devoid of any homely touches or furnishings, its only notable residents being a pair of shredded, navy curtains and a smashed chandelier.

Realising that he must have fallen into the unoccupied apartment on the fifth floor, Marcus endeavoured to regain his bearings. By using the position of the destroyed light fitting, assuming of course that it had followed a vertical track to the floor, and the location of the window as refence points, he estimated that he was on the very edge of the kitchen. By that logic, the pillar dividing the entrance hall and living room, should've been just to his left, but he knew that twisting that way was out of the equation.

Alternatively, he reached out with his good arm to feel the material of the floor, knowing that tiles would indicate that he was in the kitchen; and wooden boards would place him in the living room. However, when he made contact with the cool tiles, he also found that they were coated in an unanticipated layer of something wet, and viscid. Raising his hand to assess it in the light, it startled him to see that it was coated in blood, making it look as though he was wearing a gauntlet of liquified rubies.

The sight of it frightened him, and when he registered that the blood was his own, that fright transmogrified into something far more perfidious. Glancing down without moving his head, Marcus saw that the scarlet pool originated somewhere to his rear, and extended nearly two feet to his right, where it began to soak into a splintered, oaken cupboard. It was alarming to see so much of his blood oozing across the floor, and as he wrestled with grotesque thoughts of his own mortality, Marcus reached around his back to find the cause of his injury.

Leaning forward set the nerves in his left side ablaze, but he grimaced through it, and slid his hand around further, noticing for the first time the smooth metallic object he was leaning against. Tracing its form, he found an indistinct overlap in the metal sheeting, but that did little to dissolve the indeterminate nature of the object. Then, as he found first one, then an entire line of rivets, his memory jolted, and he recalled the jagged plane wing that had split the roof above.

Somehow, during the fall, he must've ended up with his back to it, but that still didn't explain why he was stuck. Searching further, he felt the hinging flap of an aileron move at his touch, but it felt oddly short, so he pursued its edge with his fingers. At the limits of his flexibility, just a couple of short inches away from where he'd first discovered the aileron,

Marcus's hand, along with the aluminium, ran into something moist and organic; they ran, into him.

As the revolting truth dawned on him, Marcus thought he might vomit, for the reason the flap on the wing was so much shorter than it ought to be, was because the other half of it was embedded in his back. Whether it was a figment of his imagination, or simply his cognition pointing itself to the wound he didn't know, but he thought then that he could feel the erroneous metal inside him. The notion of the metallic barbs clawing hungrily at his innards sent Marcus into a blind panic, and in his hysteria, he attempted to lift himself from its spiteful grasp, only to be dragged back down by an unspeakable agony.

He screamed then, loud and deranged, as the weight of his descending body plunged the shard of metal further in, making the gash cry fresh tears of blood. As his life force spilled onto the tiles around him, Marcus gasped, coughed, and prepared for his inevitable demise. But when another, higher pitched splutter rose up beside him, off to the left, it distracted him from his doom and he remembered suddenly why he had to stay alive.

'Ari, are you there?' He breathed, barely able to summon the strength to speak.

'Marcus, what the hell happened?' she wheezed, her voice woozy and distant.

'I think we're in the apartment, the vacant one on the fifth floor. I guess we must've fallen through when the wing caved the roof in.' He paused, trying to mask his pain with a sigh. 'Are you hurt?'

'My leg feels sore, I'm not sure why, but it moves at least. I must've hit my head pretty fucking hard though because

I literally feel like I'm experiencing a month's worth of hangovers.' She groaned. 'I'm going to lie here for a second, just whilst it wears off.'

'Worse than a night on the punsch?' Marcus asked with a snort, in spite of his pain.

'So much worse.'

'You always were a lightweight,' he joked, doing his utmost to keep the severity of his injuries from her.

'Honestly, Marcus, the stuff you come out with!' She huffed. 'If you could get paid for lying, you'd be a millionaire by now.'

'You can, can't you? I thought it was called working for the government?' he said, laughing along with her, until the wound in his back transformed the chortle into yet another rattling cough.

Drained from the short exchange, Marcus closed his eyes and rested his head against the jet wing, counting each deep breath as it came and went, in order to busy his mind and stave off the madness. Aria, it seemed, was intent on remaining still too, and aside from her own breathing and the intermittent clearing of dust from her nose, neither of them made a sound. In spite of their dormancy though, it was still anything but quiet in their tight hollow, as the rancorous sounds of combat still saturated the streets of Moscow beyond their prison of rubble and dirt.

Marcus focused on the noises, picking them apart, and with his eyes clamped shut against any unwanted visual distractions, his mind began to reshape them into better things. Whether he was defending himself against the strife of war, or merely falling prey to the first hallucination on his road to death, Marcus didn't know, but the somewhat random image of a beach from his childhood was unintentionally brought forth from the vaults of his memory.

In that vision, a screaming jet became a squawking sea bird, the reverberations of a pestilent gunshot were reimagined as a pebble, skipping across the surface of a turquoise ocean, and the lamentations of the dying were transformed into the friendly heckles of beaming fruit sellers. So vivid in his head was the scene, that it felt real and tangible, making him long to stay in the pacifistic sands of his reverie forever. As he thought about taking a seat on that sunlit vista though, something nagged at him, a sound, no, a voice, one that he knew as well as his own; but it didn't belong in his paradise.

Opening his eyes with a jolt, Marcus grimaced and exuded a clenched jawed yelp, as his rigid muscles spasmed, causing the slash in his back to tear slightly. Nevertheless, it wasn't his butchered flesh that had stirred him, it was the faint thrum of a rasping, Scottish burr somewhere above them.

'Is that Knox?' he said faintly, swallowing once, and licking his dry lips. 'Is he coming for us?'

'I'm not sure,' Aria replied with a grunt, as she turned onto her side to prop herself up. 'I mean it's definitely him, and Viktor too by the sounds of it, but I don't know if they can reach us.'

'I think they might still be in trouble themselves,' offered Marcus, listening intently to the verbose string of obscenities and rifle fire that boomed overhead.

'Not as much trouble as Tak-hing … I still can't believe he's dead,' Aria whispered, her sad recollection sounding less like a statement and more like a question, as if asking for the truth might somehow deny it.

'He was a good man, and there was something so, *human* about him, wasn't there? I barely knew him, but I miss him … and as for Cyril, Christ he's going to be devastated.'

'I know, the poor thing. It's just so, I don't even know, how do you even describe what we've seen, Marcus? I feel like we've been living lives that don't belong to us,' she said, her voice buckling under the weight of all it all.

'I don't think there's enough words in the world to tell this story, Ari, and who'd believe us if we tried?' he scoffed, with a mirthless flicker of laughter.

'I suppose it's a good job you took so many pictures then?'

'Oh shit, my camera!' Marcus said, suddenly frantic, as he reached for his neck and realised it was no longer there.

'Don't worry, it's here,' she said in a mollifying tone, scraping something up off the floor. 'I mean, it's seen better days and the lens is cracked, but I think it'll still work.'

'Just flick that switch on the top and see if the screen comes on.'

'I know how a camera works, you know?' she muttered sarcastically, as the camera beeped into life. 'There we go, see, good as new … if good means destroyed.'

'Bloody hell, thank God for that,' Marcus said, exhaling in relief. 'Just check what the first image is of please, I need to know if the memory card's damaged.'

'Ha! It's of Knox's ridiculous ambulance. I can't believe we got all the way to Scotland in that thing.' She giggled. 'Here look, I can't believe it was–' But when she caught sight of Marcus for the first time, her words jammed in her throat, and the silence of their misexpression hung heavy in the air, like bodies from a gallows.

'What is it?' he queried, feeling the shift in atmosphere.

'Your … your back,' she responded, her voice fluttering like a dead butterfly, as she continued to crawl towards him.

'Oh, yeah. I'm a little stuck, I'll admit, but my left side's just taking a sabbatical right now, that's all,' Marcus said, attempting to make light of the horrendous wound as she came near to him. 'Is it bad?'

'Just a scratch, really,' she answered with a stoic smile, but after taking a closer look; the tears in her eyes told a very different tale.

'Good, then you can show me that picture, can't you?' Marcus said, returning her smile, even though they both knew how serious the situation was.

'Don't you think we should be trying to get out of here?' Aria said, a swelling impatience tightening her voice.

'Look around us, Ari, I can't move at all, and there's no way you can budge that rubble by yourself,' he countered, trying to appear cogent and calm, but the sprig of gnarled metal in his back squeezed the breath from his words until they sounded desperate.

'You can barely even speak!'

'Listen, our best bet is to wait. They'll come for us, I know they will.'

'Not if they don't survive, they won't!' she argued, scrunching her face up in indignation. 'We need to get you out of here.'

'Please, just come sit with me, will you?' Marcus begged, straining to retain his composure, as he extended his right hand to her. 'They're still up there, you can hear them both bickering and I'm sure once Cyril and Hugo make it back, they'll come for us.'

'I hope you're right.'

'I'm always right, now shut up and come here.'

Unwillingly, she complied with his request, taking his hand and shuffling into the space between his legs, where she curled up against his hip. Being careful not to place too much of her weight on him, and doing her best to avoid the blood, she raised the camera up so they both could see the image she'd been talking about.

Displayed on the LCD screen was a photograph of the spotless, white ambulance which McRae had recommissioned, and used to smuggle them out of England. It sat on the uneven, gravelly surface of the riverside garden, surrounded by verdant leaves and daisy spotted grass, waiting to carry them off in search of the truth. Looking at it now, it seemed to both of them as though that picture belonged to another world, a more innocent, sanguine one; that was not so bereft of cheer.

'It seems like a lifetime ago since we were sat in that carpark waiting for Knox to turn up.' Aria smiled, remembering the morning fondly. 'I walked for hours to get there too, thanks to your stupid route.'

'I never was great with directions,' Marcus jested, as he reached around Aria's shoulder, and pressed a button on the camera to show the date of the image. 'I took this on the twenty first of August, can you believe it's only the twenty eighth now?'

'You're joking? I feel like we've been gone for weeks, months even, I had no idea it had only been *seven* days,' she answered, scarcely able to comprehend how much had happened in such a short space of time.

'You know what's even crazier? When we set off on this journey, we thought the whole thing was lie, some sort of convoluted plan to keep everyone at home and steal our lives, but we couldn't have been further from the truth. I thought they were being overly cautious because there were so few deaths from the virus, but after seeing Russia, I don't think they're doing enough,' Marcus said, considering for the first time just how drastically his opinions had changed.

'I just don't think the media in our country will ever give an honest report, that's why the lockdown wasn't taken seriously in the first place. How were we supposed to know who to trust when every new story undermined the last, and not a single one of them even hinted that the situation is as severe as it is. It's still bullshit, except now it's in reverse.'

'I couldn't agree more, but at least now we have the means to blow the lid off the whole thing,' he said with a tarnished sense of victory.

'What are you talking about, what means?' she questioned, unsure what his comment portended.

'The photos, look,' said Marcus, cycling through the camera's memory card. 'I took pictures of almost everything, Ari, and once these images hit the internet they'll spread like wildfire, especially if we've got Knox's influence to help us. We'll be able to warn *everyone* of what's coming.'

'You and your big ideas, Marcus, I hope it is that simple,' she mumbled quietly, seeming to retreat into herself for a solipsistic second, before turning the camera off and continuing. 'I wonder how much has changed back home?'

'You miss your sisters, don't you?' he asked after a pause, rustling through the leaves of the archetypal bush with a more precise inquiry of his own.

'Yeah,' Aria replied in a guarded tone, slightly disconcerted by how well he'd interpreted her. 'I miss everything, but I think about them *every* day, I just hope they're keeping safe, you know? Staying out of trouble,' she finished, clearly finding it challenging to discuss anything too close to her heart.

'They'll be fine, they're Bianchis, remember? They're made of tough stuff,' Marcus reassured her. 'And anyway, your dad is the most terrifying man I know, he'd never let anything happen to any of you,' he added, praying that some comic relief would still her shaking voice.

She let out a passing giggle at that, rich and smooth, and it bolstered his will, allowing him to momentarily forget that the excruciating pain in his back was worsening. However, just as that fragile wave of optimism washed over him, it found itself colliding with the cliffs of reality all too soon, shattering its sentiments to pieces, and spraying them across the rubble by Marcus's feet as Aria began to cry.

'I just don't know what I'd do if anything happened to them though, they look up to me, Marcus, and if I wasn't there to pro–' But her words merged with her sobs then, rendering her tortured voice ungraspable amongst the sounds of her hushed snivelling.

Marcus hadn't seen Aria cry since she was thirteen years old, after a particularly nasty altercation with another girl during their school lunchbreak, and knowing how far she had to be pushed to show any kind of sadness made the sound of her reticent tears all the more unbearable.

Without even a sliver of indecision, he used what little remained of his energy to pull her close to him, and even though every shudder of her body made Marcus feel as though he was being cleaved in half, he refused to let her go.

As her weeping eyes wet his ragged uniform, and his blood soaked the floor, Marcus was trampled by the loathsome march of defeat. His body was broken, they'd lost Tak-hing,

Aria was falling apart in his arms, and for what, what had it all been for?

'I'm so sorry, Ari, if I knew it was going to end like this, I would've never asked you to come.' He whispered, pressing his compunctious lips against the top of her head as he spoke.

'I don't regret coming, Marcus, it's just such a mess … such a fucking mess,' she said, her voice breaking into a whimper as she repeated herself over and over again, until nothing but incomprehensible moans escaped her.

Then the dam holding his own misery back split in two, leaving crystalline streams running over his dust-marked face. There was nothing else either of them could say, so they sat together in their tenebrous prison of debris, clinging onto one another for dear life, and expounding their deepest sorrows through rivers of tears. They cried for an unfathomable length of time, mourning for themselves, for their friends, families, the world, and all the ills that were driving humanity to the brink of dissolution.

When their waterways ran dry, and they were reduced to empty vessels, exhaustion came for them. With nothing left to give, Marcus and Aria submitted to their tiredness, drifting off into an uneasy doze as they awaited liberation; and all the while Moscow sang on, roaring the gruesome chorus of battle.

The dreams Marcus experienced during that unnatural sleep were feverish, and lucid, each of them simultaneously distinct and indivisible, making them into a maze of infinite pathways. Lost in the morass, he drifted aimlessly, finding that every line he traced connected one moment of his life with another, seemingly unrelated one, as though he was being shown a scrambled version of his own narrative.

He revisited the beach from his earlier daze, repainted his first childhood artwork, and even relived his last day at school, but amongst those crucial moments were incalculable others. For the first time since he'd lived them, Marcus saw all the prosaic seconds that had comprised his life. Those were the grains of sand that Tak-hing had told him about, the very matter of his being, distilled into its most atomic form and trapped inside a time glass. He marvelled at it, that effigy of the unrememberable memory, and the millions of tiny fragments of himself that swirled within it, observing each of them as they fell.

One by one the recollections dropped from the upper chamber to the lower, landing with a rhythmic, gentle patter as the pile grew ever larger. For a time it was dazzling; however, as the particles of his past continued to fall, Marcus was overcome with worry as he realised just how few were left in the top of the glass. He had almost run out of pieces of himself, and yet there was one more he had to give away; even if it was his last.

He woke gasping, drowning in his dreams, and reached for Aria; only to find that she was no longer huddled against him. Instead, she was kneeling down in front him, removing chunks of concrete and plaster from the wall of debris with her grazed hands.

'Ari,' Marcus croaked, his throat like a desert.

'Marcus? Shit, Knox, Knox he's awake!' she cried, her own voice hoarse, but still full of relief.

'Good, keep him talking, don't let him drift off again,' the Scotsman said urgently, as his grimy face appeared in the gap above Aria's head to speak to him directly. 'No more naps, lad, it's home time!'

'Got it, Knox,' he mumbled in reply, sounding drowsy.

'You're going to be fine, Marcus, everyone's here, they've come to get us, just like you said, remember?' Aria garbled, her words coming out in a jittery, garrulous flow.

'I remember. I'm always right, aren't I?' he slurred, unable to control his mouth.

'Of course you are, you stupid boy,' she answered, fighting to put a smile on her face as he carried on muttering incoherently.

'Knox you have to hurry, he can barely talk, and he's whiter than a ghost!' Aria shouted gravely over her shoulder.

'We're almost there, keep him holding on,' McRae bellowed back, his voice straining as he tugged at something heavy.

'Tell him that no one else is dying today, not even him, ah?' Viktor boomed.

'You hear that, Marcus? No dying today or you'll have Viktor to answer to.'

'But it's so *cold*, Ari, I just want to go back to sleep,' he said, drunk with death, his eyelids fluttering.

'Don't you fucking die on me, *Merda*!' Aria warned angrily, shaking his face, but the second she let go, his eyes closed and his head lolled to one side like that of a rag doll. 'Marcus, come on, come on … please! Don't leave me now,' she pleaded, as tears once again began trickling down her face 'Knox, he's going!'

'Right, lads, we're out of time, with me, Pull!' he yelled.

Marcus didn't really understand what was happening at that point, all he could comprehend was the feeling of slipping away, but to where, he couldn't tell. He could hear voices around him, but they were distant and muddied, as if whomever was speaking was stood on a riverbank and he was lying beneath the water.

There were other noises too, pervading the depths. Grunts of effort, tearful cries, the groaning of stone and then, suddenly, a bombastic crash followed by a torrent of light. The burning of that light, after spending so long locked in the gloom, was strong enough to force his eyes open again; bringing him back from the precipice of oblivion.

Through his murky vision he saw Aria clutching him, her face distraught, and past her in the opening they'd just created were the shadowed, panting figures of Knox, Viktor, Hugo and Cyril. Their faces were unreadable to him, but he liked to think they were as pleased to see him, as he was to see them, and although the pain in his body was slowly euthanizing his emotions, he still spoke words of gratitude. Whether his companions were able to hear him or not, he couldn't tell, but as they all rushed forwards to help him, he caught a glimpse of the sky through the window; a sky that seemed uncannily familiar.

Through a silhouette frame of jet-black girders protruding from the rubble, it looked as though someone had daubed the sky with a perse, yet rufescent paint, and smeared it until it resembled a range of mountains. The soft, bluish bases sprouted from the vastness above, throwing fuchsia and periwinkle valleys downwards until their candied, red peaks thrust low, almost scraping the roofs of the city. It was stunning, and there, liquescing on the barely visible skyline behind the clouds, was the shimmering sun, saying goodbye to the cataclysmic day it had so recently lit, and welcoming the night.

Marcus smiled slightly as he remembered the day that the journey first began, and recalled how sweet Aria's voice had been on the phone, as he watched the sun set before him. He turned to her then, gazing into her brave, beautiful face and beamed, knowing that now was his chance to finally give her what she deserved; the final piece of him.

'You said yes.' He laughed, using the last of his strength to take her hand in his. 'And you gave me everything I wanted.'

'What are you talking about?' she asked, gripping him tightly.

'I got to spend my last moments … with you.'

'I don't understand?' she said, her voice breaking as his eyes closed one last time.

'I love you, Aria.'

Then, he was still.

Epilogue

'I think I know the answer to your question,' Aria said to Knox, grinning as they waved Hugo off from the side of the runway.

'What question?' he grumbled, unsure what she was talking about.

'Dimmi, cosa vuoi di più dalla vita?' she replied clunkily. 'That's what you asked me on the first day that I met you, remember?'

'Aye, I do actually. Have you finally figured out what it means then?' the old artist smirked.

'Yeah, I have, you asked me what I wanted most from life,' she said, her pride giving her voice an almost cavalier tone.

'And what's your answer, *poppet*?'

'I don't know.'

'How profound.' He balked, chuckling rompishly.

'But, what I have learned, is that I don't think it's what I expected it to be,' she finished with a defiant smile, as she looked past McRae, to where Marcus was being propped up by Cyril. 'I think life's full of surprises.'

'I think you're right, lass. And I have a feeling that we've got many more, still to come.'

'How do you think Viktor's doing?' she asked, her tone becoming momentarily disconsolate.

'Honestly, I hate to think. He's got enough rage in him to blacken the sun, Tak-hing's death has broken whatever was left of his humanity, there's no doubt about that.' Knox sighed sombrely.

'But at least Moscow is safe again, right?'

'For the meantime, but as we've already established, that attack was clearly a distraction and as of right now, none of us have figured out what exactly they were distracting us from.'

'So, what are we—'

'Going to do now?' McRae rumbled, finishing Aria's question for her with a somewhat pretentious raise of his rocky brow. 'You're going to be quiet, or I'll be stuck here answering your questions 'til the next ice age rolls around. Now, grab your invalid, will you?' he finished, turning on his heel to head between two rows of deceased aircraft. 'The car's this way,' he called back over his shoulder.

Aria's face contorted into a look of disgruntlement as she watched the Scotsman walk away, but she followed his orders anyway, and made her way over to Marcus and Cyril. With every step her expression softened, morphing from one of malcontent into something warmer and more buoyant, until the smile tugging at her lips became irrepressible.

'Come on then, hop-along, we've got to get you home,' she joked, kissing Marcus on the cheek as she bent down to help him up.

'He is quite heavy, you know?' Cyril jibed, smiling at Aria as each of them moved to support Marcus's arms, being careful not to disturb the thick bandages tied around his waist.

'Get lost, I'd be as light as you too, if I was only three feet tall,' Marcus retorted, scowling at the pain in his back when he tried to move.

'Will you lot pipe down and hurry up? We're not out of the woods yet, there's work to be done!' Knox shouted, not even pausing to look at them.

'Or what?' Aria quipped in mock belligerence.

'*I'll drive,*' he rasped, making all of them laugh.

It was a testament to their resilience that in spite of all they'd seen, heard, done, and endured, that they could still laugh; and that alone was enough to prove that there was still hope to be found. There was a long way to go, but maybe ordinary people could change the world, after all.

A letter to the reader

Dear reader,

If you've made it to this page, then you've likely already read far too much of my waffle as it is! So, I'll keep this brief, but before you go, I'd just like to tell you a bit about how this book came to be.

I started writing Quarantine Sunsets in April 2020. The world was a bit upside down, I wasn't able to go to work, I couldn't see the people I cared about, and the end was nowhere in sight. So, I needed an outlet, and after taking a picture of a very unusual sunset during an evening walk; I had a flash of inspiration. The very next day I started writing, turned the photograph I'd taken into a book cover, which is the very one on the copy you're now reading, and the rest, as they say, is history.

What I really wanted to say here though, is that my story isn't really about the pandemic; it's about what it is to be human. It's about how we deal with the unknown, how we face things bigger than ourselves and, rightly or wrongly, the decisions we make along the way. I just hope that in these hardest of times, reading this book has provided you with as much solace, as writing it did for me.

Printed in Great Britain
by Amazon

61403440R00213